The Princess
of Celle

JEAN PLAIDY HAS ALSO WRITTEN

BEYOND THE BLUE MOUNTAINS
(A novel about early settlers in Australia)

DAUGHTER OF SATAN
(A novel about the persecution of witches and Puritans in the 16th and 17th centuries)

THE SCARLET CLOAK
(A novel of 16th century Spain, France and England)

Stories of Victorian England { IT BEGAN IN VAUXHALL GARDENS
{ LILITH

THE GOLDSMITH'S WIFE
(The story of Jane Shore)

EVERGREEN GALLANT
(The story of Henri of Navarre)

The Medici Trilogy
Catherine de' Medici { MADAME SERPENT
{ THE ITALIAN WOMAN } Also available in one volume
{ QUEEN JEZEBEL

The Lucrezia Borgia Series   MADONNA OF THE SEVEN HILLS
LIGHT ON LUCREZIA

**The Ferdinand and
Isabella Trilogy**   CASTILE FOR ISABELLA
SPAIN FOR THE SOVEREIGNS } Also available in one volume
DAUGHTERS OF SPAIN

The French Revolution Series   LOUIS THE WELL-BELOVED
THE ROAD TO COMPIEGNE
FLAUNTING EXTRAVAGANT QUEEN

The Tudor Novels
Katharine of Aragon { KATHARINE, THE VIRGIN WIDOW
{ THE SHADOW OF THE POMEGRANATE } Also available in one volume
{ THE KING'S SECRET MATTER

MURDER MOST ROYAL
(Anne Boleyn and Catherine Howard)

THE SIXTH WIFE
(Katharine Parr)

ST THOMAS'S EVE
(Sir Thomas More)

THE SPANISH BRIDEGROOM
(Philip II and his first three wives)

GAY LORD ROBERT
(Elizabeth and Leicester)

THE THISTLE AND THE ROSE
(Margaret Tudor and James IV)

MARY, QUEEN OF FRANCE
(Queen of Louis XII)

The Mary Queen of Scots Series   ROYAL ROAD TO FOTHERINGAY
THE CAPTIVE QUEEN OF SCOTS

The Stuart Saga   THE MURDER IN THE TOWER
(Robert Carr and the Countess of Essex)

Charles II { THE WANDERING PRINCE
{ A HEALTH UNTO HIS MAJESTY } Also available in one volume
{ HERE LIES OUR SOVEREIGN LORD

THE THREE CROWNS (William of Orange)
THE HAUNTED SISTERS (Mary and Anne)
THE QUEEN'S FAVOURITES (Sarah Churchill and Abigail Hill)

The Georgian Saga   THE PRINCESS OF CELLE
QUEEN IN WAITING
CAROLINE, THE QUEEN
THE PRINCE AND THE QUAKERESS
THE THIRD GEORGE
PERDITA'S PRINCE
SWEET LASS OF RICHMOND HILL
INDISCRETIONS OF THE QUEEN
THE REGENT'S DAUGHTER
GODDESS OF THE GREEN ROOM
VICTORIA IN THE WINGS

The Queen Victoria Series   CAPTIVE OF KENSINGTON PALACE
THE QUEEN AND LORD M
THE QUEEN'S HUSBAND
THE WIDOW OF WINDSOR

General Non-fiction   A TRIPTYCH OF POISONERS
(Cesare Borgia, Madame de Brinvilliers and Dr Pritchard)

The Spanish Inquisition Series   THE RISE OF THE SPANISH INQUISITION
THE GROWTH OF THE SPANISH INQUISITION
THE END OF THE SPANISH INQUISITION

The Princess
of Celle

JEAN PLAIDY

G. P. PUTNAM'S SONS
NEW YORK

G. P. Putnam's Sons
Publishers Since 1838
200 Madison Avenue
New York, NY 10016

First American edition 1985

Library of Congress Cataloging in Publication Data

Plaidy, Jean, date.
  The princess of Celle.

  Reprint. Originally published: London : R. Hale, 1967.
  Bibliography: p.
  1. Sophia Dorothea, consort of George I, King of Great
Britain, 1666–1726—Fiction.   I. Title.
PR6015.I3P76   1985   823'.914   84-27684
ISBN 0-399-13070-5

Printed in the United States of America
1   2   3   4   5   6   7   8   9   10

CONTENTS

Prologue

IN the bed the old man lay dying, staring before him with his poor, sightless eyes, murmuring incoherently as his thin yellow fingers plucked at the bedclothes. The physicians were huddled together in the ante-room pretending to confer as to what treatment they should offer; but they knew that there was nothing they could do. His hour had come, and William, Duke of Lüneberg, would not last the night.

His eight daughters were close to his bed, some kneeling, all weeping; but his seven sons were together in a corner of the death chamber, preparing to draw lots.

The macabre scene was lighted only by the guttering candles, and all were thinking—not of the dying Duke—but of the seven brothers.

In the little houses of the town of Celle, the inhabitants waited for news; some had hurried to the church to pray. It was to this church—built of brick in contrast to the wooden houses—that Duke William himself had gone regularly, for he had been a deeply religious man who had earned the name of The Pious.

Life had been pleasant in Celle under Duke William; and the people had been aware of their good fortune. Order reigned within and without the castle; and his subjects could expect justice. But the Duke was dying. And what changes would his successor bring? The people of Celle were afraid of change.

In the corridors of the castle the squires murmured together; the pages talked to each other; the serving men and maids shook their heads and looked grave. Would it be different now? For years life had gone on in its regular pattern. No one had changed it while Duke William lived, even though he had lost his wits, for there were times when he was lucid enough and then not one of his seven sons would have dared disobey him.

There had been no blaspheming in the castle nor in the town without it was punished; and lechery was something to be practised in secrecy. Life in the castle it was true had been more like that in a monastery; but it was the way Duke William had decided it should be and so it was. Meals were taken regularly; twice a day—at nine in the morning and four in the afternoon—throughout the town the trumpeter could be heard from the castle tower summoning all to the table; and anyone who did not appear at that time went without. It was the custom before each meal was served for one of the Duke's pages to walk between the tables and announce the Duke's command that all should be quiet and orderly, and that swearing, cursing and rudeness were forbidden, as was the throwing to the floor of bread and bones or attempts to cram these items into the pockets. Beer was provided, but wine was served only at the Duke's table; and before his affliction had robbed him of his senses, each day the accounts had been brought to him that he might personally study them.

Such had been the life of the castle.

And one of the seven could change it.

*　　*　　*

The candles were throwing flickering shadows on the wall. Each of the young men turned suddenly towards the bed as his father groaned more loudly than before.

"We must settle this matter now—while there is still life in him," muttered Ernest the eldest. "It would be his wish."

George, the sixth son, was promising himself that now he could go away from Celle to seek his fortune. He had often seen the carriages trundling by on their way to the Court of France carrying fashionably dressed gallants and beautiful women. How different they would be from the rosy-cheeked girls of Celle, though they were fresh and often eager; but he dreamed of elegant women, voluptuous women, versed in the art of making subtle love.

Yes, he would go away—make a Grand Tour of Europe. He would visit the Courts of France and England, and win honours on the field of battle. This was no place for a young man who would make his fortune. There was no fortune here, for only one among them could draw the shortest stick which would give him this castle and the right to marry, so that his son would inherit not only Celle but all their father's estates. It was the only way. All over Germany dukedoms such as theirs were becoming impoverished through the custom of dividing the inheritance between so many so that what had once been a sizable domain became nothing but a series of country houses. It must not happen to the Guelphs. They had all agreed on that.

So now the seven of them were drawing lots for marriage and the opportunity to give their father's estate of Brunswick-Lüneberg its future ruler.

Their father's chief minister held the sticks before them—seven sticks which could decide the future. There was a brief hesitation before Ernest took one of them.

George's turn was sixth and as he glanced down at the piece of wood in his hand he saw his destiny there.

The eyes of his brothers were all on him. The hope had left them, but it was replaced by immediate resignation because they all knew that this was the only way to keep the territory intact.

George had won. Now it was his duty to provide the heir.

*   *   *

The people of Celle were relieved; the castle retainers were overjoyed. The new Duke George had decided to make no changes. Each day the trumpeter called all to meals in the great hall; and the page walked between the tables issuing the Duke's commands which were the same as those of his father.

But the Duke himself was not in Celle. He was an adventurer this Duke and he had gone touring Europe, fighting here and there, for he had always wanted to be a soldier. "Marriage?" he said. "It can wait, for I am young yet and I have six brothers." Those brothers continued to live at the castle to save expense and waited anxiously for his return, for settle down he must very soon, or it would be necessary to call another family council and perhaps undergo another ceremony of the sticks. George was young, but it was time he produced the heir, and to do so he needed a wife.

His brothers meanwhile contented themselves with mistresses or morganatic marriages and as it was being said in Celle that the all important lot had fallen to the hands of the wrong man, Duke George returned to Celle with his bride Anne Eleanor, the daughter of the Landgrave of Hesse.

All was well, Duke George proved himself to be as good as his father—although now and then he left Celle in order to wander on the continent, doing a little soldiering here and there, but becoming domesticated enough to produce a family.

Three of his daughters died when they were children and only Sophia Amelia lived; but his four sons were strong and healthy and no one could complain that Duke George had not done his duty.

The four boys, Christian Lewis, George William, John Frederick and Ernest Augustus could often be seen riding through Celle; and the great affection between two of them was remarked on, for wherever the second son George William went, there was the youngest Ernest Augustus, and the friendship between these two was very pleasant to see.

The Brothers

In the cold dawn Ernest Augustus tried to stop the impatient pawing of his horse on the inn cobbles. He looked up at the window above and called: "Make haste, brother. The dawn is here."

When George William appeared at the window, Ernest Augustus shook with laughter. His brother half naked, hair tousled, was still the handsomest man in Celle even after a night of debauchery.

"Was *your* friend so disappointing then?" asked George William.

"Oh come, brother, you know we should be back at the castle before daylight."

A woman appeared behind him. She was young and comely. Trust George William to select the best. Ernest Augustus had become accustomed to taking what was left—one of the penalties of being a younger brother. But he bore no resentment, he would always rather be with George William than anyone else.

"I'll join you soon. Be patient a little longer, brother."

His head disappeared. There were exclamations and giggles from the open window. This was a little dangerous, thought Ernest Augustus. It was all very well to go whoring outside their own home, but they should be more careful in Celle. If Christian Lewis should hear of their adventures ... Not that he did not know that such adventures were indulged in; that was not the point. Christian Lewis himself was no monk—although life in the castle went on in the old monastic way under him as it had under their father. Yet one did not philander in Celle. That was the difference.

A movement from above and George William was at the window again. He appeared to somersault; there he was one moment, deftly gripping the sill with both hands, and the next on the ground.

"Well done, brother," said Ernest Augustus. "I never saw a man leap from a lady's bedroom as skilfully as you."

"An art acquired through long practice. You will come to it in time. My horse."

Ernest Augustus, who was holding it, nodded his head and George William leaped into the saddle.

The castle was stirring when they rode into the courtyard. The grooms tried to hide their smiles. They knew where the young men had been. There was, after all, nothing unusual in these nocturnal adventures. This was just another of them.

*   *   *

Since the death of Duke George, Christian Lewis had become the head of the household. The brothers were good friends; they were all lusty, but all in agreement that nothing must stand in the way of their house's continued prosperity. One of them would marry and produce the heir to the entire estate; it was the accepted plan.

On the day following their night adventure Christian Lewis sent for his two brothers and told them he wanted to talk to them seriously.

"You were a little noisy at the inn this morning," he announced. "You were seen leaving. I have already heard of it ... from the town. A certain man and his wife, rising early to go to church, saw you leave and heard your ribald comments on the night's adventures."

George William grimaced and looked at Ernest Augustus, who burst out laughing.

"It is no laughing matter when the townsfolk disapprove," Christian Lewis reminded them. "Why don't you two each find yourselves a good mistress and settle down."

"We have one taste in common," replied George William. "It is a love of variety."

Christian Lewis sighed. "That's understandable. But a good mistress here would displease no one and then you should go abroad for your variety."

"Abroad," echoed George William. "I confess the prospect pleases me. Abroad ... where the women are supremely elegant.

French ladies! Italian ladies! They are more elegant than our Germans. Yes, I should be very pleased to find a friend or two among them."

"I am going to marry," Christian Lewis told them. "They're forcing me to it. It is time we produced the heir, they say. That leaves you two free. I envy you."

"Dear brother, it is noble of you to take on the burden," said George William.

"I am the eldest. It is my duty," answered Christian Lewis mournfully.

"I hope, brother," put in Ernest Augustus, "that you will have a comely bride."

"A woman of virtue and good background. Worthy to enter our family. We are deciding on Dorothea of Holstein-Glücksburg."

"Good fortune, brother! May you beget many sons and a few daughters."

"Thank you. I shall do my duty."

"We shall pray for you," said George William.

"And," went on Christian Lewis, "since I shall marry and you cannot live, it seems, without a variety of adventures, perhaps you should seek them outside our territory. You and your brother should do a little travelling."

"An excellent plan. Why should we not travel together?"

"That's what I would wish. Make your plans. Have your adventures—wild as you like—provided that in your own land you conduct yourself with decorum."

Ernest Augustus's eyes were shining with anticipation. There was little that could appeal to him more than a trip abroad in the company of his handsome and versatile brother.

* * *

After the wedding of Christian Lewis the two brothers set out on their travels journeying south into Italy until they came to Venice, and so enchanted were they with this beautiful city that they decided to rest there for a while.

They took a house on the Grand Canal and were welcomed into Venetian society : two young German Princes whose manners were, at the beginning, a little uncouth, but this gradually changed after contact with what the Venetians called the civilized world. The beauty of the city—particularly by night—enchanted the two men; Venice was at that time at the height of its glory—one of the gayest cities in Europe; rich, elegant, artistic, *civilized*. The young Germans had always loved music and this interest they were able to indulge to the full.

"Who would live in Celle," demanded George William, "when he could live in Venice?"

And as usual Ernest Augustus agreed with him.

After a series of love affairs George William entered into a more permanent arrangement with a young Venetian, Signora Buccolini—a woman of beauty and a nature sensuous enough to match his own. They set up an establishment together and Ernest Augustus—always accommodating—moved from his brother's house and set up a household of his own. But while George William lived with one mistress, Ernest Augustus failed to find one who could satisfy him completely, so he had many.

It was a pleasant existence and the brothers asked for nothing better. They revelled in their good fortune in being born younger sons while they spared time from pleasure now and then to pity poor Christian Lewis, who as the eldest, had to bear the burden of the estates.

Sometimes they would talk of Celle and laugh—the laughter of complacency—recalling the monastic nature of life in the castle and poor Christian Lewis sitting at the head table in the hall at precisely nine in the morning and four in the afternoon. They had heard that he was drinking heavily—it was his one vice, it was said. So presumably he did not waste much time outside the marriage bed. Poor Christian Lewis! What a sad duty to be forced to produce the heir!

"Soon," said George William, "we should be having news of the birth of our nephew."

But there was no news; and it was not easy to go on remembering dull Celle in glittering Venice.

Signora Buccolini became pregnant and that was a matter of great interest; particularly when in due course a son was born. He was a charming child with his mother's beauty, and it was amusing to be a father.

As soon as his mistress was recovered George William gave a ball to celebrate the occasion—a masked ball with gaiety and frivolity, and the canals were brilliant with beflowered and beribboned gondolas of the guests; and the culmination was the unmasking at midnight in St. Mark's Square.

It was a dazzling ball—but one of many in that gay city and the brothers were settling down to consider Venice their home. They were beginning to speak the language well, to act and think like Venetians. It was true that Signora Buccolini was becoming a little too possessive. She seemed to believe that having borne little Lucas she should demand absolute fidelity, and it was scarcely in George William's nature to grant that. There were passionate quarrels and even more passionate reconciliations, and so the days passed.

*　　*　　*

But this pleasant way of life could not be expected to go on for ever. Although the brothers appeared to forget this, they belonged to Brunswick-Lüneberg, and it was from these far-off estates that the money came which enabled them to enjoy this sybarite existence; and one day when George William sat on the terrace of his *palazzo* one of his servants came out to tell him that a messenger had arrived with a letter for him.

George William stared at the houses opposite; he was aware of the blue sky, of the handsome woman waving a hand to him as she passed in her gondola; and an icy shiver touched him, for he knew before he asked whence the messenger came.

"My lord will see him?" asked his servant.

"In a while," he said. "Give him refreshment first." What he asked for was a few more moments to enjoy this sunshine, this gay, enchanting scene, just a moment when he could delude himself into believing that the messenger did not come from Celle and the letter he brought was not from his brother and did not demand his instant return. Instead he had come to announce the birth of a son to Christian Lewis and to bring an assurance that George William could live for ever in this paradise.

It was hopeless, of course. What good did postponement ever bring? What was the use of gazing across the broad water, along to the Rialto. He had to leave it some time, he knew.

The messenger was standing before him.

"You come from Celle?" asked George William unnecessarily.

"From His Highness Duke Christian Lewis. And it is his express wish that I put this letter into no other hands but yours, my lord."

There was no escape. George William sighed and took the letter.

It was even worse than he had feared.

What was he doing in Venice? Did he not realize that he had his duties at home? The people were growing restive. The council were sending him an ultimatum. Either he returned home without delay or his allowance would be stopped. There was even graver news. Dorothea was proving to be barren, George William was the second in age, and it was his duty not only to return without delay, but to consider marriage, for the heir had to be produced somehow and since Christian Lewis and Dorothea could not, it must be George William and his bride.

"Marriage!" groaned George William. "Who would have thought that such an evil fate would ever overtake me?"

He sat for a long time, the letter held listlessly in his hand while he stared across the canal, but this time he did not see the beauties of the city he loved; he saw the castle of Celle. Sermons and prayers regularly each day; he heard the trumpet sounding from the tower. "Come to the table and eat! Stay away and starve!" What an uncivilized way to live.

He read the letter. Was there no way out? He could see none.

He walked down to the canal and signed to his boatman. He must go to Ernest Augustus and tell him that the days of pleasure were at an end. They must both prepare to leave without delay for Germany.

*   *   *

There was trouble with La Buccolini.

"And shall I be left with the child to bring up? And how shall he live in accordance with his rank?"

He could pacify her with gifts and promises, but she was loath to let him go.

How should she know that he would keep his promises?

He swore that he would; he had kept from her the fact that he was returning home to marry; but he promised himself and Ernest Augustus that he would come back to Venice.

It was two sad young men who journeyed northward.

"You grieve only for the loss of sun and gaiety," mourned George William. "Not only shall I lose them, too, but I have to put my head into the noose as well. Marriage! Oh, brother, to think that I should ever be called on to accept such a fate."

"I shall be with you," answered Ernest Augustus. "Have we not always been together? And if I settle with a mistress, I shall be expected to live with her and be to some extent faithful, which will be almost as bad as marriage."

"Nothing," retorted George William firmly, "could be as bad as marriage."

*   *   *

The old castle rising before them, the sun touching its yellow walls, looked like a prison to George William. The people he had seen on the road looked stern and dour—quite different from the Venetians. The girls at the inns where they had rested had been amusing for a time, but how different from the passionate Buccolini.

He gazed at the drawbridge and portcullis, the moat filled with the waters of the Aller, the strip of grass between it and the tall grim walls. A prison indeed!

In the courtyard he looked at the sundial at which, in the days of his childhood, he had told the time of day; the pigeons fluttered up in a cloud of white and purple from their lofts; listlessly he was aware of their cooing call.

Nothing had changed. He felt it would go on in the same manner, day after dreary day.

The grooms were rushing to his service, genuinely glad to see him back. He was the best-loved of all the brothers because he had a natural charm which the others lacked. He was less stolid, taller, more slender than his brothers, possessed of a natural grace; the others were heavy on their feet; he could dance well; he could play the guitar; he was good-natured and easy-going. He was elegantly dressed in a manner strange to them; the cloth of his coat was finer than that which they were accustomed to see; he wore rings on his fingers and a jewelled chain about his neck; and in his train he brought foreign servants. The days must necessarily be enlivened by the return of Duke George William.

He went into the castle, Ernest Augustus beside him—straight to the apartments of Christian Lewis and Dorothea.

The brothers embraced and after the exchange of a welcome Dorothea left them and they were joined by John Frederick, the third brother who was a year younger than George William and four years older than Ernest Augustus.

John Frederick's welcome was cool. He considered his brother George William lazy and lacking in a sense of duty; as for Ernest Augustus he was just a dupe who had no will of his own.

A precarious state of affairs for the House of Brunswick-Lüneberg, thought John Frederick, when the eldest had married a barren wife and the second son had no desire but to live abroad and squander his patrimony. Passionately John Frederick wished that he had been born the eldest.

"Ah," said George William, "a family conference."

Christian Lewis replied that it seemed wise for them to talk over their affairs together before they listened to what the council had to advise.

"Advise?" asked George William. "Or insist on?"

"There would be no need to insist, I am certain," answered placid Christian Lewis, "for once our duty is made clear to us it will be the ardent wish of us all to perform it."

"I understood," replied George William ironically, "that I am to be the one to perform the duty."

John Frederick said quickly: "If you did not, there would be others to step into your place."

George William turned to smile lazily at his fiery brother. Not you, my brother, he thought. But he bowed his head graciously and turned to Christian Lewis.

"It is becoming increasing clear that Dorothea cannot have a child," said Christian Lewis. "All this time and she remains sterile. The doctors tell me that it is unlikely she will ever conceive. Time doesn't stand still, my brothers. You are thirty-three, George William. It is time you finished roaming and giving sons to Venetian women. You must marry without delay."

George William lowered his eyes. He was aware of John Frederick's smoulderingly ambitious gaze and remembered the story they had heard from their father of how when his father lay dying he and his brothers had drawn lots as to who should provide the heir. The story had fascinated them all. Sometimes they would go to the very chamber in which Duke William the Pious had died and play the scene . . . treating it as a game. There had only been four of them to draw lots; but they had insisted that their sisters play the unimportant rôles—Sophia Amelia the old man in the bed and little Anne Eleanor—long since dead, for she had died before her sixth birthday—must be the steward who held the pieces of wood for them to draw. The excitement of that game had been that they had never known who would draw the shortest stick and he who did was allowed to be the lord of them all for the rest of the day.

George William could have sworn that John Frederick was thinking of that game now—wishing they could draw lots and make it a reality. Christian Lewis was occupied with the idea of passing on his duties, and Ernest Augustus—it was certain that his thoughts were where his heart was—in Venice.

"You have decided," said George William grimly; "and I'll warrant there is something else you have determined on too. The name of this unfortunate woman."

Christian Lewis smiled. "I am sure she will reckon herself the reverse, brother, when she sees you. I have heard it said that women favour you—and what I have seen gives me no reason to doubt it."

"Well," demanded George William, still conscious of the resentful glances of John Frederick, "who is she?"

"It has been suggested that Princess Sophia, daughter of the late King Frederick of Bohemia and Elector of Palatine, would be a good choice."

"Sophia . . ." murmured George William. "I have heard she is proud. Would she take me?"

"When a woman reaches the age of twenty-eight and is unmarried, she is not difficult to please."

"Then," replied George William, "it seems possible that she would take me."

"My dear brother, we have made certain that if you travelled to Heidelberg to woo her, your journey would not be in vain."

"Then," answered George William, "it seems there is no help for it. To Heidelberg I must go. Will you be my companion, brother?"

He had turned to Ernest Augustus as he spoke. The younger man smiled. Of course he would accompany his brother. It would be one last carouse before George William accepted his responsibilities.

"You should make your preparations without much delay," Christian Lewis warned them. "The council is impatient . . . so are the people. They want to see the heir."

George William shrugged his shoulders. He was resigned. He thought of his father who had drawn the shortest stick with a reluctance which now matched his own. Perhaps it would be possible to follow his example, for he had not been completely confined to Celle even after his marriage. Yet he had been a good Duke, combining pleasure and duty. And he had given his people what they asked—four sons.

Perhaps it was not so depressing as he had once thought; and he was certain that if John Frederick took his place, he would very quickly find some opportunity to denude his brothers of their estates and fortunes. There was a look of ambition in the eyes of John Frederick which George William did not like.

Very well, he was the second son; he would do his duty.

"Well, brother," he said to Ernest Augustus. "There is no help for it and no reason for delay. Let our good people see that they can rely on us."

Within a short time of their return from Venice the two brothers were preparing to leave for Heidelberg.

*   *   *

The Princess Sophia was elated at the prospect of receiving her suitor. She remembered him well for she had seen him years ago when he had first come to Heidelberg with his young brother—an exceedingly handsome boy, with the manners of a courtier; he had danced with her and she had flirted with both boys. She suspected that this was an occupation in which they indulged as naturally as breathing. George William had played the guitar to her which he did most charmingly; and while he was in her company had made her believe that he enjoyed it more than that of any other person.

But she was too shrewd nowadays to believe that—although at the time she had been willing enough to delude herself. Well, now she was to marry him—and it was time too that they both married. She was not displeased with her prospective bridegroom—although being an extremely ambitious woman she had had hopes of a more advantageous marriage.

What joy, though, to escape from Heidelberg! It was not very pleasant being tolerated at her brother's court as the poor sister who was not particularly well endowed with personal attractions, and every year taking a few steps farther away from marriageability.

In her youth she had been tolerably handsome; but this had been completely overshadowed by the beauty of her mother. Elizabeth, Queen of Bohemia—until her husband Frederick had been deprived of his throne—had become known as the Queen of Hearts, so charming was she, and compared with such a mother the mildly handsome looks of her daughter Sophia had been insignificant. Moreover, she had been poor from birth, for the family's fortunes had been already in decline when she arrived in the world. Therefore with little to recommend her but her birth she became excessively proud of that.

Although she did not see her mother frequently—Sophia declared that Queen Elizabeth preferred her dogs and monkeys to her children—it was she who dominated the household. Her personality was such that she must attract and, however resentful Sophia felt, she must admire. It had not been much fun, moving about Europe enjoying hospitality wherever it was possible to beg it, yet Queen Elizabeth did so with grace and great charm; she even gave banquets—although this always meant the sacrifice of some precious jewels; the courtiers about them were mostly rats and mice, Sophia had grimly commented, to which of course could be added the creditors. And through her troubles Elizabeth moved serene, admired, adored—the Queen of Hearts.

She never forgot that she was an English Princess. Although, Sophia pointed out—and had her ears boxed for her impertinence—her mother was the Danish Princess Anne and her father, King James I of England and VI of Scotland, more Scots than English.

But England was the country enshrined in her mother's heart.

In England she had been an honoured princess; in Bohemia she had been Queen of a Kingdom which quickly rejected her husband and made an exile of her. Sophia had been brought up with a great admiration for England and to hope that she might go there—as a Queen.

It had not seemed an impossible dream. It was true that her uncle, Charles I, had been in conflict with his Parliament and as a result had lost his head, that Oliver Cromwell had set up a Commonwealth and that the son of Charles I, Prince Charles, was wandering from court to court on the Continent now, waiting and hoping for a chance to regain his kingdom. If ever he did, a bride would be very carefully chosen for him, but, while he was a wandering prince, he was not such a good proposition. That had seemed to be Sophia's chance.

He was a charming young man, this cousin of hers—witty, amusing, goodhearted, selfish perhaps—but what Prince was not? —gay and very licentious. She dreamed of him; so did her mother.

"One of my dearest wishes, Sophia," her mother had said to her, "is to see you Queen of England."

"But there is no Queen of England," Sophia had replied, to which her mother had shrugged her shoulders impatiently.

"Of course there will be a Queen of England. Charles will go back. Make no mistake about that. I believe the people would have him now—they are heartily sick of the Puritans already."

So the Queen had had her daughter brought up to speak English fluently; and she learned more about England than any other country; and although she had never seen it, her mother talked of it so intimately when they were together that Sophia saw it . . . saw Windsor Castle with its ancient walls, and the palace of St. James's and Whitehall where her uncle Charles the Martyr had been cruelly murdered by Cromwell's orders.

Sophia had believed that England was important to her, but Cousin Charles made no effort to court her. One heard constant stories of his amatory exploits, but there was no marriage. He was waiting, said the Queen, until his throne was restored to him; and then what chance would his poor cousin Sophia have to marry him and become the Queen of England?

So the years passed—and while Charles waited for his throne Sophia waited for a husband. There was the attack of smallpox from which she recovered, but it had left its mark on her, and her beauty was not improved.

She was beginning to despair of ever marrying, which would mean living at the court of her brother the Elector Palatine where she was not wanted, listening and often forced to take part in the squabbles between him and his wife, the poor relation, the woman whose ambitions had gone sour, who had no fortune —nothing but her pride in her birth and a love for a far-off country which she had never seen and which was becoming a fetish with her.

Thus Sophia—twenty-eight and desperate—prepared to offer a warm welcome to Duke George William when he came to Heidelberg to propose marriage to her.

*   *   *

Her maid dressed her for the meeting. It was not a new gown; there was no money for new gowns. Her mother, wandering in exile through Europe, continually suffering poverty, short of money, could not help; nor was her brother the Elector inclined to. She had her home at his court; she must be content with that. "Oh, rescue me soon, George William!" murmured Sophia. And her eyes brightened at the prospect.

While her maid was dressing her hair she studied her reflection. Her hair was rather pretty, falling in light brown natural curls about her shoulders; when she smiled she was not without charm despite the damage done to her skin by the accursed pox. It was a pity she were not a little taller, but she made up for that by carrying herself well and haughtily—as became a princess with English blood in her veins.

She hoped George William would be pleased with her. Not that it should make any difference if he were not. This marriage had been arranged and he would have no more choice than she would. She hoped he had not changed. He had been such a charming boy—as her cousin Charles undoubtedly was; and George William, she believed, although he had had countless mistresses, was not quite so profligate as Charles. His mistresses would not be important though, as long as he spent enough time in her bed to enable her to provide the necessary heirs— and, of course, accorded to her the dignity of her rank.

A servant came to tell her that her brother the Elector commanded that she join him in his apartments. She knew this meant she was to be presented to her future husband.

One last look at her reflection. If I were not pitted with the pox, she thought, I should be tolerably handsome.

She was announced, and as she came into the apartment saw her brother with George William. George William was one of the handsomest men she had ever seen.

As he bowed to her, she lifted her eyes to him, and felt an

excitement creeping over her. This was indeed the next best thing
to marriage into England.

George William took her hand.

"I find it impossible to convey my pleasure in this meeting."

He was suave, elegant, gallant.

His brother, standing a few paces behind him, was quite a
pleasant young man but eclipsed by the other's superior
attractions.

George William gave no sign of the deep depression which he
was experiencing.

He had decided in that moment that marriage was even
more repugnant than he had imagined—and he certainly did
not want Princess Sophia for his bride.

*   *   *

There was little finesse about the Elector. He knew why the
brothers were in Heidelberg and so did everyone else, so why
make any pretence about it? The house of Brunswick-Lüneberg
wanted a wife for its Duke, and there was no doubt that he
wanted a husband for Sophia. He was tired of keeping his sister;
her tongue was a little too sharp for his liking, he resented her
cost to his household : and he would rejoice to see her the concern
of someone else.

So he arranged that the young people should have a private
interview on the very day of the arrival of the Duke and his
brother.

Duke William, accepting the unpleasant duty before him,
plunged in without any preamble, seating himself beside Sophia
and taking her hand. His voice was cool as he said : "You know
for what purpose I am here?"

There was nothing of the coquette about Sophia.

"I have been told," she replied.

"Then I trust you are not displeased by the arrangements
which our families have made for us. I do assure you that if this
matter is distasteful to you . . ."

"It is not distasteful to me," she answered sharply.

He was surprised, and she turned to him laughing. "I am not
going to play the part of coy maiden. Have no fear of that. I
am nearing thirty. Time is running out. If I am going to give
my husband heirs I should delay no longer."

"I had thought . . ."

"That I was in my teens? Now come, my lord Duke, you
thought nothing of the sort. You knew my age as well as I
knew yours. Why, as soon as a match was mooted between us,

I'll warrant you discovered all it was advisable for you to know about me . . . as I did about you."

He laughed. She had a ready tongue.

"Well," he said, "there is little for me to say but : Will you marry me?"

"And nothing for me to answer but: I will."

"So the matter is settled then?"

"To your satisfaction, I hope."

"It is the successful conclusion to my mission. I had not thought to complete it so soon."

"Then, my lord Duke, have you nothing more to say to me?"

He took her hand and kissed it. His kiss was cold; and remembering all the stories she had heard of him she knew how different it might have been.

He was telling her that it was a marriage of convenience and she would not be expected to ask for more. This was surely not the way he behaved with his Venetian mistress.

And why? Because he felt no passion for pock-pitted Sophia, because he was proposing marriage only because his family insisted that he should?

Sophia was greatly attracted by him. She was longing for marriage, to be the mother of children, to attain the rank and dignity which was denied her in her brother's court. If her bridegroom were not pleased with her, she was with him.

*   *   *

The marriage contract had been signed. There was one condition. George William had explained to the Elector Palatine that he could not consider marrying immediately because he had affairs to settle, so he wished that his betrothal to Sophia should not be made public just at this time.

The Elector, afraid that any disagreement might mean he had his sister back on his hands, was amenable, and George William took his leave of his bride-to-be and with Ernest Augustus left Heidelberg.

Ernest Augustus did not like to see his brother so downcast.

"Oh come, brother," he said, "it's not so bad. You'll soon get her with child and when she has produced your son, you and I will go off on a little jaunt together."

"I have no great fancy for her," admitted George William.

"Well, 'twill not be necessary to. Cheer up. You must be in good spirits in Venice."

"Venice !" cried George William.

"The soon-to-be-married man should have his final bachelor carousal."

George William turned to Ernest Augustus and they began to laugh.

"Come on! To Venice then!" cried George William.

"There to forget the future while we revel in the present."

"Yes, we'll revel, for I have a notion, brother, that if I am married to that woman nothing will ever be the same again."

* * *

It was not even the same in Venice.

Signora Buccolini surveyed him with suspicion, as he did her. He believed she had been taking lovers during his absence.

He was changed, she told him. He was remote. His thoughts were elsewhere.

"You are in love with someone," she accused him.

"No," he cried. "I'm not. I wish to God I were."

Such a cryptic remark did not ease matters; there was an attempt to recapture the old passion, but it would not come, and the bedchamber of the beautiful Signora seemed to be haunted by the Princess Sophia.

He could not stop thinking of her. She came between him and his passion. How could I ever make love to her? he asked himself. Other princes did in such marriages. But he was different. He was at heart a romantic; he was a man of taste and elegance.

Oh, God, he thought, I could never make love to that woman! Marriage! The thought of it haunted him.

"I would do anything ... anything," he told Ernest Augustus, "to escape it."

Little Lucas, his son, was his only consolation during those days. The boy was growing up—proud and handsome; he asked questions about his father's country. George William guessed that his mother had been talking to him too freely—perhaps putting the questions into the child's mouth.

All the magic had gone from Venice. The flower-decked gondolas seemed tawdry, and the canals smelt unpleasantly. Even the women had lost their mystery; they were very little different from the German women. And he suspected his mistress was unfaithful to him.

In any case he was no longer in love with her. He had returned hoping to start again where he had left off. It was a mistake.

He awoke one early morning to find his mistress missing; he was waiting for her when she crept in before daybreak.

"So," he said, "what I suspected is true."

"And why should you think I should remain faithful to you? Have you been faithful to me?"

He said : "I did not ask for fidelity while I was away. But now I am here you prefer another man."

"Oh, you and your fine stories of your rank and greatness in Germany! Germany! What of Germany? And where is the money you promised me for your son?"

"Our son will be cared for, never fear."

"So far he has had to rely on his mother rather than his father ... albeit *she* is a woman of no standing and *he* is a Prince. Who is going to keep him when you go back to your Germany? Tell me that. Oh, I've heard rumours. There's going to be a marriage. I know. And then we shall not see our precious Duke again in Venice. He will be living cosily with his lawful wife in his German castle and I shall be forgotten, and Lucas with me."

"It is true that I have to go back home, but I'll leave a settlement for you."

"And the boy?"

"I'll take him back with me."

He had spoken without thought. How could he take the boy back to his new wife and say : "This is my son!" He was becoming impetuous. He spoke without thought. This was what came of being forced into marriage.

"Go as soon as you like," she snapped. "Or as soon as you've made your settlement. And take the boy with you. You owe it to him."

He was astonished. He had expected a passionate quarrel and the even more passionate reconciliation; but there was no doubt of it : she had her new lover and she wanted to be rid of the child. It was a sign that their relationship was at an end.

I am betrothed to a woman who does not attract me, thought George William, and I must go back to Celle with my little Venetian bastard.

Rarely had he felt so depressed.

He returned to bed and lay thinking. There was a way out of his predicament.

When he rose from his bed that morning he knew himself for a desperate man, and he was going to take desperate action.

He dressed carefully, and went out into the sunshine. He stepped across the terrace and down to the water's edge, signing to his boatman.

Along the odorous waters of the canal, through the disenchanted city to the establishment of his brother, Ernest Augustus.

* * *

Sleepily satisfied. Ernest Augustus lay in the sun on the terrace of his *palazzo* but he started up when he saw his brother, realizing from his expression the seriousness of his mood.

"Where can I talk to you in private?" demanded George William.

"Here. Why, brother, what has happened?"

"We might be disturbed here. We might be overheard. This is of the utmost secrecy."

Ernest Augustus led the way into a room; after locking the door, he drew the blinds, shutting out the bright sunlight.

"I cannot go on with the marriage," declared George William.

Ernest Augustus shook his head sadly.

"I know you think you have heard this before. But you have not. I have made up my mind. I will not marry Sophia. In fact I won't marry at all."

"You must. There's no way out of it."

"There is. That's what I want to talk to you about. *You* shall marry Sophia in my place."

"I!"

"Pray don't stand there looking stupid. I said you shall marry her—if you will. And why should you not? As long as one of us marries, as long as one of us produces the heir ... what does it matter?"

"But *you* are betrothed to Sophia."

"I think I must have had this in mind even then, because I insisted the betrothal should not be made public knowledge just yet. Listen to me, brother. You shall take my place at the wedding."

"I could not afford to marry."

"You could if I made over certain estates and money to you."

"And you would do this?"

"Ernest Augustus, if you would but take this woman off my hands I will do much for you. Brother, for my sake ... do this."

Ernest Augustus was thoughtful. Take his brother's place. Step up from the youngest brother to the head of his house—for that was what he would be if he produced the son who would inherit the family estates. Christian Lewis had a sterile wife; George William would not marry; John Frederick would not be

allowed to, either . . . and he, Ernest Augustus, would have the
honour of fathering the heir of Brunswick-Lüneberg.

But suppose at some time George William did marry?

He shook his head, but George William had seized him and
was shaking him gently to and fro.

"You must save me from this woman."

"There are too many complications."

"Nonsense! What complications?"

"I'm the youngest."

"Our father was the sixth of seven sons and yet he became
head of our house."

"That was agreed on by all his brothers when they drew lots."

"It shall be agreed on between us all . . . in just the same way."

"Would you swear never to marry?"

"I would swear it."

"John Frederick would have to swear the same."

"He shall swear it."

"And Christian Lewis would have to agree."

"My dear brother, have no fear. This shall be done in such
a way as shall give you no qualms . . . no fears of the future.
Marry this woman and you shall have the means to settle yourself and start a family. You shall be the head of our house, I
promise you."

"In that case," said Ernst Augustus, "it will be necessary for
us to return to Celle without delay. There we will draw up the
documents, for much as I trust you, brother, this is a matter
which must be signed and sealed, and our brothers must be
present at the signing–sealing ceremony."

George William clapped his brother on the back. "You are
become a man of affairs already." Then he embraced him. "How
can I thank you! It is as though a great burden has fallen from
my shoulders."

In a few days' time the brothers left Venice and travelled
northwards, little Lucas Buccolini going with them. George
William was planning to put him with foster parents; his education and future would be well looked after; his name would be
changed—perhaps to Buccow—because it would be a handicap
to the boy to go through life with an Italian name. He should
have a place in his household, but that was for later. At the
moment George William must give his mind to settling this little
matter; and once Ernest Augustus was married, he, George
William, would go off on his travels again. It would be different
though. He would miss Ernest Augustus; and he would not
want to return to Venice. Yes, everything would be a little

different, for Ernest Augustus had already changed. He carried his head a little higher; he gave orders to his servants in a more peremptory manner; he had acquired a new dignity even before he took on his bride and his new estates.

* * *

Christian Lewis was thoughtful.

"I see no harm in it," he said. "Ernest Augustus is willing to take over your responsibilities and if you will agree to his terms then, for the love of our house, let us get the terms settled without delay. We are no longer children and this marriage should take place as soon as it can be arranged."

"I will prepare my statement at once," said George William.

"There is one point that you have not considered," added Christian Lewis. "What of the lady? How will she take the change?"

George William agreed this was a matter which would need delicate handling. "A pity," he said, "that we did not come to this arrangement before I made the proposal. Never mind. It's not a man she wants but marriage. You must admit that our young brother is a fine figure of a man."

"Let us hope that she thinks so," added Christian Lewis with a smile.

"We will get the matter settled; then she shall be informed and Ernest Augustus can go to his nuptials."

"You understand all you are giving up?"

"I understand absolutely."

"You may regret."

"I shall always remember that the price I paid for freedom was worth it."

* * *

In his study George William was writing his renunciation of marriage.

"Having perceived the necessity of taking into consideration how our House of this line may best be provided with heirs and be perpetuated in the future; yet having been and remaining up to the present date both unable and unwilling in my person to engage in any marriage contract, I have rather induced my brother, Ernest Augustus, to declare that, on condition of receiving from me a renunciation of marriage for myself, written and signed with my own hand, in favour of himself and his heirs male, he is prepared forthwith and without delay to enter into holy matrimony, and, as may be hoped, soon to bestow the blessing of heirs on people and country, as had been agreed and settled between him and myself; and whereas my brother, Ernest Augustus, for reasons before mentioned has entered into a marriage contract with Her Highness Princess Sophia, which contract he purposes shortly to fulfil so I, on my side, not only on account of my word given to and pledged, but also of my own free will and consent, desire to ratify and confirm the aforesaid conditions to my aforementioned brother and promise, so long as the said Princess and my brother continue in life and in the bonds of matrimony, or after their decease leave heirs male, that I neither will nor shall on any account enter into, much less carry out, any marriage contract with any person, and with nothing else than to spend what remains to me of life entirely *in caelibatu*, to the extent that the heirs male of the aforementioned Princess and of my brother, in whose favour this renunciation is made, may attain and succeed to the sovereignty over one or both of these our principalities. For the same and truer assurance of all which conditions I have, with my own hand, written and signed this renunciation and sealed it with my seal, and thereafter handed it over with all due care to my brother's own charge and keeping."

George William read through what he had written. It appeared to embrace every point. Now he must sign it and seal it in the presence of his brothers; and then the matter would be settled, apart from informing the Princess Sophia of the change.

*   *   *

The three brothers were waiting in the apartment of Christian Lewis for the arrival of the fourth. John Frederick had no notion as to why he was being summoned, but as George William had said, it was of no great concern of his for as the third brother he had nothing to lose by the transaction.

"At last!" cried George William as John Frederick entered. "Welcome, brother. An important ceremony is about to take place."

"It is evidently a pleasant one," replied John Frederick, "judging by the look of you and Ernest Augustus."

George William glanced at his youngest brother. Good God, he thought, he *is* ambitious. He wants to produce the heir to the house. He wants to marry Sophia.

And he had been imagining this was a sacrifice his brother had been making for his sake!

So Ernest Augustus was ambitious! Well, George William was a generous man and it always pleased him better to give than to take. He was pleased therefore that Ernest Augustus was more than reconciled—gratified and delighted.

"I am all eagerness to hear," pointed out John Frederick.

Christian Lewis nodded to George William. "Explain to him," he said.

"Well, brother, it is like this. I was betrothed to the Princess Sophia."

"You mean you are no longer betrothed?"

"No longer so. I have decided to abdicate in favour of a brother."

Eagerness shot up in John Frederick's eyes.

"You understand," went on George William, "that I have no wish for marriage."

"I have always known that—and therefore it is right that you should pass on the opportunity to a brother."

"Then we are all in agreement."

"Of course it would be necessary for you to pass on not only the bride but certain monies."

"That has all been thought of. The bridegroom will have nothing of which to complain. I have drawn up the necessary documents and we shall sign them immediately."

"And the Princess has been acquainted with the change?"

"Not yet. We thought it necessary to have the agreements signed and sealed before acquainting her."

"I will ride to Heidelberg tomorrow."

"You, John Frederick?"

"As the future bridegroom . . ."

"It is Ernest Augustus who has agreed to take over the marriage."

"Ernest Augustus! But he's the youngest!"

"I have made the arrangement with him and he has given me his promise."

"But I am the next in seniority. I should be the one."

Ernest Augustus took a few paces towards his brother and said: "It's too late, John Frederick. Everything is settled now. I am going to marry Sophia."

"I'll not agree."

"You will have to. The three of us agree and you would be one against the rest."

"I agree to changing the bridegrooms, but I consider that my place in the family entitles me to be the marrying one."

"Too late, too late," said George William. "I have come to an agreement with Ernest Augustus."

John Frederick seized his young brother's arm. "You will stand aside for me."

George William took John Frederick by the shoulder and wrenching him away from his brother threw him across the room.

"Enough of this nonsense," he said. "I have the document here and I shall sign—and that is the end of the matter."

John Frederick glowered; Ernest Augustus held his breath; he could scarcely wait for the signature to be put to the paper. Those few strokes of the pen would make him in a sense the head of the house. For the first time in his life he despised his handsome, amusing elder brother. George William was a fool. He was throwing away his birthright for a mess of potage. Pray God he did not realize this until his name was at the foot of that important paper.

George William laid the paper on a table and took up his pen.

"George William," he wrote, "Duke of Brunswick and Lüneberg, April 11th, 1658."

He stood up. "There!" he cried. "The deed is done. Here, brother, is your assurance."

As Ernest Augustus took the paper, John Frederick tried to snatch it from him. The paper fluttered to the floor to be picked up by George William while the two younger brothers, caught in an angry embrace, rolled on the floor.

George William stood laughing at them for a few seconds. Then he cried: "I'll not have this solemn occasion changed into a brawl."

He put the paper on the table and went to the aid of Ernest Augustus, and together they succeeded in thrusting John Frederick from the room.

George William locked the door and stood leaning against it.

"Well, brother," he said, "there's your security. Now go to."

Christian Lewis looked grave.

"Come, cheer up," admonished George William. "This is for me a gay occasion. I want to celebrate my freedom."

"I like it not," murmured Christian Lewis, "when brothers quarrel."

*   *   *

The Elector Palatine sent for his sister.

"I have news for you," he said. "News from Celle."

Sophia sat quietly, her hands folded in her lap, but her heart beat uncomfortably. Was he going to attempt to wriggle out of his agreement? He had been lukewarm. She had recognized that.

This couldn't be yet another disappointment. How could she endure to go on living, single, at her brother's court with no hope of ever improving her position !

"Duke George William has decided that he is not fitted for matrimony."

Thank God she had always been able to cloak her feelings ! So he found her repulsive. He had taken a look at her, had reluctantly agreed to marry her, and then gone away—presumably to one of his mistresses—and changed his mind, and so determinedly that he had had the effrontery to jilt her. It was unforgivable.

Still she sat calmly, hands in her lap.

"But," went on her brother, perhaps enjoying keeping her in suspense, "they have a bridegroom for you."

She lifted her head sharply then and said in a cold voice : "What is the meaning of this ?"

"Duke George William declines to marry you, oh, not you personally. It has nothing to do with that. It is marriage itself to which he objects. Ernest Augustus, however, has no such objections."

"He has no such prospects either."

"That is not so. George William resigns more than you to him, sister. He has given him a promise not to marry, to pass over certain estates to his brother and the heirs of your body shall become the heirs to the entire estate."

"So then, nothing is changed but the man."

The Elector laughed. "You're a cool one," he said.

"Tell me, brother, is it not the Brunswick-Lüneberg estates I am marrying? Should you give your consent to my marrying one of your subjects?"

"Assuredly not."

'Well then, I shall have all that was promised me—the only difference is that they will be handed me by a younger brother. A good establishment is all I care about and if it can be secured through the younger brother, I am indifferent to the change of man."

"You're a wise woman, Sophia, and I'm glad. You can't afford to be aught else at your age. Mind you, I think you'll get on better with the younger brother."

"And why so?"

"He seemed to me more amenable. You'll make him dance to your tune, Sophia. I doubt whether you would have been able to have done the same with the other."

"Then there is nothing in the way of going ahead with the marriage?"

"Nothing at all. I will write this day to Ernest Augustus and tell him that you will be delighted to take him to be your husband. I see no reason for delay, sister. You can begin making your preparations at once."

He looked after his sister as she left the room.

Cold, he thought. Ambitious. But she would make a good wife for this Ernest Augustus. She was reasonable too, which saved a great deal of trouble.

*   *   *

Sophia dismissed her servants and sat down by her mirror studying her reflection.

So I do not attract him! she thought. He took a look at me, weakly agreed to have me, and then went away and changed his mind.

Good God! How repulsive he must find me since he is ready to throw away a large portion of his estates and his chances of ever having legitimate children—all to be rid of me.

She was not as cold as they believed her to be but as romantic as any young woman might expect to be. Before the smallpox she had not been uncomely—perhaps if he had seen her then . . .

But he had, when they were children, and he had danced with her and played the guitar to her and she had, in the manner of the very young, conceived a romantic fancy for him. When she had heard she was to marry him, she had been exultant; she had changed, become more feminine, dreamed of the future. And when she had seen him, although he had been cool to her and made no pretence that he was in love with her, she had continued to dream.

But he would not have her. Moreover, he was ready to pay a great price to discard her.

Very few women could have been so insulted. She should be grateful that the engagement had not been made public—but it would be known, of course, throughout all the German principalities and throughout Europe. Cousin Charles would hear . . . in Breda or wherever he was . . . roaming about the Continent, waiting for a chance to get his kingdom back. And he would commiserate with George William; he would say : "I understand the fellow's reluctance. She was offered to me, you know."

She would never forget how George William had insulted her.

But by good fortune there was Ernest Augustus and as nothing helpful could come of brooding on her disappointment, she must take what she could get.

Ernest Augustus! He had come to Heidelberg with his brother when they were boys. He was not unpleasant; he had some charm;

it was merely that George William eclipsed him. Ernest Augustus had been interested in her, at that time; he would have willingly been very friendly indeed. But she had looked on him as a younger brother with few prospects and had no intention of allowing her name to be coupled with his, a matter which might work to her detriment if other suitors were being considered.

That was when she was young, of course, before her complexion had been spoilt, when her mother still hoped that she would capture the Prince of Wales.

And now he was to be her husband. He was not unlike his brother. When one did not see them together he would appear very like him. In any case she had to make the best of him. She could endure no more delay. She wanted marriage quickly and children to make her position sure.

She must insist on her brother's making absolutely certain that the documents were in order; and then she must receive her bridegroom as though she was just as happy to have him as his brother.

She would do it, she had no fear.

It was only in the solitude of her own bedchamber that she allowed herself to give way to thoughts of bitterness and disappointment.

*　　*　　*

Ernest Augustus came with all speed to Heidelberg and before there could be any more delays the Elector arranged that the marriage should take place.

There were balls and banquets to celebrate the event—which the Elector informed his sister in private, he could ill afford.

"At least," she retorted, "you will be rid of me now. So this is the last expense you will have to bear for me."

The Elector did not answer, but in his heart he knew she was right.

So the wedding took place and Sophia was not entirely displeased with her bridegroom. They were the same age; and Ernest Augustus seemed to have grown both mentally and physically since he took over his brother's commitments. He was shrewd and ambitious; and that was what Sophia would expect her husband to be.

He assured her that he considered his brother's defection as the greatest luck to himself. He proved to be a passionate lover and Sophia, being an ambitious woman, reciprocated, being pleased that the foundations of her life were now settled. It was not what she would have wished; she still thought a great deal about England—but of course that country was closed to her ambitions now. She had a princely husband, who was young and lusty; and she believed that when she had her children—sons to start with, to make sure of the succession—she would be a contented woman.

They left Heidelberg—first for Hanover and then settled at Osnabrück; and it was here that Sophia was able to give her husband the joyful news that she was pregnant.

*   *   *

Sophia lay on her bed and those who served her believed that she would never leave it. She had calmly awaited this event all through the difficult months of pregnancy; and now she was battling not only to give birth but for her own life.

As she lay between spasms of agony she thought of the past, of her hopes, of her dread that she would never marry and make a destiny for herself and her children. It could not end like this.

"I'll not allow it," she told herself as she lost consciousness.

*   *   *

She heard the cry of a child and joy enveloped her, taking away her pain, leaving her limp and exhausted but triumphant.

"The child?" her lips moved, but no sound came.

And then—infinite joy—someone spoke. "A boy . . . a healthy boy."

She lay lightly dreaming; then she was aware of someone at her bedside. It was Ernest Augustus.

"Sophia," he said, and his voice seemed far off. "We have him. We have our son."

"So!" she whispered. "Then you are well content?"

"You must lie quiet. It has been a trying time."

"But he is well . . . he is strong. . . ."

"Listen. He has a good pair of lungs, they tell me. *He's* trying to tell you now."

"Show me," she whispered.

And he was brought to her and put into her arms.

The pain had been worthwhile, she thought. Gloriously worthwhile. This was the meaning of life. She would scheme for this child, plan for him; her first born.

They called him George Lewis.

Romance in Breda

GEORGE WILLIAM was restless. He had no desire to return to Venice. He was free to go where he would, for Ernest Augustus and Sophia were doing their duty for the Guelphs. They now had two sons, George Lewis was healthy, although excessively ugly, and little Frederick Augustus had joined him in the nursery.

It was amusing to watch Ernest Augustus as a father and head of the house. How he had changed! He no longer looked up to George William as he once had. He was the ambitious man on the alert to establish the position he had won by taking his brother's place, anxious to make little George Lewis's inheritance a worthy one.

He had recently succeeded to the Bishopric of Osnabrück, that See which was founded by Charlemagne. It was a strange selection, but the Treaty of Westphalia had decreed that the Prince Bishops of Osnabrück should be alternately Roman Catholic and Lutheran; and that the Lutheran Bishop should be chosen by the chapter from the house of Brunswick-Lüneberg. Thus was Ernest Augustus selected, and as it was an office bringing with it power as well as riches he had been delighted to accept. He had immediately moved his family to the Castle of Iburg and decided to make this his headquarters.

He was enjoying life. I should have made him pay me for what was done, mused George William. He made no sacrifice.

They were growing apart. Ernest Augustus was so much the married man, George William the confirmed bachelor. The only

quality they shared was their deep sensuality, for although Ernest
Augustus was married he was by no means a faithful husband. He
did his duty by Sophia, giving her every opportunity to bear
children, but it was not to be expected that one woman could
satisfy him. He was determined to live his own life and made it
clear that while every respect was paid to Sophia by his subjects,
while she might rule the household as chatelaine, he must be
allowed to go his way. Sophia understood this; she never complained at the mistresses he took; she had control of the children
and the household, and was queen in her domain. Very well, she
would not ask for the impossible.

So Ernest Augustus had done well. He even managed to travel
a little—although not too far, nor did he stay away too long. He
could see that George William was doing himself no good by his
constant absences. He liked hunting, eating, drinking and sleeping
with women. While he could get these and beget a family he was
content.

Not so George William. Restlessly he flitted about the Continent
until eventually he came to Breda, which had become known as
the home of exiles, for in this pleasant town they congregated and
lived recklessly and hopefully, as exiles will.

There was a royal set in Breda—exiled Princes and Princesses,
Kings and Queens and the nobility who had reasons for wanting
to leave their native countries, settled there. Some were rich;
many were poor; and those who might not be able to compete
with the rich hostesses of the Court of Restored Royalty in England
or that glittering opulence of Versailles, set up house in Breda and
contented themselves with offering hospitality to persons who, at
the moment, were in the shadows but full of hope of returning to
power, in which case they might remember the friends of their
needy days.

Sophia's mother, the ex-Queen of Bohemia, had stayed at
Breda; so had Charles Prince of Wales who had now returned
to England where, he had said, he was greeted so warmly
that it must have been his own fault that he had stayed away so
long.

Through the streets the carriages of the once-great or near-
great rattled; ladies dressed in the latest French fashions acknowledged the greetings of gallant gentlemen as their carriages passed
along. Every day seemed to be the occasion for some brilliant ball
or masquerade. The people of Breda were proud of their foreign
population which had brought such prosperity to the town.

George William was welcomed. He was no exile but came purely
for pleasure; his servants found a worthy lodging for him and in

the first few days he received a message from the Princesse de
Tarente inviting him to a ball.

George William was delighted. Breda soothed him; here was
grace and charm which might have come straight from Versailles.
It was different from Venice. The climate was not so clement; the
romantic canals and the delight of a masque which ended in St.
Mark's Square was missing; but there was an excitement about
Breda which Venice lacked; and he felt his spirits rising. As his
servants dressed him for the ball he knew that he had been wise to
hand over everything to Ernest Augustus. Freedom was worth
anything.

It was a splendid ball and he was received effusively by the
Princess.

"My dear, dear Duke!" she cried, holding out both hands to
welcome him. "What a pleasure this is! We are almost related
now. You were indeed a wicked one to refuse my niece. You look
astonished. Did you not know that the Duchess Sophia is my
niece?"

"It is impossible. I had thought you might be sisters."

"Now you would flatter me. Or has marriage aged dear Sophia
so much? I hear she has two splendid boys! How happy the dear
Bishop must be! And you ... oh no, you are a born bachelor and
still determined to remain one. I hope you are not contemplating
a short stay in Breda. We are two Germans, remember. After all,
I am only French by marriage. But you will meet some delightful
people ... delightful. ..."

She was ready to greet the next guest and he passed on. Such
enchanting women! He danced; he flattered; and it was like a
hundred other balls he had attended until he found Eléonore.

She was tall and her dark hair, which was very abundant, was
piled high on her head, although one curl was allowed to fall over
her shoulder; she had a dazzling complexion and sparkling dark
eyes; and George was struck by her air of dignity, which was rare
in one so young, and of modesty which was even more rare.

She spoke German as a foreigner speaks it and he knew from
her accent that she was French.

The Princess had presented him to her.

"Take care of my little *demoiselle d'honneur*," she said, "and
she will see that you are well cared for as it is your first visit to us
and we want it to be the forerunner of many."

Perhaps she was being a little mischievous. Perhaps she was
thinking of his reputation for indulging in amorous intrigue and
Eléonore's for virtue; but she as well as these two were astonished
at what happened that night.

They danced together and they talked. Those who knew George William well would have been surprised, for his manner had changed. Into his voice there had come a gentleness which had never been there before. There was a complete absence of innuendo in his remarks; he was not planning the quickest route to the desired goal. Not that she did not delight him; she did, as he had never been so enchanted; but from the first moment of their meeting this was an adventure such as he had never indulged in before. He took her to an alcove lightly secluded by foliage where he said they could talk in comfort. He wanted to know why she was in Breda, how long she had been there, how long she intended to remain, what had brought her there.

"I was at the Court of France," she said, "but we are Huguenots."

"Exiled then?" he asked.

She nodded.

"And you long to return?"

"Not as things are. It would not be wise."

"So you live here in the Princess's household."

"She has been so good to us."

"To you . . . and others?"

"To my family. My father and my sister Angelique."

"They should have called you Angelique," he told her. "It would have suited you. Though I prefer your name. But perhaps any name which was yours would become beautiful simply for that reason."

"You like to pay compliments."

"And you to receive—although I know you must grow weary of them."

"I like best the truth," she said.

"Perhaps I may meet your father and sister."

"I am sure they would be delighted. My father is Alexandre d'Esmiers, Marquis d'Olbreuse."

"Do you think he would be pleased to receive me?"

"He is always delighted to receive friends of the Princesse de Tarente. She has been so good to us. To have many friends helps to soothe the . . . *mal du pays*."

"And you suffer from that?"

"A little. Though perhaps not so much as my father. It is easier to leave your home when you are young. I think he often dreams of Poitou. He would love to go back. But how can he? His estates were confiscated after the revocation of the Edict of Nantes when Huguenots were persecuted by the Government."

"That must have been sad for your family—but I can only be glad because it has brought you here."

She was quite enchanting, and after the first shock of being with the most beautiful and attractive young woman he had ever met he began to wonder how soon he could make her his mistress.

He was too experienced to make a false step; he knew very well that he would have to be patient. He was prepared for a little delay, but because of that, the culmination would seem all the more worthwhile when it was reached.

He went warily through the evening—yet as though in a dream. And when he said farewell to the Princess he had made no assignation with her charming *demoiselle d'honneur*, not being sure how this should be done.

"I trust," said the Princess, a little slyly, "that Mademoiselle D'Olbreuse looked after you?"

"Admirably," he answered.

"I am so pleased. You look as though you have really enjoyed my little ball."

"So much," he answered fervently. "As I never have enjoyed a ball before."

She laughed and tapped him with her fan. "I am delighted. Then my little Mademoiselle did her duty. She is such a good and virtuous girl. I knew I could trust you with her ... and her with you."

* * *

Two days later he presented himself at the Princess's house and begged for an audience with her.

Once more he was received graciously. He looked about him for a sign of Eléonore. There was none.

"You are contented in Breda?" asked the Princess.

"I am not sure. It has occurred to me that I should not give myself entirely to pleasure while I am here."

The Princess raised her eyebrows and asked what he had in mind.

"My education in languages has been rather neglected, I fear. I have been thinking that while I am staying here it might be a good opportunity to remedy that in some way."

"Oh? What language did you wish to learn?"

"French. I was wondering if you could suggest a teacher."

"I doubt not I could find you one. Some old nobleman—an exile from France, very short of money—might be glad to earn a little."

"You have many French friends with you here in Breda."

She studied him archly. "As you discovered when you last visited us."

"Yes. There was one young French woman . . ."

"Ah, Mademoiselle d'Olbreuse. What an excellent idea! Her father might help you. Oh, I am not sure. They are a very proud family. You have no idea how proud some of these exiles can be. Pride seems to grow out of poverty."

"To show it perhaps is their only way of reminding others of their past splendours."

"I am sure you are right. I do not think the Marquis would care to become a teacher of French. I believe I know an old professor . . ."

"Well, I fear I should not wish to be so serious as that. He would put me through lessons which I should find beyond my powers of concentration."

"But my dear friend, you will have to concentrate if you wish to learn a language."

"I meant rather to learn through conversation . . . light, amusing conversation."

"Such as you might exchange with a young lady?"

"Exactly."

"With say . . . Mademoiselle d'Olbreuse?"

"That is what I mean."

She laughed and nodded. "Well, I could ask Eléonore how she would feel about giving you such lessons. Shall I do so?"

"I would deem it a great favour if you did."

"It would please me to please you," she answered. "After all, we are connected by marriage now. But I must warn you, cousin. Are you my cousin? Let us pretend so. It is such a pleasant, cosy relationship. I must warn you that it could only be Mademoiselle d'Olbreuse teaching you the French language. You would not be expected, however tempted, to teach *her* anything."

She laughed and went on. "She is an enchanting creature, I grant you. She is the loveliest girl I have ever seen. Do you agree with me?"

He nodded seriously.

"Consider, cousin. She will never be your mistress. Would it not be better at this stage to turn your attention towards an easier conquest? I would not have your stay in Breda clouded in any way."

"You are very kind."

"Well, we are . . . cousins, and I want to help you."

"So you will ask this lady if she will consent to instruct me in the French language?"

"If you are still sure that you want to learn it?"

"I was never more sure of anything in my life," he answered.

"Then, I shall ask her."

When he had left she was thoughtful for a while. He was a handsome fellow and well-versed in the arts of seduction. It would be interesting to see what happened now. How would he tilt against Eléonore's impregnable virtue. She could not for the life of her guess how this would end.

*   *   *

The Princesse de Tarente obligingly lent them a room. Eléonore sat on one side of the table, he on the other; he watched her gesticulating hands; he listened to her fluting voice.

"French is surely the most charming language in the world," he said. "When spoken by you," he added. "My attempts seem to provoke only merriment."

They were amusing lessons. He told her that he had never before enjoyed learning. How different it would have been had she taught him in his youth; he might have become a scholar. In spite of this, she pointed out, he was not making much progress with his French.

Every time he left that room he marvelled at himself. This was not the manner in which he usually conducted his love affairs; he was like a naïve schoolboy. Two weeks had passed and he was still taking his French lessons and she was no nearer becoming his mistress than she had been on that first evening at the ball.

But she was not indifferent to him. Behind her dignity there was a warmth of . . . friendship? She was pleased to see him; she admitted that she enjoyed teaching as much as he enjoyed learning. It was a profit to them both, she pointed out; a mutual advantage; for while he progressed a very little with the French language, she was augmenting her German.

The inevitable happened when he conjugated the verb to love.

"*Je vous aime*," he told her; and she pretended to believe that was part of the lesson.

"That is correct," she told him.

"Correct and inevitable," he said. "From the moment we met I knew meeting you was the most important thing that had ever happened to me."

He had seized her hands across the table but she was smiling at him calmly.

"I do not expect you to love me as deeply, as devotedly as I love you . . . yet," he rushed on. "But I must have the opportunity of showing you . . . of . . ."

Her eyes were puzzled. "The Princess tells me that you are in no position to make such a declaration," she said.

"You will come back to Germany with me. We will live there together for the rest of our lives . . . but not all the time of course. We will travel . . . see the world. I will take you to Italy, to England . . ."

"But how would that be possible?" she asked.

"How? We will just go. That is how."

"Then is it not true that you have taken an oath to your brother never to marry?"

"To marry . . ." he stammered.

She smiled coolly. "I see that marriage had not entered your mind." She rose. "The lesson is over. I think, do you not, that in the circumstances there should be no more."

He was on his feet and at her side.

"Eléonore . . ." He tried to embrace her but she held him off.

"I do not think you understand," she said. "We are poor . . . we are exiles . . . but my family would never allow me to enter into such a relationship as you are suggesting. Goodbye, my lord Duke, I am sorry you did not explain sooner."

With that she left him. He stood staring after her—bemused, frustrated and desperately unhappy.

*   *   *

"What can I do?" he asked the Princess.

She put her head on one side and regarded him affectionately. So handsome. Such an accomplished lover. Well, this time he had indeed met his match.

"These French nobles . . . they are so proud," she reminded him.

"I understand that. I would not have her other than she is . . . but what can I *do*?"

"You might offer settlements. They are very poor. The father's prospects are alarming . . . unless one of his daughters—or both of them—make wealthy marriages."

"If it is a matter of money . . ."

"Compared with them, my dear lord Duke, you are very wealthy and you would give a great deal to win my dear little Eléonore. But it may be that money is not enough. But we can try."

"You will talk to her?"

"I would do a great deal to make you happy," she answered.

*   *   *

The Marquis d'Olbreuse smiled at his beautiful daughter.

"It is for you to decide, my child," he said.

"But how could I accept such ... dishonour. Have you not always said that our pride is all that is left to us now?"

"I have and I mean it. But it is not easy to make a good marriage when there is no dowry. I have nothing to offer you ... neither you nor Angelique. How different it would be if we had not been driven from our home!"

"You are not suggesting that I should accept him?"

"I would not suggest that you did anything you do not want to do."

"But, father, he is asking me to become his mistress!"

"It is true. But he has talked of settlements ... and a man does not usually offer that to a casual mistress. I believe if it were possible, he would marry you."

"But, *mon père*, it is not possible."

Angelique had come into the room. She was a very pretty girl but lacked Eléonore's outstanding beauty.

The Marquis looked from one to another of his daughters and sighed.

Two lovely girls and he had not the means to set them up in life. That, he believed, was his greatest tragedy of all. Life did not become easier as the years passed. He visualized an old age of poverty, of living on the bounty of others. It was not a pleasant vista for a proud old man.

And if Eléonore accepted the offer of the Duke of Brunswick-Lüneberg? He was rich; he was a Prince—albeit a German one of a small principality. He was not the head of his house because he had an elder brother living and had signed away his own rights—but ...

Even so, he would not persuade her that here was a chance to make her family's future secure. In France a Prince's mistress was a power in the land—often more so than his wife. Eléonore was French enough, proud enough, beautiful and intelligent enough, to play the rôle made famous by so many women of her own country. In her small way she might become a Diane de Poitiers. Little pride was lost and honours were gained in such a rôle.

But the man was a German, of course; and they had not the same refinements of taste as the French nor the same ideas of gallantry.

It must be for her to choose. But if she accepted, if she played her rôle as he was sure it could be played, what good she could bring to her family!

Eléonore, who knew him so well, guessed the thoughts which

were passing through his mind. She was a little shocked; and yet she understood so well.

When she retired to her room Angelique followed her there.

"You are the talk of Breda," said Angelique. "How I envy you!"

"Then you are foolish. My position is far from enviable."

"They say that Duke George William is madly in love with you. I think he is most attractive. I don't know how you can refuse him."

"Then it is a pity he does not transfer his affections to you."

"Now Eléonore, don't be touchy. *Mon dieu!* So it is true then?"

"What?"

"You are in love with him."

Eléonore turned away angrily.

Was she? She was not sure. But Angelique had noticed something in her demeanour, some change.

If he despaired and went away, she would be quite desolate. Was that being in love?

If he had offered marriage how joyfully she would have accepted. But how could the proud daughter of a proud house agree to become a mistress?

* * *

The Princesse de Tarente watched the lovers with interest. So charming she said, in a blasé world. She was certain that in time Eléonore would relent.

She told George William so and that if he offered a morganatic marriage it might help to persuade Eléonore.

"Alas, she has had a strict upbringing and it has always been impressed on her that she must never live with any man without marriage."

"I have been a fool," cried George William. "If I had not made this contract with my brother how happily would I marry her. Nothing but my declaration of renunciation holds me back. I know that I want to live with Eléonore for the rest of my life, and I shall never want any other woman. She will be sufficient to me. My dear Princess, I cannot describe to you how much I have changed. I am a different man. Had I known it was possible to feel this passion, this tenderness, this desire for a tranquil life with one woman I should never have been such a fool as to sign that contract. I know now why I refused Sophia. I must have been secretly conscious that Eléonore was waiting for me."

"So charming!" sighed the Princess. "So romantic! You have promised settlements that would accompany a proper marriage

... you have offered a morganatic marriage ... you can do no more. I am certain that Eléonore loves you."

"Are you?" he cried rapturously.

"My dear George William, how delightful it is to be in love! Oh yes, she adores you. She would make you a wonderful wife and you would be the best husband in the world. You have learned the emptiness of mere passion, the dissatisfaction which must follow lust. You are in love, and it is quite beautiful. I believe you will win in time. I will give a ball for you both which will, in a way, set a seal on your relationship. When she knows how much all of us in Breda are with our dear romantic lovers, she may relent, for she longs to, I do assure you. Oh, how she longs to! She cannot deceive me. She is as much in love with you as you are with her."

He kissed the Princess's hands with fervour. She was his very dear friend. If he were not so wholeheartedly in love with his Eléonore he would doubtless be in love with her.

"No more compliments of that nature, my dear," reproved the Princess. "They might reach Eléonore's ears, and then she would think she was right after all—fascinating as you are—to hold out against you."

But he was grateful, he assured her. He would be grateful to the end of his days.

*   *   *

It was a glittering ball and the guests of honour were Duke George William and Mademoiselle Eléonore d'Olbreuse.

They danced together; they talked together; and made no secret of their pleasure in each other's company.

During the evening the Princess called them to her and told them that it made her very happy to give this ball in their honour.

"I want you to know, my dearest *demoiselle d'honneur,* that all of us in Breda wish you well. I want you to take this as a memento of this happy evening."

She put a medallion into Eléonore's hands—a picture of George William set with diamonds.

"What can I say?" cried Eléonore, deeply moved.

"Say what you have to say to him, my child. And that will best please me."

She left them together and George William drew her to an alcove in the ballroom as he had on the first night they had met.

"You see," he said, "you must say yes now. It is the wish of everyone that you do."

"I want to," she told him, "but . . ."

"I promise you you will never regret this step, my dearest."

"I do not believe I should, but I should never be your wife and . . ."

"There should be a marriage."

"Not legal, not binding."

"It should be binding in every way."

"And our children, what of them? I could not bring illegitimate children into the world."

"They should have every honour that I could give them."

"I do not know. I cannot say."

"But you love me."

"Yes," she answered earnestly. "I love you."

"Now I shall win. You cannot hold out against me. Eléonore, my dearest, say yes now. Let this wonderful evening be the happiest of my life . . . so far. Let it be the beginning of all my joy."

"I will give you an answer tomorrow."

"And it will be yes."

"I think so . . . I hope so . . . and alas, I fear so," she answered.

*　*　*

That was a happy night. He was sure of success. He was already wording in his mind the settlement. There should be a ceremony in every way as solemn as a marriage service. She should never have anything to regret.

He was the one who must regret . . . regret the contract he had been fool enough to enter into with Ernest Augustus. Why had he not understood then that he did not want marriage because he had never been in love, that he did not understand love before he met Eléonore!

He was angry with himself because he could not give her everything—simply everything that she desired. Still he would make up for the one lack. She should be treated like a queen.

Tomorrow he would call on her father. They would talk . . . make plans.

He lay sleepless thinking of the next day.

*　*　*

His servant was at his bedside.

"My lord Duke, a messenger."

Those fateful words. He had always dreaded them because they invariably brought disturbing news from home.

"Bring him to me, without delay."

The man stood by the bedside, travel-stained and weary, yet
with that elation in his face which was a characteristic of those
who brought exciting news—good or bad. He sensed by the solemn
look this one was forcing on to his face that this was bad news.

"My lord Duke, Duke Christian Lewis is dead."

"Dead!" cried George William struggling up. "My brother . . .
dead."

"Yes, my lord. And there is more. Duke John Frederick has
seized the Castle of Celle and has declared that he will hold it
against you."

George William leaped from his bed; fate was against him;
Eléonore was on the point of relenting; and now news had come
to him which necessitated his immediate return to his own
country.

*　　*　　*

He presented himself at the lodgings of the Marquis d'Olbreuse.

"Monsieur le Marquis, I must speak to your daughter without
delay."

"Certainly, certainly," replied the Marquis. "I will tell her you
are here."

Eléonore came eagerly into the room, but as soon as she saw
her lover she knew that something was wrong.

He took both her hands and looked into her face. "My love, I
have to return to Celle this very day. My eldest brother is dead and
the elder of my two remaining brothers has seized my castle there,
and is attempting to rule in my place. I have no choice. If I am
to keep what is mine I must go at once."

"Yes," she said, "you must go."

"And I still have not had your answer."

"I cannot decide . . . I cannot. Pray give me time."

He sighed. Then he fervently kissed her hand. "I shall be back,"
he told her. "As soon as this affair is settled I shall be with you.
But I want you to take these documents. You will then have no
doubts of my feelings for you."

"You have no need to give me further proof. I know. If only
I could reconcile all that I have been brought up to believe is
right with what you are asking and what I desire!"

He embraced her tenderly.

"You will in time," he said. "As soon as I have settled this unfortunate matter I shall come to you or better still you must come
to me. Now . . . I must leave you."

Within a few hours Duke George William was riding out of
Breda, and when she studied the documents he had left her,

Eléonore saw that he had settled on her his entire fortune in case of his death.

She wept, horrified at the thought that he might be going into battle against his brother.

If it were not for the thought of the children they might have, she would have written to him at once telling him that she would come to him as soon as he sent for her. Because of that thought, she wavered still.

*　　*　　*

Strife within the family was an evil thing. All the brothers agreed to this; but John Frederick had declared that he would be revenged on his brothers for passing him over for Ernest Augustus without consulting the family. In the past brothers had agreed to draw lots and rely on luck; but George William had acted in a high-handed manner and bestowed Sophia and all the change implied on the youngest brother. For this reason John Frederick had revolted. Moreover, George William was bringing the family into disrepute. He was never at home. First it had been Venice—and now Breda. It was time he was taught a lesson.

But when George William came riding back with all speed to Celle, John Frederick had no wish to take up arms against him and agreed that such problems as theirs should be discussed round a council table; but George William must understand that if he were to be allowed to rule his little principality he could not satisfactorily delegate authority to others; he must be present himself. These long residences at foreign places must come to an end.

George William saw the wisdom of this. He must settle down. As it happened it was just what he wanted to do ... with Eléonore.

If she would come to him, if they could set up house together, he would ask nothing more but to live quietly for the rest of his days in his own land.

The brothers met. The death of Christian Lewis meant that there were prizes to be passed round; and as a result of the conference George William became Duke of Celle, John Frederick Duke of Hanover, while Ernest Augustus remained the Bishop of Osnabrück. They were all satisfied—even John Frederick.

Now, thought George William, all that remained was to go back to Breda and bring Eléonore home to Celle.

His ministers shook their heads with disapproval when he said he was returning to Breda.

"My lord," it was pointed out, "if you left now John Frederick would claim what he did before. You would lose Celle, for although the people prefer you as their Duke your perpetual wanderings displease them. They want you to rule them, but only if you do so in person."

"It would be a short stay, I do assure you."

"It would be dangerous to leave now. You must stay at least a year before you wander abroad again."

George William was in despair. Eléonore was still unpersuaded; and it might be that only he could do the persuading.

He wrote to her at once explaining the position. There was a short delay before her answer came back, telling him that he must forget her; for she had suffered from the smallpox and her beauty was gone. He could not love her now, and she prayed that he would put her out of his mind as she was trying to put him out of hers.

Her beauty gone! He pictured her with her dazzling complexion ruined, the soft skin pitted in that disfiguring way which ruined so many who would otherwise be beauties. He wept; he mourned; and after a day or so he knew that he wanted Eléonore whether she was beautiful or not.

He wrote and told her so.

*   *   *

The Princesse de Tarente wrote to him. They missed him in Breda but they had heard that his affairs at home were no longer giving him reason for anxiety. Poor Eléonore was wretchedly unhappy. "She loves you, my dear Duke, do not allow yourself to believe otherwise. Do not believe what she tells you, for she is trying to make it easy for you to do without her. In spite of her sadness she is as beautiful as ever. She has the loveliest complexion in Breda. It breaks my heart to see her so sad, and I am sure you do not wish to break my heart, my dear."

He smiled when he read the letter.

So Eléonore was lying to him . . . for his sake . . . to make it easier.

He was determined on two things: To have Eléonore and Celle.

He decided on a visit to Osnabrück. After all, Ernest Augustus had always been his friend and Sophia seemed satisfied with her fate, so perhaps she did not hold the jilting against him.

He would ask their advice and help.

*   *   *

Sophia received him graciously. How handsome he is! she thought. Being a little drawn, a little thinner, does not detract from his charm.

He went to the nursery and saw the children. George Lewis was almost five, Frederick Augustus four—and both were healthy boys.

"What do you think of my sons?" asked Sophia, watching him closely for a trace of envy.

"You are fortunate. My brother is delighted, I am sure."

"From what I hear you are not so pleased now that you renounced your rights. Is it true that there is a lady in Breda whom you would like to marry?"

"It is true. I want to have a good talk with you and Ernest Augustus about her. I think you can help me."

"Help you? You need help to persuade the lady?" Sophia's laugh was a little harsh. So he is in love! she was thinking. He could not contemplate marrying *me*. He preferred to give up his rights to escape *me*. And now if he is as enamoured of this French creature as rumours say, he is feeling he acted a little hastily. He is wishing he had thrown me over without bothering to find a husband for me!

She could have hated him—if he was not so handsome, so much more charming than Ernest Augustus, if she had not decided when she had heard she was to marry him, to fall in love with him.

"You will hear what I have to suggest?"

"The contracts stand firm," she replied grimly.

"Naturally. I did not mean in that way. George Lewis is all attention."

"He is an intelligent child."

"Two intelligent children! Lucky Sophia! Lucky Ernest Augustus! I am sure you will want to help *me* to be happy."

George Lewis was holding up a wooden sword.

"Uncle," he said, "I shall be a soldier."

George William lifted the boy in his arms. What an ugly little fellow he was, but his eyes were bright.

"We will go to war together, nephew."

"I shall come too," piped up Frederick Augustus.

"Of course."

"Come," said Sophia, "dinner will soon be served. And afterwards we shall talk together."

They left the nursery and George William went to his apartments in the palace.

They are contented, he thought; Sophia owes me no grudge and Ernest Augustus should be very grateful to me. They will help me.

*   *   *

They had eaten well of sausage and red cabbage with ginger and onions—a dish to which, during his sojourns abroad, George William had grown unaccustomed.

He thought longingly of the French cooking at the table of the Princesse de Tarente. But he must not think of Breda—only as to how he could bring Eléonore out of it.

He noticed that every time he saw Ernest Augustus, his brother was changing. He was getting gross with too much good living—greasy German food, and the heavy ale they drank. He hunted frequently, travelled occasionally; and took his choice of the women of his court. A typical ruler, thought George William. How different his own life would be with Eléonore!

And Sophia? She was dignified, never forgetting her royal blood, and as long as everyone else remembered it she did not care that her husband was blatantly unfaithful. She ruled the household and would never allow any of his mistresses to attempt to dominate her. She was the woman supreme in the castle; and as long as Ernest Augustus granted her that, he could go his own way. Now of course she was hoping for more children. Two were not enough; for this reason Ernest Augustus must spend certain nights with her.

It was an amicable arrangement and Ernest Augustus was pleased with his marriage.

Sophia kept her feeling to herself, which was as well, for George William had no idea of the emotions he aroused in her, and when she said that she wanted to help him, he believed her.

When they were alone together he explained the situation to them both.

"A pity she is a Frenchwoman," said Ernest Augustus. "I never trusted the French."

"Oh, come brother, we know the French have been our enemies. But that is not the fault of Mademoiselle d'Olbreuse and her family. Why, they are *exiles* from France. Louis has had them driven out. That should make you friendly towards them."

"You think that we can help you?" asked Sophia.

"Yes, by inviting her here. Treat her with respect. If you did so she would understand that, in spite of the circumstances, she was being given all the honours that would be due to my wife."

"She would not be your wife," put in Ernest Augustus quickly. "That is quite out of the question."

"I know. I know," replied George William wearily. "I have sworn that I will not marry. But I could marry . . . morganatically. You could have no objection to that."

"The documents would have to be very carefully drawn up."

"Naturally."

How time changed people! thought George William. Here was Ernest Augustus, wary and suspicious; and a few years ago he would have done anything in the world to please his adored elder brother.

"Well, should we ask her here?" said Ernest Augustus to Sophia.

She was pleased that he bowed to her decision in matters such as this; it was payment for refusing to hear the giggling and other noises which came from his bedroom.

"We shall have to consider this," she said slowly. "To take her under our protection might be misconstrued."

"How so?" demanded George William.

"Oh, it is easy to make trouble. Look how John Frederick almost succeeded in snatching Celle from you. If you had not returned when you did who can say what might have happened."

"You must do this for me," insisted George William. He laid his hand on her arm.

She was conscious of the hand there—yet successfully she hid her reaction.

How he pleads for her! she thought angrily. He pleads for her as eagerly as he rejected me!

"We will consider," she said coolly.

"And you will give me your answer . . . when?"

"Tomorrow."

*   *   *

"I shall expect you tonight," Sophia told Ernest Augustus. "There is this matter to discuss."

He nodded. It was time they slept together again, and he had no other project in mind for the night.

In her bedchamber he sat on the bed watching her.

"Well?"

"I think we should invite this woman here."

"You would be prepared to do that?"

"I think it would be good if he lived with his mistress. That is all she can ever be, of course. We must make sure of that."

"Naturally it is all that she can be. I have his signature on the documents."

"I saw a look in his eyes tonight. Ambition, I said. And I fear ambition."

"But he has signed the documents. I have them under lock and key."

"There they must be kept. But he has changed; and we must

be careful. When he signed over his rights to you he was a feck-less young man, wanting merely to flit from one adventure to another. Now he has become serious. He wants this woman to be his wife. What do you think he will want next? Children. And once he has them he will want estates for them."

"Which he can't have."

"Which," agreed Sophia, "he can't have. But that won't prevent his wanting them. And this woman ... she will want them too. Our George Lewis is the heir; but what if George William has a son?"

"George Lewis will still be the heir."

"George William is rich ... richer than you are ... in spite of what he has assigned to you. I'd rather Celle than Osnabrück. And Celle must be for George Lewis."

"So it shall be."

"We have to be careful. That is why I want that woman here. I want to see what manner of creature she is who has worked this change in him. And I want her to know that it is useless for her to dream. She is a nobody and I am a Princess of a Royal House. I have English blood in my veins."

"Oh, how you go on about the English!"

"I happen to be proud of my connection with a proud people."

"Who murdered your uncle!"

"That was a few of their leaders. The people are now happy to have my cousin Charles back on the throne. I am proud of being English, Ernest Augustus, and I don't care who knows it. They at least have one King to rule over them ... they are not split into all these principalities which are not worth much alone. That is why George Lewis must inherit as big an estate as possible. He must have Hanover, Celle, Osnabrück ... the whole of the Brunswick-Lüneberg inheritance. And that woman will try to prevent it if she can, because if she should have boys of her own ... You see my point? I am going to ask her here. I am going to show her that if she comes into this family she comes on the wrong side of the blanket and need have no fine ideas of what *her* children will get, or *she* will get for that matter. She comes as the Madame of the Duke of Celle—not as his wife. That's what I want her to know and that is why I am going to ask her here."

"So you are going to help our lovers?"

"Yes, I am going to help them, because I think it is a good thing that George William settles down to produce a few bastards and remembers that they have no inheritance because when he passed me over to you, he passed over his rights with me."

"You sound as though you would punish him for rejecting such a prize."

"Punish him! I care not enough to wish for that. I'm satisfied with the way everything turned out."

"A pretty compliment, my dear."

She came and stood before him—unseductive yet inviting.

"We will have a large family," she said. "Two sons is not enough."

*   *   *

There was excitement in the Olbreuse lodgings when the letter arrived from Osnabrück.

Eléonore hastened to show it to her father.

"It can mean one thing," said the Marquis. "You are accepted by his family. This is the Duchess herself; and she is a Princess. It is couched in a very welcoming manner. This means that all is well."

"It means a marriage which will not be accepted as one."

"My dear, many morganatic marriages have been made before."

"My children would have no rights."

"You are clever enough to see that they do, I am sure."

Eléonore looked at her old father. What it would mean to him if she accepted this invitation and married George William, she well knew. The first thing George William would do would be to settle a pension on the Marquis. He had said as much; and she trusted him to keep his promises.

She looked at Angelique—so gay and pretty. What chance had she of making a good marriage as the poor daughter of an impoverished Frenchman—aristocratic though he might be, even though the French nobility was of as high a social standing as a German Prince, and often more cultivated and civilized! Not that she would criticize her German Prince; his absence had taught her how wretched she was going to be without him.

Her family was urging her—but more insistent than anything else were her own inclinations.

"I will go to the Princess," she said. "She has been so good to us and her advice will help me make up my mind."

The Princess received her with pleasure; she read Sophia's letter.

"My dear Eléonore," she cried, "of course you must go to Osnabrück. This letter means that Duchess Sophia accepts you— and if she does so will every German. This is telling you that although you cannot be his legal wife because of contracts he has made preventing his marrying, in every other way you will be treated as such."

"You . . . you almost persuade me."

The Princess laughed. "My dear *demoiselle d'honneur*. You know you have made up your mind. You love this man. Don't be afraid of love, my child."

Eléonore went solemnly back to her father's lodgings. The Marquis and Angelique looked at her expectantly.

"I shall write to the Duchess Sophia at once," she said. "And now . . . I am going to prepare for the journey to Osnabrück."

The Marquis's expression relaxed. Angelique flew at her sister. "Oh, Eléonore . . . how we are going to miss you!"

"You, Angelique, will not. I am to be treated with all honour. Therefore I need my own *demoiselle d'honneur*. Who better to fill the rôle than my own sister?"

Angelique burst into tears of joy and when Eléonore glanced at her father she saw that he too was weeping.

Tears of joy! Tears of relief! Eléonore herself could have joined in. The decision was made. I will never be parted from him again as long as I shall live, she thought.

* * *

George William stood beside the Duchess Sophia at the foot of the great staircase in the Castle of Iburg, his eyes bright with pleasure and emotion. She seemed more beautiful than she had in Breda; there was a serenity in the lovely dark eyes and when they met his he knew without a doubt that she truly loved him.

This is the happiest moment of my life, he thought; and then immediately : It would have been happier if I had been receiving her at Celle, if I could have offered her a true marriage.

But she had come to him at last—and he was thankful. He vowed to himself that he would spend the rest of his life making her so happy that she would not notice what she lacked.

Sophia's pleasant smile hid her rancour. Oh yes, she thought, she is beautiful. I don't believe I have ever seen a woman more so. If she had been offered to him in the first place he would never have handed her over to his brother.

"Welcome to Osnabrück, Mademoiselle d'Olbreuse," said Sophia in good French.

Eléonore made a graceful curtsey. Everything she does she does perfectly, thought George William. A haughty piece for all her good manners, Sophia was thinking. Well, Mademoiselle, now you are here, you will have to learn your place. Fancy French

manners won't have the same effect on me as they do on my besotted brother-in-law.

George William had taken Eléonore's hands and embraced her
before them all and Sophia was aware that those watching were
softened by the scene. All the world loved lovers—except Sophia
and Ernest Augustus. And beauty and charm such as this French
woman possessed could always arouse interest and sympathy—
unless of course they had the opposite effect and stirred up envy.

Eléonore presented Angelique to Sophia who gave the young
girl a smile and told her that she was pleased she had accompanied
her sister to Osnabrück. And now she would take Eléonore to her
own apartments that they might talk together for a short while
before she conducted her guest to those which had been prepared
for her.

In Sophia's private chamber coffee and salt biscuits were served.
This intimate tête-à-tête was an honour Sophia reserved for her
friends. It was a sign, George William was able to tell Eléonore
afterwards, that Sophia had taken a fancy to her and wanted
everyone in the castle to know it.

Afterwards Eléonore was conducted to her own apartments
where Angelique was already waiting for her. When they were
alone Angelique sat on the bed laughing.

"Oh, Eléonore," she cried, "I'm so glad we came. These Germans . . . so plump . . . so *slow*. George William is not like one of
them. He is different. But I like them, sister. I am so glad that we
are here."

Eléonore smiled at her sister's exuberance. She too was glad
they had come.

*   *   *

Those were happy days. George William rode with her in the
countryside, walked with her in the gardens of the palace, and
they talked incessantly of the future.

There was to be no delay in the ceremony, which, George
William declared, should be like an ordinary marriage. He had
documents drafted and redrafted until they pleased him, then he
showed them to Eléonore.

"I want all the world to know that the only reason this is not
in every sense a true marriage is because I have given my oath
not to marry."

She was gratified, but she was also deeply in love, and there
were occasions when she wanted to have done with documents
and ceremonies and go away with her lover.

Sophia helped a great deal during those days, often inviting

Eléonore to her chamber for coffee and salt biscuits when she made her talk of France and her childhood and she herself talked of England ... the country which she had never visited but to which, she assured Eléonore, she belonged more than to any other. She spoke fluent English. Her French was good but her English better. "My mother was English ... an English *Princess* before she became *Queen* of Bohemia. It is in my blood ... this affinity with England. And when the blood is royal ..." There were times when Eléonore suspected that Sophia was trying to underline the difference between them. Then she thought she was mistaken and George William's devotion would make her forget everything else.

Ernest Augustus insisted on studying the marriage documents with his lawyer.

"No loopholes mind," he cried. "His renunciation stands."

"There is no intention to evade it, your Highness," he was told.

"Make sure there is none ... make doubly sure. My brother has always kept his word, but he was never before devoted to a woman as he is to that one. He's capable of anything for her sake."

Sophia joined him. She was of his opinion. Carefully she studied the papers.

"Well, my dear," she confided to Ernest Augustus, "I would call this in the language of the dear lady herself an anti-*contract de mariage*!"

Ernest Augustus laughed with her. They saw eye to eye over this matter as naturally they should. George William was not going to be allowed to evade his agreement by one line; and George Lewis was destined to be the heir of Brunswick-Lüneberg.

And so the morganatic marriage took place and the married pair continued at Osnabrück.

"It is as well," said George William, "to do so for a while. It will stabilize your position."

Eléonore agreed.

* * *

"Madame von Harburg!" said Sophia. "Well, it is as good a name as any for a woman who, call herself what she will, is still not his wife."

"He wants her to have a title and he has an estate of that name," pointed out Ernest Augustus.

"I am aware of that. But it makes no difference to me. She is Mademoiselle d'Olbreuse."

"I hope you will not call her by that name. It would cause trouble with George William if you did."

"My dear husband, I have no wish to let George William know my true feelings. That would indeed put him on his guard. We have to be careful."

"And he is as much in love with her as he ever was."

"Give him time to fall out of love!" said Sophia with a snort of laughter.

"Sometimes I wonder whether he ever will. He is not the man he once was. I scarcely recognize him as the carefree fellow who used to accompany me on my journeyings."

"You've both changed," Sophia reminded him.

It was true. George William had once been the leader, now he was proving himself a man with a soft and sentimental streak in his nature. Ernest Augustus had changed too. The young man who had adored his brother and was eager to follow him in every way was learning to despise the one-time hero. Ernest Augustus would never love anyone to such an extent that he was ready to sacrifice everything. Sophia suspected that George William would do just that for his Eléonore and, illogically, while she applauded the growing shrewdness of Ernest Augustus, she longed for the devotion of which George William was capable.

When George William presented his wife with a carriage drawn by six horses, Sophia declared that she must take firm action.

"Why," she complained to Ernest Augustus, "when she rides out she appears to be finer than we are."

"It is George William's wish."

"I can see that, and we shall have to show people that whatever fine jewels she wears, even if she has a carriage drawn by *twelve* horses she is not royal—nor can we treat her as such."

When Sophia drove out she never allowed Eléonore to ride in her carriage; and she explained when there were others present: "You see, my dear, you are not the Duchess of Celle; and therefore the people would not expect to see you ride with us. I am sure you will understand."

Eléonore, whose pride was great, was beginning to resent Sophia's allusions and to wonder whether she was after all the good friend she had once pretended to be. George William was growing more and more devoted as the weeks passed, but he still believed that they should continue at Osnabrück for a while. In fact, when he remembered how antagonistic his subjects had been when he had brought home his Venetian servants, he felt very uneasy as to how they would receive his French wife. It was so much better, he pointed out to Eléonore, that they remain under the protection of Ernest Augustus for as long as possible.

Eléonore yearned to have her own household. She found the manners of this court crude; she could not bear the smell of the food they ate and when the bowls of greasy sausages were served on masses of red cabbage she felt nauseated. She turned from the cloudy ale which they so much enjoyed and as a compromise she had set up a little kitchen in her own apartments where she and Angelique cooked some dainty dishes.

Even so she must appear at meals and as she listened to the champing of jaws and saw the eyes alight with greed and the grease running down the chins of the eaters she turned away in disgust.

Sophia had pointed out to her, most graciously, that she could not sit at the table with herself, Ernest Augustus and George William, for naturally the people would object.

"You and your little sister will sit at another table. I am sure you will understand."

Eléonore was inwardly incensed, but she said nothing and agreed to sit at the table indicated.

Sophia had made one special concession. "You may remain seated while we eat," she had said. "The rest of the company must stand and not eat until we have finished. But in view of the great esteem in which we all hold you, we should not expect you to stand."

Eléonore often wondered afterwards how she endured such slights. George William would watch her unhappily, and she knew that never had he regretted so much his folly in signing away his birthright. She had no wish to make him more unhappy on that score, so she pretended that this treatment did not upset her as much as it did.

Sophia came to her apartment after having eaten sasuages and red cabbage to inspect the dishes which Angelique was cooking.

She sniffed with amusement. "So that, I suppose, is what you call French cooking."

"It *is* French cooking, Madame," answered Eléonore with dignity.

"And you are going to eat that!"

"To us it seems as good as greasy sausages do to you."

"French tastes!" laughed Sophia; and ever afterwards when she had finished eating she would nod in Eléonore's direction and cry: "Now, my dear, you may be off to help your little sister with the saucepans."

Several months passed and the vague slights which were heaped upon Eléonore were bearable only because she was beginning to know her husband better than ever and what she discovered delighted her.

There came the day when she was certain that she was pregnant.

Everything seemed to change for her then. She had accepted insults for herself, but she never would for her child. *She* had changed; she had not become less proud but far more shrewd and she knew these people were her enemies—and George William's. They gloated over their triumph. They were determined that she should remain a woman without status, her children illegitimate; and she was going to fight with all her might for the sake of this unborn child.

"George William," she said, "our child must not be born here. That would be an evil omen. He must be born under his own roof. I have heard the Castle of Celle is very beautiful. Take me there. Let me be in my own home for these months of waiting."

George William agreed with her that the time had come to move; in any case his greatest wish was to please her.

So they left Osnabrück for Celle and when she saw the yellow walls of the old castle her spirits rose and as they came into the courtyard and the tame pigeons fluttered round them, Eléonore was happier than she had ever been.

"I feel," she said, "that I have come home."

*   *   *

On a golden September day her child was born.

"The most beautiful little girl in the world," declared George William.

The child was brought to its mother and she examined it eagerly. Perfect in every detail!

"George William," said Eléonore, "the bells should be ringing throughout Celle."

"I shall order it to be done."

"You should bestow gifts on your subjects. Give an entertainment . . . a ball . . . a banquet. I want them all to know what a great occasion this is."

"We will do it."

"I am so happy. I shall lie here thinking how happy I am . . . and how all Germany must know what an important event this is."

"What name have you decided on? I should like her called after you."

Eléonore smiled. "No, that would never do. She must have a

German name. I thought of Dorothea after your eldest brother's wife ... and Sophia ... because so many in the family are Sophia."

"After the Duchess Sophia who was our hostess for so long. It is a gracious gesture."

"Yes," said Eléonore smiling. "She shall be Sophia Dorothea. They are pleasant together. My little Sophia Dorothea who must have the best in life."

"Sophia Dorothea," repeated George William; and as he agreed with Eléonore in all things he did in this.

*   *   *

"What a fuss!" cried Sophia. "What a pother ... and all for the birth of one little bastard! What are they trying to tell us? That she is not? Ha! They may tell us all they will but that cannot alter facts."

She rode over to Celle to see the new baby.

A pretty child, she had to admit.

She herself had just had the good fortune to bear a child. "A son," she told Eléonore proudly. "Now you are going to be envious."

"No. Now that we have our little daughter we would not change her for any boy."

An oft repeated protest! thought Sophia grimly. And an absurd one. What ambitious woman would not rather have a son than a daughter! But perhaps if the child was a bastard ...

"My little Maximilian William is a bright little fellow. I'll swear he already knows me."

"I am happy for your sake."

"And I for yours, my dear. And the child is to be Sophia Dorothea. A good German name. You were wise in that. In fact, I begin to think you are full of wisdom."

"You flatter me."

"That is one thing of which I am rarely guilty. It is rather a fault of you French than of us English. You look surprised. But I am English, you know. My mother was an English Princess. It is sad news I have from my friends there. While this child was being born London was being ravaged by fire. It lasted four days they tell me and thirteen thousand houses as well as ninety churches were razed to the ground ... and only a year ago they were suffering from the Great Plague."

"I had not heard this news."

"Why should you? You are not English, but I see that I am well informed of what is happening in my cousin's country."

'I heard it said that the plague was a visitation because of the morals of the King."

"Morals of the King!" said Sophia, her eyes flashing with rage. How dared the woman . . . this unmarried mother . . . how dared she have the effrontery to criticize a King . . . and a King of England at that! "My dear Madame von Harburg, it is not for lesser folk to judge Kings. A king it seems must have his mistresses—as men will, One does not blame *them* for a natural custom."

"But I thought you would wish to hear what I had heard since you are always pleased to hear of England," replied Eléonore quietly.

Conversation was a little strained afterwards, and Sophia very soon took her leave.

She was thoughtful as she rode back to Osnabrück. We shall have to be very careful of that woman, she thought. She could be dangerous. She was always too clever, pretending reluctance in order to make herself more precious. Now she's a tigress with a cub to fight for. She will fight.

Sophia was right. After she had left Eléonore lay in her bed thinking deeply of what she could do to make her little Sophia Dorothea the equal of her cousins of Osnabrück.

The Rival Courts

THE people of Celle were content with their Duke and his wife. They had naturally been a little suspicious of the foreigner at first, particularly when she appeared to be somewhat fastidious and so elegant. One glance was enough to show that she did not belong to Celle and they had resented this.

But she did not appear aware of their resentment; when she rode through the town she smiled and acknowledged their greeting in a manner which was strange but which could not fail to charm them; and during the first months of their return the main topic of conversation was the Duke and his Madame, as they called her; it was significant that later they changed that to his Lady.

Even the Frenchwoman's strongest critics admitted that she had wrought a miraculous change in their Duke. He had ceased to be a feckless wanderer, and appeared to care so much about his little community that he rarely left it; and it was comforting to know the Duke and his family were in residence. It was a reminder of those days when Duke William the Pious had been alive, although nowadays the trumpeter did not announce meals twice a day from the tower, and affairs were conducted very differently in the castle. It was all being Frenchified but, say what one liked, that meant elegance, greater comfort and more courteous manners; and the people of Celle were adjusting themselves very happily to the new *régime*. Then when the child had been born there had been celebrations in which they had all joined and very soon the Duke's Lady was riding through the town in her carriage and the little girl was with her; she enjoyed listening to compliments on the child's health and beauty.

She had decided that there should be alterations to the old castle; and the Duke, ever willing to indulge her, had agreed. This had meant the employment of local workmen and an era of prosperity began. All those who went to work at the castle were charmed by the Lady who seemed to be interested in them and their way of life; and although she was gradually changing everything so that the Castle of Celle resembled a miniature Versailles instead of a rather comfortless German schloss, they were interested and eventually delighted. It was gratifying to think that their castle, their Duke and his Lady were different from others.

It was so pleasant merely to look at her in her silks and velvets; and the little girl who was becoming so pretty, and very like her, was a delightful creature too. The Duke doted on them both and it was easy to see that he could scarcely bear them out of his sight. How extraordinary when they considered how other Dukes kept mistresses and lived in a state of extravagant coarseness. Their Duke was a faithful husband—and his romance with the charming Eléonore was smiled on throughout the principality.

There was another delight enjoyed by the inhabitants of Celle which was denied others. Eléonore had opened a theatre in the castle and with the help of her sister Angelique she arranged that plays and musical entertainments—such as those played before Louis XIV—should be performed in Celle. And not only were the castle staff admitted but the townspeople too.

Yes, the people of Celle were pleased with the state of affairs at the castle; George William was forgiven his earlier neglect and it was not forgotten that his reformation had been brought about by this charming Frenchwoman.

During the five years since the birth of Sophia Dorothea, while she had been gradually winning the approval of her husband's subjects, she had given birth to other children who had not lived and it became evident that Sophia Dorothea was going to be an only child. This necessarily meant that all her devotion was given to this girl—and because George William followed Eléonore in everything, he also adored the child almost to idolatry.

There was one element of unhappiness in Eléonore's life; she had known it would be thus and it was the very reason why she had withstood George William's pleading for so long. Loved as the little girl was, she was illegitimate, and this fact was going to bar her from making the brilliant marriage which Eléonore wanted for her.

As they sat on the terraces, or wandered arm in arm through the gardens, this was the continual theme of their conversation. Again and again George William reproached himself for his impulsive act in signing away his birthright; again and again Eléonore assured him that he must not blame himself.

"Regrets are useless," she said. "We must plan. Fortunately you did not give everything; and you are richer now than any of your brothers. Money is very useful, my dearest. We must use it to buy the best for Sophia Dorothea."

A kinsman of George William's, Anton Ulrich, Duke of Wolfenbüttel, had written telling them that he proposed calling on them and was bringing with him his son Augustus Frederick who was sixteen. He thought they might have interesting matters to discuss.

"It can mean one thing," said Eléonore. "He wants a betrothal between Augustus Frederick and Sophia Dorothea."

George William agreed that if this were so, it was an excellent proposition, for Wolfenbüttel was a senior branch of the House of Brunswick; and if Duke Anton Ulrich was contemplating marrying his son to their daughter, it could only mean that he was ignoring the little girl's illegitimacy.

"You would agree?" he asked.

"It would be an excellent match. I should want her to be happy though . . . as we are. I would never wish her to marry against her will, however brilliant the match."

George William leaned towards her and kissed her. The servants had grown accustomed to these gestures of affection; they thought them odd in a German Prince, but regarded them as the French influence, and in any case they were an outward sign of that harmony which it was to the advantage of all to maintain.

"But," went on Eléonore, "I am pleased that Anton Ulrich should make the suggestion. We shall consider it with pleasure."

He laughed indulgently. How like his Eléonore—who, in law, had no standing, whose beloved daughter was illegitimate—to talk of considering an offer from a German Duke who was of a senior branch of the Brunswick family.

The sounds of arrival were in the courtyard. How calm she was, how unhurried!

When Anton Ulrich appeared she rose to greet him with the grace of a Queen; and Anton Ulrich who had been prepared to dispense with certain ceremonies in the circumstances, found himself quickly reverting to them.

"Welcome to Celle," said Eléonore.

Anton Ulrich presented his son—a pleasant youth who was completely captivated by the beautiful Eléonore and unable to hide the fact.

"We are honoured that you should visit us," said George William.

"We have heard such accounts of the court you hold here that we could no longer stay away."

It was indeed a little court, thought Anton Ulrich. The banquet was not only magnificent but tastefully served.

He noticed that although the lackeys still wore the Celle livery—yellow stockings, blue coats trimmed with grey lace, and gold or silk buttons according to their rank—as they did in the days of William the Pious, they looked different. He suspected their liveries might have been new for this visit. Yes, George William of Celle was a rich man; they must get round this matter of the daughter's illegitimacy in some way for the child—bastard or not—would inherit all this wealth which could be put to good use in Wolfenbüttel. Moreover, it was always advantageous when principalities were joined, and even the estates which remained George William's allied with theirs would make one very powerful unit.

The table talk was elegant and although the German dishes were served, there were others—rather mysterious but far more pleasant to look at than sauerkraut and smoked sausages and the usual red cabbage, ginger and onions. There was wine—French wines too—as well as the cloudy beer they drank so much in Germany.

And after the banquet there was a theatrical performance in which the Lady and her sister took parts—as did the enchanting little Sophia Dorothea. A precocious child, Anton Ulrich noted, as children were apt to be who were very certain that they were doted on.

"An excellent entertainment," he said. "Why, cousin, you're a regular little King in this court here in Celle."

"It's a good life," admitted George William, "and I ask no other."

When Anton Ulrich found himself alone with George William and Eléonore he came to the point of his visit.

"Your daughter is a child as yet but you will wish her to marry early. I thought we might consider the advantages of a match between our children."

"Augustus Frederick is ten years older than Sophia Dorothea," pointed out Eléonore.

"A mere nothing, my dear cousin. She is bright and intelligent beyond her years. She will be ready for early marriage."

"You suggest that we should examine the advantages," went on Eléonore. "There is no harm in doing that."

Anton Ulrich glanced at George William. Did he then allow his wife to manage his affairs? It seemed that he did for he was nodding his assent to all that Eléonore said.

"It would please me very much to see a marriage between our houses. Your daughter would acquire rank and I'll be perfectly frank, cousin, I doubt not that she would bring with her a good dowry."

"All that we have will be hers one day," admitted George William solemnly.

"Well then, let us consider these matters."

As they talked a flush appeared beneath Eléonore's smooth skin. This could mean only one thing. Duke Anton Ulrich did not regard Sophia Dorothea as illegitimate, for by the German law a prince of a sovereign family could only marry a princess or a countess.

Did this mean that this was how Sophia Dorothea was regarded throughout Germany? Did it mean that the morganatic marriage was regarded as a true one?

It was too much to hope for. Anton Ulrich needed the wealth Sophia Dorothea would bring. But the betrothal must be accepted, Eléonore decided; and it must be soon, for the future of Sophia Dorothea depended on it.

*　　*　　*

When they were alone in their bedchamber she spoke to George William about the importance of this.

"I believe," she said, "that Anton Ulrich expects us to do something about having our daughter legitimized. Augustus Frederick could not marry her unless she were. I fancy he was telling us that by the time she is marriageable this must be done."

"If only I had not been such a fool . . ." sighed George William, sitting on the bed and staring at the tips of his boots.

Eléonore sat beside him and slipped her arm through his. How often had she heard him say those words! He meant them sincerely; but this situation demanded more than words.

"There is one who, would he but give his word, could make it possible for us to marry."

"You mean . . ."

"Your brother Ernest Augustus."

"But . . ."

"We would take nothing from him. We might even pay for

his consent. That should attract him. If he would release you from your promise not to marry, that is all we would ask—and if he did release you, then nothing would stand in our way. We could marry, Sophia Dorothea would be legitimized . . . and that is all we would ask."

"You think he would?"

"Not easily. He would have to be heavily bribed, I doubt not. But your brother the Bishop is very . . . bribable."

"Do you propose that I should go and talk to him? My dearest, I have hinted it a thousand times."

"No, let us send Chancellor Schütz. He is a loyal minister and will make a good ambassador. Let him sound your brother, and if we fail . . ."

"Yes," he said, "if we fail . . . oh, my love, how could I have been such a fool!"

"You were not a fool. How much worse it would have been if you had *married* Sophia."

"God forbid."

"How much more difficult our position would have been then. No, do not reproach yourself, my love. What is done is done. It is the future with which we have to concern ourselves. And if this fails then we will try something else. If I have to plead with the Emperor himself, I intend to have my daughter recognized as legitimately yours."

"You will succeed, my love. Do you not always?"

Eléonore was determined to, and soon after Anton Ulrich rode away from Celle, assured that Sophia Dorothea would be legitimized by the time she was of marriageable age, and that George William's wealth, which was increasing year by year, would be hers, Schütz left too, and his destination was Osnabrück.

* * *

Sophia was seated with her six maids of honour embroidering an altar cloth, for she had never approved of idleness. One of the maids read aloud as they worked, for, decreed Sophia, although the fingers were busy the mind should also be occupied.

In actual fact she was paying little attention to what was read, for her thoughts darted from one thing to another. Was the allowance of one hundred thalers given to these maids of honour too much? The household accounts which she examined herself were always a shock to her. The tirewomen, the chambermaids and the maids of honour . . . to think of a few, were so costly. And then, more so than ever, the gentlemen of the household. That was Ernest Augustus's affair, but this was one characteristic they shared; they both deplored the high cost of the household. But since George William had returned to Celle and set up his elegant Frenchified court there, the court at Osnabrück must have some standing.

It was perfectly easy to see, Sophia had pointed out to Ernest Augustus, that George William wanted visitors to go to his castle and think of him as the head of the house. And since they would find Celle so much grander than Osnabrück, they would begin to get it into their heads that Celle was the leading court of the house of Brunswick. Hence, Osnabrück must vie with Celle—and a costly business it was. Cupbearers, chamberlains, gentlemen-in-waiting—and the thalers mounting up.

In addition there were the nursery expenses. Over the last years the inhabitants of this important part of the household had increased. George Lewis, now eleven years old, and Frederick Augustus aged ten, had been joined by Maximilian William, now five, Sophia Charlotte, three, and Charles Philip, two. They must have their governors, tutors, fencing masters, dancing masters and pages as well as their attendants.

Thalers, thalers, whichever way one looked, thought Sophia.

She sighed and said: "That's enough."

The maid of honour who had been reading, promptly closed the book and Sophia, setting aside her needlework and signing to another of the maids of honour to put it away, left them and went to the nursery.

She was rather anxious about that eldest son of hers. He was intelligent enough, but so unattractive. His brother Frederick Augustus was charming in comparison and Sophia secretly wished that he had been the elder.

She found George Lewis, instead of sitting at his lesson books, directing a campaign across the schoolroom table—his brother Frederick Augustus in the rôle of opposing general. Little Max William and Sophia Charlotte had evidently been assigned other rôles in the campaign and, poor little mites, they did not appear to be enjoying them.

Frederick Augustus sprang to his feet when his mother entered and made the courtly bow which he had been taught; but Sophia's eyes were on George Lewis, whose brown face had flushed a little as he lumbered awkwardly towards her, and clumsily made his acknowledgment.

Sophia made a note: I must speak to Platen about him.

"Where is your Governor Platen?" she asked.

George Lewis shook his head implying that he did not know.

"Do not shake your head at me, sir. Have you no tongue?"

"Yes, I have."

"Have what?" demanded Sophia.

"A tongue."

"Should you not give me some title when you address me?"

"Yes . . . Madam."

"I am glad you deign to do so. I never saw such manners. And what is this game you are playing?"

"I am a general," piped up Frederick Augustus. "You see, Mother, my men are facing those of George Lewis but I fear he has manoeuvred his forces into the better position."

"It is a pity he cannot manoeuvre his manners a little more expertly." Sophia gave a loud laugh. "I want to see Platen. You go and find him and take him to the antechamber. I will be there shortly."

Frederick Augustus went off and Sophia gazed in dismay at her eldest son who continued to stare down at his feet. "George Lewis," she said impatiently, "why do you stand there? Why don't you say something?"

"What do you want me to say?" he mumbled.

Sophia Charlotte had toddled up to her mother pulling Charles Philip with her; and Max William was waiting hopefully for his share of her attention.

"I want you to say something which will tell us that you are not the complete oaf and boor you seem to be."

She turned to Sophia Charlotte.

"Mamma . . ." said Sophia, her pretty face flushed with excitement. Sophia picked her up. How pretty she was! and Charles Philip was pulling at her gown too.

Sophia sat down and took the young ones on her lap while Max William sidled up.

"Well, my son," said Sophia, "what were you doing in the campaign?"

"I was a general . . . a little one."

"And you have left the battle?"

He rubbed his finger on the soft material of her skirt and smiled up at her shyly.

"Perhaps that is because you were only a little general, my son."

Max William lifted his shoulders and laughed childishly. Sophia laughed with him; and the little ones joined in.

They were delightful, these children of hers . . . all except George Lewis who had no manners, no grace; he had now gone back to the table and was moving the toy soldiers there with a concentration that meant to imply he found them more interesting than anything else in the room.

He should be whipped, thought Sophia indignantly. He was a boor. How had it happened? His tutors and governors were to blame. But were they? She had told Ernest Augustus that she was beginning to suspect no one could make anything of George Lewis.

When he had been a baby she used to say she loved him because he was so ugly. It was amusing perhaps for a baby to be ugly, but when the baby grew up and became an uncouth, ill-mannered boy that was another matter.

Frederick Augustus came back and said that their governor was awaiting the Duchess's instructions and was in the antechamber when she wished to see him. So Sophia took leave of the children and went to join their governor.

Baron Frank Ernest von Platen was a mild man, but an ambitious one, determined to raise himself in the royal household. He saw an opportunity of doing this when he was appointed to the post of governor to the children of the reigning house. Being cautious he had become wealthy, and Ernest Augustus was inclined to favour him.

"Ah," said Sophia, "so here you are."

"At your service, madam."

"I want to talk to you very seriously about George Lewis."

Platen looked grave.

"You may well look as you do. I find his progress most unsatisfactory."

"He is not as bad as he seems, Madam."

"I hope not, for then I should despair; but it is necessary for a Prince to appear *better* than he is . . . not worse. Don't you agree?"

"I am in complete agreement."

"And yet this pupil of yours is a boor without the grace to behave with ordinary good manners."

"Madam, he is George Lewis. If he makes up his mind to act in a certain way then he will do it. Let me say this that his knowledge of military history is good; that I am sure he has great courage. But there are some subjects in which he has no interest. And he refuses to try to excel in light conversation."

"He is eleven years old. I should not have thought it was for him to lay down rules as to what he should and should not do."

"He is a Prince, Madam. Already he knows his mind."

"Then he will have to learn, will he not, that it is not his place to make decisions?"

"He can be very stubborn," said Platen. And vindictive too, he thought, when he is crossed. George Lewis would remember a score for years, Platen was sure; and that was a point to remember when it was certain that one day he would rule in place of his father.

"Something will have to be done. How is his English?"

"I am uncertain, Madam. Perhaps you would wish to speak to his tutor?"

"I would," she said.

"Then, Madam, if you will excuse me, I will find him and send him to you."

Glad to escape, Platen went out and in a few minutes returned with John von dem Bussche, the Princes' chief tutor.

"Now," said Sophia, "I am asking how my eldest son progresses with his English."

"Not at all, Madam, I fear."

"Not at all! But he must speak English. It is almost his native tongue."

"He has no aptitude, Madam. He is tolerably good at other languages but English seems to be beyond him."

"He must speak English. It would be such a disgrace if he did not. He is part English, as you know. I wish him to study not only the English tongue, but English history, for that is the history of my family."

The two men caught each other's eye. Sophia's preoccupation with England and the English was well known through the palace. It might even be that the recalcitrant George Lewis knew this and that was why he shut his mind to all things English . . . and in particular their tongue.

"Well, you will see that he learns his English. And I am most disgusted by his awkwardness. If you wish to keep your posts at least teach him how to bow and move with some grace. He may have to go to England one day and I would be most ashamed for my relations there to see my son as he is today. I can tell you this, that my cousin the King of England is one of the most charming men in the world. His manners are perfect . . . and they always were. I would wish my son to be as my cousin."

"In this matter of manners?" murmured John von dem Bussche with a daring which made Platen wince. Really, he would have to be a little more careful if he wished to keep his post. To refer to the blatant immorality of Charles II before his cousin Sophia was a little dangerous.

Sophia saw fit not to notice the lapse.

"Let this be attended to," she said.

Then she left them to go to her husband, for this matter of her son's unfortunate character weighed deeply on her mind.

Ernest Augustus was sleeping after a heavy meal; she could smell the sauerkraut about his clothes and person as she approached.

"Ernest Augustus," she said, "wake up. I am disturbed."

He started and looked at her in surprise. "My dear, this is hardly the time . . ."

"You were very preoccupied when I wished to have a chat with you before."

This was a reference to his current intrigue with Esther, one of Sophia's *femmes de chambre*. She was mildly irritated, wishing that he would look a little higher in his *amours*.

"Well, what troubles you?"

"George Lewis troubles me, and he should trouble you too."

"Is anything wrong? I thought he was in good health."

"His health's rude enough—the trouble is so is he. His manners are disgusting; he makes no progress with the English tongue; he shambles like an idiot; he gapes, and stammers. . . . In other words, he is an oaf, a boor . . . and something should be done about it."

"What?"

"Perhaps he should be sent abroad on a grand tour."

"Well, that might be possible. I suppose you're thinking of sending him to England."

"To England!" cried Sophia. "I should be ashamed. To my own people . . . and him such an oaf! You know Charles with his gracious manners!"

"I have heard he performs superbly in the bedchamber."

"He is a King and must have his diversions. He is not the only one who spends much time and energy in that room."

Ernest Augustus was quiet. He marvelled at her tolerance. It was one of her greatest virtues in his eyes. But he did not want to abuse it.

Sophia went on: "George Lewis is not ready yet to go to England, but I trust in good time he may be. It would seem that my cousin Charles's wife is a sterile woman, and that he'll get no issue from her."

"He does very well outside the marriage bed. Ha, ha."

"Which shows that the fault does not lie with him. We are not a sterile family. I wonder if he ever remembers that I was once promised to him. That would give him food for thought when he considers *my* nursery."

She was a little indignant that Charles had not asked her hand in marriage, and in spite of the fact that she was so proud of her connection with him she bore him some resentment. Yes, she was a proud woman. Ernest Augustus was glad to discover her vulnerability.

"He seems carefree enough and he has a brother."

"Yes," said Sophia, "with two daughters. Who knows, one of them might do for George Lewis."

"That would delight you! An English wife for George Lewis!"

"And, has it occurred to you, if one of those girls were Queen it might be the crown of England for George Lewis."

"You set your ambitious ideas very high, Sophia."

"That's what ambition is, my dear husband. I want George Lewis to be ready . . . if fortune should be good to him. His boorish manners shock me deeply. Something must be done. I think that as soon as it can be managed he and Frederick Augustus should do a tour of Europe. Not England . . . no, no. . . . He must improve before he goes there. But perhaps Italy . . . France. . . . What do you say?"

"I think you're right, as you invariably are. If there was more money, if they were a little older . . ."

"It is a matter to be considered then?"

"Most certainly."

As they were discussing the possibilities this might open up for their sons, a messenger came to tell them that Schütz, Duke George William's ambassador, had arrived at Osnabrück.

*　　*　　*

Ernest Augustus had rarely seen Sophia so angry as she was when Schütz had stated his case.

"My lord Chancellor," she said, "I am sure my husband the Duke will willingly show you the documents which your master has signed, in which he swears never to marry."

"I know of the existence of such documents, Madam, but my master is asking your indulgence."

Ernest Augustus put in : "But there is no releasing him from his vows. If I did so he would still have to face his conscience."

"My master has satisfied his conscience, my lord Duke. His great concern is for your help in this matter."

Sophia nodded at her husband who said : "What you ask is quite impossible."

"We are surprised, Herr Schütz," added Sophia, "that you should have allowed yourself to be the carrier of such a request."

"Madam, I follow my duty which is best to serve my master."

"By advising him to break his vows!"

"All he asks is that his marriage may be recognized as legal and his daughter legitimized."

"All he asks is to break his solemn vow," cried Sophia. "And my husband and I are agreed on this : the answer is no."

*   *   *

Schütz returned to Celle to report that it was useless to hope for any help from Osnabrück because both Duke Ernest Augustus and Duchess Sophia had made up their minds to do everything to stop the marriage.

"Well," said Eléonore, "at least we know what to expect. As a matter of fact, I very quickly learned that Sophia was an enemy. She never forgave you for passing her over to Ernest Augustus and me for winning the affection you could not give to her."

"So," sighed George William, "it is useless to fight."

"There I cannot agree," said Eléonore. "This is where the fight begins."

"But if Ernest Augustus will not release me . . ."

"We shall go higher than Ernest Augustus."

"You mean?"

"The Emperor."

"Eléonore !"

"Why not? What harm can it do? I am sure he will be sympathetic if I state the case precisely. In any case, it is what I intend to do."

"My dearest, you are a very determined woman."

"I have to be. I have my daughter's future to think of."

*   *   *

To the surprise of George William, Eléonore received a reply to her letter from the Emperor Leopold.

He understood, he said, and he sympathized; and what she asked was by no means impossible. He was, however, very busily engaged. He was faced with wars which had to be his main preoccupation. He had to fight the Turks and the King of France—to whom he knew Eléonore, although a Frenchwoman, had no reason to be grateful. He was sure that Eléonore's husband would be as glad to help him as he would be to help Eléonore if he had the opportunity. Firstly of course he must settle his pressing affairs. He was in need of men and arms. If the Duke of Celle could help him, he could rest assured that he would do everything in his power to repay such a service.

When Eléonore read the letter she gasped with surprise. To write to the Emperor had been the defiant gesture of a desperate woman and she had never dared hope for such a reply.

Well, here it was. George William must first send men to help
the Emperor—and then his reward should be considered.

She ran to George William who read the letter in amazement.

Then he looked at Eléonore, his eyes shining with pride.

"You are a wonderful woman," he said.

"And you will do this?"

"My dearest, the Emperor can make a bargain with you; rest
assured that I shall do everything ... just everything in my
power ... that you ask of me. Leopold shall have his troops."

This was the first step, thought Eléonore. She was certain that
she would take the rest unfalteringly to victory.

*   *   *

Sophia from Osnabrück declared open warfare, no longer pretending to be Eléonore's friend.

She blamed Ernest Augustus for not striking an even harder
bargain when he had had the chance. He should have robbed
George William not only of his right to marry and some of his
estates but all of them.

For the dismal truth had to be faced that George William was
much richer than they were and although he kept his Frenchified
court he had not a nursery full of children with their necessarily
expensive household to keep up.

All they had was their idolized petted Sophia Dorothea.

"She must be a spoiled brat!" fumed Sophia. "And if Eléonore
has no more children she will be a very rich one when she inherits
all they have."

And not content with making her the richest of heiresses
Eléonore was trying to bestow legitimacy on her as well. No wonder Anton Ulrich was licking his lips. She dareswore he was cursing the fact that the pretty little thing was not of an age to be
snapped up right away.

Sophia wrote to her niece, Elizabeth Charlotte, who having
married Louis XIV's brother was now the Duchess of Orléans.
She had known Eléonore when she was at the Court of France and
being of a malicious and mischievous nature she was delighted to
write to Sophia about her, inventing scandal, which seemed to be
what her aunt wanted.

These letters passed frequently between them and Eléonore was
the subject of them. They gave vent to their hatred by referring
to her as "that piece of flesh", "that clot of dirt", and remarking
how scandalous it was that she should be trying to make a position
for herself in the court of a German prince—even though a minor
one.

"You had better tell me all you know of this woman," Sophia wrote, "for can you guess what she is trying to do? She is trying to make her marriage to my foolish brother-in-law legal so that little bastard of hers can have a title and make a brilliant marriage. We owe it to our house, to our blood, to prevent this."

Elizabeth Charlotte, not finding sufficient scandal on which to feed her salacious and ever greedy mind, was not averse to inventing it. What had been her duties in the household of the Princesse de Tarente, did Sophia think? What was the Princesse de Tarente doing in Breda? Anyone who lived in her house automatically cast aside their reputations. Did Sophia know that? Elizabeth Charlotte could tell stories of a certain page at the court of Louis XIV. Eléonore had done everything she knew— and that was a great deal—to marry him; she had failed of course and now was doubtless glad since she had succeeded in making a fool of the Duke of Celle. And in the household of the Princesse de Tarente—what had been the relationship between the Princess's husband and that clot of dirt?

With delight Sophia read these letters to Ernest Augustus who did not believe them.

"Whether you believe them or not we must do our best to make others do so."

"Do you think you will? You only have to look at her to know that she is quite incapable of such acts ... not only for virtue's sake but for that of her dignity, which is very great."

"Well, we shall see."

When the rumours reached Celle Eléonore knew whence they came. Still she was distressed and, to show his utmost belief in her, George William decided to buy more estates which, because they were outside his inherited territory, he would be at liberty to leave where he wished. These he would leave to Eléonore. But even before he could make the purchase it was necessary to get the consent of Ernest Augustus to make the transaction.

George William was sad to see the change in his brother. When he called to tell him of his wishes, he reminded him of the old days when they had wandered about Europe together.

"Why, brother," he said, "then you would have done anything in the world for me."

"Then," replied Ernest Augustus, "we hadn't a care in the world. And if I have changed, then so have you. You used to be adventurous, ready for anything ... now you have been a quiet old married man."

"Well, I have responsibilities."

"And so, brother, have I."

"I did not think you would ever be so hard."

"I did not think you could ever be so sedate."

"It but shows what circumstances will do to us. Now this matter of Wilhemsburg . . ."

"You propose to buy the island so that you can leave it to Madam von Harburg."

"That is my idea."

"It is a very rich and fertile island."

"That is why I wish to acquire it."

"If this deal goes through I should need a little . . . commission. I am making a great concession in agreeing to the purchase . . . and I have a big family to keep, George William."

George William sighed.

Yes. Ernest Augustus had certainly changed.

*   *   *

Having acquired the island George William then set about making a pedigree for his Eléonore. He sent for a French genealogist and offered him a high price if he could prove that Eléonore was descended from the Kings of France. This was expertly done and made public.

When Sophia saw it she burst into loud laughter and immediately sent a copy to the Duchess of Orléans, who saw that the matter became a great joke at the French Court. The Duchess thereupon set about drawing up a genealogical tree for her cook to prove, she said, that she had descended from Charles the Bold. Eléonore realized that she and George William had been rather foolish over this matter, but the rift between the Osnabrück and Celle courts was wider than ever.

Eléonore and Sophia ceased to meet unless it was absolutely necessary, and then their demeanour towards each other was glacial.

Several years had passed since Sophia Dorothea's informal betrothal to Anton Ulrich's son, but Eléonore was not wavering.

Eventually she was going to win the Emperor's consent to legitimizing her marriage and the birth of her daughter.

To make sure of this George William himself took a troop of his men to fight under the Emperor when it was made clear that this was the wish of Leopold.

Eléonore endured the loneliness without him; even this, she thought, is worthwhile for the sake of Sophia Dorothea.

The Adventuress

In the coach which was trundling along the road to Osnabrück sat two young women and a man who was clearly their father. The elder of the girls was about twenty-three years old, the younger sixteen. They were handsome, and the elder in particular had an air of alertness; her large eyes were watchful as now and then she glanced out of the window at the passing countryside.

"You will find this a change after Paris," said her father.

"Doubtless," answered the elder.

"I loved Paris," said the younger.

"But Paris, my dear Marie," her sister caustically reminded her, "did not love you."

"How I should have loved to have been at court! I don't think there could be another place this side of Heaven to compare with it. You thought so too, Clara. Admit it."

"Heaven for me would be where I was treated as an angel."

"And you were told rather plainly that you weren't wanted. I'm surprised, Clara, that you did not stay and fight."

"My silly little Marie, do you think I wouldn't if we had had a chance. Papa had it from Montespan's agents themselves that we had better get out or it would be the worse for us."

Their father sighed. "It was no use going against them," he agreed. "I had hoped to get you both settled in France. I foresaw a brilliant future for you . . . but it did not come about."

"And quite rightly," said Clara, who obviously ruled the family. "We should never have been allowed to go near the King. French etiquette is the most rigorous in the world. It will be different in Osnabrück."

"Clara's right," agreed Count Carl Philip von Meisenburg. "Heaven knows what they would have trumped up against us. Men and women can be quickly eliminated in France. A *lettre de cachet* . . . and a man is whisked away and never heard of again. I saw that we had to get out . . . and quickly."

"And all because," added Clara, "you have two beautiful daughters!"

"Beautiful girls are not such a rarity at the Court of France, my dear. I happened to have a daughter who was both beautiful and clever. That would be regarded as a threat . . . and was."

"Well, to hell with Paris. To hell with the Roi Soleil. We'll try our luck in Osnabrück."

"Osnabrück!" sighed Marie. "Who has ever heard of Osnabrück."

"We shall see that people hear of it," Clara reminded her.

"Oh, Clara, I really believe you will."

"You must always listen to your sister, Marie," said their father. "She will know what is best to be done."

"I was rather attracted by Osnabrück when I heard about the Prince Bishop," admitted Clara.

"Ernest Augustus—Prince Bishop of Osnabrück," murmured Count Carl Philip.

"A man," went on Clara, "who seeks to set himself up as a Grand Monarque."

"He hates the French," put in the Count. "His great enemy is Louis. And yet . . ."

"And yet," finished Clara, "he would be like Louis in every way. I heard he tries to make a miniature Versailles at Osnabrück, that he keeps his mistresses and tries to deceive himself that they are as glorious as Madame de Montespan. I am sure he will be interested in two young ladies recently come from Paris . . . wearing the latest Paris clothes, looking like court ladies . . . and ladies of Louis' Court at that . . . clever, beautiful, shining with French gloss."

Count Carl Philip slapped his thigh.

"You'll do well for yourself, daughter. You'll settle the family's fortunes, I'll vow."

"His wife is ageing; she has borne many children; and although she has her own way in some matters she is tolerant about others. One need not fear her."

"The Duchess Sophia accepts the fact that men—rulers that is —must have their mistresses."

"She is a wise wife. I long to make the acquaintance of Ernest Augustus."

Clara lay back against the upholstery of the coach and closed her eyes.

She was excited. The thought of adventure always stimulated her. It had been disconcerting—more than that, humiliating—to be turned out of Paris as they had been; and yet in a way it was flattering. Why had they been ordered to leave? Because those sycophants who surrounded the King of France had been afraid of them, afraid that she, Clara Elizabeth von Meisenburg, might attract the King's attention and acquire too much influence over him. Beautiful women attracted the King's attention, but it was those who possessed brains as well as beauty who were feared.

They saw in her the makings of a King's mistress—not the sort of woman with whom he amused himself for a few weeks but a King's mistress who could become the most important woman in the country; and everyone knew that it was the woman who became the King's chief mistress who ruled the King and therefore the country.

Clara knew she possessed all the qualifications to rule. It was humiliating therefore to be turned from the glittering Court of France to try her talents in a smaller one.

Yet they were wise to come. There had been too many enemies in France. At Osnabrück they would not be recognized for what they were until the field was won.

She had already decided that she would take Ernest Augustus; and for Marie—there was the son, the Crown Prince, who was as yet a boy, and said to be sullen. Probably he was inexperienced. With herself advising the Prince Bishop and Marie having his eldest son in thrall, it would mean that the Meisenburg girls were ruling as they were surely meant to.

The coach was coming into Osnabrück, and the entire family were eagerly looking about them.

"It is not like Paris," complained Marie.

"Fool!" snapped Clara. "Did you expect it to be?"

"Now girls," murmured the Count, "no quarrelling. Remember, the family must stand together."

The coach came to rest before an inn which looked small and mean to the girls.

"Our lodgings," said the Count, "until we can find a better."

They alighted and the host came out to greet them.

Visitors from Paris! This was an important occasion. The best
rooms available? Most certainly!

Clara stood looking about her disdainfully; the smell of sauerkraut floated out from the kitchens.

"Ugh!" she murmured. "One realizes one is not in Paris."

*   *   *

It was not so easy to conquer Osnabrück as the Meisenburgs
had fancied. The Duchess Sophia kept a sharp eye on who was
admitted to the castle; and she saw no reason why Count von
Meisenburg and his daughters should be welcomed there. They
came from France, and she was not enamoured of the French.
Now had they come from England she might have received them
very kindly. They were not rich and were forced to take a humble
lodging, and it seemed during that first year of their residence at
Osnabrück that this fortress was as difficult to storm as that of
Paris. In Paris they had at least been considered dangerous; here
they were ignored.

Clara would pace up and down the bedroom which the girls
were obliged to share and clench her fists in rage. "We're wasting
time, I tell you. Precious time."

Clara was indeed, thought Marie, rejoicing in her seventeen
years which was very different from twenty-four.

"All we get is news of the court; all we see is the Prince Bishop
passing by."

"He did look up at the window and smile as though he liked
you," ventured Marie.

"As though he liked me!" cried Clara. "If only I could get a
post as maid of honour to the Duchess!"

But there seemed to be no hope. The Count did his best, but
the Duchess Sophia had no desire to add to her household.

The sisters saw the departure of the Crown Prince and his
brother for the Grand Tour with their governors Platen and
Bussche.

"The younger brother is the more handsome," commented
Marie.

"But it is the elder one who is more interesting to us."

"I should not care to go to bed with him!"

"Then you are a fool. You should at this moment be planning
how you can."

"Clara! Those wild plans! Do you think there is ever going
to be any chance of carrying them out?"

"I tell you I am not going to sit at windows watching processions all my life. I am going to be part of them ... and right in the centre."

Marie sighed. There had been a time when she believed that Clara would get everything she set out for. Only now was she beginning to doubt.

*   *   *

Life was dull in Osnabrück. Why had they ever come here? Clara asked her father twenty times a day. He was asking himself the same question. They had very little money. Who, he asked in return, would have believed that in a place like Osnabrück it would have been so difficult for three talented people to get a hearing?

The fact was, pointed out Clara, that they were too talented. People were suspicious of them.

Their French manners were noticed as they passed through the narrow streets; their French clothes sniggered at publicly and admired in secret.

There came the day when the Princes returned from the Grand Tour and there was to be a fête at the castle to welcome them.

As they had travelled abroad it would be amusing to show them something foreign—something similar to what they had probably seen on their travels. It would prove that Osnabrück had something to offer which was not very different from that which they had seen abroad.

A visitor from the castle called on the Count von Meisenburg. He had been in France, had he not? He had two daughters— very attractive young ladies by all accounts. If they would care to join in the fête they might do so. Perhaps they could sing some songs in French which would amuse the young Princes.

Would they!

Clara was almost wild with joy.

When the visitor had left she cried : "This is the opportunity for which we have been waiting. Now ... if we don't go on from here, it will be our own faults."

*   *   *

There was great activity in the Meisenburg lodgings. Silks and laces were strewn across the floor. They had to make their own gowns for they could afford no dressmaker; and, as Clara had said, what they wore should be a secret. They wanted no one copying them.

Did Marie realize the importance of this occasion?

Marie assured her forceful sister that she did.

"You are going to be dressed in this lilac silk. See. It does become you. You look so pretty . . . prettier than any of the girls here. You must. And make sure that you smile at the young Prince. He has to admire you so much that he is determined to make you his mistress."

"He is so young and . . . very ugly."

"Be grateful that he is. It should be all the easier for you."

Marie grimaced, but one did not disobey Clara.

Clara, losing no opportunity, called at the castle and sought an interview with those who were arranging the fête. She pointed out that she wanted to know how much time was to be allotted to her and whether she and her sister were to perform before the Duke and the Duchess.

While she was explaining her reasons for coming, Frank Ernest von Platen, the Princes' governor, looked in, and as he appeared to be treated with some respect Clara made herself gracious and asked if he could help her.

"If I could be of any assistance to you it would give me great pleasure," said Platen gallantly.

Clara lowered her bold and beautiful eyes. "I am sure you can. My sister and I are recently come from France and we have been summoned to perform at the fête."

"You must be the daughter of the Count von Meisenburg."

"How clever of you to guess! Because we have come from France we have been summoned to perform in the French manner for the Princes' entertainment."

"I can see that we are all going to be very fortunate."

"You are kind to say so, but my sister and I are a little disturbed because we are not quite sure what is expected of us."

"I am sure you will only have to appear to enchant."

"Everyone, alas, is not so kind as you . . . er . . ."

"Platen. Frank Ernest von Platen, Governor to the Crown Prince and his brothers."

"Oh!" Clara's eyes were sparkling. "You can help me then. Are we expected to perform before the Duke and Duchess?"

Platen was thoughtful. "Well . . . er . . ."

Clara's spirits began to sink but she rallied them. "I will be frank with you. We are not very rich. You know what it is to be of noble birth and poor. We came here to seek places at court and so far have been unable to get even a hearing there."

"The Duchess Sophia keeps a stern grip on the affairs of the household."

"Yet I feel that if I could get some opportunity of showing her that I would not disgrace her household ... I and my sister that is. My sister is beautiful."

"I can believe that—if she resembles you."

"She is very like me ... but younger."

"I am sure your years—although I refuse to believe they are many—have added to your charm."

"What pleasant compliments you pay! I did not know it was a German habit. It makes me happy though for I know that you will help me."

"All I can."

"I want to make sure that my sister and I have an opportunity of showing our talents to the Duchess ... and the Duke."

"Then you should perform early in the entertainment, for the Duke may grow tired of it and retire early."

"Could this be arranged?"

"I might arrange it."

"And shall we perform in the hall of the castle?"

"If it is warm and sunny it will be out of doors. What will be the title of your performance?"

"Pastorale."

"Fräulein von Meisenburg presents Pastorale ..."

"No ... no. Pastorale Ordonée par Mesdemoiselles von Meisenburg. You see the point is that we have just arrived from France and it is for this reason that we are given the opportunity."

"I shall see that you have every opportunity, *Mademoiselle* von Meisenburg."

She flashed her brilliant smile at him.

"We shall meet again," he said.

"I hope that we shall," she answered.

When she left the castle she was elated. At last she had a friend inside—and an important one since he was the Governor of the Crown Prince.

As she stitched at her blue silk gown she thought a great deal about Frank Ernest von Platen. There was something about him that appealed to her. The weakness of his mouth perhaps. He would be malleable.

*   *   *

In the castle grounds the shepherdesses in their elegant French style costumes held the attention of the assembled court. The smaller of the two was very pretty indeed; her hair, piled high on her head, with a curl falling on one shoulder, was adorned with flowers; her cheeks had been delicately and expertly tinted; her eyes very slightly blackened to make them look bigger than they actually were.

Her sister, equally elegant—perhaps more so—yet lacked Marie's dainty charm. Her enormous dark eyes flashed brilliantly but anxiously over the assembled company.

She was thinking : We *must* make our mark !

While she danced—as they had been taught in Paris—while she sang in French she was aware of the impression Marie was making on the Crown Prince, who goggled at her, his mouth slightly open, his eyes lascivious. Poor Marie ! thought Clara, yet rejoicing. But he was such a boy—he couldn't be much more than thirteen. Ready to experiment, of course. But a boy of thirteen was of little use.

Clara's eyes were on the Duke; that was why she noticed him yawning slightly. Was it failure again?

The Duchess Sophia was smiling graciously. The young women had a certain grace and she was glad of it. They spoke good French, but to hear French spoken like that always reminded her of her enemy at Celle and her thoughts slipped from her immediate surroundings to wander far afield. What would Madame von Harburg think of next? What new move would startle them? Madame von Harburg was becoming too friendly it seemed not only with Duke Anton Ulrich of Wolfenbüttel, but with the Emperor Leopold.

The two sisters had approached the Crown Prince and they were singing in their pleasant voices a song of welcome.

George Lewis liked it. Sophia watched him almost licking his lips over the younger girl. He would be another such as his father. She sighed. Well, they must have their mistresses. As long as he married the wife she would choose for him, what did it matter what mistresses he had? He was young as yet, though. Thirteen. Far too young to set up a mistress. Let him content himself at the moment with serving girls—which she believed he did. A necessary part of the masculine existence.

How hard these women were trying. Surely they weren't trying to seduce George Lewis !

She glanced at Ernest Augustus. He was nearly asleep.

"For heaven's sake," she murmured, "try to look a little interested."

"Ah yes. Very charming. Very charming."

What could one expect, Sophia asked herself. He was not as young as he would like to pretend to be. He still hunted for long hours; he attended to his business; and then he was awake half the night with some young girl in his bed. He had gone back again to Esther. What was it about that slut? Sophia wondered. Perhaps because she was so obviously a slut. Well, what mattered it. If it were not Esther it would be some other.

The pastorale was over. The women were taking their bows. George Lewis looked on slack-mouthed and his governor Platen and tutor Bussche were applauding wildly.

"Some evidently enjoyed the performance more than you did," whispered Sophia to Ernest Augustus.

"Excellent idea . . . these entertainments. Keeps them happy."

"There is no doubt,' replied Sophia, "that it makes some among them very happy indeed."

*   *   *

Back in their lodgings Clara tore off the blue satin gown.

"So much wasted effort!" she cried.

"Oh Clara, how can you say that?"

"The Duke was asleep."

"I thought the Prince was quite amused." Marie took up a mirror and studied her round pretty face.

Clara slapped it out of her hand. "You little fool," she said, "what good was that? He's a baby. What good will he be?"

"He'll grow up."

"So will you . . . and so will others. I tell you there is not a chance in this place. We'll get out. I shall speak to Father about it right away."

"Where should we go?"

"Somewhere where they are more appreciative of our talents."

"I hear that at Celle the Duke is only appreciative of his wife and daughter."

"I was not thinking of Celle."

"Where then?"

"I shall have to think. One thing I do know is that this place is no good to us."

Their father came into the room. "My dear daughters," he said, "you were magnificent."

"You would appear to be the only one who thought us so."

"Nonsense. I heard nothing but talk of you both."

"Much good that will do us."

"You have made an excellent impression. For what more could you hope?"

"That I had been able to keep the Duke awake."

"He is much occupied with affairs of state."

"A large part of his affairs are conducted in his bedchamber."

"Well, what do you expect?"

"That he might have spared a glance for us. Surely we are a little different from his fat German sows?"

"Hush Clara."

"I will choose when I am to be silent."

The Count quailed before his daughter's anger. It was recognized in the household that Clara ruled it; and it had been so for the last five years.

"The Duchess seemed to like your performance," suggested the Count placatingly. "It might be that she will offer you a place . . ."

"Because we dance and sing well? I doubt it . . . I very much doubt it. Listen. We must start thinking very seriously. Osnabrück is of no use to us. We must move on. We have wasted enough time already."

"I doubt we should have the money to pay our debts."

"Debts! We shall have to leave without, then. I am not going to stay here . . . wasting my time."

A servant at the door had already scratched twice unheard.

Clara turned to scowl at the woman. What had she overheard? What had they said about their debts? This was maddening—quite frustrating.

"These were left by messengers from the castle, Mademoiselle," she said.

Clara snatched the packages.

One was addressed to herself, the other to Marie.

Clara opened hers first, still retaining Marie's.

Inside was a brooch set with small gems—a pretty glittering thing. There was a note with it. Would she accept this small token of a big admiration? He had listened entranced to her performance. He had never been so enchanted in his life. He trusted that he might call on her. It was signed Frank Ernest von Platen.

Laughing, Clara opened Marie's. There was a brooch a little like the one Platen had given her; with a similar message of admiration and hope for a meeting in the near future. This was signed John von dem Bussche.

Clara threw the gifts and the letters on to a table. Marie and the Count ran forward to look at them and Clara watched them in silence.

They turned to her expectantly and she said : "Well, we set out to capture a Duke and a Prince. Our efforts have not entirely been lost. We have our consolation prizes."

The Count said : "And you still plan to leave Osnabrück?"

"No," said Clara, smiling. "I think I should like to stay a while in Osnabrück."

*　　*　　*

It was not, of course, what she had hoped for; but she did not despair.

There was an old proverb she had learned in France. *Petit à petit les oiseaux font leurs nids.* She must remember it. Platen was besotted. He had never known anyone like her. And Bussche felt the same for Marie. Clara was energetic; she discovered all she could about these men. The fact that they were in charge of the Princes should give them influence at court, and that was very desirable, providing of course they had the wit to use it. This she doubted. Platen was a weakling, and weakness she despised, for it was a fault of which no one could accuse her. But there could be occasions when weakness in a husband might be one of his greatest assets, and it was often the best possible arrangement when an ambitious wife had a pliable husband. Platen was longing to be her husband, and Marie was being interestedly courted by his friend and fellow governor Bussche. There was no mistaking their intentions.

The Count timorously asked his daughter what she thought of this situation.

Clara replied : "It is not one I planned. It has happened. But I don't think for one moment that being a married woman will be a hindrance to my plans ... rather a help."

The Count stared in astonishment at his daughter. So she was still aiming at ultimate power.

"Platen believes that he will have no difficulty in finding a place in the Queen's household for his wife."

"I see."

Clara laughed at him. "It's one way of storming the castle."

A few months after the sisters had performed the pastorale in the castle grounds Clara married Platen and Marie, Bussche.

From that it was an easy step to the household of the Duchess Sophia; and as it was one of his wife's dearest wishes that she should become one of the maids of honour, as soon as a place was vacant, her doting husband procured it for her.

Thus was near-failure turned to success; and Clara could begin the real business which had brought her to Osnabrück.

The Little Scandal

SOPHIA DOROTHEA awakened early and stretched luxuriously in her bed. It was a golden September morning—and her birthday.

For weeks there had been hushed whispering in the castle; her parents had exchanged glances when certain things were mentioned and she knew they were thinking of the pleasant surprises for this day. The servants had been bustling importantly for weeks; exciting smells rose from the kitchens; and the people in the town called their greetings to her when she rode out with her father or mother—and even they seemed to be sharing in the fun.

It was comforting; it was delightful—in fact it was the happiest thing in the world to be Sophia Dorothea of Celle.

Her mother was the most beautiful woman in the world; her father was the most indulgent father; and she was their adored and only child. Sometimes she wished that she had brothers and sisters, but if she had of course she would have lost a little of her importance. Would it have been worth while? That was one of the problems of Sophia Dorothea's world. There had been occasions when the household had been hushed; when she had believed that there might be a brother or sister; but all this had come to nothing and here she was—reigning supreme—the little Queen of Celle, as they called her in the town.

There would be entertainments at the castle all day. Everyone must know what an important day it was. The day on which was celebrated the birth of Sophia Dorothea.

Sophia Dorothea laughed; she gazed at the mantelpiece supported by four cupids; there had been a time when she was very small when she had believed that they were actually holding it there; she used to lie in bed and wait for them to move, wondering whether the mantelpiece would come crashing to the ground. Her mother had explained that the cupids brought love. There was certainly love in the castle. They all loved each other so dearly—Papa, Maman and Sophia Dorothea. There never had been such love as they shared—so Maman said; and because of it they would be happy ever after.

"For ever and ever," sang Sophia Dorothea.

She slipped out of the bed in the alcove and padded across the room, through the open door to the schoolroom. Her apartments consisted of three rooms leading out of each other—bedroom, schoolroom and parlour. In the schoolroom were two large windows and she loved to kneel and look out to the lime trees and the moat. The moat was to make them secure, Maman had said, secure from the wicked uncle and aunt at Osnabrück who did not love them.

Sophia Dorothea enjoyed shivering at the thought of the wicked uncle and aunt of Osnabrück; it gave real meaning to the security of Celle and made the love of her parents so much more precious.

There was going to be a ball today; she knew because of what was being done in the ballroom. Perhaps beyond the moat down in the wooden houses of the town people were waking and saying: "Do you know what today is? It's the seventh birthday of Sophia Dorothea, the little Queen of Celle."

And they would put on their best clothes and come to the castle, and she would be with Papa and Maman and everyone would smile and call greetings in German. She liked French better because she always spoke it with Maman when they were alone; but of course she must speak German sometimes.

Voices from without. It was too early yet. But the door was opened and there was Maman, her arms full of parcels and behind her Papa with his equally full.

They came into the apartment.

"So she is out of bed!"

She hid behind the curtains and then leaped out on them. They had thrown their parcels on the bed and Maman had lifted her in her arms.

"Happy birthday, my darling."

"Happy birthday, my darling Maman," answered Sophia Dorothea; for Maman had said they would always share everything—joys and sorrows, so it was equally her birthday.

Eléonore had to control her emotions as she looked at this child who grew more beautiful every day. Her hair was black, her eyes large and sparkling; her face a perfect oval, her skin so smooth and fresh; but it was more than that—a grace, a charm, a daintiness, which Eléonore assured herself was entirely French.

She loved this child so fiercely that her affection for George William seemed almost insignificant by comparison.

"I am here too," said George William. "Happy birthday, my dearest."

"Thank you, Papa."

She loved him very much but she did not share with him as she did with Maman. She could love only one person best.

"And what were you doing out of bed?" asked George William with mock sternness.

"I was having a look at a birthday morning."

Then they laughed together and sat on the bed opening the parcels.

*   *   *

There was a ball in the evening to celebrate the occasion, and Sophia Dorothea would open it with her partner.

She would remember all the steps taught her by her dancing master, who would be watching with apprehension; but he need not worry. She loved to dance.

Her partner was a tall boy—the most handsome boy she had ever seen, she decided.

He held her hand lightly and he had smiling eyes. She was glad he was a partner.

The others were falling in now—Papa and Maman dancing together; and Aunt Angelique with her husband the Comte de Reuss. Sophia Dorothea did not love Aunt Angelique greatly; she was not as beautiful as Maman and inclined to be a little resentful of all the devotion that was showered on her young niece. Sophia Dorothea had heard Aunt Angelique refer to her as *une enfant gâtée*.

She was not spoiled. Maman did not think she was—nor did Papa—and Sophia Dorothea was sure they knew far better than Aunt Angelique. She wondered if her companion thought so.

"Do you?" she asked forgetting that she was speaking her thoughts aloud.

"I did not quite catch ..."

"Do you think I am a spoilt child?"

"I do not know you well enough, but that I hope to remedy. If you are not, which I am sure is the truth, that is because you are too sweet-natured and sensible to be; and if you are—well, then it is the fault of others."

Sophia Dorothea's laughter rang out. "What funny things you say."

"I am glad they amuse you."

"You do not live in Celle?"

"I am going to for a time."

"What is a time?"

"One year . . . two years . . . three perhaps."

"That I shall call living in Celle. I am pleased."

"Why?"

"Because I like you. You shall always dance with me when there is a ball."

"Thank you."

"Do I dance well?"

"Most excellently."

"What are you, besides a dancer?"

"A soldier."

"Have you come here to fight?"

"To learn to fight and . . . other things."

"Why?"

"Oh, because it is a custom in noble houses for sons to be brought up away from home."

"Then you will live here? You will be as my brother."

She put her head on one side and smiled at him. Another one to love her, to spoil her? She was pleased. "This is the happiest birthday of my life," she announced.

The dance was over and she must take her partner to her mother; she wanted Eléonore to know how very happy she was.

"But first," she said, "I must know your name, for how can I tell my mother who you are if I do not know?"

"It is Königsmarck," he said. "Philip Christopher Königsmarck."

"Come," she said, and slipped her hand in his. "I will show you to my mother."

Eléonore was looking for her and she cried: *"Maman,* look. This is my new friend."

*   *   *

The days were more exciting. Sophia Dorothea would run to the window as soon as she was awake and see if Philip Königsmarck were in the grounds of the castle. If he were he would wave to her. They rode together; he told her about Sweden and it was interesting to hear of countries other than France, of which her mother talked so frequently, and Italy, which came so often into her father's conversation.

Philip told her of the great family of Königsmarck and how they were known throughout Europe as great soldiers.

Life had become more exciting since that seventh birthday when she had first met Philip.

*   *   *

It was Angelique who was responsible for what happened. Sophia Dorothea did not know this or her dislike for her aunt would have turned to hatred.

Angelique came to her sister's apartments one day and said : "Eléonore, I should like a word in private with you."

Eléonore looked in surprise at her sister and asked what was troubling her.

"Sophia Dorothea," answered Angelique.

Eléonore turned pale. "What do you mean?"

"Oh, don't distress yourself. She is well enough ... too well perhaps. I passed her in the stables a few moments ago with that Königsmarck boy. It was that which made me decide I must speak to you."

"What are you talking about, Angelique?"

"Has it occurred to you that Sophia Dorothea is somewhat precocious and that Königsmarck is sixteen years old ... almost seventeen?"

"You surely are not suggesting ..."

"In a childish way Sophia Dorothea is in love with the boy."

"As long as it is in a childish way ..."

"But he is not so childish, is he?"

"My dear Angelique !"

"Oh, you are like all mothers. Your child is different from all others. Hasn't it occurred to you that these two at least might experiment?"

"What are you suggesting?"

"Only that I saw Sophia Dorothea throw her arms about him and declare he must never, never go away."

"She is a baby."

"Very well, if you are prepared to allow her to run risks ..."

"You know I would never allow her to run risks."

"Moreover, what do you think is the motive of Count Königsmarck in sending his son here? Sophia Dorothea will be a considerable heiress."

Eléonore was uneasy. "Thank you, Angelique," she said. "I will think about this."

*   *   *

When her sister had left her Eléonore went to the window and looked out across the moat.

She *is* precocious, she thought. There could be trouble. She is so lovely and he is a remarkably handsome boy. Sixteen. Rising seventeen. Scarcely a boy.

Eléonore went to find George William, who was sitting in the sunshine near the open window; he looked up and smiled as she entered.

"There won't be many more days like this, this year," he said, as though excusing his laziness.

"So you are making the most of them?"

He reached for her hand and looked up at her affectionately. "Something troubles you, my darling?"

"It's what Angelique has just said about Sophia Dorothea and Philip Königsmarck."

"What could she say?"

"That the Königsmarcks have sent him for a purpose . . . marrying our daughter. And that Sophia Dorothea is a little too fond of him and he is no longer merely a boy."

"And this disturbs you?"

"You know that Sophia Dorothea is for Augustus Frederick of Wolfenbüttel."

"That will not be for a year or two."

"She is very fond of this boy, George William. Suppose she grew too fond of him?"

"My love, you are talking about a child. They change their affections every week."

"I haven't noticed Sophia Dorothea do that."

No, thought Eléonore, Sophia Dorothea had loved her mother steadily since she had become aware of her. She was not one to change her devotion.

"Well, what is it you wish to do, my dearest?"

"I think it would be wise to find some pretext for sending the boy away. One thing I could not bear would be for our child to be hurt. It would be terrible if she discovered a fondness for this boy and then was forced to take Augustus Frederick. What I want is for Philip Königsmarck to go . . . and we must invite the Wolfenbüttels here more often. I want our daughter to know the man she is to marry, I want her to learn to love him before she is taken away from us. Well, what do you say, George William?"

"You have spoken, my dear. We will diplomatically dismiss young Königsmarck and Augustus Frederick shall take his place in our daughter's affections."

Eléonore stooped and kissed him.

"Thank you," she said. "You make me feel so . . . safe. I know that while we stand together nothing can harm us."

*   *   *

The years began to slip by. Sophia Dorothea had been so deeply distressed when Philip Königsmarck left Celle that Eléonore knew how right she had been to send the boy away. But Sophia Dorothea was a child still and Eléonore set out determinedly to make her forget her loss. She did not entirely succeed in doing this, and for a long time after Philip had gone, Sophia Dorothea would refer to him rather sadly. "Philip would have said that." "Philip would have done it this way."

Angelique had been right. Sophia Dorothea, living so much with older people, was a precocious child.

Augustus Frederick often came to Celle and he and Sophia Dorothea were good friends. She did not find the exhilaration in his society that she had found in that of Philip Königsmarck, but at least she liked him and Eléonore was satisfied that her beloved child would be spared the horror which so many princesses and heiresses had to endure—of being married to a stranger.

George William had left Celle to go and fight once more for the Emperor who had hinted that he would appreciate such help, and Eléonore was always uneasy while he was away; she was always afraid that there would be some sort of attack from Osnabrück and that she would be unable to defend herself. Often she dreamed of Osnabrück—crazy dreams dominated by Sophia as a giantess and Ernest Augustus as an ogre, storming Celle when George William was away and trying to rob her of her precious child. These dreams were ridiculous by the light of day, of course; but she was always a little anxious when visitors arrived at the Castle until she had ascertained that they did not come from her brother-in-law and his wife.

She and Sophia Dorothea were constantly in each other's company. She herself taught the child—it was an excuse to be together. Sophia Dorothea was growing up into a vivacious, intelligent and extremely charming young woman. Each day she grew more beautiful; and it was not only her mother who thought so. She was gracious always to the townsfolk and it was easy to see how she charmed them. Eléonore had longed for a large family but she believed that in this one child she had all that she desired.

She wanted everything for her—wealth, honours, happiness. But first, she assured herself, happiness. She had acquired it; so must her beloved child.

It did not occur to her that George William was a little jealous of her devotion to their daughter; it did not occur to her that he ever could be. She believed that he was as devoted to Sophia Dorothea as she was. This was not so; George William was proud of his daughter; he indulged her; but he could not love a child as much as he loved a woman; and in the last years the thought had come to him that the older their daughter grew, the less time Eléonore had to spare for him.

He had had proof that she loved Sophia Dorothea more than she loved him, for when the Emperor wished him to go to war, Eléonore wanted him to go. She did not say so; she had wept at his departure; but she believed that it was his *duty* to go, because of the absolute necessity of pleasing the Emperor and getting their reward, which was the legitimization of Sophia Dorothea.

For the sake of this then, he must go to war; and Eléonore wanted him to go.

He hid his resentment; did he not love his daughter too? He fought valiantly; he did everything in his power to win the Emperor's approval; and he knew that he had succeeded.

When he returned to Celle, Eléonore was radiantly happy to welcome him, and all his resentment faded. There was his beautiful daughter waiting to fling her arms about him and to jump up and kiss him and tell him what a handsome soldier he was and how happy they were to have him home.

He wondered then how he could have entertained such foolish thoughts for a moment. They were one family, and the good of one was the good of all; and each time he saw his wife and daughter afresh he was struck by their beauty which in his eyes exceeded that of all other women.

He had news for Eléonore and he could scarcely wait until they were alone.

"I have seen the Emperor," he told her.

It was wonderful to see the way in which she opened her eyes so wide and watch while the colour flooded her face.

"Yes," he went on, "I so distinguished myself in battle that I had a private audience."

Eléonore threw herself into his arms.

He kissed her forehead and her throat and then he said : "But you do not seem to be interested in what he said?"

She was out of his arms, staring at him.

"He said : 'Commend me to your Duchess. I trust she is well.' "

"He . . . he called me your . . . Duchess?"

George William nodded.

"Then he means that he regards me as your wife."

"I think it was a hint. He was telling me that he was pleased with me and that I had earned my reward."

"You are the most wonderful father in the world."

"I would rather you thought I was the most wonderful husband."

"Both," she cried ecstatically. "Both!"

*   *   *

George William had been right in his assessment of the Emperor's intentions. Quickly on his return followed letters granting Eléonore the title Countess of Williamsburg and legitimizing Sophia Dorothea.

Ernest Augustus and Sophia were furious when they heard this news, but there was nothing they could do against the Emperor's decisions, although Sophia told her husband that they would have to be more watchful than ever, or that sly French Madame would outwit them yet. It appeared she had been writing to the Emperor. What impertinence! And she had managed to bewitch him with her pen as she had poor George William with her beauty.

They must indeed be very watchful.

*   *   *

Sophia Dorothea sat before her mirror watching the effect of a red rose in her dark hair. It was very becoming. She could not help being aware of her beauty; people would stare at her when she rode through the streets with her parents; and her maids told her that she was going to be as lovely as her mother.

One of the pages had even told her that he would willingly die for her; he was such a handsome page that she had given him one of the flowers she carried and he had replied that he would keep it until the day he died.

Sometimes she thought of Philip Königsmarck—only she could not remember exactly what he looked like now. When she read of the old gods and heroes of the North she would think of him. She remembered him as all that was brave and noble. He was like Sigurd riding through the flames to awaken Brynhild, or Balder the Beautiful dying pitiably from the sprig of mistletoe thrown from Loke's malicious hands. I shall never forget him, she would say to make herself feel sad. It was sometimes pleasant to feel sad in the castle of Celle because it was such a rare emotion.

While she dreamed one of her maids brought her more flowers and would not say who had sent them.

"They have been gathered from the gardens," said Sophia

Dorothea. She knew it was the page. How bold! How daring! But then Sigurd and Philip Königsmarck were bold.

A note fell from the flowers; she laughed and read it. It said that the writer would die for her. "He's already told me that," she said. She was the most beautiful creature in the world and he only lived to serve her. He signed his name boldly.

"Well," said Sophia Dorothea. "He is a very bold young man."

But she kissed the note and slipped it into a drawer. Then she went down to join her parents.

*   *   *

When the Emperor had granted the legitimization of Sophia Dorothea, Ernest Augustus had agreed with Duchess Sophia that they must be more watchful of what went on at Celle. "For you may depend upon it," pointed out Sophia, "French Madame will not stop at this." Ernest Augustus had agreed, and as a result they had planted spies in the castle of Celle. A maid here, a page there —all occupied in moderately menial tasks so that they would call little attention to themselves. One of these—a maid who had been posted to the apartments of Sophia Dorothea—was quickly aware of the devotion of the romantic page; the woman saw the flowers delivered, saw Sophia Dorothea with the note—for it had not entered the girl's head that she could have any enemies in her father's castle and she was very careless—and immediately she was alone in the room the maid went to the drawer into which Sophia Dorothea had thrust it. She read it but put it back, and then went to the person who could cause most trouble : the Countess of Ruess.

Angelique pounced triumphantly on the note and carried it to her sister.

"There, you see. That is what is going on."

"Where did you find this?"

"In your daughter's apartments."

"You mean you . . ."

"I found it. Let it rest there. You should rejoice that I did so, for now you can no longer be blind."

Eléonore summoned her daughter, and showed her the note.

"Oh, that is from one of the pages," Sophia Dorothea explained.

"But he is telling you he is in love with you!"

"Oh yes," said Sophia Dorothea.

Eléonore looked in horror at this beautiful girl. "But my darling, do you not know what this means?"

"It means that he would die for me. He says so."

Innocence! thought Eléonore. Absolute innocence! But there was need to protect her.

"If ever anyone in the household—or anyone else for that matter—writes a note such as this to you, you must bring it to me at once."

"Yes, Maman."

"There! Do not look so worried. It is over. But remember in future that you must tell me what is going on. Have we not always shared everything?"

Sophia Dorothea threw her arms about her mother. "Oh yes, Maman; and we always will."

"Now, my precious, that is well. Think no more of this."

"And if he sends more notes you want me to bring them to you? I hope you won't scold him, Maman, because he is really a very good page."

"He will send you no more," said Eléonore.

She ordered that the page was to be put into one of the castle dungeons until it was decided what should be done with him.

After a few days he was banished from Celle.

"It is better," said Eléonore, "that this affair should be forgotten as soon as possible."

But meanwhile the spy had reported the incident to Osnabrück.

*   *   *

Duchess Sophia was delighted to hear of the scandal.

"But is this not exactly what we should have expected from them?" she demanded of Ernest Augustus.

He merely shrugged his shoulders. "I would expect it from any. It is the way of the world."

Acid retorts sprang to the lips of Sophia, but she silenced them. Ernest Augustus was willing to treat her with respect as long as she acknowledged him the head of the house; she was prepared to do this as long as she had her way where she wanted it; but to achieve this she must work to some extent underground. He liked to follow his masculine pursuits—hunting, travelling a little, eating, drinking, fornicating; but at least he was growing more and more shrewd as the years passed by; yet he could never feel the venom she did for his brother's wife. He thought George William had been a fool, and still was over the woman; but he had no desire to indulge in blacking the characters of Eléonore and her daughter.

Eléonore was clever; the child was pretty by all accounts and it was the most natural thing in the world that a page should fall in love with her. As long as that fool of a brother of his didn't try to take anything back that he had forfeited, Ernest Augustus was willing to live at peace and without rancour.

But Sophia did not intend to forget the incident. It could, she believed, do some harm to the family at Celle, for when people were in a delicate position it was always easier to besmirch them than if they were living normal and conventional lives.

Sophia declared that since Sophia Dorothea's mother was merely the Madame of the Duke, it was not to be wondered at that the girl showed herself to be indiscreetly promiscuous.

She eased her annoyance by writing to the Duchess of Orléans. "What a pity that we ever asked that clot of dirt to our court. If we had not George William could not have brought her to Celle. We could have found some other *catin* for him who would have known her place. But never fear. Give Mademoiselle Sophia Dorothea a little while and she will provide us with something to talk of. She is a little *canaille*. You will see."

Sophia could trust the Duchess of Orléans to spread the story of the page, embellishing and garnishing it to give it a more shocking flavour.

And so the story which Eléonore had been at such pains to keep secret reached the ears of Anton Ulrich.

"It is time Sophia Dorothea was married," was his comment.

But here was a dilemma. Sophia Dorothea had been legitimized, but still her parents were not properly married. This seemed a serious drawback in the eyes of Anton Ulrich and he rode over to Celle to discuss the matter.

*   *   *

Seated in the apartments of George William and Eléonore, Anton Ulrich looked out past the lime trees to the moat and said : "I do not think the Emperor would deny the permission. Already he has shown himself friendly to you both."

"There is Ernest Augustus to consider," pointed out George William.

"But if it was the Emperor's wish and he was to lose nothing by the marriage, I do not see how he can object."

"We could try," suggested Eléonore.

"And," said Duke Anton Ulrich, "if I added my pleas to yours, and explained the circumstances to him, I do not think he would deny us what we want."

"And my brother ..." began George William uneasily.

"Well, we might try the Emperor first; and if we get his consent, then we can begin to consider where your brother comes into this."

"Let us try it," cried Eléonore with shining eyes.

Duke Anton Ulrich turned to her; he respected her drive and determination far more than he did her husband's. George William, he decided, had grown soft over the years. He was more enamoured of peace and quiet than perhaps it was good for a man to be.

*   *   *

Anton Ulrich's suggestion proved a good one. The Emperor had no desire to put anything in the way of the marriage, providing the two brothers could work out an amicable solution.

Ernest Augustus sat long with his lawyers. It was difficult to oppose the marriage since the Emperor was agreeable; but he was going to see that his interests were well looked after.

Messengers went back and forth between Osnabrück and Celle, and at last a document was drawn up in which Ernest Augustus agreed that George William should be joined in holy matrimony with Eléonore von Harburg, the Countess of Wilhelmsburg; and that their daughter should bear the arms of a Princess of Brunswick-Lüneberg.

But there was uneasiness at Osnabrück as great as there were rejoicings at Celle, where the most elaborate arrangements were made for the celebrating of the wedding.

And there in the church at Celle amidst glittering ceremony George William led Eléonore to the altar; and they were solemnly married.

Duke Anton Ulrich, with an important following from his own court, was present; so was the rather bewildered Sophia Dorothea, who was enjoying an experience denied to many—being present at her parents' marriage.

Everyone was happy and Eléonore radiant; she had achieved success at last. Her daughter a Princess; herself a legitimate wife.

When she saw the children together—her beloved daughter and Anton Ulrich's son—she exulted. Anton Ulrich had proved himself to be a good friend to her and when the houses of Celle and Wolfenbüttel were joined they would be far more powerful than the court at Osnabrück.

Even on such a day she must recall her enemies and when she thought of them it was not Ernest Augustus whom she dreaded but Sophia.

But this was a day for rejoicing. A day of triumph and perfect happiness.

Her triumph was even greater when the Emperor Leopold came to the neighbourhood and Eléonore was presented to him. He was charmed by her; he was delighted with her success; and he bestowed upon her the title of Duchess of Celle.

Now she had everything. There was nothing more to fear. She was invulnerable; no one would dare cast slights at her again.

But the Duchess Sophia was going to lose no opportunity of keeping the newly created Duchess of Celle where she, Sophia, considered she belonged.

Clara Triumphant

CLARA VON PLATEN was awaiting her opportunity; she had no doubt that when it came she would step right into the place she had chosen for herself even before she had come to Osnabrück. Having married Platen she was committed to Osnabrück; there could now be no packing of bags and going on to seek her fortune. Why should she? Although she had had to wait longer than she had first thought, she was very near now to her dream's fulfilment.

The court at Osnabrück was suited to her taste. It seemed that every petty Duke and Princeling imagined himself to be a Grand Monarque. Louis had a great deal to answer for! Everywhere there were attempts to turn German castles into palaces of Versailles, and the glitter and allure of the French Court—albeit that Louis was an enemy—was slavishly imitated. There were fireworks displays, masques, banquets, plays in the gardens and the great halls. When news seeped through that this and that had been done at Versailles, sure enough there would be an attempt to produce it at Osnabrück or Hanover where Duke John Frederick, the third brother, now reigned. In fact, John Frederick was the biggest Frankophile of them all. He had even become a Catholic, had put up statues in the gardens of the Palace at Hanover, commanded that Mass be sung in the churches and invited French singers and dancers to be his guests.

Ernest Augustus did not go so far as that, but he had his love of ostentation. He could not afford to spend as lavishly as John

Frederick because he had a large family of six sons and one daughter, whereas John Frederick had no son and of his four daughters only two were living. George William was the only brother who did not set out to make a small Versailles of his castle; and this was strange considering he had a French wife. All was good taste and charm at Celle in contrast to the often vulgar displays of Osnabrück and Hanover.

But Clara was pleased with the manner in which the Osnabrück court was conducted. She herself loved display; and she did not forget that it was due to the fact that she and her sister had recently come from France that they had been given an opportunity to display their talents.

Now as waiting woman to the Duchess Sophia she had an occasional opportunity to study her quarry. Ernest Augustus pleased her. He was a man of lusty appetites and she would know how to satisfy them. Her sensuality was second only to her ambition; and she did not see why she should not indulge the former while serving the latter. Once Ernest Augustus had tried her, her fortune would be made; for she would make sure that he should discover her to be unique. The experience must be such as he had never enjoyed before. But how make sure of that? If his eyes rested on her lightly as they had done on the unfortunate Esther—unfortunate because Clara had decided that her reign would soon be over—he would make up his mind that here was another of his light o' loves and that would be all she could ever hope to be. A man had to be made aware that he was getting something specal before he would believe he was.

"How?" she asked herself.

She would wear some entirely French and exciting garment. Yes, that—but clothes were not enough. She had to seduce his mind before she seduced his body.

For this purpose during those first weeks in the service of the Duchess Sophia, she actually kept out of Ernest Augustus's way; and instead ingratiated herself with Duchess Sophia.

An intelligent woman, thought Sophia. Discreet and oddly modest. She complimented Platen on his marriage; and remarked to Ernest Augustus that George Lewis's governor was cleverer than she had thought.

Ernest Augustus while commenting that he had not made such a good job of George Lewis, fairly admitted that he doubted whether anyone could. He was glad that she had a high opinion of Platen because he was thinking of making a minister of him. A quiet efficient fellow—those were the sort he liked to have about him.

This was triumph, Clara decided, as well as a sign for her to go forward, and when Platen received his promotion she insisted on hearing everything that took place. She was astute, shrewd and single-minded; and she was working to one end, to attract Ernest Augustus and to set up in Osnabrück that institution which was so much a part of the admired Court of France, the *maîtresse en titre*. Clara was yearning for that rôle—the woman who by wit, charm, brains and beauty, ruled the King and therefore ruled the country.

It was naturally simpler here than it would have been at Versailles. There were no rivals for one thing. Silly little girls who giggled together about what had happened to them in the Bishop's bedchamber were welcome to their brief triumph.

She saw that she had been wise to marry. Frank Platen was no fool; he was merely a coward. He wanted a peaceful existence, free from conflict. In a few weeks she had dominated him; and while he was a little disappointed to find his marriage was not what he had hoped it would be, he was continually being astonished by the astuteness of his wife.

"We are working together," she told him. "I'm going to make you the chief minister. I'm going to get you a resounding title. A count, I imagine. Yes, I would like to be a countess."

He had laughed. "The things you say, Clara."

"I say what I mean," she told him fiercely.

She listened to his accounts of meetings; she told him what he should say; she even phrased his speeches for him, pithily, wittily.

He began to be noticed; he, little Frank Platen, who had hitherto not been of any great importance, to be singled out by his fellow ministers, by the Bishop himself.

"If the Bishop asks you who thought of that, tell him your wife."

He looked at her in astonishment. "I have my reasons," she said.

"What reasons are those?"

"You will see."

He obeyed her; it had become a habit to obey Clara.

"Your wife seems to be an extraordinary woman, Platen," said Ernest Augustus one day.

"She is, my lord."

"In the Duchess's bedchamber, is she?"

"Yes, my lord."

"I believe the Duchess is pleased with her."

"I think that to be so."

"Well, you look pleased with yourself. I must meet her one day."

Platen reported this conversation to Clara.

She laughed. "He shall," she said.

*   *   *

Ernest Augustus was dozing in his private study. He had eaten too much and had retired hither on the pretext of studying some state papers but actually to sleep.

I'm getting old, he thought, yawning.

He could hear the music coming from the great hall. Music was played during meals now. He had always loved music—good stirring German music; but of course the taste now was all for the French.

Too much red cabbage, he thought; too much beer. The French drank wine. Well, he thought, we don't want to become as French as that.

He smiled, thinking as he often did of George William over at Celle. What was he doing now? Sitting down with his wife and child like any peasant. No, not like a peasant, of course. In the utmost luxury, for George William was the richest of all the brothers—and quite a bit of that fortune would go to that little French bastard of his unless he and Sophia could think of a way of preventing it—in the room, made gracious by Madame Eléonore who would be seated in her chair, her delicate white fingers working at her tapestry; and the girl would be seated on a tabouret either at his feet or hers; and they would be talking about the affairs of the castle. A charming domestic scene . . . if one cared for domestic scenes. He could not imagine himself and Sophia indulging in them. Theirs was not that sort of marriage—no idyllic love affair without end, but a good marriage of two people who understood each other. She had her way in anything that did not interfere with his comforts and needs—and the same for him.

Let George William keep his domestic bliss—his beautiful wife, his pretty—and if accounts were true—coquette of a daughter.

A gentle scratching on the door. He frowned, having no wish to be disturbed. Who had dared open the door without an invitation to do so?

A woman stood there. He had seen her before; she was one of Sophia's women. Good figure, bedworthy, he had marked her down for future dalliance. But when he wanted a woman he would summon her; he did not expect to be disturbed thus.

"My lord . . .'

Her voice was low, exciting in a manner new to him.

"What do you want?"

"I heard that Your Highness wished to see me."

"Then who carried such a message?"

"It was my husband, Frank von Platen."

"Ah! So you're Platen's wife?"

She came to his chair, bowed before him, making sure that her dress fell away from her full breasts as she did so.

An invitation? wondered Ernest Augustus, slightly surprised, remembering how demure she had been.

"I didn't send for you now," he said.

"My husband said you would like to meet me some time."

He laughed. "At a more appropriate time," he said.

"My lord, I thought this . . . a most appropriate time."

"Most wait until sent for."

"You will find that I am not like . . . most."

Her eyes were brilliant; she had cleverly made them look bigger than they actually were. What a body! he thought. She would have skills. And she came from France, he remembered, although she was a German. This meant that she had the airs and graces without the pride of his sister-in-law Eléonore. Now, there's a woman I could never fancy, he thought. He realized that he had already come to the point of fancying Platen's wife.

"Your husband often mentions you," said Ernest Augustus. "He seems to value your judgment."

"At least it is valued by one of Your Highness's ministers."

There was a meaning behind her words. He was a little fascinated and his annoyance at having been disturbed was fast disappearing.

"I see that you have other gifts to bestow on your husband . . . besides advice."

"It is a pleasure to give what is appreciated."

"And you find him appreciative . . . enough?" He regarded her lazily.

"Who can ever have enough appreciation?"

Surely there was no mistaking her meaning? Women were of course eager to please the most important man in the principality, but he sensed this one was different. He would discover later what she wanted. At the moment there was no need to go beyond the obvious step.

He held out a hand and she took it. He drew her down so that she was forced to kneel before him.

"You have come to offer me . . . advice?" he asked smiling.

"If you need it . . . it is yours."

"And if I do not?"

She shrugged her shoulders. "All need the help of friends."

"The Bishop needs it from his minister's wife?" he asked.

"He may at some time. He may need other things she has to offer."

"I think that very likely. And they will be given freely."

She bowed her head.

"But it must be remembered that she likes . . . appreciation?" he asked.

"She would be wise enough to know it is foolish to ask for what would not be freely given."

He brought his face close to hers and looked into her eyes.

"You are a strange woman," he said.

"You have quickly discovered that."

"I would like to know more of you."

"And I of Your Highness."

He put his hand on her shoulder; touching her skin, his fingers probed lightly; but in spite of the lightness he could not hide the fact that he was excited.

"Well?" she said faintly mocking him, he fancied.

He answered with another question. "When?"

"You are the lord and master." Again that hint of mockery.

"Tonight. I shall be in my bedchamber . . . alone."

"It shall be my duty . . . my pleasant duty . . . to see that Your Highness is . . . not alone . . . for long."

*   *   *

When Clara came out of the Bishop's apartment, the first signs of dawn were in the sky; she walked lightly past the sleeping guards; they were aware of a passing figure but paid little heed. A woman coming from the Bishop's bedchamber was not a very unusual occurrence. It was wiser not to look too closely; she might not like it; she might whisper a word into the Bishop's ear one night—it was easy enough—and there would go the hope of promotion.

Clara was pleased with herself. There would be no going back now. She had startled him. Hers was a sensuality matching his own and she had given it full rein. It had been amusing. She would not waste her energies on a man like Platen—Ernest Augustus was different. She had been making love to Power and that had aroused all her ardour.

He had let her go reluctantly, but she had insisted. Yes, insisted. It was as well to set the pace from the start. Of course she was not such a fool as to imagine she could arrogantly command him. He had been having his own way too long to accept that.

But she would govern—in her own subtle way; and it might well be that he would know and simply not care.

What a night! She wanted to laugh aloud. She had startled herself as much as Ernest Augustus. She had been born to be a courtesan. She knew it. She had all the tricks of the trade; and they were inherent. Louis did not know what he had missed. Poor Louis with his mincing French harlots who would never know the verve and vulgarity of a German whore.

She opened the door of the apartment she shared with Platen. Poor ineffectual Platen! His day was done. She would never share his bed again; and he might as well know it.

"Clara!"

He was awake, waiting for her. Fool! He might have had the grace to pretend to be asleep. How ridiculous he looked with his thin hair sticking out in all directions from under his night cap, his eyes pale and bulging, his pasty face, his gaping mouth.

"So I awakened you?"

"Where have you been?"

"Employed in useful occupation," she said flippantly.

"Clara, I insist . . ."

"You insist. Now, Frank, don't be foolish. You insist on nothing —nor shall you ever where I am concerned."

"I want to know where you have spent the night."

"So you shall. I have no intention of making a secret of it. Soon it will be known throughout this court. Soon everyone who wants the smallest favour will know it has to come through me."

"I don't understand."

"Oh yes you do. We've hinted it, haven't we? You wanted it as much as I did . . . or if you didn't you're more of a fool than I take you for."

"Do you mean that you've been with . . ."

"With His Highness, yes."

"You have . . ."

"I have."

"Clara!"

"My dear little shocked husband, you are now a cuckold. Don't look outraged. It's a pleasant thing to be as you will learn. The best thing to be if you can't be a noble Duke or Prince or King is a cuckold, as many a man throughout the world has come to realize."

"Clara, I'm horrified."

"You don't appear to be. I can see the speculation glinting in your eyes and well it might. Why do you think I married you?

I married you for this. Now listen to me, Platen. We are going
to make our fortunes. I'll make you the richest man at this court.
I'll make you the Bishop's chief minister. I will, I tell you. You
should go down on your knees and thank me for this night's
work."

He was staring at her and she laughed.

Weak! weak! she thought. And excited. At last he is discovering he has ambition. He was afraid of it before—but now he has
someone to tend it for him . . . he really is rather excited.

Despicable! she thought.

Then : Thank goodness. It means we shall not be plagued by
petty irritations.

*   *   *

In the schoolroom with its windows overlooking the moat,
Sophia Dorothea sat with her attendant, Eléonore von Knesebeck,
idly glancing at the books before them.

Eléonore von Knesebeck had become her greatest friend; and
although she was a few years older than Sophia Dorothea she
was less precocious; she had a pleasant face without beauty; and
she and her family were very happy that the young Princess had
taken such a fancy to her. Sophia Dorothea had felt the need of a
friend near her own age and Eléonore von Knesebeck filled that
need perfectly. As her father was one of George William's councillors it had been agreed that Eléonore should share Sophia
Dorothea's lessons and that the friendship between the two girls
should be encouraged.

Since the little Knesebeck had come to her apartments Sophia
Dorothea had found life much more interesting, for her friend
was more in touch with the world outside the castle than she
herself could be and there was nothing she enjoyed so much as
startling Sophia Dorothea with news of it. It was from Eléonore
von Knesebeck that Sophia Dorothea learned so much about the
court of Osnabrück, and that enchanted castle ruled over by the
ogress had grown more realistic but none the less sinister. Sophia
Dorothea now knew that Clara von Platen had become the
Bishop's mistress-in-chief and everyone at the court was a little
afraid of her; she knew that George Lewis, the Crown Prince,
was a little monster who was like his father in one way only—
and that he indulged this trait with the serving girls in his father's
household. She knew that the Duchess Sophia was a tyrant in her
own way, ruling apart from Ernest Augustus.

Sophia Dorothea liked to listen and shiver ecstatically; and to
be thankful for her beloved parents and peaceful Celle.

The two girls were talking idly now of the court at Osnabrück for it was a subject that fascinated them both.

"My aunt and uncle never visit us here," said Sophia Dorothea. "Sometimes I wish they would. I should love to see them."

"They are jealous really," put in Eléonore. "Celle is richer, more cultivated and more beautiful than Osnabrück; and you are more cultivated and more beautiful than any of their children."

"They have a lot and poor Maman and Papa have only me."

"Quality is better than quantity," declared Eléonore; and the two girls laughed.

"Of course I shall not be here forever," sighed Sophia Dorothea. She frowned; she could not visualize a home that was not this castle. The idea of waking up in a bed which was not in the alcove and from which she could not see the mantelpiece supported by four cupids seemed impossible. But it must come, for there was a great deal of talk about her betrothal.

"You'll not be far away," Eléonore soothed her.

"You'll come with me when I marry."

"I shall come. We've said we'd never be separated, haven't we?"

"All the same I shall *hate* going. I wonder if Augustus Frederick would come here and live?"

"Well, he'll be the heir of Wolfenbüttel. Heirs usually live in their own castles. But it is near. You'd be home in a day."

"I'd always remember that; and if I didn't like it, I should just come home."

"But you do like Augustus Frederick?"

"H'm. He's all right." Sophia Dorothea stared dreamily out of the window. "Eléonore, do you remember Philip Königsmarck?"

"Who?"

"He was a boy who came here once. We were great friends. He went away though. And he didn't say goodbye properly. I wonder why."

"People come and go."

"I should have thought he would have said goodbye to me."

"When was this?"

"Long long ago. I believe he was really Sigurd. He left so mysteriously. He was handsome, very handsome; he rode a white charger . . ."

"And he rescued you from a ring of fire?"

"You're laughing at me, Eléonore. But I've never forgotten him."

"You dreamed it. I don't suppose he was any better than Augustus Frederick really."

"Do you think I did dream it?"

"You do change things a little ... from what they were, you know."

"Yes, I believe I do." Sophia Dorothea sighed. "The fact is, Eléonore, I never, never want to leave Celle."

"But you want to grow up, have a family of your own. You don't want to be a child forever."

"I don't know. I don't want anything to change. I used to think it never would. Birthday mornings when I wake up and think of all the secret treats they are planning, and Maman and Papa come in with all the presents ... I want it to go on like that forever."

"Which it can't," said Eléonore practically. "Oh, look, there are riders approaching the castle."

The two girls were at the window watching.

"It's the Wolfenbüttel livery," said Sophia Dorothea. "What message do you think they are bringing?"

"They are coming to tell the Duke and Duchess that Duke Anton Ulrich is coming to pay a visit with Augustus Frederick."

Sophia Dorothea made a little grimace.

"Their livery is not as charming as ours."

"Nothing outside Celle is as charming as inside," answered Eléonore von Knesebeck.

"It's true."

"Except at Versailles where everything is so much more wonderful even than at Celle."

"Maman was at the French Court; she was banished from it and she is happier at Celle than she has ever been anywhere else." Sophia Dorothea turned to Eléonore von Knesebeck and hugged her suddenly.

"What is it?"

"I just thought that I am so like Maman that I shall never be happy anywhere but at Celle."

"You're shivering."

"Yes ... so I am. Is it not foolish of me? Do you know, Eléonore, I always feel like this when messengers come to the castle. I am always afraid of what messages they will bring."

"There's nothing you need fear while you're in Celle."

"No, of course not. There is only the old ogre and the ogress from Osnabrück we need fear."

"And they cannot touch you."

Sophia Dorothea laughed and went back to the table; she and Eléonore von Knesebeck were sitting there together when the door opened and the Duchess came into the room. Sophia

Dorothea, jumping up to greet her mother, saw at once how agitated she was.

"Maman," she cried. "What is wrong?"

"Bad news, my darling."

Sophia Dorothea threw herself into her mother's arms; the Duchess stroked her daughter's hair while Eléonore von Knesebeck stood apart uncertain what to do.

"Dear Augustus Frederick is dead. He has been killed in battle at Philipsburg fighting for the Emperor. My dearest, this is a terrible blow to us all."

Sophia Dorothea hid her face against her mother's bodice. She felt bewildered. Augustus Frederick . . . so young, so vital . . . dead. It was bewildering. Never to see him again . . . never to hear him speak.

"This is such a shock," said her mother, stroking her hair.

It was some time later when Sophia Dorothea thought : There will be no marriage now. I shall stay at Celle where everything is safe and happy.

*   *   *

The Duke of Celle was with his chief minister, the Count of Bernstorff, in that small, very private apartment where they were wont to deal with matters of state, discussing the recent death of Augustus Frederick and what effect this was likely to have on the relationship between Celle and Wolfenbüttel.

"I believe that Duke Anton Ulrich hopes that this will not change anything," said Bernstorff.

"I do not see how we can be so close as a marriage between his son and my daughter would have made us."

"He is still hopeful, my lord, of uniting Celle with Wolfen-büttel. I'll guess that Wolfenbüttel already has plans for the Princess Sophia Dorothea's dowry."

"I have no doubt," said the Duke wryly.

"The Duchess has a very high opinion of Duke Anton Ulrich." Bernstorff laughed lightly. "They are sworn allies."

"We are all good friends," answered the Duke.

Bernstorff lowered his eyes; he did not want to betray himself by an expression. He was excessively vain, certain of his own powers, longing to take a bigger part in the government of Celle; and although he was the Duke's chief minister again and again he found himself in conflict with the Duchess.

The Duke was easy-going and luxury loving; all he wanted was to be left in peace. What a pleasant state of affairs that would have been—but for the Duchess. She was unlike her husband; she

it was who had decided that there should be this alliance with
Wolfenbüttel. It was not that Bernstorff doubted the good of that
alliance for Celle; but he was not so much concerned with the
good of Celle as the good of Bernstorff. What he did not care for
was continually to be forced to accept the will of the Duchess. It
insulted his vanity—which was the ruling passion of his life—to
have to be subordinate to a woman.

And the trouble at Celle was that the Duke so doted on his wife
that he was ready to follow her advice in all things.

What Bernstorff wanted was to acquire a fortune, become a
landowner, to be supreme in his own little world. It was not easy
to build up a fortune in Celle, yet but for the Duchess it might
have been. A bribe here ... a bribe there ... and it might have
been possible to build quite a fortune out of bestowing places;
the easy-going careless Duke would never have been the wiser.
But the Duchess was aware of what went on—and so he hated
her. If he could do her harm, if he could make the Duke swerve
one little bit in his devotion to her, he would feel he was making
some headway. That had seemed impossible—but now he was
not so sure.

"Very good friends," he said now; and cautiously added : "And
I doubt not, my lord, that very soon there will be another bridegroom to replace the one we have lost."

"Which bridegroom is this?"

"Duke Anton Ulrich has another son, my lord. I heard the
Duchess say that he is nearer the age of Sophia Dorothea—so I
am hourly expecting an announcement."

"There has been no arrangement."

Bernstorff permitted himself a slight laugh. "Oh no, my lord,
but since the *Duchess* has so obviously made up her mind ..."

He did not finish the sentence; he had said enough. The Duke
frowned slightly.

At last he was getting home the point he had been trying to
make over the last months with delicate innuendoes and insinuations.

The Duke was beginning to understand that in the opinion of
his minister he was a man subdued by a forceful wife. A
henpecked husband. Madame gave the orders; the husband
obeyed.

It was not very pleasant, and it was clear that the Duke disliked it.

That little touch of resentment should be fostered. It could
grow big.

*   *   *

John Frederick, Duke of Hanover, was drunk. There was nothing very unusual in this; his attendants had often seen him stagger from the table and stand at the window of his palace and look out on the grounds with admiration.

"Louis would have to admire that . . ." he often muttered.

Louis XIV had no more devoted admirer throughout Germany than John Frederick of Hanover. Hanover was in truth a *petit* Versailles for he had been quite slavish in his imitation.

In his gardens he had erected statues and fountains; many foreign guests filled the court; he had even become a Catholic, which delighted Louis so much that he had given him a pension.

When he was very drunk John Frederick would talk of my friend the King of France with maudlin tenderness.

His subjects accepted this attitude with phlegm. The entertainments were amusing; and there was always plenty of beer to drink. In fact the only German characteristic John Frederick seemed to possess was his love of beer; and only when he was drunk did he revert to old habits and then he would throw off his French manners and those about him felt that he was one of them.

He sat one evening over supper drinking as usual, talking of his adventures in Italy and how such and such was done at the French Court; and suddenly he grew tired and said he would retire to bed.

His attendants sprang to help him for it was clear that he was in a state to need their help; and as he stood up, his glass still in his hand, he fell sprawling across the table.

Before they could get him to his bed he had died.

* * *

"So," said the Duchess Sophia, "John Frederick is dead. At least he died like a good German—with a glass in his hand. And because he is dead, Hanover is ours."

It was true. John Frederick had left no male heirs and because George William had signed away his birthright, Hanover with all its riches fell to Ernest Augustus.

Sophia was delighted. There was no point now in staying in little Osnabrück. The court moved into the Hanover Palace with as little loss of time as possible.

* * *

"Hanover is yours," said Clara, lightly running her fingers over her lover's body. "Now you will have a setting worthy of your state."

"I'll admit," Ernest Augustus told her, "that it is going to suit us better than Osnabrück."

"The Duke of Hanover!" cooed Clara. "I fancy you will like that title better than Bishop of Osnabrück."

"I was never meant to be a Bishop."

"So, my dear, it would seem."

"Nonsense, the Popes had their ladies."

"They were wise men."

"And self indulgent."

"Aren't we all?"

He was silent for a while savouring her caresses. He was becoming more and more devoted to Clara. She was different from any other woman he had known.

"George Lewis will have to leave the army now," said Ernest Augustus.

"Oh yes, he must certainly be present when you are crowned Duke of Hanover."

"He is growing up. Scarce a boy any longer."

"In a year he'll be twenty-one." Clara was thoughtful. When George Lewis came home he would be a power in the land.

*   *   *

When Clara called at her sister's apartments, Marie greeted her warmly; her husband was receiving many favours due to the fact that Clara had become Ernest Augustus's mistress; and Marie, who had always obeyed her sister, knew that she must do so even more zealously than ever.

"I see all is well with you," said Clara, "and that you are enjoying the married state."

Marie nodded, and Clara regarded her complacently. She was very pretty. Far prettier, thought Clara, than I could ever be. But I have something more useful. Brains, the ability to see ahead and grasp the advantage before it is too late and someone else has seen it and taken it.

"John is a good husband?" asked Clara.

"Very good. We were lucky to go to the fête as we did and meet our husbands..." Marie stopped, wondering what the relationship between Clara and hers could be at this time, for everyone knew she was Ernest Augustus's mistress.

"Very lucky," agreed Clara. "But luck is seizing opportunities, and it doesn't stay with you because you are special favourites. Oh no. You have to work for it."

"You have worked very hard, Clara."

"There must be no complacency. Every day Ernest Augustus relies more and more on me."

"And Frank?"

"Frank! Don't be so absurd. He gets as much out of this as anyone, so of course he is content."

Marie opened her blue eyes very wide. After all the years we were together and I tried to instil a little sense in her, thought Clara in exasperation, she is still an innocent.

"It is your turn now, my dear," went on Clara.

"Mine?"

"That's what I said. The Crown Prince is coming to Hanover for the coronation."

"I expected he would."

"You can depend upon it that some clever woman at the court will know how to get her talons into him."

"He likes women, so . . ."

"Yes, that's a good point. He'll be important. He is nearly twenty-one; and that means that he will have a say in government. He'll be brought up to rule. Now will be the time. He must be with us. I wouldn't want someone working against me in Hanover."

"You think he will?"

"No, because he'll be stopped."

"You'll stop him?"

"Don't be obtuse. How can I when Ernest Augustus is my affair. George Lewis will be yours."

"Mine! I don't understand."

"Don't be so childish. You're very pretty so it'll present no difficulties. . . . He'll be willing enough. And it isn't to be the affair of a night or two either. You must see to that."

"But Clara . . . !"

"Don't play the innocent. You knew that we came to Osnabrück to make ourselves agreeable."

"But there is John . . ."

"He will understand as Frank does. Believe me, Frank thought he should protest at first. I soon silenced him and he saw where his own advantage lay. I'll deal with your John if you can't yourself. But not a word until it is a certainty. Now when the Crown Prince comes to Hanover you must be ready. You must give him no chance to stray elsewhere. He is young and therefore may be impressionable. Be prepared."

"Clara . . ."

Clara took her sister by the wrist and twisted her arm quite gently, but it was a reminder of punishments inflicted when Marie was a child, and meant that she must go on obeying Clara as she always had, for to disobey could bring unpleasant consequences.

Marie was weak and without morals. Such an adventure as was being suggested had its interest, and if she need not worry about her husband's reactions, and if she could enjoy an intrigue and feel that she was helping her family, she was not really averse to the idea.

*　　*　　*

George Lewis was riding sullenly towards Hanover. He had no wish to return there. He knew that he would dislike court life and the court of Hanover would necessarily be so much more grand than that of Osnabrück. Dancing, mincing in and out of levies, playing the courtier!

George Lewis uttered a coarse expletive. Being so much with the army had made him coarse. But he was at home with his soldiers and popular enough with them for he was at his best in camp where men had come to respect him; he was intrepid and never asked of his soldiers what he would not do himself; in fact he was always one to take the first and biggest risk. He could be relied on, although he was so young, and he was known to be just. That was the life for him. Even his father had complimented him when he had fought at Consarbrück. And Maestricht and Charleroy were battles with which he was remembered.

On the battlefield he was a leader of men; he knew it and they knew it; and his vanity was gratified. It was only when he was at court, with people who fought each other with words, that he was at a loss and the brave soldier became an uncouth boor.

To hell with their clever phrases, their tricky jokes. He wanted none of that. He liked to sit on a bank surrounded by men, eating sausages and black bread and talking about the battle : how it had been fought, how it might have been fought; where they had shown cunning; where they had faltered; talking too of the women they would have. That was a man's life. No dancing in the French fashion; no titillating conversation, no hiding behind fans, showing shocked surprise as though it were not known towards what end everything was leading. A waste of time, thought George Lewis. Why indulge in that? There was the woman and the man. They both knew for what purpose they were together. Therefore get on with it without preamble. He had no doubts of *his* abilities in actual performance; it was all the stupid gyrations, all the overtures and innuendoes, all the advancing and retreating, all the pretty manners, in which he failed.

And why worry about that, for of what use were they? They

were all directed towards the same end and if it could be reached without bother, why go through them like performing animals?

That was what George Lewis told himself when he rode to Hanover. There would be plenty of women and that was all that mattered.

But when his horse was taken from him and he entered the Palace and he was aware of the Frenchified atmosphere he quailed, and his expression became more sullen than ever. He tripped over a tabouret which in his annoyance he had not seen, and cursing with a soldier's oath he kicked it across the room.

Fortunately it came to rest before his parents appeared. He shambled over to them, his face red from the exertion.

How awkward he is! thought Sophia. What will they think of him when he goes to England? Charles is so graceful.

Uncouth as ever! thought Ernest Augustus. He belongs in the camp and always will.

"Welcome, my son," said Sophia.

George knelt before his parents.

Sophia was thinking: Let us get this ceremonial greeting over as soon as possible. A pity Frederick Augustus isn't Crown Prince. He would have made a better showing. How did we get such a one as this?

George Lewis was on his feet.

"You'll wish to go to your apartments before dinner."

George Lewis said he would.

"Then I want to hear how the army is getting on."

The young man's face brightened.

At least, thought Ernest Augustus, he's a good soldier.

*   *   *

The Duchess Sophia followed Ernest Augustus into his apartments and shut the door, signing to the Duke's attendants that she wished to be alone with her husband.

"Well?" said Ernest Augustus.

"His manners haven't improved."

"Do you think anything on earth would improve his manners?"

"I always hoped."

"My dear, you are over-optimistic. George Lewis will always be what he is—a bore and boor."

"What can we do about it?"

Ernest Augustus shrugged his shoulders. "He'll be a good soldier. Let us be thankful for that. It's a useful occupation when you have a principality to protect."

"How will he be in his relations with other states?"

"Let us hope he has good advisers."

"At least," said the Duchess, "he is fairly safe as far as women are concerned, for no woman of culture and education would attract him. It will be serving girls for him."

"Don't be too sure of that. He'll be the Duke of Hanover one day. I fancy that will make up for his uncouth manners."

"What I meant is that the sort of women who will attract him will be those who are not interested in state affairs; and that is all to the good."

The Duke looked over his wife's head. Was this a reference to Clara? If so, he would ignore it. Sophia knew that one thing he would not endure was interference with his affairs.

"In any case," went on Sophia, "it is time he married."

"I agree with you there."

"The King of England has no legitimate heirs and I do not believe he will ever get any. That wife of his is barren, depend upon it. All this time and not one son. And when you consider how many strong sons the King has given to other women . . ."

Ernest Augustus nodded in agreement.

"And," went on Sophia, "what of James?"

"James has children."

"Two daughters—Mary and Anne. He does not seem to be able to get a son that will live."

"Well?"

"Mary is married to my cousin's boy, William of Orange. And . . . so far, there are no sons there either."

"It's early yet."

"Still no sons."

"What are you driving at?"

"The Princess Anne is unmarried."

"You mean you want George Lewis to have her?"

"It would be an excellent match. It could so easily happen that George Lewis came to the throne of England."

Ernest Augustus smiled at her with amusement. "And that," he said, "is where you would rather see him than anywhere in the world."

"Don't forget he has English blood in his veins, through me."

"You, my dear, would never allow me to forget it."

"I want him to try for Anne."

"And you think Charles and James would have him?"

"Why not. He is their kinsman."

"They might possibly look higher than a petty Duke of Hanover."

"There is no harm in trying."

Ernest Augustus shook his head. "To go over there, to be paraded like a stud bull. How do you think he would fare? Imagine Charles exercising his wit on him! I'm not so enamoured of the English."

"My dear husband, are you mad? You are not comparing the Dukedom of Hanover with the crown of England."

"You're looking far ahead, Sophia. Charles has to die without legitimate heirs. I admit there is every possibility that he will. James has to die without a son. That is certainly not likely. And if he does he has two daughters. Mary is already married to Orange. She also has to die without heirs; then would it be Anne's turn; and if George were her consort, I admit that he could share the crown. After all he is actually in the line of succession—though some way back."

"Through me," Sophia reminded him with a satisfied smile.

"Through you, my dear. But have you forgotten that not so long ago these English allowed their king to be murdered?"

"It was that villain Cromwell. They have since deeply regretted it. Look how they adore Charles!"

"Well, Charles happens to be larger than life. He happens to have charm and wit and a seraglio which the English people find colourful—particularly after years of puritan rule. If they ever had our George Lewis they would quickly discover that he was no Charles."

"He is a good soldier. Besides, he is young yet. His manners may improve. Particularly if he went to England."

"*If* he went to England. Are you suggesting that he should go?"

Sophia nodded.

"You have spoken to him of this?"

"Certainly I have not. He is only just come home and naturally I should speak of it to you first."

"To try for Anne . . ." mused Ernest Augustus.

"Well?"

"I am not eager."

"But why not?"

"I don't think they'd have him. He'd make a fool of himself."

"Oh, come, why shouldn't a Prince visit a kinsman's court?"

Ernest Augustus was silent. "I'll think about it."

Sophia's eyes narrowed. Discuss it with Clara, she wondered; she pictured them lying side by side in his big bed, making love and then talking politics. What Clara said would be important to him. Well, Sophia was not having that. She had no objection to his taking the woman to bed, but that should be for one purpose and it did not include deciding the future marriage of the Crown Prince who, Sophia would have him remember, was her son as well as his.

"I think," said Sophia, "that until we have come to some agreement on this matter this should be a secret between us two; and even when we have decided on action we should take only one other into our confidence—and that is George Lewis."

Ernest Augustus looked into his wife's face. He admired her. He was fortunate in his marriage. And she was right of course. If they decided George Lewis should go to England, and if the King of England would not accept him as his niece's husband, they did not want the whole world laughing at the Crown Prince of Hanover.

Moreover he had not entirely decided that George Lewis should go to England.

"You are right," he said. "We will discuss this at greater length —and it shall be a matter between us two."

Sophia bowed her head. In the same way as Ernest Augustus was satisfied with her, so was she with him.

*   *   *

George Lewis was bored with the dancing. He could never dance gracefully and had been the despair of all the dancing masters who had attempted to instruct him.

He had eaten well; his father had questioned him about the army and that had been interesting; but there was nothing else at court to attract him except the women; he had been eyeing a few of them and selecting those who might be his kind.

His mother had talked as usual of England—how everything that was done there was so much better than everywhere else. He remembered how she always had talked like that. It bored him as did quite a number of people in spite of the fact that she was supposed to be witty and very learned. That in itself of course was of no interest to him.

Beside his father was a woman of whom he had heard—Clara von Platen. He could see that his father was more taken with her than he had ever been by any other mistress; it was understandable; she had personality. Her glittering eyes were alert as though she missed nothing and at the same time she conveyed a deep sensuality which was not lost on George Lewis.

She was not the sort he would go for. But sitting next to her was a very pretty girl. Her gown was cleverly cut to show a seductive figure; her large eyes were soft and what George Lewis always thought of as full of promise. There was a pretty girl indeed.

He asked who she was.

"She is the Platen's sister."

"Sister of my father's whore?"

"Yes, sir. She is married to John von dem Bussche. You remember him?"

"I do. He tried to teach me languages among other things. He didn't succeed."

"His wife, sir, might be more successful if she tried to teach you."

"She'd teach me nothing I don't know."

"She's aware that we're talking of her."

It was true. The beautiful eyes were on them; and they stayed on George Lewis. He felt excited at once. She wasn't clever like the sister; she was pretty; and, oh yes, he'd enjoy teaching her. Rather amusing that. He reckoned old John von dem Bussche was better in a schoolroom than in a bedchamber; and he hadn't really had much success in the former, poor man.

Poor man! But he had no right to marry a pretty girl like that.

"Shall I tell her Your Highness wishes to speak to her?"

"No," said George Lewis. "I will arrange that myself."

The evening had now taken on an interest. He would speak to her soon; he would let her know that he had no intention of making a lot of pretty speeches; he was a man who believed in taking the shortest cut to the bedchamber.

They danced after the meal. It wasn't easy for him to act secretly because everyone would be watching him, so he made no attempt to.

"I don't care for dancing," he said, his eyes, taking in the voluptuous curves of her young body, explaining more than words what he did care for.

She lowered hers and said : "Nor I, Your Highness."

"I've been watching you."

"I saw you. I . . . I hope you were not displeased."

"Oh, I was pleased. I hope to be more pleased."

She giggled, understanding.

"Let's take a turn in the gardens, shall we? There are too many watching us here."

She agreed willingly.

"Come on," he said, and they went out.

*　　　*　　　*

Clara came to her sister's apartments.

"Well?" she said.

"All's well," answered Marie.

"Already?"

"He's not one to wait. I was afraid he would get impatient and go elsewhere. You said that wasn't to happen."

"Still ... But perhaps you're right. You must see that you don't lose your grip on him."

"I don't think so."

Clara laughed and gave her sister a little push. "I can trust you, I know."

"And what about John?"

"Leave John to me. I'll get Frank to speak to him. This is after all, a family affair."

Marie was nothing loath. She was tired of John, and George Lewis the crude and forthright lover was virile enough to make up for his lack of manners; moreover, Clara was now delighted. The task of ministering to the sexual needs of the house of Hanover—which were considerable—was in the hands of the Meisenburg sisters, which was after all the reason why they had joined this court in the first place, so she might say Mission Accomplished. Only of course the important part in such an operation was not only attaining one's goal, but holding it against all comers.

That was the task for the future.

*   *   *

Clara recognized the power of the Duchess Sophia and had no wish to challenge it. Now that Marie was firmly established as the mistress of George Lewis and she herself was even more firmly that of Ernest Augustus she was deeply concerned with holding those positions; and she realized that the most likely direction from which such a threat could come would be from the Duchess Sophia.

She was almost modest with Sophia; as soon as she came into the Duchess's presence she was the demure maid of honour and never betrayed by a look or a gesture the power which was hers.

Clever woman! thought Sophia; and she respected her for it.

Clara would go further. She would let the Duchess see that when she did use her influence with the Duke it was in his wife's interest.

Sophia's admiration for England was well known; in the opposite direction was her dislike of Celle. The latter she did not speak of as she did of the former but it was none the less fierce for all that.

Clara therefore allied herself with the Duchess in her dislike of Celle and as she was eager to show Sophia that she stood with her in this, decided to do something about it.

Ernest Augustus's infidelities were becoming fewer. Occasionally he discovered a pretty girl—usually among his wife's attendants—and he would take her to bed. His old mistress Esther was not entirely forgotten. On such occasions Clara would spend half the night pacing up and down her room cursing the object of the Duke's interest, but in the morning she greeted her lover with the same tenderness as she had always shown him.

She knew that the least little resentment on her part would be the beginning of discord between her and Ernest Augustus, and she wanted him to think of her as a woman to whom he could come back; she wanted to be a habit with him . . . as a wife was. Clara was determined to consolidate her position and nothing must prevent that.

Ernest Augustus, in fact, seemed more fond of her than ever after temporarily straying; and she was coming to believe that it was not a bad thing after all for him to try others and realize her greater worth. These little flights of his did not disturb her as much as they had once done. But she was always alert, determined never to run the risk of becoming a nuisance to him.

For this reason she allied herself with the Duchess in the matter of Celle. Knowing the value of the spy, she had already set several in places where she thought they could be most useful; and when it was reported to her that Minister Bernstorff in Celle was dissatisfied with the influence the Duchess of Celle had over her husband and had shown on more than one occasion that he was attempting to break it, she was very interested.

Bed was the safest place in which to discuss secret matters and it was there that, one night, Clara broached the subject.

"The harmony of Celle is breaking, I hear. Trouble in paradise . . . so I am told."

"You are like God, Clara," laughed Ernest Augustus. "Omniscient!"

"Well, I have my friends to tell me what is going on in places which are important to my lord."

"And what do they tell you?"

Clara nuzzled up to him. "That Bernstorff hates the Duchess . . . hates the influence she has with the Duke. That everything has to be approved by her before it can be carried through. He hates her."

"He's jealous of her."

"I believe you have a soft spot for her."

"She's a very beautiful woman."

"Ha! And that excuses her highhandedness."

"I've noticed that beautiful women are often highhanded."

"In the service of their lords and masters."

"It seems to me that some would be the lord and master."

"That is how it is with Madame of Celle. She is the ruler and it is this which Bernstorff resents."

"Why doesn't he get out then?"

"He prefers to stay and fight. Besides, where else would he go? He is making some progress, I hear. The Duke is at last beginning to ask himself whether he is not a little under the thumb of his beautiful Duchess."

"You are sure of this?"

"Certain, my lord. I have had it from several sources. The Duke is a proud man . . . although lazy."

"But he is deeply enamoured of that woman."

"Deeply enamoured, yes. But . . . at the same time he is beginning to realize that she is governing Celle in his place. He has no desire to put another woman in her place; he merely wants her to let him have his."

"It has made a rift between them?"

"Not exactly. But he is showing a little firmness here and there; he does not always fall in with her wishes. Bernstorff is responsible. An ambitious man, this Bernstorff. He would be on the side of those who paid him best."

"You are sure of this?"

"Almost certain. We should pay him to work for us. Then we should know everything that was going on in Celle. You realize that she is working for alliance with Wolfenbüttel. An alliance between them and Celle and they would be more powerful than Hanover. The Duchess is all for it. She doesn't trust us. George William is soft . . . and lazy. He's sentimental too. She's a clever woman that Duchess. She's far more clever than her husband. She wants this alliance, and she'll get it, if we're not careful, by marrying her precious Sophia Dorothea to Anton Ulrich's son. The eldest died, but what does that matter? There's another. I think we have to be watchful."

"Clara," he said, "you have your eyes open."

"In your service."

"In our service. We're together, eh?"

She kissed him lightly. "For ever and ever amen," she added, and although her tone was light, she meant it to be a pact between them.

He pulled her to him and held her close. She was a wonderful woman, his Clara. She had everything to offer; and in addition to those voluptuous and intensely satisfying charms she was a politician.

"What do you suggest?"

"That we sound Bernstorff. Offer him some bribe."

"Such as?"

"He wants to be a landowner. So he'll want money. But at first . . . to show that money would be following, let it be a rich present. You have a gold snuff box studded with diamonds. If that were sold it would buy quite a bit of land. Let us try him out with that; and I've no doubt that in exchange we shall have a front seat—in spirit—in the council chamber of Celle."

"Let us try him out with the snuff box then. It will be well if I am not concerned in this."

"Of course you must not be concerned in it. I will arrange it."

"What should I do without you?"

"That is a problem which, at the moment, you have no need to consider."

He laughed. "My little minister!" he murmured.

"One thing more," she said. "When we have settled this little matter . . . satisfactorily, the Duchess Sophia should be taken into our counsels. I am sure she will give the scheme her approval."

Ernest Augustus sighed luxuriously. He was a lucky man. He had a mistress who combined an excessive sensuality with wisdom and to crown it all she was without jealousy of his wife.

A Mission to London

GEORGE LEWIS was summoned to his father's apartments and found his mother there with the Duke. They were alone so he guessed that what they had to say to him was secret.

Both parents shuddered inwardly as he lumbered in.

What will they think of him? Sophia asked herself.

Perhaps it's time he travelled a little, was Ernest Augustus's inward comment.

"Now George Lewis," said his father, "your mother and I have something to tell you. It's time you married."

"I thought that was coming," answered George Lewis with a slow smile.

"You understand that your wife must bring you a good dowry, and that your father and I are seeking the best possible."

"It is always so," answered George Lewis.

"This is a matter between the three of us," said the Duke. "At present it should not go beyond this room. Your mother believes that the Princess Anne of England would be a very suitable wife."

George Lewis whistled. In the manner of a stable boy, thought his mother with disgust.

"It is by no means certain that you would be accepted," she said sternly. "But you understand it would be a very desirable match."

"A match with England," George Lewis replied, slyly looking at his mother. "Nothing in the world could be more desirable . . . to you."

"There is a possibility—if you married the Princess Anne—that you might inherit the throne of England," said his father.

"There is even a possibility—remote, I admit—that even if I don't marry her I might do that."

"So you are aware of it," put in Sophia with grim satisfaction.

"Madam, you have told us time out of number how closely we are related to the royal family of England and you have seen that we're scarcely likely to forget it."

"It is something to be proud of. When you have seen London and compared it with Hanover you will understand what I mean."

"When do I set out?" asked George Lewis.

"Wait a minute," cautioned Ernest Augustus. "As I told you in the beginning, this is not to be known outside this room. It will be announced that you are going on a tour of Europe. That is something which any young man of your birth and rank would naturally undertake and I might say this, that in your case it is more necessary than in most. The fact that you go to England as a suitor to the Princess Anne is to be a secret so far. It may well be that you are found unacceptable. In which case you do not want to be made a laughing stock. Keep this secret. You are going on a Grand Tour of Europe and naturally you will visit your kinsfolk in England. But when you reach England you will at once make yourself agreeable to the Princess Anne."

George Lewis grunted. "I'll tell no one the real reason."

"Then you must make your preparations." Sophia was smiling complacently. "I will have a talk with you and look over your things myself. What a pity that you did not try to make a little progress in the English tongue. They are inclined to dislike those who can't speak their language."

"If I marry an English woman," declared George Lewis, "she will have to speak my tongue."

"That attitude," his mother admonished, "will not carry you very far with the English."

George Lewis smiled at her. Everyone knew how she idolized that race. George Lewis had no such feeling for them.

He remembered then that he would have to leave Marie. Never mind. He'd soon find someone to take her place. He must not tell her why he was going. There was little fear of that. George Lewis rarely indulged in much conversation when they were together.

Already he was wondering what the Princess Anne was like.

*   *   *

Clara was rueful. No sooner had she arranged that George Lewis should be comfortably settled with Marie than he was to go away. Well, there was nothing to be done about that; and it was the custom for young men in his position to tour Europe. She only hoped that he did not get too much taste for France and Italy as his father and uncle had done.

She warned Marie that she must not sulk or annoy her lover in any way; but must make him realize that no matter where he went would he be able to find such a mistress as herself.

"When he comes back, it must be to you," said Clara.

Meanwhile preparations for George Lewis's departure went on and Sophia was gratified when she received a message from her kinsman William of Orange.

He had heard, he wrote, that George Lewis was about to set out on a tour of Europe, and as he believed he was including England, doubtless he would have to pass near Holland. William would be very disappointed if his kinsman, George Lewis, did not call on him. He hoped that George Lewis would have time for at least a week's visit. He and his wife, the Princess Mary, were looking forward to making his acquaintance.

"You must go," said Sophia. "You can't have too many friends."

So George Lewis said farewell to a regretful Marie who was not too sad to make the parting unpleasant, and promised him that she would be counting the days to his return and that she would pray he would not forget her, for she knew there was not another lover in the world to be compared with George Lewis.

George Lewis muttered that he would not forget her; and he would soon be back.

Then he left Hanover and set out on his travels.

*　　*　　*

When George Lewis arrived at The Hague he found a very warm welcome waiting for him. This was more unusual than he realized, for William of Orange was a cold man, never effusive; yet he had commanded his wife Mary to make much of the Crown Prince of Hanover and, although she had wept for days when forced to marry him, she now obeyed him absolutely in everything he commanded.

Moreover, she was very pleased to have an opportunity for gaiety. There was little enough at the court of The Hague where William set the fashion, and Mary, who had come not so very long ago from the court of her gay uncle Charles II, missed the balls and banquets and general fun-provoking occasions which had come back into fashion with the Restoration of the Monarchy.

George Lewis was pleased with his welcome. William suited him in a way. Taciturn, hunchbacked, pale-faced and far from attractive, he made George Lewis feel like a romantic hero in his presence; and since, although his manner was cold to others, he was pleasant to his guest, George Lewis was delighted with his host. As for Mary, she was quite charming. If her sister Anne were anything like her, George Lewis would be ready to begin his wooing without delay.

It was Mary's pleasure to show him the Palace of The Hague and the gardens which William himself had planned. William was very interested in architecture, she explained. Was George Lewis? He shook his head. No, he was a soldier.

It was a very good thing to be, answered Mary, since he had a principality to protect. He would find a great deal in common with William who was a great soldier too. Doubtless George Lewis had heard of his exploits.

"As we have of yours," Mary hastened to add. "We all remember how you conducted yourself in the Battle of the Bridge at Conz. It was the talk of the army. I believe you were only fifteen at the time."

George turned and mumbled something unintelligible, but he was pleased.

He had done well at that battle where he had proved that he was a natural soldier.

"Well now, of course you are here on a different mission. That's if you have a mission at all. Or are you just doing the Grand Tour for pleasure?"

"It is a grand tour for pleasure," muttered George Lewis.

"And you are going to England. You will enjoy meeting your relations."

"Oh yes."

She looked wistful. "England!" she said. "It still seems like home to me. Does that surprise you? Do you think I should regard Holland as my home now that I am married?"

"Well, my mother has never been to England but she still thinks of it as her home because her mother was English."

"My great-aunt Elizabeth. She was so lovely, we always heard. It was very pleasant hearing tales of the family. Is it not a pity that we all have to be separated."

"It's always been so."

"Ah, I cried when I left home ... cried and cried ... and my dear sister Anne was too ill to know that I had gone. If you see

my sister Anne, will you tell her how I long to see her? Will you
remember me to her very specially?"

"If I see her," he said cautiously; but she was alert, watching
him.

"You will, of course?"

He shrugged his shoulders. He had respected his promise not
to speak of the real object of his visit.

"She is a charming girl," said Mary.

He nodded again.

"Gay, affectionate—and pretty."

She was watching him closely, but he congratulated himself
that he betrayed nothing.

＊   ＊   ＊

Later Mary said to her husband : "I talked to him and although
he is so clumsy he betrayed nothing."

"You can depend upon it," said William gravely, "that he is
being sent over on approval. If your uncle likes him he'll have
Anne. Who else is there for her?"

"Poor Anne!" sighed Mary; then she cast down her eyes,
flushing, remembering how many people, only such a short time
ago, had said Poor Mary.

"He's not much of a catch," admitted William. "But that
mother of his is after Anne. I am certain of it. We mustn't allow
it."

"I don't think Anne would care for him."

William gave his wife a contemptuous look. As though it were
a matter of Anne's caring!

"We must do our best to stop it," he said.

"Yes, William."

He looked at her with narrowed eyes. He was not going to
explain. He had not yet tamed her and he was even a little
uncertain of her. He would not forget easily—nor forgive—the
spectacle she had made of herself weeping for everyone to see
when he had been introduced to her as her future husband.

He had married her because there was a hope that she would
one day be the Queen of England and although she was the elder
sister, she had not yet produced an heir. This meant that if she
died before him, and Anne married and had children they would
come before him. Therefore he wanted to put off Anne's marriage
as long as possible; and certainly he would prefer her not to
marry a man who—like himself—was in the line of succession.

First of all he had to find out whether his surmise that George was going to England as a suitor for Anne was correct; and if it were so he had to stop it.

He said coldly that he had a state matter to which he must attend and left his wife, bewildered and unhappy, as always; but he had forgotten her as soon as he left the room. He was planning how he could make George Lewis betray his secret.

*   *   *

Hollands Gin was the answer, for like a good German George Lewis found it irresistible.

There he sat, side by side with William, while William's specially selected friends carried on the conversation.

They talked of England and the Princess Anne, sister to their Stadholder's wife.

"You can be sure that the King of England and the Duke of York are considering it is time she married."

"She is seventeen—and marriageable."

"Wasn't there some talk about the Earl of Mulgrave?"

"Oh yes, Mistress Anne became rather romantic about the fellow and he was sent away on a trip to Tangiers."

"I believe the Crown Prince could let us into a secret."

George Lewis was pleasantly happy. He had seen one of the Princess Mary's attendants whom he fancied, a nice, plump Dutch girl. She had seemed as though she would be willing.

Hollands Gin. Willing girls. It was a good life.

Someone was leaning forward smiling at him, implying that he was a fellow who knew how to enjoy himself. He'd have a good time before he settled down.

"Settled down!"

"The Princess Anne would be as good a wife as her sister the Princess Mary."

"I'd see to that," he boasted.

"Ha, ha." They were laughing sycophantishly. "She'll know who's the master, you can swear on that. You'll soon show her."

"I'll show her," he said.

"Does she know why you're coming?"

"I don't know. My uncle or her father may have told her."

"Well, well. Good luck to you. Good luck to the bridegroom."

"Good luck," said George Lewis smiling fatuously and laughing into his Hollands Gin.

*   *   *

William looked grimly at his friend and chief adviser William Bentinck.

"Well, do you agree now?"

"He's admitted it. Your Highness was right. He's going wooing the Princess Anne."

"And he'll get her unless we do something to stop it. We'll have to get our friends working at Hanover. Did you find out who was open to bribes?"

"There is the woman at Hanover, Clara von Platen. She could be very useful. She's Ernest Augustus's chief adviser under the bedclothes, and with a man like Ernest Augustus this carries more weight than the council chamber. She would work for us if adequately rewarded. Then there is Bernstorff at Celle. He is disgruntled but mostly against the Duchess. He's already in the pay of Ernest Augustus so would most certainly be ready to be in ours."

"Get working on them right away."

"That they may help in preventing this marriage, yes."

"Is there someone who might be a good match for George Lewis?"

"Well, there is a cousin. The Duke of Celle's daughter. I imagine it would be an attractive match for both the fathers. You see, it would join up Hanover and Celle and you know how these little German princelings like to sew their lands together. It's an old German custom."

"That seems a good idea."

"Get our agents out to Hanover and Celle at once and tell them that they are to work without delay for a marriage between Hanover and Celle. Then ... we must see our people in London. We have to make sure that no pretty little romance is allowed to flourish between my fat sister-in-law and this handsome young princeling."

Bentinck laughed. "It shall be done," he said.

*   *   *

George Lewis was sorry to leave the hospitable Dutch; but he guessed that his English relations would be as pleased to see him.

It was a dismal day when the boat which carried him lay off Greenwich and he was surprised that his mother's cousin, the King of England, had sent no one to welcome him. It was very different from the arrival in Holland. His mother had warned him that the first thing he must do when he reached England was get in touch with his uncle, Prince Rupert, who would, if it were necessary, introduce him to the English Court; and since it seemed he would need some introduction George Lewis sent one of his men ashore with a letter for his uncle.

Rupert returned with the messenger. So this, thought George Lewis, was the Prince with the fabulous reputation : Rupert of the Rhine, who had fought for his uncle Charles I and his cousin Charles II and was known as one of the greatest soldiers of his day ! As one soldier to another, George Lewis was impressed.

Prince Rupert, being just past sixty, was also past the days of his glory. There were the remains though of handsome looks and his garments were so elegant that George Lewis could only stare with open mouth and marvel that great soldiers should choose to deck themselves out in such a fashion. His coat was of scarlet velvet richly trimmed with silver lace—the same lace trimmed his satin breeches; but his face was gnarled with time and weather and went ill with such finery.

But he was still one of the greatest soldiers of his day and was now one of the King's privy councillors. A man of influence and just the person needed to introduce a rather shy young man to a foreign court.

"So ..." he said, his eyes cool and appraising. "You are George Lewis. Your mother has written to me much of you."

But she hadn't told him what a country lout he was or Rupert would have suggested teaching him a few gracious manners before sending him to England.

"She talks of you continually ... and England."

"It is to be expected," replied Rupert. "Well, your reputation has travelled before you. You like war and women, so we hear."

"Who does not?" murmured George Lewis with a sheepish grin.

"Most of the King's courtiers are very partial to the second though they have little taste for the first."

"Why," said George Lewis, "they know not what they are missing."

Rupert waved a hand impatiently. "You are fortunate to come at this time. The people of England will review your suit favourably."

"Oh ... why?"

"Because, my dear nephew, James, Duke of York, is making it very plain that he has embraced the Catholic religion—and one thing the people of this country will not tolerate is a Catholic King. Therefore the fact that you are a Protestant will count in your favour."

"Well, I have yet to see the Princess."

What a boor ! thought Prince Rupert. Clumsy manners. Clumsy speech.

"I don't know that I shall like her," went on George Lewis.

"Not like her! Don't be a fool, nephew. She's the best match that could come your way."

"Well, we have something to offer, you know."

A brash boy! thought Rupert. Hanover! Was that to be compared with the possibilities of the crown of England!

"It is rumoured that Mary may never have a child. And in that case . . ."

"Anne will be Queen and I the consort. But I don't know whether it is not more gratifying to be a Duke in my own right in Hanover than a Queen's consort in England."

"They might make you King, since you are in the line of succession and William and Mary have no children and your son and Anne's might be the heir to the throne. What do you think of that?"

"I'd like to see something of the country before giving my opinion."

"You are very sure of yourself, nephew."

"If I'm not sure of myself no one else will be."

Arrogant! Vain! Quite unaware how uncouth he was. Charles would poke sly fun at him. The whole court would laugh at him behind his back. And he would be too stupid to know it. What chance had he of marrying Anne?

"I think," said Rupert, "that I had better prepare the King for your arrival. Then I will take you to court. In the meantime you had better make my house in Spring Gardens your lodging."

Thus George Lewis landed in England.

* * *

George Lewis's plan was to look for a house in England but no sooner had the King heard of his arrival than he sent a messenger to the house in Spring Gardens to say that on no account must George Lewis look for a lodging. One was already waiting for him at Whitehall and here Charles would receive him as soon as he arrived and it was His Majesty's wish that during his stay in England he should live at Whitehall "*en cousin*" as he expressed it.

George Lewis was pleased to hear this, but Rupert looked on with a rather sardonic smile, for the more he saw of George Lewis, the more he wondered how he would fare at Whitehall.

So, in company with Prince Rupert, George Lewis went to Whitehall, and as soon as he arrived he was conducted to the King's presence chamber. There surrounding the King were some of his ministers and courtiers—all bejewelled and beribboned, bewigged and befeathered. The makers of ribbons, feathers and lace must be reaping fortunes in England, thought George Lewis; also the makers of rouge patches and such aids to beauty if the appearance of the women—and some of the men—whom he had passed on his way to Court were any indication. The people of England had determined to deck themselves in fine feathers after the homespun years of puritan rule, and even after some twenty years they still seemed to delight in show.

George Lewis was aware of Rupert's stern eyes upon him as he approached the King and looked up into the merriest pair of black eyes he had ever seen; they were set in a brown face, marked with signs of high living and laughter. The mouth was cynical yet whimsical, worldly yet kind. It was the most distinctive face George Lewis had ever seen.

"Welcome to England," said Charles. "Now you must give me news of my cousin, the Duchess Sophia. How fares she in far off Hanover. It is most generous of her to spare you for our pleasure."

George Lewis mumbled in French—the language in which Charles had spoken—that his mother was well and that she had given him a letter which he was to hand to the King and no other.

Charles held out a white ringed hand.

"I shall take it to my private apartments where I may read it in solitude."

George Lewis was staring goggle-eyed at the women. He had heard of these women. Louise de Kéroualle the French spy; the Mancini woman who was said to be the most beautiful in the world; and Nell Gwyn the saucy play-actress. All different, yet all arrestingly attractive, they made a background for this King, notorious for his love of wit and women.

The black eyes were summing up George Lewis; the King was thinking : Poor Anne. It will be sad for the child if she takes this one. He'll be as bad in his way as William is in his. Rough as a stable boy. Crude in manners, lusty as ... a King of England without his finesse, without his adoration of the opposite sex. No, I cannot allow my dear little Anne to go to this one.

"Now you will give us news of your parents and of Hanover. We are all eager to hear."

George Lewis began to talk of Hanover, giving a factual account of such details which could only bring yawns to the lips of his listeners until Charles said : "I see you are such an entertainer that you will enchant my friends all through the night if I do not stop your narrative." He added in English : "And I see too that you have deluded some of them into the belief that it is already night. Buckingham, pray suppress your snores; they are scarcely elegant."

"Your gracious Majesty, I have discovered a cure for sleeplessness."

"His Grace is complimenting you on your discourse," said Charles to George Lewis.

"I do not understand the tongue you speak," muttered George Lewis.

Buckingham went on : "His Highness should talk of Hanover. 'Twould be of greater service to the sleepless world than opium."

"I will conduct you to the Queen," Charles told George Lewis. "She will wish to greet you."

So in company with Charles, George Lewis strolled through the apartments of Whitehall until they came to the Queen's; and there was the black-eyed Portuguese lady—Queen of England. Barren, thought George Lewis, which was her most interesting characteristic in his eyes because it was the reason why he found this visit so important. She was gentle and kindly and when he attempted to kiss her robe, she made a show of struggling gracefully with him as though to prevent him and gave him her hand to kiss instead. It all seemed rather foolish to George Lewis who in any case considered it undignified for a man to kiss the hem of a woman's gown; but it seemed it was the practice here and the black-eyed King, whom he was beginning to distrust because he could not understand him, seemed to expect it.

Charles slipped his arm through that of George Lewis after the latter had attempted a little conversation with the Queen and her ladies and said that he guessed he was eager to meet the Princess Anne. But perhaps he had met enough of the family for the time being, so if he would present himself in the royal apartments the following day, his niece would be very happy to greet her kinsman.

*   *   *

London was attractive, thought George Lewis. He liked the glitter and excitement of the streets. He liked the women with their exposed bosoms, their faces painted and patched and their eyes welcoming. They displayed themselves at windows, while fat comfortable looking women below urged him to enter their houses as he passed by. He did not understand their language but in this sort of barter speech was unnecessary. His uncle Rupert had warned him not to get into trouble over women, because that was exactly what had happened to William of Orange when he had come over to this court. There had been quite a scandal when William—made drunk by some of the King's mischievous friends —had broken the windows of the maids of honour's apartments

THE PRINCESS OF CELLE

and tried to get at them. And that was William of Orange—a man not greatly enamoured of woman. What was likely to happen to the lusty stable boy from Hanover!

"These people," warned Prince Rupert from his bed, for he spent much time in bed of late, he told George Lewis, since he was troubled with his legs, "like to play their jokes; and never so readily as on naïve young foreigners. So beware."

George Lewis would take care. That was why the streets attracted him more than the court, particularly the fashionable Mall where the King appeared in the mornings, either showing his skill at the game of pell-mell, or walking among the people who addressed him without ceremony while the hawkers called their wares. The flower-girls, milk-maids and orange-girls strolled through the crowds; and all seemed concerned with some game of flirtation and assignation.

It was a fascinating city, George Lewis decided. The stalls with the goods for sale, which naturally included a surplus of ribbons and laces and patches for the face; the ballad sellers who sang their songs as the printed sheets fluttered in the breeze; the play-houses and the excitement always surrounding them; the coaches which trundled through the crowds with their patched and painted occupants often pulling down a window to shout to a friend or drop a handkerchief to someone in the crowd with whom an acquaintance was desired.

It was colourful, foreign, exciting—and there was nothing like it in Hanover.

All the same George Lewis was wary. He had no wish to be made a fool of as his kinsman William of Orange had been.

He was eager to see the Princess Anne for he had begun to wonder what it would be like to live in this city and fancied it would be a little to his taste.

Charles greeted him with affection.

"Ah," he said, "now to the Princess Anne. I shall show my fondness for you by giving you leave to kiss her."

"To kiss her cheek?" asked George Lewis.

The dark face was illumined by a brilliant smile. "Her lips. It's an English custom. You'll find we have some very pleasant English customs. But then doubtless you have equally pleasant ones in Hanover."

George Lewis felt awkward, being unsure whether the King was laughing at them.

And there was the Princess Anne—plump and rosy-cheeked, with short-sighted eyes, quite pretty and yet inclined to view him with suspicion. She was remembering how they had hustled her sister into marriage and was wondering whether they intended to do the same with her. She had heard unfavourable reports of this young man who was the son of her father's cousin Sophia. Definitely she did not care for him; she compared him with the Earl of Mulgrave for whom she had experienced very romantic feelings and who had recently been sent to Tangiers because of this.

"Now," cried Charles. "Salute the lady."

George Lewis saw the criticism in Anne's eyes as he surveyed her coolly. If she did not like him, nor did he like her. She ought to know that their meeting had been arranged for political reasons.

Coldly he touched her lips with his, deeply conscious of the King's amused glance.

"Well met!" said Charles. "Now perhaps you would care to take the Princess to the alcove there and talk to her of the virtues of Hanover."

George looked sullenly at the Princess, who gave him a cold stare.

They sat down where indicated and he talked in French.

She answered that she was not fluent in that language and would he please speak in English.

He had no English, he replied; and she regarded him superciliously as though to say that those who could not speak the English tongue were to be greatly pitied.

The conversation was spasmodic until the King sent one of his courtiers to rescue them.

* * *

Bernstorff, Chief Minister of Celle, stared into the blazing fire in his private apartment and thought of the future.

He would be rich. Ernest Augustus had shown that he would reward him amply. Locked away in a drawer of his cabinet was a snuff box of gold and diamonds which would fetch a great price when he sold it; and he would as soon as he found the right buyer, and that was only a foretaste of what was to come, so Clara von Platen had implied; and all knew what close counsels she kept with her lover.

He would have land of his own; he would be independent of any man—his own master, making his own rules. And it would not be long, for now there were opportunities of wealth from other sources.

The emissary from Holland had made it clear to him that if he could persuade the Duke of Celle to agree to the marriage of his daughter with her cousin George Lewis, he would be very well rewarded indeed.

And why not? He would deserve the reward, considering that the Duchess loathed Hanover and everyone connected with it and she would never allow her cherished daughter, her precious ewe lamb, to be offered up as a sacrifice to the whims of others. It was a mighty task: To persuade the Duke against the Duchess and to break off the alliance with Wolfenbüttel and make another with Hanover! Most people would say he was attempting the impossible. And so he might have been—a few years ago, even a few months ago.

The Duke loved his Duchess as devotedly as ever—as a wife and a woman. Previously though he had looked upon her as a goddess. Bernstorff believed he had succeeded in modifying the Duke's adoration. Little by little over several years he had gradually worn through that pedestal on which the Duke had set his wife. She was beautiful still; a devoted wife and mother, nothing could alter that. But was she the omniscient being the Duke had one time believed her to be? He was certainly a little resentful because of her; she was the one who dictated the policy of Celle. It was ridiculous that this state of affairs should continue—so Bernstorff had pointed out. Ridiculous was the word—for there would always be ridicule for the man who allowed a woman to rule him. By her attitude the Duchess reduced the Duke to a mere cypher; she should know that it was the Duke's duty and privilege to rule his own state.

The Duke had come to see this. Now and then he had insisted on having his way, which was sometimes opposed to the Duchess's wishes. Not that he necessarily desired it urgently; but it was a matter of principle, as Bernstorff pointed out; as for Bernstorff he was always ranged on the side of the Duke against the Duchess.

And now this matter of the wedding. What were his Dutch friends thinking of? Didn't they know that George Lewis was in London for the purpose of meeting the Princess Ann? It was safe therefore to suggest the possibility of the marriage, for it was most unlikely ever to take place.

He made a few hasty calculations trying to discover how long it would be before he had enough money to become a landowner. If it were possible to bring about a marriage between Celle and Hanover that time would move considerably nearer.

Why had his Dutch friends asked for this? Had they some special knowledge of affairs? Could it be that all was not going as Sophia and Ernest Augustus had hoped when they sent their son to London?

He rose from the fire and went along to the private apartments of the Duke, where to his relief he found his master alone.

"Come in, Bernstorff," said the Duke, looking up from the book he was reading. How he liked an easy comfortable life! thought his minister. That was why it had been so easy for the Duchess to dominate him. On the other hand it was why it would not be difficult for any strong-minded person to do the same.

"You have something on your mind?" asked the Duke.

"I have been thinking for some time what a pity it is that there could not be an alliance between Hanover and Celle."

"Between Hanover and Celle! How would that be possible?"

"If the Crown Prince married our Princess the family quarrels would be over and the two principalities joined as one, and all the Brunswick-Lüneberg estates brought together again as the family always wanted them to be."

"Impossible," smiled George William.

"Not impossible at all . . . if the two young people married."

"You can guess why George Lewis is in England now."

"Hoping for the Princess Anne."

"Do you think Charles will agree?"

"I hope not."

"What, Bernstorff?"

"It has occurred to me that you would be glad to see an end to the strife in your house, that you would like to be on the terms you once were with your brother."

"Well . . . it's a dream, Bernstorff."

"Great and blessed events often begin as dreams."

"You're very romantic tonight, Bernstorff."

"I cannot help thinking how pleasant it would be to see the two Houses in harmony."

"I admit it would be pleasant, but the Duchess would never agree. She has been too humiliated by the Duchess Sophia and in such a manner as she will never forget. She is determined on an alliance with Wolfenbüttel. Anton Ulrich has always been a good friend to her. Moreover, the Princess herself is becoming accustomed to the young man and her mother will never allow her to be married where she has no inclination."

"She could grow to like her cousin."

"George Lewis is scarcely attractive. But what nonsense we are talking, Bernstorff. Soon we shall have a triumphant announcement from Sophia that her first-born is to become the husband of an English Princess. Won't that make her happy?"

Bernstorff laughed. He could see that he had sown speculation in the Duke's mind. George William would be pleased to see a union with Hanover, for was it not the wish of every German princeling to keep the family estates intact? And he was an easy-going man; he hated being on bad terms with his brother and would welcome an opportunity to get back to the old friendship.

"I think, much as she loves the English, she would be equally happy to see Celle and Hanover united."

"Never. You don't know Sophia. And we have been on very bad terms."

"Only on . . . account of the Duchess."

It was daring; it was underlining a truth. The Duke frowned and Bernstorff wondered if he had gone too far.

"The Duchess has of course suffered great provocation," said Bernstorff hurriedly. He laughed a little uneasily. "She would not be pleased with me if she knew I had made such a suggestion. I pray you will not betray me, my lord."

George William laughed. "Rest easy. I shall say nothing."

*   *   *

Clara waited for the secrecy of the bedchamber before she made her attack.

"Have you heard the news from England?" she asked.

"News, what news?"

"They have passed the Exclusion Bill in the Commons but it has been rejected by the Lords and the King has dissolved Parliament. No Exclusion Bill, and James to follow Charles as King of England—Catholic though he may be."

"Far off politics don't concern me."

"With George Lewis trying his luck for the Princess Anne?"

"What do you think this will mean?"

"That George Lewis will be unacceptable as a husband for Anne. As a matter of fact I have heard rumours . . ."

"Come, Clara, have you spies everywhere?"

"In your service, my lord."

"Ah, Clara, what should I do without you? What did I do before you thrust your attentions upon me?"

"Why concern yourself with the lamentable past? Here I am at your service and this I tell you : George Lewis has not made a favourable impression."

"Who expected him to? If he ever did it would be the first time in his life."

"They won't have him. He'll be sent packing with his tail between his legs."

"Charles wouldn't so insult his dear cousin Sophia."

"Let us see that he doesn't have a chance to."

"You mean we should send for him?"

Clara nodded.

"On what pretext?"

She was silent for a while and then plunged. "There is one plan which is very dear to you, I know. There is one thing in your life which you greatly regret."

"We were talking of George Lewis."

"This concerns George Lewis. You deeply regret your quarrel with your brother the Duke of Celle. In fact, now that I know you so well I believe you regret that more than anything that has ever happened to you in your life."

"You say this, Clara, when I am telling you how much I regret not meeting *you* earlier."

"That is past and rectified, but this quarrel still exists. I should like to see an end to it; I should like to see Celle and Hanover united. I should like to see friendship where there was once enmity, and the old tradition of one ruler for one family back with us."

"Clara, what are you saying?"

"That there is a Princess at Celle who will inherit vast wealth and land; and there is a Prince at Hanover who might marry her."

"George Lewis marry Sophia Dorothea! Clara ... are you serious?"

"Deadly serious."

"And you think the Duchess Sophia would agree to this?"

"No. She has set her heart on that paradise ... England. But England is not for George Lewis. That is very clear to me. We should draw him out while we can do so with dignity and this alliance between Celle and Hanover should at least be considered."

"It's so ... unexpected."

"Good plans often are."

Ernest Augustus whistled softly under his breath.

"Clara," he said, "you're a brilliant woman."

"My brilliance is at the disposal of Your Highness," she answered.

"But ..." he added.

"But it's a hare-brained scheme," she finished for him. "Perhaps. But at least worth brooding on. Pray you, say nothing of it to the Duchess Sophia. She would never forgive me if she thought I had suggested such a match."

"I will certainly say nothing. In any case she would never agree."

"We will talk of it together ... just the two of us. We will weigh up the advantages against the disadvantages. It will at least be amusing."

*   *   *

The Princess Anne sat before her mirror while one of her ladies helped her put on her gloves. This was one of the Villiers girls with whom she had been brought up, the eldest of whom had gone to Holland with Mary and, so it was said, became William's mistress—although it was hard to believe William would ever possess one.

"My fan?" said the Princess.

"Here, Your Highness."

"Thank you."

"How becoming is the blue, Your Highness."

Anne smiled; she was always friendly with her attendants and rarely stood on ceremony.

"Even this young man from Hanover would surely admire that."

"You think he does not admire . . . often?"

The girl looked embarrassed. "I . . . I'd rather not say, Your Highness."

"Why, what mystery is this?"

"It is just a tale, like as not."

"I wish to hear it."

"It is foolish talk, Your Highness."

Anne was suddenly authoritative. "I have said I wished to hear it."

The girl bit her lip. "It was said Your Highness that this young oaf . . . forgive me, Your Highness, but his manners incense me and all your friends . . . it is said that he found you . . . repulsive and that is why he was so uncouth at the meeting."

"He found *me* repulsive!" cried Anne, rising, her pink cheeks flushing to crimson. "I tell you that I found him positively nauseating. I wouldn't marry that man if he were the King of France."

"Ah, Your Highness, he could never be mistaken for the King of France who I hear is as courtly and gallant as His Majesty himself . . . or almost."

"I will go and see His Majesty. I will tell him that nothing on earth would induce me to marry this German boor. I will tell him I will die rather. I would rather leave the Palace and go and live as a seamstress . . . or a laundress."

"I am sure His Majesty will never allow you to do that, Your Highness. But I have heard that he too has no great admiration

for this fellow." She had begun to tremble. "You will tell no one
that it was I . . ."

"Rest easy," said Anne. "I will tell no one anything but that I
refuse to marry this German."

Anne picked up her fan and went from the apartment and her
attendant sat down to write a letter to her sister Elizabeth in
Holland to say that she had done as she was told and she believed
it had succeeded right well with the Princess.

                    *   *   *

From a window of her husband's study Eléonore watched her
daughter on horseback in the company of Eléonore von Knesebeck.
They dismounted, a groom took the girls' horses, and arm in arm
they entered the castle.

"What are you smiling at?" asked George William, coming
over to stand beside her.

"Our daughter," she said. "I believe she grows more lovely
every day."

"More and more like her mother," said George William, fondly
slipping his arm through that of his wife.

"In September she will be sixteen," went on Eléonore. "I think
it is time she married."

"Sixteen . . . is it possible?"

"Possible! It's a fact. I think Sophia Dorothea is ready for
marriage. Perhaps we have sheltered her a little but she will want
to be loved. I sense that in her; and I should like to see her
happily settled."

Recalling secret conversations with Bernstorff, George William
was a little uneasy. He had not dared mention to the Duchess the
suggested match with Hanover.

"Oh, she is young yet," he parried.

"You are like all fathers. They want to keep their daughters
children for ever."

"No, I would not say that."

Eléonore turned to smile at her husband. "But I would. I think
something should be done soon, though. A definite betrothal.
Anton Ulrich is getting a little impatient."

"Fifteen . . . it is young!"

"I do not mean for an immediate marriage. We shall need
several months to prepare."

George William began: "Er . . ." But it was too difficult. He
guessed what her reaction would be. Stark horror. He loved her;
he could not bear to upset her. And yet, one part of him remembered the look in Bernstorff's eyes. Did the whole of his court and

that of Hanover laugh at him behind his back for a man who was under his wife's thumb? If this could have been the case secretly, he would not have cared. He realized he was a weak man. He had always been a pleasure-seeker; now he wanted peace and comfort. When he joined with Eléonore he had made a very happy life for himself and he wanted it to remain so.

Eléonore had turned to look at him. "I do not believe you are eager for this marriage."

He plunged in then. "It seems wrong to me somehow. She was affianced to the brother and then he died. It seems . . ."

"Oh, but she was merely promised."

"Yes, in a way it makes a sort of affinity."

"That's absurd."

He frowned a little. Yes, she did attempt to override him. But almost immediately his petty annoyance faded for she had put her arms about his neck and laid her face against his. "Oh, my dearest, we both love her too much, I sometimes think. We both want everything to be absolutely perfect for her, and that makes us over-anxious."

He held her in a tight embrace. "It's true," he said. Now, he told himself. Now is the time. Mention the advantages of a match with Hanover. He tried, but the words would not come.

Procrastinate! Play for time! That was his rule of life.

"I don't want to hurry anything," he heard himself saying. "Let's wait awhile. Let's wait . . ." he calculated. Six months? He could do a great deal in six months. He might even talk to her, bring her round to his way of thinking. "Let's wait until September," he said.

"September," said the Duchess. "Her birthday. Yes, that's a good idea. We will announce the alliance with Wolfenbüttel on her birthday."

George William pushed aside unpleasant thoughts. September was six months away. He had always been a man to live in the present.

*　　*　　*

Bernstorff met Clara von Platen riding somewhere in the twenty miles which separated Celle and Hanover.

"Well," said Clara, "you have news?"

"Anton Ulrich grows impatient and the Duchess does too. She is working for a definite betrothal."

"And George William?"

"He is holding it off but has not plucked up courage to speak to her."

"If we are not careful she will affiance the girl to Wolfenbüttel and then it will be too late."

"I know."

"Well, cannot you do something to stop it?"

"If you knew George William you would understand my difficulties. He can't bring himself to disagree with her when he's face to face—although depend upon it if we could get him alone . . . if she would go away . . . then we would have the agreement."

"Is there no hope of her going away?"

"They are never separated. Besides, she could not be persuaded to leave her beloved child."

"And you don't think she could be persuaded? After all, a match with Hanover and a possibility—vague I'll admit—of the girl's becoming a Queen if ever George Lewis had the throne of England, must surely be a better proposition than a marriage with Wolfenbüttel."

"But the girl has quite a fondness for the Wolfenbüttel boy and that counts with the Duchess. We do not hear very good reports of George Lewis."

"What do you mean?"

"Coarse, crude manners and too many mistresses. Sophia Dorothea has been brought up, surrounded by affection and French manners and such like. The Duchess wants her to be treated like a precious piece of porcelain when she leaves the parental roof."

"The girl had better come out of her shell and live."

"So say I. But try saying it to the Duchess."

"So you think he'll agree with this Wolfenbüttel match?"

"He'd like to for the sake of peace. But he has a great desire to be friends with his brother as apparently they were very close to each other in their youth."

"Yes, I've heard of that. Ernest Augustus would like to take up the friendship too."

"And George Lewis?"

"What of him! He's ready to be a prize stud on occasions, provided on others he's allowed to roam around in search of his own choice heifers. He doesn't count. Nor does the girl."

"She does with her mother."

"You must keep us informed. If this does not come off you'll be a great deal poorer than you might otherwise be."

"I know."

"Keep me informed of the slightest incident."

"I will."

They said goodbye; and Bernstorff riding back to Celle was a very uneasy man.

*   *   *

Ernest Augustus came to his wife's apartments, waving a batch of papers in his hand and frowning deeply. He signed to her attendants that he wished to be alone with the Duchess.

"Something is wrong, I see," said Sophia quietly.

"Wrong! Indeed yes. This little jaunt of our son's to England is going to be very expensive and I have to pay for it."

"But if . . ."

Ernest Augustus held up a hand. "Don't deceive yourself. I fear you miscalculated there. There'll be no English marriage for George Lewis; and it has been a very costly matter to discover what I felt to be the truth even before he embarked on his fool's errand."

"Fool's errand! I refuse to believe it. And you thought it an excellent idea that he should go."

"I gave way to you, it's true."

"But what has happened. He has been received at Charles's court. He has even had lodgings at Whitehall."

"Yes, and I hear that the Princess Anne will have none of it. The Duke of York is back at court after his exile in Scotland; the Exclusion Bill has not been made law. There are even rumours that Charles in secret does not frown on Catholicism. He has given Mary to the Protestant Orange and he is not inclined to give Anne to a German Duke even though he is a Protestant. That is how I see it."

"But how can you be sure?"

"They've given him a consolation prize—a Doctorate of Laws at Cambridge. And can't speak a word of English! It's as though they are poking fun at him. If he had studied a little more and learned some English he could at least have given some account of himself. But he cannot. What hope has he? He must come home before he is made to look more foolish than he already does."

"You are telling me that you propose sending for him."

"I have already done so."

Sophia's face was flushed with anger, but Ernest Augustus thrust the papers into her hand. "Take a look at these. Then you will see how much this fruitless journey has cost me. Then you will see that George Lewis must come back to Hanover and find a bride nearer home."

The Duchess Sophia stared at the figures. She could have wept with rage. To her they represented the end of a dream. She realized it now; from the time her ugly little George Lewis was a baby she had dreamed of his ascending the throne of England.

And Ernest Augustus was angry. She had involved him in unnecessary expense. He would not forget this in a hurry. If he had not listened to her, George Lewis would never have gone to England to make a hole in his father's purse and a fool of himself.

*   *   *

It was good to be back in Hanover, thought George Lewis. He liked London but he could never understand the people. They laughed too much and, he believed, at him. Did they find everyone amusing who did not speak their tongue and who didn't follow their customs?

There had been one of their customs which George Lewis could follow very well.

He saw Marie at a window of the palace as he rode towards it. She was leaning out with apparent eagerness, and behind her stood her sister the Platen woman, who was becoming more and more important to his father. She was watching him and Marie, but he had little thought to spare for her.

His father greeted him grimly; he was still calculating the cost of his journey; his mother was solemn, regarding his empty-handed return as a tragedy.

George Lewis listened half-heartedly to their greeting. His mother wanted to hear all that had happened to him at the English court; his father wanted to know how much money he had spent.

A dreary home-coming, thought George Lewis, except for the fact that Marie had made herself very visible to him and had clearly implied how eagerly she was waiting for him.

*   *   *

The Duchess Sophia shut herself away the better to forget the tragedy; she read a great deal and wrote letters to learned friends all over Europe. She had so counted on the marriage between her son and the English Princess and could not imagine what had happened to make plans go awry. It could only be George Lewis's uncouth manners. How she wished that one of the others had been the eldest son!

Ernest Augustus with Clara von Platen in attendance talked to his son about the English visit.

"Bah!" he said. "Let them keep the girl. There are other fish in the sea."

George Lewis grinned. "She was not exactly beautiful and was very spoilt."

"Yes, those two girls were spoilt. Well, William knows how to tame the elder."

"I would have tamed the younger."

"Let's not upset ourselves over that."

"His Highness is right," said Clara. "He would have known how to deal with this . . . Anne."

George Lewis gave her a friendly leer. He guessed Marie had been discussing his prowess with her. What he liked about Marie was her lack of prudery not only in deed but in word. He guessed her sister was the same—perhaps more so.

"You'll have to look near at hand for a bride," said Ernest Augustus.

George nodded.

"What about your cousin over at Celle?"

George Lewis's jaw dropped. "Not . . . ?"

"Yes," put in Ernest Augustus impatiently. "Who else could be at Celle but your cousin Sophia Dorothea?"

"Oh *no* . . . !"

"Why not? She's an heiress. It would be good to end our quarrels."

"We already inherit from my uncle."

"She's a considerable heiress in her own right. And don't forget all the possessions her mother has managed to amass."

"I wouldn't want the girl."

"Why not? She's a beauty."

"Fancy French manners."

"You would soon change those," laughed Clara.

He gave her his slow smile, but he shook his head. "I wouldn't want the girl."

"You have to think of Hanover, my son, not your likes and dislikes. This English jaunt has cost me more thalers than I like to think about."

"Sophia Dorothea!" breathed George Lewis.

"Yes, think about it. But one thing to remember. Don't let your mother know anything of this. Don't forget how set she is on an English wife for you."

"She's still mourning for the Princess Anne," said Clara. "Give her a chance to recover."

"Sophia Dorothea!" breathed George Lewis and slowly shook his head.

The Fateful Birthday

ELÉONORE had been uneasy all through the summer. There was a change in George William. Occasionally she would see the stubborn set of his jaw; he would disagree with her in a pointless way as though he were anxious to show her that she could not have all her own way. She was hurt, for she had never sought to dominate. Her great desire now was for the happiness of her daughter. For this reason she often invited Duke Anton Ulrich to Celle and with him came Augustus William, the boy who was now his eldest son. Eléonore's one idea was to make the two young people the best of friends so that marriage between them would not be the shock it was to so many young people in their positions. She talked often to her daughter of her own romance and the great love which had arisen between the Duke and herself; she wanted a union as romantic and as enduring for her beloved daughter. And she had thought George William did too.

But he had become evasive; he had already postponed the betrothal; he spent more time lately shut up with Bernstorff who was a man she had never been able to respect. Perhaps George William was growing old and did not always feel as healthy as he used to. That might change him, make him a little moody.

But now the summer was passing and Sophia Dorothea's birthday was almost upon them; she had made up her mind that on that birthday the betrothal should take place.

September was a beautiful month—the most beautiful of the

year to Eléonore; and the fifteenth, that important date had always been celebrated more lavishly than any other in the calendar.

This September should be the most lavish of them all, decided Eléonore. She would invite the Wolfenbüttels to the celebration and the people of the town would crowd into the castle and its grounds to enjoy the festivities and to hear the good news that Celle and Wolfenbüttel would be joined together forever in friendship because of the alliance between the Crown Prince of Wolfenbüttel and the Princess of Celle.

She went to her daughter's apartments where Eléonore von Knesebeck and Sophia Dorothea were laughing together over some secret joke.

Fraulein von Knesebeck immediately became serious and bobbed a curtsy when the Duchess appeared. Eléonore said: "The Princess will send for you when you may return."

Sophia Dorothea smiled at her mother. "You sound a little serious, Maman."

"Just a little," Eléonore agreed. How lovely the child was! she thought. But a child no longer. Sophia Dorothea's young body was in bud, ready to burst into bloom. What a beautiful woman she would be. A Princess, well educated, of courtly manners, she would turn Wolfenbüttel into a little Versailles—not a travesty of one as some of these German princelings had provided for themselves, but one of which Louis himself would not disapprove. She was more French than German—versatile, charming, graceful and gracious. May she be happy, prayed Eléonore.

"You will soon be sixteen, my darling," she said.

"But you would .1ot look so grave if you had come to ask me whether I should prefer a ball to a play."

"No, that is no matter for gravity; and we shall decide it soon. It is this, dearest: You are not a child any more."

"I am glad you realize it, Maman. You have been inclined to treat me as one."

Eléonore in a sudden burst of tenderness held the girl against her. "It is because you are so precious to me."

"I know. I know. Is it this marriage you want to discuss?"

Eléonore nodded.

"I thought so. It is to be soon?"

"Well, as we said, you are no longer a child. We should announce your betrothal on your birthday and the marriage should take place soon afterwards."

"And I shall have to leave Celle?"

"My dear—Wolfenbüttel is only a few miles distant. You will

be a constant visitor here and I there. You don't imagine I would allow anyone—even your husband—to keep *us* apart."

"No, Maman. I don't. But husband..." Sophia Dorothea shievered. "I don't like the word."

"My darling, but you like Augustus William?"

"Yes, I like him. He's very agreeable. He's very kind and says he adores me."

"So you find him acceptable?"

"I would rather stay as we are, but I know I have to marry, so since that is so I'd as lief take Augustus William as anyone." She laughed suddenly. "You know when they were talking about the Princess Anne and George Lewis ... Maman, I felt so sorry for her and that made me almost love Augustus William."

Eléonore laughed. "I am glad of anything that makes you love him. He is good and you will be happy with him. Girls can't stay young and with their mothers all their lives."

"More's the pity."

"You won't think that when you have your babies."

"Ah ... babies!" murmured Sophia Dorothea.

Eléonore took her daughter's hand and said softly : "You see, my love, I want to talk to you about this. I'm going to persuade your father to agree to the announcement of the betrothal on your birthday. I feel a little uneasy ... I don't know why ... unless it is because I hate losing you. But I won't of course when you marry Augustus William. He is like a son to me even now, and his father has always been my good friend."

"So it is to be soon after my birthday then."

"Yes, but say nothing to anyone, even to little Knesebeck as yet."

"Why not?"

"I just have a feeling that it is better not."

"Maman, when I marry, Eléonore von Knesebeck will come with me, won't she?"

"Of course if you wish it."

"I do wish it. It would be good if you could come too."

Eléonore laughed. "My darling, your husband would say he was marrying your mother as well as you. Moreover, what of your father?"

"*He* would never be able to do without you."

"I shall pray," said Eléonore solemnly, "that you are as happy in your marriage as I have been in mine."

* * *

Why was she uneasy? She was not sure. Sophia Dorothea was not really unhappy about her forthcoming marriage; she accepted

the fact that she had to marry and the Crown Prince of Wolfenbüttel was of her age, a good-looking boy, in love with his bride-
to-be. Two young people like that would be happy; and when
the children came, Sophia Dorothea would wonder how she could
ever have thought the life at Celle offered her all she wanted.

She would speak to George William without delay. She went
to his study and entered unceremoniously as she always did.
George William was in deep colloquy with Bernstorff who looked
up in astonishment at her. Why? Did he expect her to petition
an audience with her own husband? She had been accustomed
to seeing George William rise to greet her with pleasure and, no
matter who was with him, invite her to take a share in their discussions, to listen courteously to all that she said.

George William *had* risen; he took her hand and kissed it—as
tender as ever.

"We have a little business to finish, my dear."

She was mildly astonished. It was a way of telling her that in
her presence the business could not be conducted.

"I will see you later," she said gravely; and she was aware of
the smug expression in Bernstorff's face as he stood there waiting
for her to depart until he could resume his chair.

She passed out of the study frowning.

Yes, there was a change; and she was uneasy.

What business did her husband and his minister discuss from
which she must be excluded?

*   *   *

She chose the time to broach the subject when Bernstorff could
not interrupt them. In the connubial bed she was safe; and there
George William was the lover as he had always been.

"I want to settle this matter," she told him. "The time is getting
close."

"Time?" he said gently, sleepily.

"The birthday will soon be here."

"Ah, the birthday."

"I have invited Duke Anton Ulrich and his family to the
celebrations . . . naturally."

"Naturally."

"Dear Sophia Dorothea, she is reconciled to Augustus William
although not anxious to leave her home. We should consider that
the greatest compliment she could pay us. My dearest child! I
have always been concerned for the time she should leave us. I
knew what a wrench it would be for her. We have been so happy
together, have we not?"

"Very happy," agreed George William.

"And I pray that she will be too. I trust Anton Ulrich as I could very few people, I am so fond of Augustus William and he is of Sophia Dorothea. Who could help it? I am so *relieved* that she should marry so close to us. We shall be able to keep an eye on her ... it won't be like losing her."

George William stirred uneasily; he was glad of the darkness. How on earth could he approach the matter of a match with Hanover? He thought of George Lewis that uncouth young monster—crude and coarse ... and their dainty little Sophia Dorothea in such hands. The project seemed impossible here with Eléonore. And the child was reconciled to marriage with Augustus William. How could he say to Eléonore : But a match with Hanover would be so much more advantageous. Of course it would, but not to Sophia Dorothea. Eléonore would never consider it.

He had half promised Bernstorff. But then who was Bernstorff? Only his minister, his servant. Why should he be afraid of Bernstorff?

"So," went on Eléonore, "I want to announce the betrothal at the birthday."

George William was silent, his heart beating rapidly and uneasily.

She put her arms about his neck. "I want it to be a happy day. You remember how she has always loved her birthdays? Do you remember when she was four and we explained together what a birthday was? I can see her now ... sitting there, those lovely dark eyes so solemn while she listened and how she looked at us so trustingly."

Yes, he remembered. He had been a fool. Sophia Dorothea's happiness and that of Eléonore—for the two were synonymous— were all that mattered. Of course he would never seriously agree to give their beloved child to George Lewis, the monster of Hanover.

"And she sat between us on her little bed ..." he added, "gripping your hand and mine."

"It has been a wonderful life since we came to Celle," said Eléonore. "I want her to know happiness like that."

He agreed, of course he agreed. But he thought of all the secret conversations with Bernstorff, all the advantages of a match with Hanover.

"I knew you would agree that the announcement should be made on her birthday," said Eléonore.

Inwardly he cried out : But I can't. I have half agreed to the match with Hanover. But how could he say those words which would shatter the happiness of his beloved Eléonore and his dearest Sophia Dorothea? And yet . . .

But Eléonore was laughing softly, having no idea of the conflict within him.

"We will go ahead with preparations," she said. "I shall hate losing her, but Anton Ulrich and dear Augustus Frederick will soften the blow . . . not only for us but for our dearest child."

What could he say? Nothing. So he remained silent.

*   *   *

Celebrations for the birthday were going on and the excitement had extended to the town of Celle where the people were decorating the streets. Bells were heard at all hours for the ringers were practising the special carillon to be performed in honour of their Princess.

This was to be the most important birthday yet and although no definite announcement had been made it was being whispered that there was a special reason for it. Frequently the equipage from Wolfenbüttel had been seen riding to the castle and Duke Anton Ulrich was popular in Celle; he had a charming young son who pleased the people even more than his elder brother had done because he was nearer the age of their beloved Princess.

Bernstorff was growing more and more uneasy. Duke George William brushed aside the subject of the Hanoverian alliance every time he broached it; the Duchess Eléonore had an air of excited contentment; she treated Bernstorff as she always had with the respect due to his position in the Government and was perhaps a little more cordial towards him. He took this as a bad sign.

It was two days before the birthday when he broached the matter of the Hanoverian match with George William. He had found it difficult to secure a private audience before that and suspected that George William avoided him, which naturally made him more uneasy than ever.

With great luck he found the Duke alone and begged a word with him.

"My lord," he said, "it would not be too late now to extend an invitation to your brother of Hanover."

"It is too late," answered George William.

"At least George Lewis might be invited. He can have no quarrel with the Duchess."

"She would never agree to invite him."

"I am sure that they are waiting for a move."

"For what reason?"

"In our little affair, my lord. Hanover would welcome the alliance. George Lewis ... he would come to it when his parents had persuaded him ... and now that the Princess will be sixteen ..."

"Listen, Bernstorff. That affair is off."

Bernstorff grew pale. He saw those rich lands—the dream of an avaricious imagination—slipping away from him. He would be in bondage for the rest of his life. If he brought about this marriage he would be rewarded by Ernest Augustus and better still by William of Orange. And all this was being snatched from him because once more the Duchess was dominating her weak husband.

"But, my lord ..." he stammered.

"Yes, it would have been a good match, but my daughter is promised to the heir of Wolfenbüttel and she has a fondness for the boy so the Duchess is of the opinion that in these circumstances it is better for the child to be happy."

"The Duchess!" Bernstorff could not control himself. "And your opinion, my lord ..."

The Duke shrugged his shoulders. "I confess I would rather be allied to Hanover than Wolfenbüttel. I should have been delighted to be reconciled to my brother Ernest Augustus. We were such friends in our youth."

Oh, God! thought Bernstorff. No reminiscences! This is no time for them.

"It is, of course, you, my lord, who will decide."

Again he saw the look flash across the Duke's face. He knew what his minister was implying. Affairs of state have to be decided by women's sentimental whims. George William saw in that moment all the advantages of the match with Hanover; he was remembering that all Princes and Princesses must accept marriages of convenience. He had intended that this should be so—but once more he had given way. He felt ashamed of himself. He had no will of his own. The Duchy of Celle was managed by Eléonore and everyone knew it.

"It is too late now," he muttered. "The betrothal to Augustus William will be announced at the birthday."

Stunned, pale with rage and frustration, Bernstorff took his leave.

* * *

He must put up a fight. There was too much at stake to allow everything to be lost. Bernstorff shut himself into his private apartment; he paced up and down. What could be done at this late hour? Anton Ulrich and his family were making their preparations to leave Wolfenbüttel; in two days' time it would be too late, for once the announcement of the betrothal had been made George William would never withdraw it; nor would Ernest Augustus accept a girl who had been betrothed elsewhere. Two days in which to save a plan—a fortune for himself ... and for Clara von Platen!

Ah, there was the answer. Clara had as much to lose as he had. She, too, was in the pay of William of Orange; she, too, wanted George Lewis kept close at hand so that she could control his affairs through her sister as she herself did those of Ernest Augustus.

He must get a message through to Hanover with all speed for he knew that Clara would work as zealously as he himself could do.

He sat down at his table, wrote a rapid message explaining what was happening at Celle, and then sent for his servant.

He stood at his window watching the man ride away to Hanover.

*   *   *

Clara rushed into Ernest Augustus's presence scattering all those servants who were with him.

"My dear Clara, you look distraught," said her lover. "What's that you have in your hand?"

"Distraught! And so will you be when you have heard. This is a message from Celle. Do you know what is happening? Their little pet will be sixteen on the fifteenth and her devoted Maman is arranging to announce her engagement on that day."

Ernest Augustus's smile faded. He was now as eager for alliance with Celle as Clara and Bernstorff.

"To ..."

"Exactly," stormed Clara. "To the Wolfenbüttel boy. They are such good friends and the little darling will not mind leaving dear Papa and dearest Maman for such a nice little fellow."

"Clara, calm yourself."

"Yes, my dear. We must both be calm. We must think how to frustrate this plan."

"But George William has agreed to it."

"She has persuaded him. Bernstorff has done his utmost to make your poor feeble brother see that he is just a cipher in the hands of that woman, and to some extent he has managed it, but she only has to get him alone and she'll have him dancing to her tune."

"Nevertheless George William has agreed to the betrothal."

"Yet he would prefer George Lewis as his son-in-law. He is very eager for the alliance. It is merely that she has overruled him . . . as usual."

"Well, what can we do now?"

"We have to stop the announcement."

"How?"

"By your going over to Celle and offering George Lewis for Sophia Dorothea."

"And the Duchess?"

"We do not have to persuade her. That would be an impossibility in any case. George William is desperately anxious to be on good terms with you. He longs to see one government between Celle and Hanover."

"That would come automatically with his death when Celle will go to George Lewis."

"But he wants to make sure that his daughter loses nothing. In every respect the alliance between Celle and Hanover is perfect; and George William realizes it."

"But the Duchess . . ."

"A sentimental woman. She imagines her daughter *loves* this Wolfenbüttel boy. And you must admit that George Lewis is scarcely the sort to attract a girl who has been brought up as Sophia Dorothea has."

"He might have done more to make himself agreeable."

"You ask the impossible. He could not make himself agreeable however he tried . . . that is to a girl brought up like the Princess of Celle. I believe he gives a good account of himself in some quarters. But we waste time. What can we do? Someone must go to Celle."

"Who?"

"Someone who is strong enough to make George William see how important this match would be. Someone strong enough to make him forget his sentimental desire to please his wife and spoon-feed his daughter."

Ernest Augustus was looking at her. He thought her magnificent with her alert brain, her grasp of affairs, and coupled with it that overpowering sensuality, that skill and knowledgeability which made her as deep a joy to a man such as he was in the bedchamber as in council.

She was the one who would put the case to George William—but how could he send his mistress? George William, like the faithful married man he was, would object to her, before he saw her; he might even refuse to receive her. No, for all her brilliance Clara would not stand a chance.

Clara was looking at him speculatively. He was the obvious choice. Clara narrowed her eyes, picturing Ernest Augustus ordering that the coach be prepared for him to go to Celle. News of his arrival might well reach the castle before he did and Eléonore would have no doubt of the reason for his journey. She would be prepared, and if she had an opportunity of making her husband promise not to give way, she would surely succeed.

Clara said : "The Duchess Sophia must go."

"Are you mad? She knows nothing of this. She hates the Duchess of Celle. She has never forgotten that the Duke refused to marry her, turned her over to me, even giving me his birthright to elude marriage, and then fell in love with Eléonore and made such efforts to marry her. You know women. Do you think Sophia will ever forgive that? Besides, she wants an English bride for George Lewis."

"She has seen that she cannot get one."

"But this proposed match between George Lewis and Sophia Dorothea has always been kept a secret from her. She has no notion."

"Then she must have a notion . . . quickly. For she is the one. If she will go to Celle, if she will talk to George William he would not be able to resist her."

"She would never do it."

"She would if she were made to see the importance to Hanover of this marriage."

"And who could make her see that?"

"You . . . her husband."

"Do you think . . . ?"

"My dear, you are no George William. Sophia is the daughter of a Queen and doesn't forget it. Moreover, her mother was the daughter of a King of England—which to her is the highest honour in the world. Her beliefs give her an unsurpassable dignity. She and she alone could bring George William to our side . . . even now . . . providing she is able to do so before Eléonore discovers what is going on."

"I should have to explain to her what we have been planning these last months."

"Never mind. She accepts you as the master. There you have been wiser than your brother. She . . . the great Sophia . . . has never sought to meddle unduly in your affairs. She did over this English visit and see what a failure that was! It is something to bear in mind when you talk to her. She is humble at the moment because of it. You could explain to her the desirability of this match; you could make her see the part she has to play. This is the right moment while she remembers the disaster of the English visit and all the money it cost you. Rarely has she been so humble as she is at this moment—nor will ever be again. You must go to her. There is no time to lose. You must bring her to our side and she must not waste a minute. The sooner we can get her riding to Celle, determined to make that marriage, the better."

Ernest Augustus looked at his mistress. Clara had genius; he had never been more sure of it than at this moment.

* * *

Sophia looked at her husband with astonishment. "A marriage with Celle! Have you lost your senses. Celle! Our enemies." She smiled suddenly. "That woman who calls herself the Duchess would never agree."

"She has to be made to."

"It is absurd. I'll have nothing to do with such a plan."

Sophia pressed her lips firmly together and held her head high. She implied that although she made no complaint at the immoral life he led and even allowed herself to be on tolerably good terms with his reigning mistress, he must never forget the respect due to a granddaughter of a King of England.

She rose and would have left him but he barred her way.

"You will listen to me," he said; and detecting the firm tone in his voice, she wavered. In spite of her birth she had no power that did not come from him; and the recent insult from England still rankled. They did not want her son; they did not consider him worthy of marriage with Anne. It was a bitter blow to her pride to know that they did not regard her as an important member of the family. Ernest Augustus had always treated her with respect; he had made only one demand, that she did not interfere with his sexual life. This had suited her, for she only desired him in her bed for the procreation of children and in that respect he had not failed her, for she had her family.

She must be careful not to alienate Ernest Augustus. She must remember that although Clara von Platen never forgot her place in the presence of her mistress, Clara was the real power. Ernest Augustus had come from Clara. This was their plot; and now they needed her.

She said slowly: "It could never come about."

"It could if you helped."

"I? What could I do?"

"Everything. You underestimate your power if you do not agree. You have rank and dignity. You could talk to George William and he would have to listen to you."

"Do you suggest that I should go humbly to your brother and beg him to consider our son for his daughter?"

"Not humbly, but in the utmost pride. Let me show you what I feel about this marriage. George Lewis must marry soon and where can we find a bride for him? The English project failed"— Sophia winced—"miserably. It has been nothing but an expense and a loss of dignity into the bargain. Everyone is laughing, you can depend upon it, at George Lewis's attempt to win the Princess Anne. They're saying he came home a little less arrogantly than he set out. That is not a pleasant state of affairs. Well, we must show that even if the English refuse him, there are others who are eager to accept him."

"And you think they will be eager at Celle, do you?"

"George William will when you have spoken to him."

"*I* . . . speak to him?"

"Yes and soon. For if we do not the girl will go to Wolfen-büttel. Now that is another problem. What do you think our position will be with Celle and Wolfenbüttel in alliance against us? We must stop that, if nothing else."

Sophia was silent. It was true that an alliance between Wolfen-büttel and Celle would not be good for Hanover. They needed money—the exchequer was low; and Sophia Dorothea was a considerable heiress. Sophia imagined the contract which could be drawn up—it might be as beneficial to Ernest Augustus as that long-ago one which gave him the standing of an elder brother although he was a younger. And Eléonore? Eléonore wanted the match with Wolfenbüttel, and to bring off one with Hanover would be the biggest defeat that woman had ever suffered. It would bring the daughter on whom she doted to Hanover; it would put Sophia Dorothea completely in their power.

An opportunity to humiliate the woman for whom George William had pleaded and petitioned, schemed and fought to marry, by the woman whom he had pledged his future to avoid.

Sophia laughed harshly.

"I see," she said, "that this marriage with Wolfenbüttel should be prevented. I will order the coach to be prepared and I will leave at once for Celle. There is very little time."

Ernest Augustus seized her hands and kissed them fervently.

"I knew I could rely on you."

Less than half an hour later he and Clara stood side by side watching the coach lumber out of the courtyard and along the road towards Celle.

*   *   *

It was already the afternoon of the fourteenth and it might be that by the morning of the fifteenth Anton Ulrich with his family and retainers would be in Celle. Once he was there and the announcement made it would be too late.

Sophia sat back impatiently against the upholstery of the coach and rehearsed what she would say ... if she arrived in time. She would see George William ... alone. If that woman were there it would be impossible. She pictured Eléonore as she had last seen her—elegant and beautiful and so assured of her husband's devotion. Not only, thought Sophia bitterly, had he married her, but he had been faithful to her. How different was Ernest Augustus! That disgraceful Platen woman was his chief minister, for her husband did what his wife told him, as well as his chief mistress. And even she could not satisfy him completely. How humiliating that many a sly-eyed serving girl among her own household, many a waiting woman had been Ernest Augustus's mistress—even if only for a night or two. Eléonore had no such degradation to endure. She was supreme in her own home, with a doting husband only too willing to be subservient to her so that it was necessary to pay a skilful spy to attempt to dislodge her.

But George William was wavering—if Bernstorff could be believed—and indeed he could, for George William had shown some interest in the Hanover alliance to which his Duchess was so vigorously opposed.

Oh yes, Sophia was going to enjoy her mission; and she was determined that it should succeed.

The coach lumbered to a standstill and she was almost thrown from her seat.

"What has happened?" she cried, drawing down the window and putting out her head.

Several of the lackeys were standing in the road.

"The road's impassable, Your Highness. The recent rains have made a bog of it."

I shall be too late, she thought. Already the afternoon is drawing to its end; and tomorrow is the birthday.

Celle was only twenty miles from Hanover, but if the road was blocked it might as well be a hundred miles.

"We must go on," she insisted.

"Yes, Your Highness, but not on this road."

"Well, is there another?"

"If we make a detour."

"Should we get there before dark?"

"Your Highness, it's an impossibility ... and we don't know what other roads will be like."

"I tell you you must get me there tonight."

"Yes, Your Highness. If you will excuse me, Your Highness..."

She sank back against the padded seat. The possibility of delay maddened her—she, who such a short time ago had had to be persuaded to take this step! Now that she had seen a way of vanquishing her enemy she longed to succeed. There would be a match between Celle and Hanover. Only let her get to Celle.

The coach lurched. She sat waiting. One of the men was at the window.

"We have pulled out of the slush, Your Highness. We're turning back and we'll strike off in another direction."

"Tell them not to waste a moment."

"Yes, Your Highness."

"They'll be well rewarded if they get me to Celle before morning. If not ..."

"Yes, Your Highness."

The coach was rattling along at a good speed. She planned what she would say. It must be to George William alone; she would find some way of excluding the Duchess. Language, of course! She would not speak in French nor in German, but in low Dutch of which the Duchess could not understand a word.

Darkness had fallen but she did not stop the coach to ask how near they were. She sat upright, her lips growing grimmer as she rehearsed her part ... in low Dutch.

The night was long; the jolting of the coach irksome; and when she saw the faint sign of light in the sky she despaired. Then she heard the shout and looking from her window saw the castle rising out of the mist and at that moment the coach was riding through the narrow streets of the town, past the sleeping houses —though here and there a head appeared at a window to see who the early visitors were.

The castle sentinels saw the Hanover coach which they recognized by the coat of arms and the liveries. The drawbridge was lowered, the portcullis raised; and the Duchess Sophia came into the castle of Celle.

*   *   *

The Duchess Sophia left the coach and entered the castle. The guards stared at her in wonder. They knew her, of course and were overawed. But at such a time and unannounced! What could it mean?

Sophia peremptorily demanded : "Where is the Duke?"

"Your Highness, he has not yet risen.'

"Take me to him."

"Madam, he is in his bedchamber."

"Take me to him," insisted Sophia.

"But . . ."

Sophia looked surprised. "Take me at once to his apartment," she ordered, and the trembling page dared do nothing but obey.

In the ducal sleeping apartments the Duke, who was an early riser, was up and at his dressing table. When the page scratched at the door, one of his servants opened the door and was about to reprimand the page when he saw the Duchess Sophia. He stood staring as though petrified.

"What is it?" demanded the Duke.

But Sophia was already striding into the dressing room, and it was George William's turn to stare.

"Your Highness," he stammered, "what does this honour . . ."

"It means," said Sophia briskly, "that I must speak to you. I have come to congratulate you on the birthday of your daughter."

"This is a great honour, but so unexpected . . . and . . ."

"And at such a time," finished Sophia grimly. "I have been riding all night."

"Then you must be exhausted. You must be given an apartment where you can rest and refresh yourself."

"The road was impassable. Hence my arriving at such a time. I should have been here yesterday."

"We can only rejoice that you have come," he said. He was about to summon a servant, but Sophia laid a hand on his arm.

"One moment. I have to talk to you on a matter of great importance. Where is your wife?"

"She has not yet risen." George William waved his hand to an open door. Sophia looked towards it and rage filled her. They had always used this apartment like the devoted married couple they were. He had just left the big bed which he had shared with her for seventeen years . . . ever since he left Osnabrück— the faithful husband, who had once been as reckless a rake as Ernest Augustus. Well, Madame Eléonore was going to get a shock now.

"George William," called Eléonore, "who has arrived?"

Sophia went to the door and looked in at the bedchamber. It was magnificent—furnished in the French style; and there in bed was Eléonore, her abundant dark hair falling about the pillows, her magnificent shoulders and arms bare, her luminous eyes startled. It was a shock to discover how beautiful she was; even more so, it seemed to Sophia, than she had been in the days of her youth. Now she was poised and serene. Those years of married happiness had given her that—love, happiness, the assurance that the man she had married was devoted to her.

I might have been in her place! thought Sophia.

Perhaps she was more perceptive than Eléonore. She knew that Ernest Augustus was the shrewder ruler, that he was mentally more brilliant than his elder brother. George William was weak in comparison—brave on the battlefield but weak in his emotions. But Sophia was in no doubt which she would have chosen as her husband had she been permitted such a choice.

And so she hated the beautiful woman in the bed—hated the elaborate room with its elegant furniture and the ceiling decorated with the Leda and the Swan legend; if she had been determined when she endured that difficult journey between Celle and Hanover she was doubly so now.

"I have come to congratulate you on your daughter's birthday," she said, and without giving Eléonore a chance to reply she turned to George William and said in low Dutch: "I must speak to you at once . . . and alone. It is of the utmost importance."

"My wife . . ." he began.

"Alone," insisted Sophia.

"But . . ."

"I beg of you, listen," She glanced towards the half-open door and then to the dressing table. She advanced to this and sat down; he followed her.

"This is of the utmost importance," she said quickly, "to you and to your brother. First I want your promise that if you do not agree with me, you will say nothing of what I am about to suggest."

"I promise," answered George William.

Sophia went on: "We have always been weakened by this enmity between our houses. I want it ended and it is for this reason that I am here. I know that you, too, deplore it. So does Ernest Augustus. Then why should it exist?"

"I have always wanted friendship with Hanover!"

"It can be achieved, immediately and forever by a marriage."

George William drew away from her, but she was not easily defeated. She then began to expound on all the advantages which would come to Celle and to Hanover. It had always seemed unfortunate that he had thrown away his birthright. But Celle and Hanover would be as one—one government—and Sophia

Dorothea would be the Duchess of Hanover so that she would have lost nothing by that long-ago arrangement. George William must see the advantages. She had ridden all through the night to tell him; she implored him not to make a mistake. He could so easily do so now. She believed that if he gave his daughter to the Wolfenbüttels that would be the end of his power. Ernest Augustus who so wanted the girl for his son would never be reconciled.

There was another point. Both George William and Ernest Augustus had fought well for the Emperor and he was pleased with them. Jointly they might be granted an Electorate. What glory for the House of Brunswick-Lüneberg! They could not both receive an Electorate and it would only be if they could be simultaneously rewarded that this could be so. And how could this come about but through a marriage between Celle and Hanover?

She was triumphant seeing him wavering. He longed for reunion with Hanover. He had been devoted to Ernest Augustus and wanted a return to the old relationship. Sophia noticed as she went on talking, that although he had at first cast uneasy glances towards the communicating door, he had ceased to do so.

He was coming round.

She plunged in again—stressing the advantages. He saw them very well, for who could not, since they existed. He had always been attracted by the alliance with Hanover. It was simply because his Duchess had decided against it that he had allowed himself to be persuaded.

"You know, George William, in your heart that if you do not agree to this you will regret it all the days of your life."

He hesitated.

"Why do you falter? It is the Duchess. I know she is friendly with Anton Ulrich. He was respectful to her before your state marriage and she cannot forget it. But we must not allow such petty things to spoil the chances of our children. It is for you to decide ... for *you* ..."

"Yes," answered the Duke. "It is for me."

A door had opened and Bernstorff, his eyes alight with speculation, stood on the threshold.

"My lord ..."

"Let him come in," said Sophia rapidly. "He is a man of good sense and we will hear what he has to say."

"Come in," said the Duke.

Bernstorff feigned great surprise as he bowed low but he could not hide the triumph in his eyes. George William quickly explained why Sophia was here.

"God be praised!" cried Bernstorff.

"So you will join with me in persuading His Highness?" said Sophia.

"Your Highness, I shall for ever thank God and you for this day."

Yes, he thought, when I ride round my acres, when I gloat over my possessions, I will thank the Duchess Sophia, for we had all but lost and now we shall succeed.

"So you share the opinion of the Duke and Duchess of Hanover?"

"I am convinced, Your Highness, that this proposed marriage would be the greatest advantage that has ever come to Celle."

They both watched George William covertly; his eyes were moving towards the communicating door.

"It is for Your Highness to decide. . . . Your Highness alone," insisted Bernstorff.

"That," said Sophia, "is why I know we shall succeed."

"Yes," said George William, turning to face them so that he could no longer see that door. "It is for me alone. And I have made up my mind."

"Yes?"

"There shall be this match with Hanover."

Sophia drew a deep breath; a faint colour had started to show beneath her pale skin, and her eyes were brilliant.

"The Duke has spoken," said Bernstorff.

"And we know that he is a man who will keep his word," added Sophia. "Oh, this is a happy day for me, and for Ernest Augustus."

George William was frowning a little. "The young people . . ." he began.

"Oh, the young people! They will learn to fall in love. After all, it is what we all have to do. They will thank us for arranging such a marriage in the years to come."

"Yes, it will go well . . . in time," said George William.

Was he already regretting? wondered Sophia. But he had given his word. Bernstorff was a witness to it. He could not in honour retract now.

"Now," said Sophia, "I could rest happily for a while. It is early yet."

"An apartment is ready for you," said George William. "You must refresh yourself and rest a while. Allow me to conduct you there."

Sophia put her hand in his.

"Come," he said; and without a glance at the door behind which Eléonore must be waiting with the utmost trepidation, he led the Duchess Sophia from his dressing room.

*   *   *

Having seen the Duchess Sophia to her apartment where she would rest a while before joining George William for breakfast, the latter returned to his apartment where he found Eléonore, now dressed, waiting for him.

"What has happened?" she cried. "What has the Duchess Sophia been saying to you?"

George William's elation faded because it gave him pain to hurt his wife, but he had thoroughly convinced himself now that he had been subservient to her wishes too long, and much as he loved her was determined to have his way.

"She came with a proposition," he told her, "to which I have agreed. Sophia Dorothea is to marry George Lewis."

Eléonore stared at him in shocked disbelief.

"Yes," he went on, "it's true. I have always been in favour of such a match and what could be better than an alliance with Hanover?"

"George Lewis!" whispered Eléonore as though she were dreaming. "That . . . *monster*!"

"Oh come, my dearest. He is but a young man."

"Yet we have all heard of his profligacy and his stable manners."

"Exaggeration! What would you expect of Ernest Augustus's son?"

"Some culture!" she said. "Some courtesy!"

"It is there all right. He is at the time enjoying a young man's freedom. He likes women. He'll grow out of it."

"I can't believe you have promised our child to him. Tell me it is not true."

"It is true."

"But without consulting me!"

"My darling, you are wise as I have learned, but where our daughter is concerned you are a little besotted. You treat her still as though she is a baby. She will look after herself."

"She will need to if ever she goes to that . . . that . . ."

"Pray calm yourself." She had never heard him speak to her sternly and with something like cool dislike. What had happened on this September morning, she asked herself, to ruin everything that was dearest to her?

She thought: I must be dreaming. This could never happen to me . . . to us.

"Calm!" she cried. "I *am* calm. It is you I think who are verging on madness."

"My dear Eléonore, prepare to make the Duchess Sophia welcome. Shortly she will be rested enough to take breakfast with us. Then she will be ready, I am sure, to talk to you of this match."

"What use of talking if it is already made."

"I thought you would wish to hear what advantages would come to our daughter when she is the wife of George Lewis."

"I see nothing but tragedy."

"You are talking like a fool."

"You are the fool . . . the heartless fool. How can we face our daughter?"

"She will have to learn to accept what her parents have chosen for her as many of us have had to do before her."

"Not both parents!" she said. "Only one of them. And I believe that parent was determined to marry where he wished." She looked at him appealingly. Had he forgotten the passionate courtship, the years of love? How could he do this to the fruit of that love—the daughter whom he loved, if less passionately, less exclusively than she did? Exclusively! When she looked at him she felt that she could hate him if what he had promised should really come to pass. Their beautiful cultured daughter in those crude coarse hands!

George Willam would not be tempted. He was afraid. He must stand firm, he told himself, particularly now. If he did not he would be a laughing-stock throughout Hanover. He had given his word. He had to keep to it—yet, witnessing the distress he had caused his wife how ready he was to waver! Knowing his own weakness he could only fight it with anger.

He said: "You have ruled too long in Celle, my dear. It is my turn to show you who is in command here."

"George William . . . I can't believe this is you. . . ."

"I have long been aware that you believed you could lead me by the nose."

"What is happening to you . . . to us?" she asked, and the tears in her voice so unnerved him that he turned sharply away from her and stared from the window.

Why had he done this? He had been led into it by the eloquence of the Duchess Sophia, by her condescension in riding through the night; he knew of the advantages of a match with Hanover; every point Sophia had brought forward was true . . . but if it caused his wife such distress he wished wholeheartedly that he had never agreed to it.

But he must show everyone that he was not led by his wife, that he had a will of his own, that when he wished to show that he was master everyone—even Eléonore—must accept this.

He said coldly : "You should go to your daughter. You should tell her of my arrangements for her future. She will have to be prepared to meet her uncle and cousin immediately."

There was a stricken silence. He believed that she was weeping for their daughter. He said her name so quietly that it was strangled in his throat. Then he turned but she was no longer there.

*   *   *

Sophia Dorothea, awake early on her birthday morning, lay in bed listening to the sounds of the castle. They were different from usual which indicated that this morning was different from others. The great day of the year; the birthday of the spoiled and petted Princess of Celle. That was what Eléonore von Knesebeck had called her. "It's true," said the Knesebeck. "There was never a Princess so doted on in all history."

"Well," Sophia Dorothea had retorted, "am I not worthy of such adulation?"

She would dance before her mirror, bowing and curtseying, admiring. She was very pretty—more than pretty, beautiful; she was told so, not only in words. She had seen the looks in the eyes of Augustus William who was soon to be her husband.

She was going to enjoy all the ceremonies of the wedding. Augustus William would be her willing slave and her mother had assured her that she would not be separated from her. The spoilt and petted Princess of Celle would be the same of Wolfenbüttel. Dearest Uncle Anton Ulrich declared he envied his son; he would be ready enough to do the spoiling.

"And we shall not be far from Celle," she had told Eléonore von Knesebeck. "We shall visit frequently." She had smiled, thinking of the celebrations there would be on such visits. "And you will be with me."

Such a marriage would not be an ordeal—just a change; and as a married woman she would have a freedom which even in her beloved Celle she lacked.

And here was the sixteenth birthday; she smiled at the four cupids and remembered other birthdays. The ritual had always been the same. Her parents came in with her gifts and they sat on the bed and opened them together, and the church bells rang out and the whole town of Celle rejoiced; and when later she rode in the carriage with her parents through those decorated streets, everyone would cheer their Princess; and the townsfolk would dance for her and sing for her and show her their devotion in a hundred ways.

The dor opened; she sat up in bed.

"Maman . . ."

Her mother's arms were empty; she looked as Sophia Dorothea had never seen her look before—as though she were ill, as though she walked in her sleep. It could mean only one thing : Some terrible tragedy had come to Celle and as thoughts rushed into her mind she was certain that her father was dead, for only the greatest calamity in the world could make her mother look like that.

"My darling !"

She was in her mother's arms. Eléonore was holding her as though all the Furies were after her. She kissed her again and again, suffocating her with the intensity of her emotion.

"Maman . . . Maman . . . is it my father?"

Eléonore's body was shaking with her sobs. She nodded.

"He is dead. . . . We have lost him?"

"No . . . no. . . ."

"Then it is not so bad."

Eléonore released her and taking her by the shoulders looked into her face; then she said : "My dearest, your father has agreed that you shall be married . . . to . . . your cousin George Lewis of Hanover."

Horror seized Sophia Dorothea, robbing her of speech. She saw a monster with protuberant eyes and big slavering jaw . . . which was as she had always imagined the cousin whom she had not seen for years. She had heard accounts of his conduct though; in the castle of Celle there had been many stories of George Lewis. The servants had sniggered when his name was mentioned. She had pictured him as an ape—able to indulge in certain disgusting functions and little else.

George Lewis who had been caught with a servant girl when he was fifteen in *flagrante delicto*. George Lewis who already kept his mistresses, who had gone to England and been obliged to return because he was unacceptable to the Princess Anne. And they would give *her* to George Lewis.

It was a mistake. She did not believe it. It was some sort of joke—some play, some charade.

"Augustus William will rescue me," she said.

"Oh, my God! What shall we do when they arrive?" cried

Eléonore aghast. "They may be here at any moment now. What shall we tell them?"

"Maman, this is not true, is it?"

"What would I give that it were not."

"Not George Lewis!"

"My darling, you have to be brave. This morning the Duchess Sophia arrivd from Hanover with . . . propositions. I was not consulted. Your father has given his consent to this marriage."

Sophia Dorothea was realizing the truth now; it wrapped itself about her like an evil dream of her childhood. It was like being lost in the forest when the trees took on the shapes of monsters and their branches became long arms to catch her and imprison her . . . for what torment she could only imagine.

"I won't," she said. "I won't."

"Oh, my darling . . ."

They held each other firmly. They wept.

"Maman! Maman! . . . never let me go," sobbed Sophia Dorothea.

*   *   *

George William took breakfast with the Duchess Sophia who was now rested after her journey.

"And your Duchess?" she asked.

"She is with our daughter."

"Breaking the good news?"

"She is explaining to her the advantages of the match."

"What a grand birthday present."

"Of course," said George William, "it is a somewhat sudden change of plans."

"But none the less welcome for that."

George William was eating little. He shifted uneasily in his chair. "Perhaps . . ." he began.

But the Duchess Sophia interrupted him. "I sent one of my men riding back to Hanover with the good news. I trust he will not have such a wicked journey as I did. But although the roads are so soggy it is easier on horseback than in the coach. He will soon be there with the good news. The bells will be ringing in Hanover this day, I'll warrant you. And Ernest Augustus will soon be here with George Lewis. What a pleasure it will be for you, George William, to entertain your brother once more."

"I shall enjoy being with him again."

"Joy for you and joy for the young people. I have a gift for the bride. I want you to present it to her with my compliments. It is a miniature of her bridegroom set with diamonds and the diamonds are exquisite. I am sure she will appreciate *them*. George Lewis's virtues are not in his looks, I fear. But I doubt not that such a beautiful girl as I hear your daughter is, will soon enchant him."

The sound of trumpets suddenly rang out.

"The watcher of the tower has seen the approach of a cavalcade. That is our welcome."

"A cavalcade! It can scarcely be the bridegroom and your brother. My messenger won't be at Hanover yet."

"It is Duke Anton Ulrich with his son and retainers. They come to celebrate my daughter's birthday."

"You must go and greet them. I understand. I will remain here. They will not wish to see me."

She was smiling sardonically as uneasily George William rose and went down to the staircase.

In the hall he found Eléonore; she seemed so changed that he wanted to tell her that this morning was a nightmare and together they would fight their way out of it. But she did not look at him; he noticed the traces of tears on her face, her unusual pallor, and that her lovely hair was slightly disordered. She seemed like a stranger.

And there was Duke Anton Ulrich with the handsome young Augustus William at his side.

"Well met!" he cried; and then stood still staring at Eléonore, it being so obvious that something was wrong.

"My lord." It was Eléonore who spoke. "We have disastrous news."

Anton Ulrich caught his breath and Augustus William cried: "Sophia Dorothea . . . she is . . . ill?"

"Sick with grief," said Eléonore.

And then George William, remembering his new determination, coldly took command. "Today it has been decided that my daughter shall be betrothed to George Lewis of Hanover."

Augustus William turned pale and reeled as though he had been struck, while Anton Ulrich's hand went to his sword and he cried : "I would like an explanation of this."

"It is simple," said George William. "The Duchess Sophia of Hanover arrived here this morning with proposals from Hanover and these I have accepted for my daughter."

"She was promised to my son!" cried Anton Ulrich.

"It is true we discussed the possibility, but nothing definite had been decided on."

"My son is here . . . I am here . . . to celebrate your daughter's betrothal to him!"

"That cannot be, for she is promised to George Lewis."

"So you have deceived us . . . led us on. . . . You have . . ."

"I have decided," said George William. "It is often that matches are discussed between parents and come to nothing."

Anton Ulrich turned in bewilderment to Eléonore. "And you . . . you are in agreement?"

She shook her head. "I suffer more than you can understand. She is my daughter . . . my gently nurtured daughter. . . . She is to be given to this . . ."

George William said coolly; "There is nothing more to be said on the subject. If you will enter . . ."

"I certainly shall not," cried Anton Ulrich hotly. "We have been insulted enough. This shall not be forgotten." He turned and signing to his son they walked to their horses.

The trumpeter on the tower stared in astonishment at the sight of the cavalcade which he had so exuberantly welcomed such a short while ago, now galloping away.

Strange events were taking place in the castle of Celle that morning.

*   *   *

Sophia Dorothea lay on her bed staring helplessly at the ceiling.

She had wept until she was exhausted. That this should have happened on her birthday was so extraordinary. Those days she looked back on as dreams of delight had led to this grim nightmare.

Everything had changed. Her mother, who had seemed like a benevolent goddess, all powerful, all loving, was all loving still but stripped of her power, and therefore a different being. Where was her father who had always been so indulgent, who had loved to watch her riding or dancing, his eyes full of pride and love? Where was he now? He was changed; he must be, for her mother had wept and begged him not to allow her to be given to George Lewis and he would not listen.

Her mother came into the room and knelt by her bed.

"Dearest Maman . . . what shall we do?"

"We must be calm, my darling, and perhaps that will help us."

"Perhaps we could run away."

"No, my pet, that could not help us."

"You will always be with me . . ."

"Always . . . always!"

"Perhaps I am not so frightened then."

"You must not be."

"Where is my father?"

"He is with the Duchess Sophia."

Sophia Dorothea shivered.

"And . . . and . . ."

"No, he is not here yet, but doubtless he will come soon."

"I dare not look into his face."

"The stories we have heard of him have been exaggerated. They often are."

"I cannot, Maman. I cannot."

"There, my dearest. Try not to cry. Let us try to think clearly . . . to plan together."

"The only plan I can think of is to run away. Perhaps Augustus William will rescue me. He is coming today."

"He has been. He came with his father. They have been told and have ridden away."

"So we are deserted!"

The door opened and George William stood looking at them. Sophia Dorothea threw her arms about her mother and looked at him fearfully.

"What nonsense is this?" he said, advancing to the bed. "I have birthday presents for you."

"There is only one thing I want," cried Sophia Dorothea. "Never to have to see George Lewis."

"What nonsense have you been filling her head with?" the Duke demanded of his wife.

"She has heard rumours of this bridegroom you have chosen for her."

"Rumours! What are rumours? Lies . . . all lies. Now, my child, this is great good fortune. You are going to be the Duchess of Hanover in good time. You will be rich and powerful . . ."

"Stop! Stop!" cried Sophia Dorothea. "I cannot bear it."

"You stop this screaming," commanded her father.

"Cannot I even weep in my misery?"

"I will have no more of these histrionics. You, Madam, are responsible. You have filled the girl's head with absurd stories. Anyone would think I was handing her over to a monster."

"He is an evil monster!" cried Sophia Dorothea. "I hate George Lewis. I love Augustus William. Oh, Father, please let me marry Augustus William."

It was a return to the old wheedling which had always been so successful in the past. He had never been able to resist giving her all the silly little gee-gaws she had coveted. It was only now when she wanted something which was of real importance that she was refused.

Only a changed man could have refused her. But he was

changed. So was her mother. Oh, yes, devastating change had come to the castle of Celle that September morning.

"Let there be an end of this nonsense," said George William. "I have a gift here from the Duchess Sophia. You should feel honoured. She is a great lady and she has ridden through the night to wish you a happy birthday and bring this present to you. Look. It is magnificent."

"A miniature?" cried Sophia Dorothea, her attention caught by the sparkling ornament in her father's hand.

He held it out to her, smiling. "There! Is it not magnificent? A picture of your bridegroom set in gold and diamonds. Could you have a more delightful gift?"

Sophia Dorothea looked at it—the heavy sullen face, that even the flattering brush of an artist could not make pleasant. The very diamonds seemed hard and cruel. She flung the ornament at the wall with such force that several of the diamonds were broken from their settings.

There was a brief silence while all in the room stared at the damaged miniature.

Thus, thought Eléonore, was the happiness of this family shattered on that dismal morning.

*   *   *

With the help of her mother Sophia Dorothea had dressed in the splendid gown which had been designed for her birthday. She was calmer but pale and the obvious signs of grief were on her face.

She must descend to the hall and receive the guests, chief of them the Duchess Sophia. Cold, hard and proud, she thought her; how different from her own beautiful mother! What shall I do? she asked herself, when I go from here to Hanover?

Eléonore was beside her—restrained, elegant and outwardly resigned. When she had recognized the impossibility of getting the decision rescinded she had given herself entirely to the task of comforting and advising her daughter. They must put up a good show in public; if they had to accept this fate they must be careful to make sure that they did so with the best possible grace and missed no advantage which could be snatched from it. "At least," Eléonore had said, "we shall not be far from each other; and you may depend upon it that nothing shall keep us apart. Some Princesses are forced to leave their own countries for others across the sea and they never visit them again. At least we shall not be parted like that." Sophia Dorothea took courage from her mother's reasoning; all through that wearying ceremony—

always before so joyous—she was aware of her; but she was aware of her father too, the man who had changed overnight and become her enemy.

Beside her father stood his chief minister Bernstorff, smiling and complacent because by a miracle—performed by the indefatigable Duchess Sophia—his future prosperity had been assured.

The Duchess Sophia hid her pleasure beneath an excess of dignity.

Proud Eléonore! So beautiful. Queen of Celle. Now her authority had been displaced by the woman whom her husband had scorned. It was like the settling of a long outstanding debt; and since the defeat of the enemy was so much an individual triumph, it could not fail to bring the utmost satisfaction.

Duchess Sophia could scarcely take her eyes from Eléonore to study her future daughter-in-law. Undoubtedly a beauty; she might even equal her mother when she was more mature. Spoiled, over indulged. They would alter that at Hanover.

Sophia Dorothea was thinking: When will this hateful day be over? She was worn out with her emotions, and it seemed long before she could return to the peace of her room.

Her mother came to help her undress and they were silent. Eléonore sat by her bed when she lay there, holding her hand.

"This is the last birthday in Celle," said Sophia Dorothea sadly. "I suppose the others will be celebrated in Hanover."

There was a finality in the words; she accepted her fate; from now on she knew it was useless to hope for release.

Eléonore was relieved, for she too saw the hopelessness of fighting against the inevitable.

The last birthday! Sophia Dorothea exhausted, slept; and Eléonore kissed her gently and crept away.

The Wedding

THE trumpeter in the tower sent out the welcome. There was bustle in the castle. For the first time for years Ernest Augustus, Duke of Hanover, was the guest of his brother George William of Celle.

George William forgot his remorse, so delighted was he to welcome his brother. They embraced; they patted each other on the back; they were both emotional over this reunion.

Beside his father stood that important young man, the Crown Prince of Hanover, George Lewis, the prospective bridegroom. Neither tall nor short he stood inelegantly slouching, his hands hanging at his side; his manner was as awkward as his figure; his features were heavy, his eyes dull, his mouth both sensuous and sullen.

When George William turned to him he did feel a wave of misgiving; but it was such a pleasure to see his brother that he was certain his son must have inherited some of his charm. George Lewis was young yet, a little shy, a little embarrassed. Thus it was when one was young.

"Come into the castle," cried George William. "We are longing to show you how happy we are to have you here."

The Duchess and her daughter did not bear this out, thought Ernest Augustus cynically. By God, he thought, what a beautiful woman she is! And even now in her grief and bitter disappointment, gracious. It is small wonder that George William has been so dominated by her, but well that he now realizes his mistake.

And the girl—she was enchanting in spite of her despair. Ernest Augustus thought her the daintiest, prettiest creature he had ever seen. She reminded him of the girls who had delighted him during his travels by their delicate beauty and charming foreign ways—so different from the frauleins of his own country.

And to marry that oaf, George Lewis, poor child!

And there was Sophia, triumphant, already thinking of this plan—to which he had had to work so hard to reconcile her—as her own. Magnificent Sophia! The grandest of them, believing so firmly that her English blood set her above them all in rank that it seemed it did.

Sophia's eyes were on her son. Cannot he even be gracious on such an occasion? she was thinking. After all the trouble to which we have gone! He is to get a girl who, though spoiled, must be one of the prettiest in Europe and with one of the biggest fortunes. He was the most pig-headed stubborn boy in the world who had surrounded his brains with such a thick crust that she defied any man or woman to find what was in them. Sometimes she thought he was quite stupid, he was so lethargic; at others he could be surprisingly shrewd. At least he had the advantage of being able to surprise. And now he was sullen, having no more wish to marry his cousin of Celle than she had to marry him. He would be wise enough though to accept the match for he realized the advantages it would bring.

It was the moment for the unhappy pair to be presented to each other.

They looked at each other squarely. George saw a child—a silly little girl. Her daintiness meant nothing to him; her beauty failed to move him; her slender grace had no charm for him. He thought of his big-busted Marie with the lewd eyes.

Sophia Dorothea saw the coarse jowls, the sullen eyes and she thought : He is all that I feared he would be.

The room seemed to tip drunkenly; the faces of those about her receded and then rushed towards her; she saw the face of her future husband distorted so that it looked like that of an ape as she swayed; had her mother not caught her in her arms she would have fallen to the floor.

Sophia Dorothea had fainted.

*   *   *

Platen, Clara's husband, came to Celle to help his master work out the marriage settlement; and the two brothers—each with his chief minister—were closeted together to deal with this matter. The odds were well in favour of Hanover for Platen worked zealously with Ernest Augustus to extract the utmost advantage; and Bernstorff worked with them to advance his; as for George William, he was so delighted to be on old terms of friendship with his brother that he was happy to concede anything that was asked of him.

"A marriage portion say of a hundred thousand thalers?" suggested Platen.

Three pairs of eyes watched George William's reaction to this suggestion. It was astonishing that he did not even blink.

"It seems fair enough," he said.

Ernest Augustus lowered his eyes. Platen was a good fellow. He would reward him for this; and it would please Clara. A title perhaps. Baron. Clara would like to be a Baroness.

A hundred thousand thalers and the estates which were already settled on the girl. This match pleased Ernest Augustus far more than the English one would have done. He doubted the Princess Anne would have received such a dowry.

Bernstorff had to make some pretence of working for Celle. He suggested that should the Princess Sophia Dorothea become a widow she should be entitled to a dower of twelve thousand thalers.

Twelve thousand thalers. A small sum when compared with a hundred thousand; yet Bernstorff managed to make it sound a good deal.

George William in any case was eager to be, as he said, reasonable. This was a contract between relations; they had no wish to bargain sordidly with each other.

He knew that he was passing his daughter into the best possible hands.

Then, suggested Platen, there was no reason why the marriage settlement should not be drawn up without delay and the two Dukes could put their signatures to it in company with the two happy young people.

No reason at all, agreed Bernstorff, rubbing his hands together and smiling at his master as though by so doing he could delude him into believing that they had come well out of the matter.

*　　*　　*

When Eléonore heard the terms of the marriage settlement she was astounded.

"It seems to me," she told George William, "that you are bewitched."

"Nonsense," retorted George William. "You have worked your-self into such a passion over this marriage that you condemn every part of it."

"You give away one hundred thousand thalers and all she will have if she becomes a widow is twelve!"

"She will always live in accordance with her rank, naturally."

"In accordance with her rank!" repeated Eléonore bitterly. "He has a mistress at Hanover. At least she should be dismissed from Hanover before Sophia Dorothea enters the palace there."

George William was silent.

"Well?" said Eléonore. "Do you agree with me?"

"Naturally he will not need a mistress now that he has a wife."

"Your brother has a wife but that does not prevent his having many mistresses, headed by that Platen woman."

"My dear, you are becoming hysterical."

Eléonore stamped her foot. "I insist that Marie von dem Bussche be dismissed from Hanover before my daughter arrives there."

"I will mention the matter," said George William.

"I will be present when you do, to add my voice to yours," she replied firmly.

*   *   *

The Duchess Sophia emitted a harsh laugh. "My dear Duchess," she said, "this woman is of no importance."

"She is George Lewis's mistress and has succeeded in making a scandal of her name."

"You have *odd* ideas," replied Sophia. "Men will have their mistresses. As long as their wives lose nothing by it, what matter?"

"How could their wives fail to lose love . . . companionship?"

"Such strange fancies! As you know the Duke of Hanover has his mistresses but I never allow them to interfere with me."

"My daughter has been brought up to respect the sanctity of marriage."

"A strange upbringing indeed! Why, as long as she sees enough of her husband to get herself children, what complaint could she have? She should be pleased rather that there are some who can amuse him from time to time. It will give her a little respite."

"You have cynical ideas of marriage."

"Worldly ones if you like. Perhaps at Hanover we are more worldly than you are at Celle. But I assure you that your daughter will have nothing to fear from her husband's mistresses."

"She has not yet signed the marriage agreement, nor given her written consent to the marriage. I have accepted much so far, but I shall stand against this. She shall not go to Hanover as George Lewis's wife while he keeps a mistress there."

"I think you are a little ... unreasonable."

"There are many matters on which we do not agree," replied Eléonore.

*　　*　　*

What a tiresome woman she was! said Sophia to Platen and Bernstorff. There they were with everything agreed upon and now Madame Eléonore was making difficulties over Marie von dem Bussche.

Ernest Augustus said: "Well, it is understandable. She is a fine woman and I admire the manner in which she is facing this. As for the girl ... she's pretty and should be enough for George Lewis until she is with child. I think we should concede this request."

Bernstorff added that the Duchess of Celle had spent a long time arguing with her husband on this point and that George William, from sheer habit, was turning to her way of thinking.

"Perhaps," suggested Bernstorff, "it would be wise to give way on this point."

"George Lewis will be furious if we do," put in Platen.

"I think," said Ernest Augustus, "that George Lewis's wishes must be ignored in this instance. If we give way, and we had better, for if we do not the Duchess may start working on her husband's resistance, then it will seem that we have granted a great concession. We shall say that we are ready to grant any reasonable request. Moreover I agree that George Lewis should not expect his wife to accept a mistress at this time. Mistresses will be for later. At the moment he must content himself with his wife."

"Then," said Bernstorff, "let us give way to the Duchess's request and the papers can go forward for signature without delay."

So, while George Lewis fumed in his apartment against the silly little girl he must take in place of his voluptuous Marie, Sophia Dorothea was writing the letter which, now that her mother had achieved the dismissal of the bridegroom's mistress, could be put off no longer.

It was addressed to the Duchess Sophia of Hanover and ran:

"Madam,
I have so much respect for my lord the Duke your husband, and for my lord my own father, that in whatever manner they may act on my behalf I shall always be very content. Your

Highness will do me, I know, the justice to believe that no one can be more sensible than I am of the many marks of your goodness. I will carefully endeavour all my life to deserve the same, and to make it evident to Your Highness by my respect and very humble service that you could not choose as a daughter one who knew better than myself how to pay to you what is due. In which duty I shall feel very great pleasure, and also in showing you by submission that I am,

Madam,

Your Highness's very humble and
Obedient servant
Sophia Dorothea

From Celle, October 21st, 1682."

"It is false, so false!" cried Sophia Dorothea; but she had written and signed it.

It was taken from her and delivered; and after that there was no need to delay further. Plans for the wedding went on with all possible speed.

*   *   *

All through the day the trumpeter on the tower was announcing the arrival of important guests. The townsfolk ran from their houses or leaned from their windows to watch the carriages rattle by. Every distinguished family was coming to the wedding, the notable exception being the Wolfenbüttels.

In the castle there was dancing and feasting and the gaiety contrasted with the misty dampness outside. Sophia Dorothea spent a long time sitting in her apartments alone, looking out at the trees and the grey water of the moat. She kept reminding herself that there was little time left; the day was fast approaching when this dear castle would no longer be her home. Instead of a castle she would live in the Alte Palais at Hanover where everything would be different; her mother, now quiet and reconciled, had tried to learn what she could of life at the court of Hanover so that her daughter might be prepared. "Keep your dignity. Remember you are a Princess and none will dare treat you with anything but respect. Perhaps you will learn to be fond of your husband." Sophia Dorothea had nodded because she could not bear to grieve her mother by letting her know the full extent of her wretchedness. They were both acting for each other; and Sophia Dorothea knew that in the last weeks she had been sharply jolted out of childhood forever.

Eléonore von Knesebeck was with her—a great comfort, for

there was one friend from whom she would not be parted. The little Knesebeck was fiercely determined to fight her mistress's battles.

One must begin to count the advantages. "I shall be the wife of the heir to Hanover," Sophia Dorothea told herself. "I shall not be far from home. The Duke smiles at me kindly. I think he will be my friend."

It was only thus that she could live through the days.

They had made her the most beautiful gown she had ever possessed; jewels were brought for her selection. She looked over them with her mother and they pretended to be interested.

If we did not pretend, thought Sophia Dorothea, we should be tempted to go out to the moat or the river and lie down there together while the waters made a covering over our heads.

Those were thoughts which brought a queer sort of comfort; but one knew all the time in one's heart that one would never reach that point. Life was there—and one kept a hold of it, desperately clinging to it, whatever happened.

The 21st November—two months since that nightmare day when everything had changed in the castle of Celle—was her wedding day.

The bells were ringing out; the streets of the town were decorated and the sounds of laughter and music filled the castle; but the laughter was not that of the bride or the bridegroom.

In his apartments the bridegroom sullenly kicked at a stool thinking of Marie whom these people had insisted on his giving up. How dared they presume to rule him! He would show them and their precious Sophia Dorothea that they could not do that for long. Marriage—a painful necessity. Oh well, he would get her with child quickly and his duty would be done.

In her apartments Sophia Dorothea was dressed in her wedding gown—a beautiful figure sparkling with jewels which were gifts from her father and the uncle who would soon be her father-in-law. But as she looked at her scintillating reflection she saw only her woebegone face. The candles were still burning although it was morning, so dark was that day and at least the weather was in tune with her mood.

She wanted to hold back time, to say : Now I am in Celle. Now I am merely the Princess Sophia Dorothea. Something will happen and this dreadful thing will not come to pass after all.

But the hours slipped by and no miracle came to Celle that morning.

Into the chapel she went just as the first rumble of thunder was heard in the distance and the rain began to hit the castle

walls, and there was gloom outside and gloom in the hearts of
the bride and her mother.

Sophia Dorothea looked at Eléonore, calm, restrained yet
tragic. Their eyes met and her mother smiled as though she were
saying : "I shall always love you, darling. You will always be the
dearest in my life; and we shall never be far apart. You are marrying this man, but his home is only twenty miles from Celle.
Remember that." "Oh, Maman, Maman," whispered Sophia
Dorothea to herself, "I will remember. It is all I want to think of
now."

Her sullen bridegroom scarcely looked at her. He mumbled
the words required of him; his hand was clammy and listless. He
disliked this as much as she did.

She shivered and then the lightning lit up the chapel and a
half second later the thunder broke as though it would shatter the
foundations of the castle. Guests looked at each other, Eléonore's
eyes were on her daughter. An omen?

But the castle stood firm against the storm. The ceremony continued and Sophia Dorothea of Celle became the wife of George
Lewis of Hanover.

Overhead the storm grew fainter; but the rain fell relentlessly
and outside it was dark as night.

Sophia Dorothea sat at the banquet, her husband beside her.
He glanced at her, summing her up. She was pretty, he could
not deny it. Too slender for his tastes and she'd be finicky, he
guessed, and know nothing. Still, she was pretty.

He smiled at her and although she shivered she was glad he
had at last seemed a little friendly.

She turned from him and watched the dancing and revelry of
those who could enjoy them, because, after all, they were not
being married.

*   *   *

In the state coach drawn by six magnificent horses, cream in
colour, sat the bride and bridegroom. They had traversed the
miles from Celle and were on the outskirts of Hanover; and
now they were aware of the welcome that town was about to give
them.

The people filled the streets; banners had been hung from
windows and sweet music filled the air.

"Long live the bride!" cried the people. "Oh, but she is
lovely!"

Sophia Dorothea could not help being touched by their welcome; their obvious admiration reminded her of her father's

subjects of Celle, and for the first time since she knew she was to marry her spirits lifted a little.

She smiled and waved her hand as she had at home and the people were enchanted with her.

It was a good marriage, they said, because it united Celle and Hanover and this enchantingly beautiful girl was bringing much needed wealth to Hanover.

"Long live the lovely Princess!" they shouted.

* * *

Clara watched the arrival from a window of the Alte Palais.

She was angry because her sister Marie had received orders to leave, and although her husband was to become a Baron, and she of course would revel in the title of Baroness, she was foiled because her sister would not be able to guide George Lewis.

He was to have no mistress for a while! That meant of course no important mistress. And Marie—sister of Clara—had received marching orders.

"Don't go," she had said to Marie. "Why should you? Once that Celle creature is here we shall know how to deal with her. I do not see why we should allow her to dictate to us. I will speak to Ernest Augustus as soon as I have a chance and you shall stay, rest assured."

So Marie had disobeyed the order to leave and now stood with her sister at the window to watch the arrival.

Here they came—in the state coach with its cream-coloured horses, her lover, George Lewis, and his bride. Marie drew aside the hangings and leaned out of the window as Sophia Dorothea was stepping from the coach, George Lewis awkwardly helping her out. Now they had turned to come into the palace and George Lewis looked up and saw Marie. So did Sophia Dorothea. And in that moment, instinctively she knew.

She turned to one of the attendants and said: "Who are the ladies at the window?"

She was told that they were Madame von Platen and her sister Madame von dem Bussche.

Calmly she entered the castle.

"Welcome to Hanover," said the Duchess Sophia who had returned a little ahead of the married pair to Hanover that she might be there to receive them when they arrived.

"Thank you," said Sophia Dorothea haughtily, "but I see that what was promised has not been carried out."

The Duchess Sophia was startled. The young bride seemed to have acquired a new authority.

"I regret that you should have cause to complain," said the Duchess, "but pray tell me to what you refer?"

"I am told that Madame von dem Bussche is in the palace although it was arranged that she should leave before I arrived."

"So she is still here!" The Duchess Sophia looked angry. "I regret this. But she shall be gone before the hour is out."

Sophia Dorothea bowed her head and requested to be shown her apartments, and to these the Duchess Sophia personally conducted her.

*   *   *

In her room Marie von dem Bussche was feverishly preparing to leave.

"This is disastrous!" she cried, between her sobs of anger. "I thought you said ..."

"I had no opportunity to speak to Ernest Augustus," replied Clara. "You should not have stood at the window. Then no one would have known you were here."

"She would have discovered in time. I thought you said she was a stupid girl whom you would be able to handle."

"She is merely not so stupid, but I shall be able to handle her!" replied Clara grimly.

"And then ...?"

"You shall come back and hold your old position with him. Don't fret. She'll not satisfy him. He doesn't want a French doll however pretty. He wants a lusty woman."

"So you think everything will be ... as it was...."

"Give him a little time with his bride. Then you shall come back. I'll see to it. Madame Sophia Dorothea will have to learn who rules this court."

Clara said goodbye to her sister and then went down to the banquet hall where she would be presented to the new bride— not, of course, as her father-in-law's mistress, but as the wife of his first minister.

*   *   *

Sophia Dorothea listened to the wheels of the coach which were carrying her husband's mistress far away. It was her first little triumph.

And George Lewis? He was far from prepossessing; he did not fill the rôle of romantic hero; but in his clumsy way he was not unkind; and he was far from being the ogre of her childhood.

She must accept her new life. The happy childhood was over. But when she sat at her window and looked out in the direction

of Celle she thought of her mother who would certainly be thinking of her at this moment; only a few miles separated them; and
soon perhaps she would have a child of her own.

This was not the happy marriage she had dreamed of; life had
changed abruptly and cruelly; but with each new phase the
shock grew less acute.

When I have a child, thought Sophia Dorothea, perhaps I shall
not mind so much.

"Mirror, Mirror on the Wall"

SOPHIA DOROTHEA was surprised how quickly she became reconciled to her new life. It was not that she fell romantically in love with her husband—far from it. She found him quite crude and coarse; but the rough awakening to the knowledge that she could not have all her own way had strengthened her, had made her realize a toughness in her character which no one—least of all herself—had expected.

Hanover was very different from Celle—less elegant, but more extravagant. The morals at Celle had been set by the Duke and his Duchess—the faithful husband and wife who had lived in perfect harmony until George William had suddenly decided it was time he exerted his authority in the important matter of his daughter's marriage. Fidelity in marriage had been the custom. It was natural that the court of Hanover should in the same way reflect the morals of its ruler. Ernest Augustus, the sensualist, with his *maîtresse en titre* and the minor members of his seraglio, set the fashion at Hanover as George William and his Duchess did at Celle. This was the shock Sophia Dorothea had to face.

It was amazing to her that the Duchess Sophia could tolerate her husband's infidelity with such unconcern; she did not hide this amazement which naturally irritated the Duchess who was always delighted to point out Sophia Dorothea's lack of knowledge of Hanoverian court custom. Life at Celle had been simple with George William and Eléonore living so constantly *en famille*. It was very different at Hanover where precedence had to be observed and where it seemed to Sophia Dorothea it was a greater crime to bow to someone who was only considered worthy of a nod than to seduce someone's wife or husband.

The Duchess Sophia could not forget that this young girl was the daughter of her old enemy; and she did all she could to discomfit her.

But in spite of this animosity there were compensations, the chief of which were the young people whom she discovered to be her cousins.

There was Frederick Augustus, about four years older than herself, who told her that he wished he had been the eldest son that he might have married her; he certainly had more grace of manner than his brother George Lewis—but then he could scarcely have had less. There was Maximilian William, about her own age—a boy of charm and mischief who showed her very clearly right from the beginning that he was ready to be her friend. The girl cousin Sophia Charlotte was some two years younger and very interested in the clothes her new sister-in-law had brought with her. Charles Philip was friendly, too, and so were the young ones, Christian and Ernest Augustus.

So after having been an only child Sophia Dorothea had the experience of finding herself a member of a large family—and this was agreeable.

There were times though when she was homesick and wanted to cry herself to sleep—and would have done but for the presence of George Lewis. Sometimes when she was alone with Eléonore von Knesebeck she would shed a few tears and they would talk of Celle where everything was so much simpler and yet more beautiful; then Sophia Dorothea would write a letter to her mother and tell her that she was getting along better than she expected yet how she longed to be with her!

But each week brought a softening of the pain as the life of Hanover became imposed on that of Celle. She would find herself laughing over Maximilian's tricks, or enjoying the envy of Sophia Charlotte.

There were days when nothing special happened. Then she would write letters or in her journal for her two favourite pastimes were writing and dressing up. She would lie late in bed and, after George Lewis had left, Eléonore von Knesebeck would come in and they would talk together often of Celle. They would work on their embroidery together, read a little; and of course the task of getting Sophia Dorothea dressed took a long time. She was learning to fit in with the ceremonious behaviour; she would go down to dinner with Eléonore von Knesebeck to accompany her and a page to lead the way, and would take her place at the head of the table in accordance with her rank and often earn the stern looks of her mother-in-law because she had smiled at someone who was not of high enough rank to deserve a smile from the wife of the Prince of Hanover.

But the little mistakes she made—usually by being too friendly to the humble—endeared her to most members of the court. And after the great midday meal when she often took an airing in her coach she would smile prettily at the people who came out of their houses to see her go by, and if the Duchess Sophia was shocked by her friendliness, the people were not.

They cheered her; and they were growing fond of her. She was the prettiest creature to come out of the court—and none of the paint and powder so lavishly used by the so-called beauties could compare with her natural charms. She was young and fresh; she was elegant and charming. It raised her spirits to know that she could charm these people as she had her father's subjects at Celle.

When she rejoined the company in the great hall for supper she would behave in a manner with which even the Duchess Sophia could not find fault; she danced exquisitely and even took a turn at playing the card games which were so popular.

Everyone was saying that George Lewis could not have found a more charming or more suitable wife.

Sometimes the court moved to Herrenhausen which was a little schloss in the country set in the midst of a charming park. The Duchess Sophia loved Herrenhausen and went there whenever she could; here the French custom of performing pastorales and fêtes champêtres was in vogue; and as the winter passed Sophia Dorothea took her part in these entertainments.

Opposite the Alte Palais was the Leine Schloss where the most important functions were held, as this old castle was more imposing than the Palais. Here Sophia Dorothea had her own apartments and it was while she was there with the coming of that new year, a few months after her marriage, that she believed herself to be pregnant.

Looking out at the limes and acacias, which made the banks of the river Leine so lovely in the spring, she thought that her child would bud and blossom with them; and that when the child was born she could be happy again.

Thus Sophia Dorothea began to be reconciled to her new life.

*   *   *

There was one who watched the progress of Sophia Dorothea with suppressed fury. Clara, now Baroness von Platen, had had a shock. In the beginning she had believed that she would have no difficulty in dealing with the newcomer. A foolish frivolous young girl, she had called her; a silly child who thought of nothing but pretty clothes and admiration; who hadn't the wits to placate her husband, the heir of Hanover.

I will soon put her in her place, Clara had promised herself. Marie shall come back and we shall be as we were.

But the girl was not as she seemed. For one thing she had been well educated under the supervision of her mother and was far more knowledgeable in languages and the arts than Clara could ever be.

And what use are they? asked Clara. I could show her things she had never dreamed existed.

Clara laughed at her own thoughts. She was a witch, said Ernest Augustus. She was skilled in the art of eroticism as no other woman he had ever known—not in France or in Italy. She could always surprise him. Thus she kept her hold on him.

If he accused her of infidelity she would retort: "Well, how am I to practise that I may appear perfect with you if I cannot make use of others?"

And that amused him. Ernest Augustus could forgive anyone who amused him. Besides, he was too much of a man of the world to expect fidelity from such a skilled woman as Clara.

Clara had the court in her hands. Clara could command and rule. At least so she had believed.

She had said: "Marie pines to be back at court. It is unfair to keep her away."

"It was in the agreement that she should be banished."

"Well, she was. Let her return now."

"Impossible, my dear. Besides, it would scarcely be fair to the Princess."

Fair to the Princess! What had that to do with it! *She* wanted it and it had to be denied her because it would not be fair to the Princess!

"She'll fight her own battles."

"Later yes, but she's a charming creature and I think beginning to settle."

"Poor George Lewis. He wants Marie back. After all, you have Marie's sister. Should you deny him his fun."

"To tell you the truth, Clara, I think he is beginning to enjoy his wife."

"But Marie amused him! Marie knows how to please a man. Surely you don't think Madame Prudery's daughter was brought up to do that."

"No, I don't. But I like to see her happier. She's a pretty creature."

He was smiling almost tenderly. That was what had sent up the danger signals.

So he too was a little taken with the fresh charm of the young bride! Clara would have to be very careful. She knew it was no use attempting to talk of bringing back Marie just yet.

She was a rich woman now, for her new title had brought estates with it and Ernest Augustus had been generous to one who had helped bring about the Celle marriage. The Baron von Platen was a useful man; not only was he an absolutely complacent husband but knew how to do as he was told—which was what Clara and Ernest Augustus told him. Such a minister was to be cherished. It was also pleasant to reward Clara so respectably through her husband. Clara naturally had the spending of the newly acquired fortune and she bought a house between Hanover and Herrenhausen which she called Monplaisir. She had added to it and entertained there so lavishly that she lured many worldly people to it from the court itself.

Ernest Augustus had looked on with amusement, and was often a guest at Monplaisir.

It was while she was staying at Monplaisir that she first realized what progress Sophia Dorothea was making. She had encouraged her attendant at Monplaisir, a girl named Ilse, to talk freely with her, for thus she learned trends and secrets it would not have been easy to discover otherwise although she had her spies everywhere.

Ilse herself was a good-looking young woman and enjoyed her position, and often she had been rewarded for her frankness.

But Ilse made her mistake.

There had been a ball at the Leine Schloss at which both Clara and Sophia Dorothea had been present. Sophia Dorothea representing Spring at this ball, had worn a plain clinging gown of green silk with flowers instead of jewels in her hair. Clara had been magnificent as the goddess of Plenty, jewels agleam, pearls sewn into a gown of great splendour.

She wanted to hear what had been said of the ball and what comments had been made about the magnificence of her gown.

Ilse told her she had heard that never had such a dress been seen before in Hanover. It was the most splendid gown of the ball.

And what had they said of Sophia Dorothea?

Oh, they had said of her that she was the loveliest of all the

women and that was it not marvellous that she could be so in
nothing but flowers and a piece of green silk.

Clara read the implication behind the words. She brought up
her hand and gave the astonished Ilse a stinging blow at the side
of her face which sent her reeling.

"But Baroness, you said . . . to tell the truth . . ."

"The truth. Are you going to tell me that that child in her silly
green silk was more beautiful than I in my gown? Do you know
what that gown cost, girl?"

"Yes, Baroness, I know . . . but you asked what they said and
they said she was so fresh and young and that Spring was more
beautiful than . . . than . . ."

"Than what?"

"I do not remember, Baroness . . . only that Spring was more
beautiful."

"Get away from me before I flay the skin off you!" cried Clara.

When the girl had gone she stood in front of her mirror biting
her lips. What was the use of pretending? Look at that sagging
line . . . look at those crowsfeet round the eyes—look how sallow
she was without her rouge! One could not live the life she lived
and remain fresh as spring. The girl was only seventeen in any
case. How could she hope to compete?

Narrowing her eyes she saw the features of Ernest Augustus,
relaxed, almost tender. "I like to see her happier. She's a pretty
creature . . ."

And he would not let Clara bring Marie back.

There was a time when no one at a court ball had had eyes for
anyone but her. She had been the queen in those days—and she
would not give up her place to anyone. To think that this girl . . .
this child . . . who knew nothing of the ways of men and women,
should come in and usurp her place just because she had a fresh
and pretty face and a few Frenchified manners!

Well, she would see.

At the moment Sophia Dorothea was pregnant. Soon she would
be unable to dance at the balls. She would have to stay in her
apartments and think of the child. Then Baroness Clara would
regain her old position. But that could only be a temporary victory.

She must be watchful; she would have to make plans for
Madame Sophia Dorothea if she continued after the birth of her
child to try to be the queen of Hanover.

In the meantime she could relax a little. But she must be careful. No one must know how she hated that young woman.

*   *   *

It was Clara's obsession now to outshine Sophia Dorothea. The entertainments she gave at Monplaisir had become more lavish than ever; if she discovered that certain people greatly admired Sophia Dorothea she endeavoured to invite them to Monplaisir when she knew Sophia Dorothea would be giving an entertainment in her apartments. Many had learned that it was unwise to offend Clara and that Sophia Dorothea would not blame them if they had a previous engagement; Sophia Dorothea, they had noticed, was sweet natured; she was not continually trying to remind them how important she was; on her her rank sat gracefully. It was not as it was with Clara.

Clara's gowns became more startling. She would spend hours with her women before her mirror and would emerge at least the most colourful woman at court.

She studied herself for signs of age. Her body had always been a greater asset than her face. It was still beautiful, even after childbearing; and she had had two children. Secretly she was not sure who their father was. It might have been Ernest Augustus or one of the pages whom she had momentarily desired one afternoon and had summoned to her bedchamber. It was of little importance, for Baron von Platen, that most complacent of husbands, obligingly accepted paternity. But the point was that childbearing did not improve the figure, and Clara had always been inclined to be sallow.

She bathed each day in milk and because she wished to earn a reputation for generosity and good deeds among the people, she allowed the milk in which she had bathed to be distributed to the poor—with bread to accompany it.

She liked to linger in her bath of milk for she felt that the longer she remained there the whiter her skin would become and one day as she lay planning what dress she would wear to put Sophia Dorothea into the shade, she called Ilse, but the girl did not come and Clara rose, put a wrap about herself and went into the adjoining chamber. The door was open on to the garden and what she saw horrified her. Ernest Augustus was leaning over Ilse, who was seated under a tree, and he was talking to her most confidentially, his hand resting on her shoulder; he was smiling— so was Ilse.

By God! thought Clara. My own maid!

She stepped into the garden, curbing her fury as she went.

"I trust I have not kept Your Highness waiting?"

Ernest Augustus turned to smile at her. He was not quick enough though. She saw the lust in his eyes. For Ilse! What had that little slut to offer? Youth! That was the answer. Youth!

She was obsessed by youth ever since she had been so blatantly reminded of it by the creature from Celle.

Small wonder that Ilse had been so insolent lately, telling her how people had thought the simply clad Sophia Dorothea more beautiful than the glorious Platen.

So ... Ilse was trying to take her place was she? She would show her!

Coolly she told the girl to go and bring refreshment for His Highness; Ilse obeyed as though in a dream. Then Clara took Ernest Augustus to her bedchamber and made savage love with him, to remind him that he would never find anyone as skilled as she was.

She made sure that Ilse brought the refreshment to them while they were in bed—that was a warning to Ilse.

When he had left she sent for the girl who might have been deceiving herself that her mistress had not noticed her duplicity.

"Come here, slut," said Clara.

Then she took the trembling Ilse by the hair, threw her across the bed and beat her until the girl cried out for mercy.

"Mercy!" cried Clara. "What mercy do you expect? How far has it gone? You had better tell the truth."

"There is nothing, Baroness. Nothing. He noticed me for the first time this afternoon and spoke to me. It was because he was waiting for you."

"And you did not come to tell me he was here?"

"He told me to wait a while."

"I see, and during that while ..."

"You came out, Baroness."

"In time!" laughed Clara. "You go to your room, girl, and stay there. Don't dare move from it until I say you may."

Ilse lost no time in running away. She tried to assure herself that the incident was not important. It was merely that the Baroness's rages were more frequent and more violent now that she was no longer considered to be the most beautiful lady of the court. Ernest Augustus had implied that he liked her. That was well. It would doubtless only be for a short time, but one did very well even so. Look at Esther! Although she had gone back again and again. Why not Ilse?

The Baroness's rage would pass. But she knew very well that Ernest Augustus took girls now and then; it did not alter his relationship with the Baroness.

While Ilse was thus musing a guard appeared at her door.

"What is it?" she cried.

"Fraulein," he told her, "I have orders to arrest you. You will follow me."

On the orders of the Baroness, Ilse was conveyed to prison.

*　　*　　*

The guard was sorry for a pretty girl like Ilse. The poor girl seemed quite stunned; it was such a sudden transition from the splendours of Monplaisir to the spinning house of a prison.

She kept saying: "I'm innocent ... innocent...." And he wanted to do something to comfort her.

He took an opportunity of speaking to her the day after she had been admitted, while he was guarding the women at their spinning.

"What have you done?" he asked.

"I've done nothing ... nothing.... The Duke stopped and spoke to me in the garden, that was all. And she saw us...."

The guard nodded. He had heard stories of the ruthless Baroness von Platen.

"He liked you, eh? Well, you could send a message to him telling him where his little chat has landed you. He's out of Hanover for a few weeks ... but when he comes back ..."

"A few weeks!" cried Ilse. "Must I endure this for a few weeks ... when I've done nothing ... when I've had no trial ... just because the Baroness hates anyone younger than herself."

"I don't reckon she'd want him to know she'd had you put here."

He looked at her; she was a pretty girl; but she wouldn't be for long if she stayed here, and he'd like to serve the girl a turn.

"Leave it to me," he said; and winked. He strutted away; he liked to feel he was engaged in intrigue.

*　　*　　*

It came to Clara's ears that her serving girl Ilse was going to petition Ernest Augustus explaining that she had been wrongfully imprisoned.

Clara was thoughtful. So far she had been able to manage Ernest Augustus, but he had refused to allow Marie to come back, and was showing a certain fondness for Sophia Dorothea. Undoubtedly he was getting fonder of younger women as he grew older—a natural habit, she supposed; but it did mean she would have to be more careful. As far as Ilse was concerned she realized she had been a little hasty. She should have kept her temper and quietly rid herself of the girl, sending her somewhere where Ernest Augustus would not have seen her again, and that would have been an end of the matter. It was all the fault of Sophia Dorothea whose coming had made a difference and set up this worship of youth in susceptible Ernest Augustus. Well, now she must settle this Ilse matter finally and she did not want the girl petitioning Ernest Augustus, who must quickly forget that he had ever seen the creature.

Immediate action was necessary.

That day she ordered that Ilse, as a disreputable woman, be drummed out of Hanover, and as a result the unfortunate girl was taken from prison, marched through the streets to the sound of discordant music, right out of the town—never to return, in accordance with that custom which had persisted for many years.

Ilse could not believe this was happening to her; she was bewildered and frightened, having nowhere to go. She realized as she stumbled along what a fool she had been to incur the wrath of the Baroness von Platen.

Exhausted, disillusioned and almost wishing for death, at length she came to a farmhouse where she begged food and shelter. This was given in exchange for work; and there she stayed a while, wondering what to do next.

*   *   *

October had come and Sophia Dorothea waited in her apartments for the birth of her child; it was a year and a month since that birthday when her life had changed so drastically and now, if she could have a child—a healthy child to whom she could devote herself—she would regret little.

Eléonore von Knesebeck was with her; the Duchess of Celle was on her way to Hanover; Duke Ernest Augustus had sent gifts and told her that he was awaiting the happy event with great eagerness; even the stern Duchess Sophia, riding back to Hanover from Herrenhausen, had expressed approval of such a prompt promise of the heir's delivery.

"Oh, Knesebeck," she said, "one grows used to Hanover."

"Then one can grow used to anything."

"My mother should be here soon."

"If she had her way she'd be here all the time."

"Except when I pay my visits to Celle. Oh, Eléonore, I am a little frightened. Is it very painful, do you think?"

"But it'll soon be over and imagine you . . . with a baby of your own."

They laughed together and Sophia Dorothea walked to the mirror, leaning on Fraulein von Knesebeck, and they compared her present state with the sylph who had arisen on that birthday morning to learn she was to be a bride of Hanover.

It no longer seemed a tragedy and they talked of it until Sophia Dorothea thought the pains were starting and a flustered Fraulein von Knesebeck hurried to call in the women.

*   *   *

Sophia Dorothea lay back exhausted but she was aware of the excitement in the bedchamber.

"A boy," they were saying. "A healthy boy."

"My darling!" It was her mother at her bedside.

"Maman, you are here then?"

"Yes, my darling. I have been here all the time. And you have come through well and you have a lovely boy."

"I want to see him."

"And so you shall."

Sophia Dorothea held him in her arms and the Duchess Eléonore thought she was like a child with a doll—her precious daughter, a mother. It seemed incredible and yet it made her so happy. The match with Hanover was not so tragic after all; George William was constantly telling her so; they had become reconciled, but she would never forget his harshness to their daughter and could not completely return to the old happy ways. Her whole life now was centred round her daughter.

There were others coming into the bedchamber. Ernest Augustus was there with Duchess Sophia and of course the chief minister Platen and his wife. The stories one heard of that woman were hard to believe on occasions like this when the Baroness remained at a discreet distance from the Duchess Sophia and behaved as if she were merely her efficient lady-in-waiting. A clever woman. Eléonore would have been very disturbed if she had been the mistress of George Lewis instead of his father. But George Lewis had been behaving like a good husband. Doubtless there were minor infidelities—a serving girl here and there (they would be very much to his taste, doubtless) but at least Sophia Dorothea was not asked to submit to the indignity of seeing a woman set up over her. But George Lewis was as crude as ever; his manners were appalling and apart from his love of music— which seemed inherent in all Germans—he had no appreciation of the finer things of life. Still, he was behaving in a manner they had dared not hope for; and of course it had had its effect on Sophia Dorothea.

Ernest Augustus seemed really fond of his daughter-in-law and George Lewis was strutting with pride in his new importance.

George William was delighted with this state of affairs and his affectionate eyes constantly informed his wife : I told you so.

The christening was a splendid occasion and it seemed a happy choice that the new baby should be christened George Augustus, after George William and Ernest Augustus—his two grandfathers.

The Duchess Eléonore remained with her daughter until after the christening and, before she left, a visit to Celle had been arranged.

* * *

Ernest Augustus was surprised when one of his servants asked permission to put a paper into his hands. This was not the channel through which documents usually reached him, and before he touched it he asked whence it had come.

"It was given to one of the servants by a poor woman, Your Highness. She said you would remember her and help her if you knew of her plight."

"I'll look at it some time."

When he opened the letter he found that it was from a woman who had once been a servant of Clara's. He could scarcely remember what she looked like, but his memory was faintly stirred. He had seen her in Clara's garden at Monplaisir once and spoken to her. Yes, he had had plans for her, for she had been a pretty creature. Then Clara had come out and found them together. Very vaguely he remembered.

So Clara had dismissed the girl from her service because of this; moreover she had imprisoned her for a while and later had her drummed out of Hanover. Rather drastic treatment for a little speculative conversation. What was the matter with Clara? She had never before minded a little waywardness because she knew he was well aware that there was not another woman like her in Hanover—possibly not in the world. However, she had treated this girl rather badly. He wondered why? Was there something very special about her?

He considered the plea. She was crying for help. She was penniless; at the moment she was working as a drudge in a farmhouse. Would he give her permission to return to Hanover and perhaps find her some humble position in the palace?

He considered.

She must have been pretty or he would not have noticed her in the first place but try as he might he could not remember what she looked like. There were many attractive girls at hand—and what would Clara say if he brought this one back? There would be trouble.

He had no desire for trouble—nor for a girl whose face he couldn't remember.

He made up his mind; she should have a small gift of money.

This he arranged to be sent to her with a warning that she would be wise not to return to Hanover.

*   *   *

After the birth of the baby George Lewis grew closer to his wife. The child was a bond between them; they were both so proud of him. Ernest Augustus, too, was a frequent visitor to the nursery; and when he found his daughter-in-law there he would stop and chat to her about the child's future.

He was growing more and more fond of her. Her beauty was so appealing. His wife could rant as much as she liked about "that piece of dirt" as she called the Duchess Eléonore, but George William's wife knew how to bring up a girl and, moreover, this one had inherited her mother's beauty. As a connoisseur of female charms Ernest Augustus could not fail to be impressed by those of Sophia Dorothea; and the fact that his relationship to her put her out of range of amatory adventure enhanced rather than diminished his admiration.

The growing respect and affection the Duke had for his daughter-in-law was noticed—and of course Clara was aware of it.

In her daily milk baths, at her dressing table, she considered her own charms and the fear that they were diminishing did not increase her good temper; she made vicious plans for the downfall of Sophia Dorothea but was unable to put them into practice. The most infuriating aspect of the situation was not so much Ernest Augustus's regard for the girl but George Lewis's, and her inability to bring Marie back to court. If she could have provided George Lewis with a mistress whom she could have commanded, Sophia Dorothea could be so humiliated that she would be running back to Celle to Maman in a very short time.

But George Lewis remained the almost faithful husband whose minor infidelities were of no importance; and with each day Ernest Augustus grew more fond of his charming daughter-in-law. She had heard though that the Ilse creature had written to him and although he had given her some small gift he had advised her not to come to Hanover. A victory, though a small one. But enough to show her that Ernest Augustus still had some regard for her, and if she were careful she could continue to hold her place. But she must be careful.

She had done her best to poison the mind of Sophia Charlotte,

George Lewis's only sister, against Sophia Dorothea. It had not been difficult, for it was as galling for a young girl as for a woman to see herself continually compared with another to her own disadvantage. Sophia Charlotte had been prepared to be quite unpleasant to her sister-in-law since she had become so jealous of her. Sophia Dorothea, who was very impulsive, Clara noted with glee, had shown quite clearly that she disliked her sister-in-law; and the animosity between them grew.

Another enemy, thought Clara. Very soon I shall bring Marie back and then we shall see. One by one they shall turn against her and then she will commit some indiscretion—for she is indiscreet. That was easy enough to see.

But then Sophia Charlotte was married to the Elector of Brandenburg—a brilliant marriage which delighted her parents more than it did Sophia Charlotte; and that meant that after the brilliant festivities she left Hanover.

One enemy the less. George Lewis went away to the army and a new pattern was set at Hanover. Sophia Dorothea spent a great deal of time with her son, living quietly, occasionally visiting Celle or receiving her parents in her home.

Ernest Augustus, who had always loved to travel, and since the marriage with Celle when he had command of Sophia Dorothea's large fortune was able to do so, decided that he would like to visit Italy again. The Duchess Sophia was perfectly capable of governing in his absence; and she was very pleased to have the opportunity.

So Ernest Augustus left Hanover for Venice, accompanied by the Platens and other friends and a few ministers, while the Duchess Sophia remained behind at Herrenhausen to govern from there. Sophia Dorothea reigned supreme in the Alte Palais or, when she gave entertainments, in the Leine Schloss. Visits to Celle were more frequent than ever; and life was very tolerable indeed.

*   *   *

Sophia Dorothea was in her apartments one day writing to her mother when Eléonore von Knesebeck ran into the room to tell her that messengers from Venice had arrived.

"Well," said Sophia Dorothea placidly, "I doubt that will concern us."

"I believe some high personage is among them."

"Who?" asked Sophia Dorothea anxiously.

"Not the Duke . . . nor the Platen woman. You can be sure one would not be here without the other."

"The Duchess is receiving them?"

"Yes, but she will expect you to put in an appearance."

At that moment there was scratching at the door and one of the pages announced that General and Madame Ilten had arrived at Hanover from Venice and the Duchess Sophia knew that the Crown Princess would wish to welcome them.

"Well," said Sophia Dorothea, when the page had left, "now perhaps we shall have a little gaiety in the Leine Schloss or even at Herrenhausen."

And she went down to greet the General and his lady.

When she heard what news they brought she was at first astonished and then delighted.

Duke Ernest Augustus thought that she must be feeling a little lonely at Hanover with so much of the court absent and that she must be in need of a little holiday. He wished her to prepare at once to leave Hanover in the company of the General and his wife and come to Italy where he would be most happy to see her. There was another reason why he wished her to be there : George Lewis had arrived from the army and would naturally be eager to see his wife.

She had never before been very far from Celle or Hanover, and the prospect of visiting a foreign city and one reputed to be as beautiful and romantic as Venice was exciting.

She turned and hugged Eléonore von Knesebeck. "What are you looking so glum about? Of course you'll come with me!"

She threw herself into a fever of preparation. The dresses she would need! The jewels!

But after the first excitement had worn off a little she thought of the less pleasant side of this adventure. She would leave her baby in Hanover, she would be far from her mother, and there would be reunion with George Lewis; she remembered it was almost a year since she had last seen him.

* * *

Sophia Dorothea was discovering herself as well as Venice. She was meant to be gay. How different was this city—a group of islands rising from the sea—compared with Hanover. The weather was clement; every day she awoke to see the sun bathing the buildings in a golden light—usually at midday, for she retired late after the balls and banquets which her father-in-law gave in his *palazzo* on the Grand Canal.

How excited she was by all the exotic sights! She would gaze in rapture at the marble palaces on the water's edge, at the gondolas gliding past on the Grand Canal, at the Rialto where on more than one occasion, masked and wrapped in a concealing cloak, she and Eléonore von Knesebeck had wandered together.

Ernest Augustus was delighted with her excitement.

"My dear," he said, "I feel I am seeing it for the first time through fresh young eyes. I did not know how jaded I had become."

He would have her with him as much as possible—his honoured little guest.

Clara was watching carefully. She would soon have to take action against Madame Sophia Dorothea. She had been enjoying Venice until the girl had come, for Venice was a city for adventure. She had had her Venetian lovers and would have others. Each day brought new promise of excitement; and now here was this girl to delight Ernest Augustus with her naïve pleasure in foreign places!

She gleefully noticed that the resumed relationship between husband and wife was an uneasy one. It had never been one of passionate devotion, certainly, rather of compromise—and now they were both a little older (Sophia Dorothea must be nineteen) and compromise was not good enough. George Lewis had returned from the army where doubtless he had indulged in many a ribald adventure and was even more coarse than when he had been away; as for Sophia Dorothea she had had a year free from his unwanted embraces and was showing even less inclination for them than before. She had not become less fastidious—but more so.

George Lewis often looked sullen when his eyes rested on his wife. She was undoubtedly lovely, but he was unappreciative of her sort of beauty. The beautiful paintings in the palaces here and the architecture meant little to him. They were just pictures and buildings; and the charm of the Piazza San Marco was solely the opportunity of finding a willing woman there.

Sophia Dorothea was different. What could be expected of one brought up by the cultured Duchess of Celle? She was deeply aware of the beauty of Venice, but at the same time she was willing to throw herself, with all her newly awakened youthful zest, into the enjoyment of a life hitherto unknown to her.

The carnival was in full progress. Sophia Dorothea blossomed in the thrill of it all. Ernest Augustus bought her a Venetian gown and Venetian jewels because he wanted everyone to appreciate the beauty of his daughter-in-law. Why not, thought Clara, it was her money he was spending, though no one would have thought it, so magnanimously did he bestow his gifts, so charmingly and gratefully did Sophia Dorothea receive them.

Clara observed that Sophia Dorothea was something of a coquette. And why not? The Venetians were well versed in the arts of flattery—something of which George Lewis had never heard. This intricate preamble of flirtation and invitation was unknown to him, and Sophia Dorothea would naturally find it as exciting as all the novelties she was experiencing.

Perhaps, mused Clara, it would be possible to bring about the downfall of Sophia Dorothea through a lover.

While she was pondering this George Lewis had to leave for Naples and Ernest Augustus decided that before he himself returned to Hanover, which state matters demanded he should before long, he would like to show his daughter-in-law Rome.

Thus while George Lewis travelled to Naples, Ernest Augustus and his party went to Rome.

*   *   *

Sophia Dorothea found Rome as enthralling as Venice and it was Ernest Augustus's great pleasure to show her this city. Clara looked on with disgust. He was like a boy, riding in his magnificent carriage through the streets with his excited daughter-in-law beside him. Of course this rôle was a minor one in the days of Ernest Augustus. He must entertain lavishly wherever he went —and since the Celle marriage he had money to spend. He had come to Italy on state affairs naturally and had arranged that troops of his soldiers should work for the Venetians; he had charged a high price, for the Hanoverian armies had a good reputation; and now he felt affluent and he had always been a man who, having money, liked to spend it.

So the entertainments he gave in Rome were every bit as splendid as those he had given in Venice, and Clara had ample opportunity of trying out a little experiment she had planned for the downfall of the girl who was in her thoughts too often for her peace of mind.

There could be no doubt that the most admired woman in the party from Hanover was the Crown Princess Sophia Dorothea, and all Clara's splendid jewel-decked gowns and cosmetics could not alter this.

There was a man—not particularly young for he must be approaching forty—in Rome at this time who was noted for the gay life he led; he was tremendously wealthy and spent his life going from one adventure—mostly amatory—to another. But at the same time his wit and his bravery were a legend.

Clara, dancing with him at one of Ernest Augustus's balls, noticed with inward anger that although he paid her delicate compliments and might be prepared to spend a few hours of the night with her if she pressed the matter, his attention was not with her. He might deceive others by his burning looks and flattering compliments but she was as skilled in this art as he was and she could not be deluded.

There was someone else on whom attention was directed and she could guess who it was.

"You have noticed our little beauty," she said.

He answered: "How happy you must be to have such an enchanting creature at your court."

"But naturally," answered Clara. "It gives us all great pleasure merely to look at the pretty creature."

"So fresh . . . so *vestal.*"

"Oh, she is a mother, so she scarcely qualifies for that description. Did you ever see anyone so abandonedly joyful?"

"Rarely."

"You have not met her?"

"It is a pleasure I am storing up for myself."

"You should not leave it too long. The Duke might decide that we return to Hanover."

"That would be calamitious. To be deprived of your society . . ."

"And not having discovered the delights of that of the Princess."

"You alarm me. I have never been so conscious of the passing of time."

"Come, I will present you to her."

"Why are you so good to me?"

His eyes, crinkled attractively with the first signs of too-good-living, smiled into hers. They understood each other. She who had been the fairest was so no longer; she could not hide from him the fact that she hated her rival. What did she want? The fresh young beauty defiled! He was sure—his infinite knowledge helping him in this deduction—that Sophia Dorothea had never had a lover before. The husband could scarcely be called that. The enchanting Princess was unawakened . . . physically; and when awakened she would be more enchanting than ever.

Jealous Clara was offering him the exquisite task of bringing understanding of the ways of love to the delightful creature. He was always a man to accept a challenge.

* * *

"How delightfully you dance! I could swear you learned in France."

"My mother was French."

"So you are partly French. No wonder I felt drawn towards you."

"Perhaps my mother knows you. She knew most of the noble families of her country."

"Heaven forbid."

He raised his eyes to the ceiling and Sophia Dorothea laughed as she danced a few steps from him, returning as the dance ordained, to put her hand into his. "Have you such a shocking reputation then?"

"Completely shocking. If your mother knew that your hand was in mine at the moment she would send out the guards of Celle to arrest me."

"She would do no such thing. She would invite you to Celle to discover whether you were as wicked as your reputation."

"Then I should be able to tell her that having met her beautiful daughter I was set on the path to reformation."

"So I have that effect on you?"

"In the subtlest of ways."

"Pray explain."

"All my life I have flitted from one adventure to another, seeking . . . I now know always seeking."

"Seeking what?"

"What was the object of every knight's search: The Holy Grail."

Again she laughed, gaily, youthfully—innocently he thought; and innocence was a quality so attractive because one longed to destroy it. "Monsieur de Lassaye," she said, "it surprises me that you should be in search of the Holy Grail."

"It was symbolic," he said. "It means Perfection. That is what I seek and mon Dieu, I believe I have found it. I never heard anyone laugh as you do, nor saw such beauty in a face."

"And I have heard of your adventures . . . in love and in war."

"They were the adventures of the seeker."

"What a dull life he will have when he reaches his goal!"

"Madame la Princesse, I assure you that his life will only then begin."

No one had ever spoken to her thus before; she was excited; the ball, the carnivals, the admiration in the eyes of men and particularly this man who attracted her, had alarmed her a little. He had the air of having lived through a thousand adventures such as she, with her limited experience, could only guess at.

"I . . . I don't know how you can be sure of that," she said.

"I could assure you . . . by proving to you."

"But, Monsieur le Marquis, what have I to do with this?"

"Everything, Madame la Princesse, everything!"

She was faintly alarmed; he came too close; she thought his
eyes were like those of a satyr and she was conscious of a great
urge to know more of him, to understand something of the world
of romance and passion of which he was a habitué. Lust as
practised by George Lewis had shocked her; the Marquis de
Lassaye would give it a different name, a different aspect. She
felt as though she were standing at the edge of an inviting lake,
the waters of which were lapping about her feet. She longed to
plunge in and float effortlessly, lightly supported by the exciting
Marquis; but she greatly feared that one as inexperienced as she
was would quickly be submerged.

But while she stood at the edge, gently dabbling with her toes,
she was safe.

So she listened to his talk and the more she listened the more
excited she became; and that night as she lay in her bed she
could not sleep for thinking of him and the possibility of sharing
his adventures.

*   *   *

He was always at her side. His conversation was stimulating to
her senses and her mind. He told her about his estates in France
and life at the court of Versailles. There was nowhere else in the
the world like it. She should come to Paris. He was sure Louis
would be delighted with her; he was addicted to beauty and
such as hers would startle even the Court of France.

It was all so pleasant to listen to. Her mother had talked so
often of France and never had she met anyone who knew that
country so well; even her mother had been long exiled from it.
But all this conversation was leading towards that inevitable end.
She contemplated it and shivered, for once it had been reached
there was no turning back. She thought of her mother who believed
that husbands and wives must be faithful to each other and had
brought her up to believe the same. But then her mother had
married a good and charming man who had loved her deeply;
theirs had been as romantic a story as any could be. It had been
easy for her mother. But how would she have fared married to
a man like George Lewis who, in Naples, was no doubt playing
the usual rôle of unfaithful husband.

But his affairs had no bearing on hers. She was excited by this
man; and although she drew back from taking the plunge, it was
very pleasant to stand on the brink contemplating it.

*   *   *

"A letter," said Eléonore von Knesebeck, giggling happily. "No need to ask whence that came."

"He has dared to write to me!"

"He would dare anything," cried Eléonore sighing.

"I believe *you* are in love with him."

"It would be easy to fall in love with such a man."

"If my mother could hear you, Fraulein von Knesebeck."

"If she could *see* you, Madame la Princesse . . ."

They laughed together. Eléonore von Knesebeck was a good companion, a good friend, they had grown up together and she could not imagine her life without her, but was she wise, was she discreet? She was the sort who would go along with her mistress in an affair like this, urging her on to recklessness. Such a thought sobered Sophia Dorothea.

"Sometimes," she said, rather breathlessly, "I am a little frightened. Where is this leading?"

"Why should you not enjoy your life? Others do. Look at Baroness von Platen. She has a good time."

"I should not care to be like her," said Sophia Dorothea.

"Oh she is wicked they say. Do you know what they call her in Hanover: *Die Böse Platen*. They know it. There was that poor girl Ilse."

"Yes, I heard about Ilse. No, I should not care to be like the Baroness von Platen."

"Are you going to read this letter?"

Sophia Dorothea took it. It was written in flowery terms, and was both eager and hopeful.

She thought: If we progress at this rate in a week he will be my lover.

Before Fraulein von Knesebeck's astonished eyes she tore up the letter.

*   *   *

She was aware that Clara was watching her . . . hopefully. Did Clara want her to become the mistress of the Marquis de Lassaye? Why? Was it because she wanted to bring her down to her level? Was it because she hated her so much that she wanted to make trouble?

Sophia Dorothea was frightened. *Die Böse Platen* indeed! Was it not Clara who had presented the Marquis to her?

She was cool to him when he approached her. He was wounded, but she could not explain to him—nor had she any wish to. She wanted to leave Rome, and was suddenly filled with a desire to see her son.

Perhaps she had been too long away.

The Marquis was more than hurt; he was angry. He was not accustomed to being so slighted, and he had wagered with Clara that the Princess would be his mistress in a matter of weeks.

That girl is sly, thought Clara. Too cautious to take a lover. Well, we shall see what happens when the right one comes along.

Meanwhile Ernest Augustus was restless. State matters called him back to Hanover and he could not stay away indefinitely.

He told Clara to make ready for the journey home and apologized to Sophia Dorothea for taking her away from her pleasures.

"I have a fondness for Hanover," she told him; "and I long to see little George Augustus."

Not George Lewis, Ernest Augustus noticed; for his son should be back in Hanover by the time they returned. Well, who could blame her for that? She would be more dissatisfied with her husband than ever now she had seen how charming and gracefully some people behaved.

But she had her son. He hoped she would soon have more. He told her that it had been a pleasant sojourn and her company had given him pleasure.

It delighted him to have a beautiful daughter-in-law whose dowry had made him so rich.

*   *   *

So back they came to Hanover and life went on as though there had been no interruption.

Very soon Sophia Dorothea became pregnant and in due course her daughter was born.

A daughter was a great disappointment and there was not the ceremony that had attended the birth of George Augustus, but Sophia Dorothea was delighted with the child.

She was named after her mother who gave herself up entirely to the care of little George Augustus and Sophia Dorothea.

George Lewis found no pleasure in his wife's society, nor she in his. After their separation she seemed more remote than ever and he to her more coarse.

She was less docile than she had been and often did not hide the repulsion he aroused in her. She allowed it to be known that she found him coarse and uneducated. Clara saw that her comments always reached him.

Thus during the months which followed the birth of little Sophia Dorothea relations between the Crown Prince and Princess of Hanover became very strained.

Schulenburg Selected

ELÉONORE, Duchess of Celle, was writing to her daughter when one of her servants came to tell her that a woman had come to the castle and begged an interview.

"Madame, she is so persistent and refuses to be sent away."

"In any case she should not be sent away," said the Duchess. "Bring her to me."

The young woman was brought to her and Eléonore saw at once that although she appeared thin and was clearly wretched, she had at one time been good-looking.

As soon as she was brought to Eléonore, she fell to her knees and remained there.

"You are in need?" asked Eléonore gently.

"Dire need, Madame."

"Well, they shall give you food."

"Madame, I want more than food. I want a chance to tell you how I came to be in these circumstances. I could tell you so much about . . . Hanover and the Princess and . . ."

"What are you saying?" asked the Duchess.

"That I was in the service of the Baroness von Platen and there I knew something of the intrigues which went on around the Crown Princess, your daughter."

"Your name?" asked Eléonore.

"It is Ilse, Madame. I was falsely imprisoned by the Baroness because the Duke of Hanover noticed me. Since than I have been persecuted."

"First you shall eat," said Eléonore. "Then you may tell me your story."

So it was that Eléonore learned how Ilse was imprisoned and drummed out of Hanover through the wickedness of the Baroness von Platen. But what interested her more was Ilse's certainty that the Baroness was working against her daughter and was jealous of the Duke's friendship for her.

Sophia Dorothea was so innocent she might not recognize wickedness when she saw it. She must be warned against this woman.

Eléonore gleaned all she could from Ilse and offered the girl a place in her household which Ilse gratefully accepted.

News travelled quickly between Celle and Hanover and Clara had her spies planted in every branch of the Celle household; so she soon knew that Ilse was installed there and was moreover betraying to the Duchess of Celle details of the private life of Clara von Platen.

*   *   *

From Herrenhausen, the Duchess Sophia looked on world affairs and the centre of these for her was England. Ever since as a child she had listened to her mother talk of England she had dreamed of herself as Queen of that country. Although she had never seen it she could picture it all so clearly. Whitehall in sunshine or the steamy mist of the nearby river; Hampton which Wolsey had first made sumptuous and then passed over to his King; Kensington; crowded streets which had been made merry during Charles's reign with milkmaids and maypoles and ladies and gallants. She read in English in order to keep herself fluent; she talked with the English ambassadors; and visitors from that country were made especially welcome.

During the last years her excitement had increased because Charles had died and James his brother had been turned from the throne by William of Orange and James's own daughter Mary, because the people of England refused to have a Catholic monarch. Sophia herself was thankful that she was a Protestant. For religion itself she had little feeling. It was useful to keep those less intelligent than herself in order; therefore it served a good purpose. But she would have been like Elizabeth of England ready to adjust herself, or Henri Quatre of France who had declared Paris to be worth a Mass. They were the wise ones. And what ruler had served England better than Elizabeth? What King had served France better than Henri Quatre? Louis—le Roi Soleil—could not compare with his great ancestor for all his magnificence and grandiose schemes of conquests.

England, that mecca, had become less remote in the last years. Sophia felt that she was approaching that moment when she might reach out her hand and take it. For William and Mary seemed unable to produce an heir. Neither was healthy and the Princess Anne was almost an invalid. All that was needed was for these people to die without heirs and since the English would not tolerate a Catholic monarch the Duchess Sophia would be the next in succession.

One day messengers might come to Hanover, kneel before her and say : "Your Majesty . . ."

Queen of England. Ruler of that island which had filled her dreams since she was a small child !

But there was one fear : encroaching age. How ironical if that call came when she was too old and infirm to leave Hanover ! Then the honour would go to one who would have no appreciation of it : George Lewis.

And how would George Lewis fare in England? He had already given some indication when he had gone to woo the Princess Anne and had returned so ignobly.

This German custom of making the eldest son sole heir was sometimes an infuriating one. It would be impossible of course to give to any of her other sons the honour of the English throne if it ever came to that. The line of succession could not be tampered with. But how she wished that George Lewis was not the eldest. Frederick Augustus was more attractive; Maximilian was charming and amusing, though mischievous; and Charles Philip the next in age was a delightful boy. He had more of a sense of duty; his manners were good. She loved her children—with the exception of George Lewis, and Heaven knew she had tried enough to love him but he made it difficult—but of them all Charles Philip was the favourite. He was now in his mid-teens, a handsome boy who could be grave as well as gay.

Why, oh why had not Charles been the first-born ! She believed that she could have faced with serenity the prospect of seeing herself too old to ascend the throne of England if she could have contemplated Charles taking her place.

When the boys talked to her contemptuously of their eldest brother, when they deplored the fact that the bulk of their father's possessions would go to him, they were very dissatisfied, and how could she help but commiserate with them?

*   *   *

If Sophia Dorothea found her husband growing more and more
uncongenial, at least she found pleasure in the society of his
brothers. Her two special friends were Charles, who was the most
charming, and Max, who was amusing; and she enjoyed entertaining these two in her apartments.

It was no use trying to hide from them that she suffered from
the boorish treatment of her husband. They knew and condemned
his behaviour.

"Where he picked up his manners I can't imagine," said
Charles.

"In the army," answered Maximilian, springing to his feet,
saluting and marching round the apartment managing to look
so much like George Lewis they were all helpless with laughter.

"Max ... you shouldn't!" reproved Sophia Dorothea, for of
course they were not entirely alone; they never were, and in the
antechamber some of her women and the Prince's servants would
be together. Eléonore von Knesebeck was with them too although
very often she sat with her mistress, being no ordinary attendant,
but, as Sophia Dorothea called her, "the confidante". No one was
more indignant about the behaviour of George Lewis than Fraulein von Knesebeck and she was apt to complain—not always with
discretion—about it to people who would delight in carrying tales
either to the spies of Clara von Platen or to the friends of George
Lewis.

"I made you laugh at least," retorted Maximilian, settling
himself on a stool and looking up at her. "And to think that he
will one day be the ruler of us all. We will be nothing and be
forced to obey him ... George Lewis!"

"You talk too much, Max," Charles warned him.

"It's my open nature. There are intrigues going on all about
us. Why shouldn't we talk of them? Grievances should be brought
out of the dark places and examined. How otherwise can we have
the remotest chance of rectifying them?"

"How can you rectify the law of the land?" asked Sophia
Dorothea.

"Sweet sister," cried Maximilian, kissing her hand, "it has been
done."

"My mother would be with us, I believe," said Charles.

"Depend upon it!" replied Maximilian. "Whither her sweet
Charles goes there would she be."

"Indeed she would not—if she felt him to be in the wrong."

"Would she fight for her rights?" asked Maximilian. "She
accepts *die böse Platen* almost as a friend."

"She is watchful," suggested Charles.

"Yes, but to see the way that woman leads our father would infuriate most wives."

"Our mother is not merely our father's wife."

"No, no! Whisper it. She may be the future Queen of England!"

"Hush. Indeed you talk too much, Max."

"Very well, we will leave our mother and talk of Platen. I would like to see her put away. Who would not? She is clever. Sometimes I think that there are women who far exceed our sex in cleverness. My mother, cultured, shrewd, aloof. I am sure she rarely fails to get her away. And Platen, that painted whore of Babylon ... that ..."

"Hush!"

"I will not hush, brother. Is she not painted? Is she not a whore? And has she not made a Babylon of Hanover? It is not even that she is our father's faithful mistress. *She* is the one to watch. She blooms most youthfully. Have you noticed how her complexion grows ruddier and ruddier ... and more like a rose every day."

"She becomes raddled," said Charles.

"Yet she would have us believe it is just the glory of youth. They say though that a good test of whether a lady be rouged or not is to apply water in which peas have been boiled to her cheeks. The water is squirted into the victim's face and the rouge immediately turns to green or some such shade."

"What nonsense!" cried Sophia Dorothea laughing. "And why put to the test what we well know to be truth."

"To discountenance a fiend who has done her best to harm a sweet princess," cried Max, bowing low and kissing the hand of his sister-in-law.

"I advise you not to incur the anger of Madame Platen. Have you never heard what happened to a serving girl of hers named Ilse?"

"Sweet sister, I am no serving girl. I am a Prince of Hanover who is about to be robbed of his rights because of some old custom of our land. Now if I were passing over my inheritance to our handsome Charles here perhaps I should not be so enraged ... or should I? Who shall know because I am not. I am passing it to George Lewis ... who, Madam, although he be your husband, an honour which he has done nothing to deserve, I find the most loathsome toad in Hanover."

"Stop making speeches, Max," commanded Charles. "I will call some of them to make up a card party."

*   *   *

There was a large assembly in the great hall. Supper was over and there would be some dancing and games of ombre or quadrille. Clara was magnificently gowned and behaved as though she were the Duchess, for neither Ernest Augustus nor the Duchess Sophia were present. As for the Crown Prince and Princess, Clara had little regard for them, and since everyone knew by now that if they wished for any concessions it was well to obtain them through the Platens—which meant through the Baroness naturally —they were all prepared to pay her homage.

Her velvet and satin gown was of a deep scarlet shade which made her dark hair look magnificent; she was certainly the most colourful woman in the room, her cheeks aflame, her eyes blackened, her lips scarlet.

George Lewis had arrived with his wife, but he was soon slouching in a corner having no desire either to dance or play cards.

Sophia Dorothea had decided to play and was settling down with Fraulein von Knesebeck and Charles Philip when Maximilian approached Clara. Clara was unsure of Maxmilian. She suspected him of being an enemy and tales of his disrespectful comments concerning herself had been brought to her.

He bowed over her hand, and lifting eyes which were full of mischief cried : "How beautiful you are tonight, Baroness!"

"Thank you," she answered cautiously.

"Such blooming health. Tell me how do you acquire it? I should dearly love to know."

Then lifting his right hand in which he was holding a bottle he squirted what she believed to be water into her face.

There was a tense silence through the hall. Sophia Dorothea had half risen in her chair and murmured : "Oh no, Max . . ."

"A little test," Maximilian was saying. "Pea water, Madam, which I found in the kitchen."

Clara put her hand to her face and hurriedly left. As she went she heard the irrepressible titters; she ran to her apartment eager to shut out the roar of laughter which she knew must be filling the hall.

*   *   *

She faced Ernest Augustus.

"I have been insulted by that boy. I'll not endure it. Pea water! And right in my face! My dress is ruined. He must be severely punished for this."

"Max is a problem," murmured Ernest Augustus.

"He is, and I am learning quite a lot about that young man. But in the meantime I want the whole court to know that no one insults me and escapes punishment."

"What can one do with such a boy?"

"Boy indeed! He is old enough to know better. But let him be treated like a child. That will wound his dignity more than anything. Shut him in his room and let him live like a prisoner on bread and water. It should help to curb his spirits."

Ernest Augustus as usual agreed with his irate mistress and as a result Maximilian found himself locked in his room for three days, there to brood on the folly of making public attacks on the dignity of his father's mistress.

*   *   *

His servants were fond of him and eager to show their devotion, and even at the risk of being betrayed to the Baroness von Platen they smuggled his two brothers to his room. Frederick Augustus, being the eldest, felt much more strongly than the others about being passed over in favour of George Lewis and he believed that the rest of them should band together to protest against this.

"See how we are treated!" he cried. "You play a small joke on our father's mistress and you are locked in your room on bread and water. Are you a child to be treated so?"

"I am not and I'll not endure it. Tell me, what should we do?"

"We should make plans," suggested Frederick Augustus. "After all I am but a year younger than George Lewis. Are we going to give up everything for that boor?"

"Never!" cried Max.

"Then let us put our heads together."

The schemes were scarcely serious, but they discussed them zestfully, for it soothed their wounded vanity to plan. They did not know that they were being spied on; that almost every damning word they uttered was carried to Clara.

*   *   *

Clara had been receiving mournful letters from Marie who had now become a widow. She was bored. Hadn't Clara promised her that she would bring her back to court to give her an opportunity of being George Lewis's dear friend once more?

Clara was ruminating on the desirability of this and cursing the fact that a promise had been given to ban Marie from court at the time of Sophia Dorothea's marriage to George Lewis, when she heard that the young men had been plotting together.

She considered how best this could be used to advantage, and when she considered the friendship between Sophia Dorothea and her brothers-in-law, she had an idea. She could scarcely wait to

see Ernest Augustus, but decided to choose the best time of all for
secret conversations which were destined to end in the extraction
of a favour.

So it was at night that she talked to him.

"Your sons are growing troublesome," she told him.

"That affair of Maximilian," he began.

"Oh that . . . that was a childish folly not meant to be taken
seriously."

She put her face close to his and with a sensuous movement let
her fingers stroke his back.

"I fear they are banding against you."

"What . . . the boys!"

"Well, you see why. They think George Lewis gets too much
and they too little."

"He is the eldest. Don't they understand that?"

"They understand the custom but that doesn't mean they like
it."

"Their likes and dislikes are not important."

"To them they are."

"What have you discovered?"

"That their plots are a little more than boyish pranks."

"They will be watched."

"You may trust me to do that. But there is someone else involved. She is very friendly with them and they are constantly in
her apartments. It is there they meet to hatch their little plots.
You know to whom I refer?"

"Not Sophia Dorothea?"

"Yes, your angelic little daughter-in-law is not averse to plotting against you."

"Oh . . . she is incapable of that."

"Is she? She is quite capable of luring your sons on. She's a
deep one, that little bird of ours. I have never been deluded by
all the dainty charm . . . as you have."

"So she has been planning against me?"

"She has brought a fortune to Hanover and doesn't forget it.
Perhaps she feels she should have some say in how that fortune is
spent."

"My dear, you exaggerate."

"I don't think so. She hates George Lewis but is very fond of
her brothers-in-law. It would be a sort of revenge on him for
being what he is—the biggest boor in Christendom—and on you
for spending the money which she looks on as hers."

"I can't believe she is vindictive."

"You have always thought so highly of her, but you'll learn.

My dear, there is one thing I want to ask of you, and I do beg
of you to grant this small request."

"Well?"

"It's Marie ... my sister. She is bereaved and so sad and
lonely. Is it still necessary to banish her?"

"It was the promise given ..."

"So long ago. And did not your daughter-in-law promise to be
dutiful? And she has been plotting with your sons. If they were
not so young and flighty that could be dangerous. Let Marie
return. I ask it."

Ernest Augustus grunted and rolled on to his back. He was
staring into the darkness thinking of his sons, growing up plotting
against him. And Sophia Dorothea—the lovely girl whom he had
begun to think of as his daughter—working with them! Clara
exaggerated, of course, because she was jealous of Sophia
Dorothea's youth. But, by God, if the girl was ungrateful to him
why should he bother to protect her from the possibility of her
husband's giving up his casual mistresses for a permanent and
clever woman who would attempt to rule him?

"Let her return then," he said. "She has been banished for a
long time ... and she is a widow now."

Clara exulted in the darkness. Victory! Now she could go into
action against her enemy, and Ernest Augustus, piqued by her lack
of affection for him, would shrug his shoulders and let his dainty
daughter-in-law take care of herself.

*   *   *

There was a brilliant assembly in the great hall. Clara was
there, so were the Crown Prince and the Princess. The Princess
was seated at the card tables; and the Crown Prince, surrounded
by a group of his friends, young men as crude as himself, was
yawning and idly surveying the women.

The Princess was intent on her cards and Clara noticed that
Charles Philip was at her table.

Now was the moment. She signed to a plump young woman
who had come into the hall and taking her by the hand approached George Lewis.

"I wonder," said Clara smiling gaily, "whether Your Highness
remembers my sister, Madame von dem Bussche?"

George Lewis looked startled.

"Oh, yes, I remember her."

Marie curtsied, leaning forward to show her half-exposed bosom
to better advantage and lifted her big and beautiful eyes to his
face.

"I thought perhaps Your Highness would wish to know that she is back at court."

"I'm glad," he said.

Clara took Marie by the hand and made her advance a few paces to stand beside George Lewis. Then she left them together.

"The court has changed a little since I left."

"It's a long time," mumbled George Lewis.

"To me it has seemed a lifetime. But I solaced myself with memories of Hanover . . . and Your Highness."

"Yes," said George Lewis. Erotic images came and went in his mind. He had grown up since those days. His sexual education would never stand still. And here was Marie back again—the woman whom he had remembered during those first weeks of marriage when he had been sullen and angry with his wife because she was not his mistress, when he had tried to impose Marie's physical presence on that of his wife in order to make love to her —and failed because his imagination was not strong enough to be of much use to him. But there had been many others since Marie.

"I was wondering how much everything had changed. I haven't seen the gardens yet. They must be very pleasant. I hear that His Highness the Duke has had many changes made since your marriage enabled him to."

It was a mistake. George Lewis did not like references to the great affluence which Sophia Dorothea had brought to Hanover. He frowned and looked at Marie; she had grown older and she did not stir him as she once had.

"I was wondering if Your Highness would be so gracious as to show me the gardens . . ."

It was an invitation—a reminder of alfresco meetings.

He hesitated; he was not quite sure whether he wanted Marie to be his partner for the night. In fact he had had his eye on another young woman and she was only waiting for the summons.

Clumsily he agreed to escort her but the cool evening air was not conducive to passion and in his crude way George Lewis made it clear during that garden walk that he had no intention of returning to the relationship which he had once enjoyed with Marie.

*   *   *

In the apartments assigned to her in the Hanover Palace Marie lay on her bed and gave way to her passionate rage.

"So I have been kept away too long! Why did I ever come back? They are all laughing at me. They know what's happened.

And at the moment he's doubtless sniggering about me with that low German whore . . ."

"Be silent," said Clara. "It's a bitter disappointment, I admit. I can't see that you've become less attractive while you've been away."

"He's changed. He's more of a boor than ever. There's only one thing I'm thankful for. I don't have to submit to him and his soldier's lust."

"Don't be an idiot, Marie. You came here to continue as his mistress, and if you had been able to get back into favour we should have had him on leading strings. That was what we wanted, for now that he's getting older he's beginning to become more important in Hanover. Has it ever occurred to you what would happen if Ernest Augustus died? We should be where we were when we first came to Osnabrück. Do you remember? The poor Meisenburg girls . . . looking for a place?"

"We should never go back to that . . . with all you have managed to put away."

"No, but there are many people here who would like to see me lose my power. It's a great blow that George Lewis doesn't want you now."

"What am I going to do? Stay here . . . and hope?"

"It's too undignified. I'll have to find a worthy husband for you and you can settle down to be a virtuous wife."

"Well, providing he's rich enough . . ."

"He will be."

"And what of George Lewis?"

"He's a problem. Imagine if one of my enemies became his mistress. Then there would be trouble."

"It mustn't happen."

"Don't worry. I'll see that it doesn't. But it's a blow, my dear sister. I had counted on you."

*   *   *

Clara was delighted to discover Ermengarda Melusina von Schulenburg, the daughter of a poor nobleman, who believed that it might be possible to make her way at court. She had been presented to the Baroness at Monplaisir and as soon as Clara saw the girl she was interested in her.

She welcomed her to her house and suggested a visit, and while Ermengarda was with her Clara devoted a great deal of time to her, which was very flattering.

Clara would give the girl tasks which brought her to the bedchamber but she was always careful that she did not appear on those occasions when Ernest Augustus called at her house.

It seemed to Clara, who since Marie's failure had been desperately seeking the right girl, that she had found her. She thought a great deal about Ermengarda. In the first place she was outstandingly beautiful and just a little stupid. No, perhaps not stupid but . . . malleable. She was the soft clay which Clara could mould, and would therefore be the perfect tool. And she had more than the prettiness that had been Marie's when she was nineteen. Ermengarda was a beauty—statuesque and beautifully curved, a goddess. She was entirely German—a Valkyrie without the fire and spirit—a docile Brynhild. Her hair was long, abundant and fell to her waist in rippling waves—vital strong hair; her features were large but regular, her eyes a vivid blue and enormous.

Although she was a startling beauty she was yet retiring, though not too much so. She was even modest, and in spite of her physical perfection she would make George Lewis feel powerful. She was the perfect woman.

But she must be trained. No quick in and out of bed for Ermengarda. She had a position to hold and Clara was determined that she should hold it—never forgetting who had groomed her for greatness, always remaining grateful to her benefactress.

There were conversations in the bedchamber.

"Ermengarda, my dear, how graceful you are! Your beauty should take you a long way."

"Oh thank you, Baroness."

"Thank rather Providence which gave you such power."

"Power, Baroness?"

"There is power for you if you know how to use your beauty, my child. I knew how to use mine and you see what has happened to me."

"But you are so clever. I am rather stupid, I fear."

"Men frequently prefer stupidity to cleverness, particularly if they are rather stupid themselves. I think that if you allowed yourself to be guided . . ."

"Guided, Baroness?" Even the way she frequently repeated what was said had a charm of its own. It made her seem more docile, or more stupid. Clara was pleased with her.

"I am fond of you. I would always help you if you came to me. Ermengarda, promise me that you will always come to me to tell me of your troubles . . . and of your successes. I look upon you as my child."

"How kind you are to me, Baroness, and I thought . . ."

"That I was not kind. It is my enemies who say that and I grant
you I am not kind to *them*. But we shall remain friends, Ermengarda. Now promise me that we shall."

"I promise."

"And I know you are one who, having given your promise,
would never break it. Tell me would you like to be like me ...
rich and powerful?"

"Oh yes, Baroness."

Clara laughed.

"Sit down, my dear. Now I will tell you something. You can
be, you know."

"I would not be clever enough."

"Didn't I say I should always be at hand to help you and didn't
you promise to bring all your troubles to me?"

"Yes, but that wouldn't make me like you, Baroness."

"Bah! Nonsense, child. How would you like to have a lover?"

"I think I should like it."

Clara closed her eyes and whispered : "A great Prince ... the
first in the land. How would you like that?"

"A Prince!" murmured Ermengarda. Repetition of course,
but ecstatic. This is my woman, thought Clara.

"The Crown Prince of Hanover would adore you."

She waited in trepidation. George Lewis was such a boor. Was
the girl going to shrink in horror?

But now she was looking expectantly at the Baroness. Clara
sat up in bed and smiled at her protégée.

"I should love to see his eyes when they discover you."

"You think ..."

"I think he'll want to make you his mistress."

"And, Baroness, what should I do?"

Clara leaped out of bed and caught the girl by the wrist. "You,
my dear child, will do exactly as I tell you."

*   *   *

Everyone was talking about the beautiful Fraulein von Schulenburg whom the Baroness von Platen had brought to court. She
was one of the loveliest girls seen there for a long time. Sophia
Dorothea might be more beautiful in some eyes but the little
Schulenburg or rather the big Schulenburg, was the typical German beauty.

Moreover there was nothing arrogant about her; she was be-
comingly modest, even shy; there were many men at court who
would have made approaches to her but from the first it was
seen that George Lewis had his eye on her.

George Lewis was enchanted with her; and she seemed so with him, in a bewildered way as though she could not believe such good fortune as to attract him could possibly be hers.

He was at her side during the evening of dancing and card playing or listening to music, and often was seen riding with her.

The Princess Sophia Dorothea had never interested herself in her husband's women; her attitude towards them had been one of cool indifference which perhaps she had learned from Duchess Sophia; so she refused to see in Fraulein von Schulenburg anything different from the scores of other women who had caught her husband's fancy temporarily.

But George Lewis's feeling for Ermengarda was different from that which he had felt for any other woman—even Marie von dem Bussche. Ermengarda to him was the perfect woman; since he had first met her he had scarcely been aware of any others. Although she was so beautiful she was so humble—what a perfect combination! She made no attempt to hide her pleasure in the attentions of the Crown Prince; she made no demands; she only sought to please. Her beauty to him was perfect. She was taller than he was but as a man of slightly less than medium size he liked big women. In her company he became less clumsy, even tender.

Clara was as delighted with her as George Lewis was; and Ermengarda remained as humble towards the Baroness as she had been in the days when she first came to Monplaisir. It could not have been better if Marie had stepped into her old place.

Now George Lewis was provided with a mistress who had come to stay and this must necessarily mean the diminution of Sophia Dorothea's power. But Clara wanted more than this; she wanted to humiliate Sophia Dorothea publicly—she wanted to force her to accept Ermengarda; and she set about planning to do this.

* * *

First she must keep her promise to Marie who must have a husband found for her without delay. It was, in a way, an insult to the family to have Marie the neglected mistress even though she had been supplanted by the woman Clara had chosen.

General Weyhe was a man of great wealth and great ambition, with a large estate a few miles from Hanover. He would know that marriage into the Meisenburg family could bring him all sorts of opportunities and as soon as Clara suggested this would be the case, he was ready to discuss terms with her. It was simple : marriage with Marie. She was a beautiful woman and sister to the Baroness Platen; all wise men knew that Clara was at the right hand of Ernest Augustus when honours were handed out at Hanover.

General Weyhe did not take long to consider. He was present at several entertainments at Monplaisir and at court; and he was seen to be constantly in the company of the widowed Marie von dem Bussche.

No one was surprised when it was announced that they should marry.

*   *   *

It was Clara who helped Maria plan for the wedding. It should be one of the grandest weddings of the year, she decided.

"You do not wish people to think that you are mourning because George Lewis prefers Fraulein von Schulenburg."

"They won't think that. Marriage with a rich general is more rewarding than being mistress even to a Prince."

Clara smiled complacently. She had marriage to a rich man and was the mistress of a Prince; moreover she had the satisfaction of knowing that she had made her husband rich.

"That is a sensible way to look at things," she said. "The wedding should be celebrated at the General's house which is so suitable for a grand occasion. The whole court shall attend and the guests of honour shall be the Crown Prince and Ermengarda von Schulenburg."

Marie looked in astonishment at her sister. "And . . . the Crown Princess?"

Clara laughed with satisfaction. "Oh, I had thought of her. She must be there. But if Ermengarda is the guest of honour how can *she* be?"

"But George Lewis will have to come with Sophia Dorothea."

"Why?"

"Because it will be what is expected . . . etiquette and . . ."

Clara's laugh brayed out again. "It is not what I expect," she said. "George Lewis is so enamoured that naturally he will be with his Ermengarda all the evening. They'll be seated together at table; they will lead the dancing. . . . After all it is what George Lewis would wish."

"But the Princess . . . Why Clara, you have planned this!"

"Of course I have planned it. On your wedding day our pretty little Sophia Dorothea who is always implying how much better they arrange everything in France will see this little French custom in Hanover. The *maîtresse en titre* is more important than the wife in France. At your wedding, my dear, this will be the case in Hanover. And the whole court shall know it."

Clara's eyes blazed with vindictive delight. Here was the opportunity at last. Revenge on the woman whose fresh young charms had called attention to her own waning ones. Sophia Dorothea would begin to learn what it meant at Hanover to humiliate the Baroness von Platen.

* * *

Sophia Dorothea was aware of George Lewis's infatuation for Ermengarda. It was the talk of the court, and Eléonore von Knesebeck was always the first to pick up such gossip.

"Well, he has had mistresses ever since I married him," said Sophia Dorothea.

"This one is different," pointed out Eléonore. "*He* is different. He's devoted to her. They go everywhere together. Everyone is talking about it."

Sophia Dorothea shrugged her shoulders. "As if I cared what he does. As long as he keeps away from me that's all I ask."

But it was a different matter when the invitations to the wedding of Marie von dem Bussche and General Weyhe were issued. Sophia Dorothea received hers and pondered on it. Should she attend the wedding of a woman who had been her husband's mistress—although it was before her marriage? She remembered the day when she arrived at Hanover—the frightened bride— and how she had looked up at the window and seen Marie von dem Bussche watching her with such a malevolent expression that she had felt a shiver of fear. Marie had been ordered to leave at once but obviously she had been furious that she should have to do so—as was her powerful sister, the Baroness von Platen.

"They don't want me at the wedding," she said, "any more than I want to go."

"But I suppose you will go, as all the court will be there."

"I suppose so," answered Sophia Dorothea. But she changed her mind when Eléonore von Knesebeck discovered that the guests of honour were to be George Lewis and Ermengarda von Schulenburg.

"How dare she do this!" cried Sophia Dorothea. "There has never been anything like it!"

Eléonore pointed out that in France a century ago Diane de Poitiers, the King's mistress, had been given the place of honour frequently over Queen Catherine de' Medici.

Sophia Dorothea was white with anger. "That girl is not Diane de Poitiers."

"But George Lewis dotes on her and everybody wants to please

him, particularly now he is taking over more and more from his
father."

"I think I see what is intended here," said Sophia Dorothea.
"Clara von Platen wants to insult me, and she wants to do it
publicly. I am to be invited with George Lewis and his mistress
and they are to be given the honours while I am treated as a
guest of minor importance."

"What are you going to do?"

Sophia Dorothea was silent for a while and then she said : "Of
course I cannot go to this wedding. I shall decline the invitation."
She frowned. "But I cannot believe that they will dare to treat
this Schulenburg girl as though she is more important than George
Lewis's wife."

Eléonore lifted her shoulders. "It is what is intended. Platen
has always hated you."

Sophia Dorothea turned to her friend. "Eléonore, you must
go. You must tell me all that happens."

*   *   *

Sophia Dorothea was alone in her apartments. How desolate
the palace seemed. It was because there were so few people in
it, most of them being at General Weyhe's mansion for the
wedding celebrations.

She sat at the window looking out into the darkness. She could
picture the scene—the splendour of a rich man's mansion, in
which he was entertaining the court. Ernest Augustus would be
there. The Duchess Sophia had declined the invitation and was
at Herrenhausen. Clara would have arranged everything. She
could picture the elegant gowns, the glitter of jewellery; the
feasting, the toasting and dancing. George Lewis, flushed, his lust
written on his face for all to see and that girl whom one could
not hate because she was so amiable and foolish, just smiling at
him as though he were Sigmund or Sigurd or one of the great
heroes of legend.

And Clara would be watching slyly, thinking of the absent
guest for whose benefit this had been arranged, and although she
were not there, she would be in everybody's mind. She had denied Clara the supreme triumph, but she could not prevent her
plot succeeding. At the wedding they would be talking of the
Crown Princess. They would know why she had stayed away, and
would understand that from now on she was of no importance
at the court, for George Lewis had publicly proclaimed his pre-
ference for Fraulein von Schulenburg; and Ernest Augustus
allowed this to happen.

Clearly Sophia Dorothea would be of little consequence in future at Hanover.

Peering through the window she thought of Celle and the happy days of childhood. How different it would have been had she married the man her mother had intended her to! They would have been kinder to her at Wolfenbüttel. If only she could go home and be with her mother. What bliss it would be to take the children and go right away from all this conflict. She would never be happy while Clara von Platen ruled at Hanover; she would never be happy while she was married to George Lewis.

She went to the nursery where the children were sleeping— George Augustus and Sophia Dorothea; when she was sad she could go to them and then everything that had happened seemed worth while—even marriage to George Lewis.

*   *   *

When the court party returned to Hanover Eléonore von Knesebeck came straight to her mistress to give her account of the wedding.

Eléonore was indignant. George Lewis had been so blatant in his fondness for Emengarda; and as for the host and hostess they had made them the guests of the occasion, so that it was like celebrating a wedding between George Lewis and Emengarda von Schulenburg rather than Marie von dem Bussche and General Weyhe.

Eléonore had to admit that the Big Schulenburg had looked magnificent. Her gown! Eléonore had rarely seen such a gown. Sophia Dorothea might have considered it somewhat vulgar but everyone had been commenting on it. And there were diamonds about her neck—a present from George Lewis. "It is rarely *he* gives presents. But he had made it quite clear to everyone that there never had been a woman in his life to take his fancy as this one does. Everyone was flattering her, complimenting her. They are saying that she will be another Clara von Platen—only a more pleasant one. She just sits and simpers and looks at George Lewis as though he is some sort of god. It seemed to me that the whole purpose of this wedding was to show everyone how your husband dotes on this woman."

"I shall not endure this humiliation."

"What can you do?"

"I shall do something. I did not come here to be insulted."

Eléonore shrugged her shoulders. "Others have had to accept this sort of thing. Look at the Duchess Sophia."

"The Duchess Sophia is an unusual woman. Although Clara

von Platen rules my father-in-law the Duchess Sophia is still the first lady of the court. Perhaps it is because she is the daughter of a queen and has connections with the royal family of England. I have not these assets."

"You can live your own life."

"At Hanover! To be insulted at every turn. I shall not endure these insults. What if I were to take my children with me and run away . . ."

"Run away. To where?"

"There is only one place to which I could go. Home . . . to Celle."

"But you are married now. Your home is in Hanover."

"Perhaps if I were tried too hard I would not stay here."

Eléonore von Knesebeck shook her head, but her eyes were excited. Often by her love of reckless behaviour she brought home to Sophia Dorothea the wildness of a plan.

Yet, thought Sophia Dorothea, if I am tried too hard . . . I won't stay. I swear it.

*   *   *

The weeks which followed were miserable. Sophia Dorothea stayed late in bed, brooding; she took rides in her carriage, her children accompanying her. All her pleasure was in them; she rarely saw George Lewis who was spending all his time with the Schulenburg woman and made no secret of it. What did she care? Sophia Dorothea demanded of herself and Eléonore von Knesebeck. One mercy was that she was spared his company. It was something to be grateful for! She was left to her reading and needlework; and after supper she would be with her own little court in the great hall, playing cards and occasionally dancing.

Clara watched with a pleasure which was marred by the fact that George Lewis's fancy had not remained with her sister; but since that little scheme had failed she could congratulate herself that the simple young Schulenburg was a grateful creature who would never forget the debt she owed to her benefactress. It might even be, Clara told herself, that the silly big creature would serve her better than Marie would have done.

It was amusing to see the haughty Sophia Dorothea humiliated. Often she made excuses to absent herself from the balls and entertainments.

Clara blossomed; her gowns were more splendid; her cheeks more ruddy and no mischievous Prince would now dare to indulge in his little pea-water joke. This was what she had worked for and she had admirably succeeded.

Listlessly Sophia Dorothea talked with Eléonore von Knesebeck in her apartments. She had no wish to go to the great hall and dance. She was tired of Hanover; she longed to be home with her mother.

"It would have been very different," she sighed continually, "if I had married into Wolfenbüttel."

Eléonore von Knesebeck agreed that it would, but she added : "You are the most beautiful woman at Hanover. They can say what they like about this Schulenburg. She's a lump of pig's bladder compared with you."

"Germans seem to be very fond of pig's bladder."

"Oh, they have no feeling for what is dainty and elegant. But some will have. Somewhere in this place there must be people who appreciate real beauty."

"And what do I care !" cried Sophia Dorothea. "I am tired. I want only one thing : to go home with the children and spend the rest of my life there."

"A fine way for a woman of twenty-one to talk !"

"Age has nothing to do with this."

"It has everything to do with it. You are young. Your life is just beginning. Come let me help dress you. And we'll go down to the hall and play a game of cards. It will cheer you."

Sophia Dorothea sighed. "I am expected down there, Knesebeck. I have to do my duty. I have to smile and be gracious and pretend I do not see my husband fondling Schulenburg and Platen sniggering behind her fan. I am tired of it."

"There now. . . . Don't, I beg of you, think of all that. Come on. The blue satin ! It is most becoming; and shall I put flowers in your hair? You will look more beautiful than any of them in spite of your melancholy."

Sophia Dorothea allowed herself to be dressed and she went down to the hall.

She had played a little cards and had a mind to dance; and as with Fraulein von Knesebeck she left the card table her brother-in-law Charles approached her accompanied by a man whose face was vaguely familiar to her.

Before she heard his name her heart began to beat faster; her listlessness was replaced by excitement; a faint colour came into her cheeks which made her dark eyes brilliant; she was indeed at the moment the fairest of them all.

"Sophia Dorothea," said Charles, "there is someone here who asks to be presented to you. He hopes you will remember him."

He bowed. "Your Highness," he said, "I hope you have not forgotten me."

"I knew you when I was a child," she said.

"I was your devoted slave then. I hope you will allow me to serve you now."

"I believe that would be a pleasure."

His eyes were as brilliant as hers; he could not take them from her glowing face. She thought: He is like some hero from the old legends—a strong blond hero. She had never seen a face so strong and yet so handsome.

"Tell me," he said, "have you forgotten my name?"

They said it simultaneously : "Philip Königsmarck."

Then they laughed and he said : "If I might have the honour of escorting you in the dance I should be so happy."

She put her hand in his. "I should be happy too."

They danced, and dancing Sophia Dorothea knew that a miracle was taking place.

She was happy again.

Murder in Pall Mall

COUNT PHILIP CHRISTOPHER KÖNIGSMARCK—handsome and adventurous—had come back, as he had always promised himself that he would, to see his little playmate who had made such an impression on him when he was sixteen years old. During an exciting life, when perhaps some love affair had gone wrong, some woman had disappointed him, he would remember the scent of the lime trees at Celle and an enchanting little girl who had adored him.

Rumours had reached Saxony where he had been staying of her marriage to George Lewis; the power of Clara von Platen; the devotion of George Lewis to Fraulein von Schulenburg; the indignation of Sophia Dorothea.

Königsmarck lived for adventure—the more romantic the better; so he left Saxony and came to Hanover, determined to set up house and stay there for a while. He was very rich, for since the death of his elder brother he had inherited the title of Count, and he was made welcome at any of the European courts on account of his money, reputation and charm.

The Königsmarcks were a famous, wealthy and close-knit Swedish family. Philip remembered early days in Sweden where he had lived with his two sisters Amalie Wilhemina and Marie Aurora; there was an elder brother Carl John, who impatiently awaiting the day when he would go with his father or his uncle, Count Otho William, to serve under them, would fight his mock battles in the nursery. Young Philip, learning his geography because his brother was always fighting his imaginary battles in different places over the Continent, made up his mind that when he was older he would join Carl John and go fighting and adventuring with him. He could scarcely wait for the day. In the meantime he must be content with the company of his sisters who adored him.

Their father was a great soldier—though not quite as famous as uncle Otho William; but when Philip was about twelve he died. Carl John immediately joined his uncle; as for Philip he was a little young but, said Uncle Otho William, there was no reason why he should remain in Sweden. He could not begin to learn the art of soldiering soon enough, and must travel. So Philip travelled, studying and learning how to be a soldier at the same time; and this was how he came to be in Celle when he was sixteen and first met Sophia Dorothea.

Returning to Sweden he had been a little disconsolate until Carl John returned from his travels. Carl John, now the head of the family, took his duties seriously and it did not take Philip long to persuade him that something must be done.

"Am I to stay here learning from books?" demanded Philip.

"Now what was it you did in Celle to be turned out?" Carl John wanted to know; but of course he knew already and there was a twinkle in his eyes. The little Princess had been attracted by him and the Duchess of Celle had thought a mere Swedish nobleman not good enough to be a match for the daughter. "Well, it was no fault of yours," went on Carl John. "You merely followed the instincts of a gallant young gentleman. You must progress in the world and then one day you may be considered worthy of any Princess."

They were good days with Carl John, who was a great talker. And what tales he had to tell. He had almost been drowned when fighting the Turks; he had visited almost every country in Europe with uncle Otho William who worked for the French and had been a Field Marshal there, as well as Governor of Swedish Pomerania. And Carl John was as dashing an adventurer as his uncle. "All the Königsmarcks are the same," he confided to Philip. "Wherever we are, there is adventure." And Philip went on dreaming of the days when he would be free to roam the world.

In the schoolroom Carl John re-enacted the bull fight in which he had taken such a noble part when he was in Madrid. He leapt about the room teasing an imaginary bull.

"There was the bull coming at me; I leaped aside. But he caught me. Gored through the thigh. A few more inches and it would have been farewell Carl John."

"I thank God it was not so."

"Why boy, then you would have been a Count."

"I prefer that you should be one."

"Bless you. There was I with the blood gushing from me . . .
but I went on fighting the bull to the end."

"I wish I could fight bulls."

"Dangerous occupation, my boy. Far better to serenade the
ladies, which I did too. Now I have plans for you. We're to leave
Sweden."

"Where are we going?"

"To England. It's a merry place since the King came back.
His court is even gayer than that of France, where there is too
much etiquette. England is gay and friendly and the King is
more familiar with his people than Louis could ever be. We shall
go to court there. At least I shall. You shall have to study for
a while. I have seen our King and he has promised to give me
letters of introduction to the King of England. You should begin
to prepare yourself for departure."

Philip often thought about the excitement of those days. To
travel was always fun, but to travel with Carl John was bliss
itself. They had taken the ship from Gothenburg, to embark
on a stormy sea and arriving at Hull they travelled straight to
London.

The excitement had ceased a little then for Philip was still
regarded as a boy and although Carl John was made welcome
by the King of England and his cronies, Philip was found a
lodging not far from Whitehall and from here he travelled to
Foubert's Academy in the Haymarket to continue his military
studies. But it was not enough for a man of his rank to be a soldier
merely, Carl John had pointed out; he must be educated as a
gentleman and for this purpose a Mr. Hanson was engaged as his
tutor, for, said Carl John, he wished his brother to take a degree
at an English University, preferably Oxford.

This was not the life of adventure Philip had dreamed of; but
he was allowed to explore the noisy streets which were gay and
vulgar and had much to delight a young man. He would wander
down the middle aisle of St. Paul's which had since the Restoration become less of a church than a promenade and market. Here
were the money lenders and the marriage brokers; he liked to
stand about and listen to their talk. "It is learning the language,"
he explained to his tutor who had been commanded to see to his
morals as well as his English. The letter writers, the vendors of
ribbons and ballads, the confidence tricksters and the thieves all
congregated in Paul's Walk; and of all the fascinating spots in

this most exhilarating town, this was the most stimulating. Chief of all there were the girls and their guardians, the ladies looking for rich lovers; Philip's handsome appearance brought him his adventures among these; but Carl John, while indulging in his own, was eager that his brother should be well protected and Philip was expected to spend more time with his books and the military academy than with young women.

But however exciting his life, Carl John never forgot to spend much of it with his brother, and Philip looked forward to those days when Carl John came to his lodgings and talked as he used to at home in Sweden. There for the young Königsmarck's edification and amusement Carl John acted out his adventures so that Philip learned a great deal about the court—about the King and his ladies and the Duke of York and his; and how the Duke of York caused anxiety by flirting with the Catholic faith. He heard stories of the antagonism that reigned between the King's two chief mistresses the cockney Nell Gwyn and the aristocratic Frenchwoman who was the Duchess of Portsmouth. It was all highly exciting and entertaining. And, said Carl John, he had a mind to settle down here and he had chosen an English lady for his bride.

This was exciting news for Philip could think of no place in which he would rather settle than in London and if Carl John married it would surely mean that they would have a home in this land.

"She is very young yet," Carl John explained.

"Younger than I?"

"Ha! Much."

"You would marry a child? Is she very beautiful?"

"I would say she is not. She has a head of red hair and is called Carrots. But she has plenty to make up for that. She is the richest heiress in England."

"So it is her money you would have?"

"Nay, don't look at me so sternly, brother. I like the girl, and I'll swear she likes me too. She's a widow already."

Philip stared at his brother. "It is all so unexpected," he explained. "I am not surprised that you are to marry an heiress, but she should be a beautiful young woman, not a carrotty girl who has already had a husband."

"The marriage was not consummated—she being of too tender an age. I shall have to fight for her for I have my rivals, but I fancy I am the favoured one."

"Certainly you must be," agreed Philip smiling fondly at his brother.

"You haven't asked her name. Well, I'll tell you. It is Lady Ogle. She married Henry Cavendish, Earl of Ogle and before that she was Lady Elizabeth Percy. What I have to do is to win over her mother, the Dowager Countess of Northumberland, before I can hope to have the girl."

"You will," Philip assured him. "But why do you want her fortune when you are already rich?"

"With my fortune and hers I should be the richest man in England. What a pleasant distinction that would be."

"Bring her to see me."

"My dear Philip you don't imagine I am allowed to escort her through London, do you? That girl is guarded as though she were the Crown Jewels. I'll swear she's worth as much."

After that, every day Philip expected to hear that his brother was affianced, but it did not work out that way. Once when his brother took him to court, he saw Elizabeth. In her widow's weeds which looked so odd on one so young, she seemed to like Carl John for her eyes sparkled at the sight of him, but the Dowager Countess was not encouraging.

Carl John told Philip that he was going to ask formally for the hand of Lady Ogle and that the King himself—who greatly favoured him—had promised to speak to the Dowager Countess on his behalf.

"That," he said, "will decide matters. She may hold out against me, but she won't against the King."

So all the next day Philip had waited for the return of his jubilant brother; but how differently it turned out. When Carl John did come to his lodging he was in a great rage. He had been dismissed by the Dowager Countess who had refused to give him her daughter, declaring that when Lady Ogle married it would be to an Englishman, for she did not like foreigners. So even the King's intercession had done nothing for him.

Never had Philip seen his brother so angry. He kept pacing up and down the room declaring that he would have his revenge, as well as the girl. Elizabeth wanted him; he swore she was weeping for him now; and he had been told to go and not speak to her again!

"But the King . . ." cried Philip. "He will command the Dowager Countess to let you be betrothed to Elizabeth."

"Not he. He avoids what is unpleasant. He'll merely shrug his shoulders and refuse to discuss the matter further. He hates any sort of trouble and he would be the first to say that it is for the girl's family to decide who shall have her and her fortune."

"Well, what are you going to do?"

"I'm going to get out of this country."

"When do we leave?"

"*I'm* going. I want *you* to stay and go to Oxford. I'll be back and I want time to think about this. I don't want to go back to court where I have been so insulted."

"You mean I'm to stay here alone!"

"Till I come back for you. You like it here. You're getting along well. You couldn't find better tutors anywhere than Hanson and Foubert. Work hard and I'll be back with you soon."

It was no use trying to dissuade him; he was going to join a foray against the Moors and Philip could not accompany him there, so he must perforce carry on with his studies and dream of the day when he would be a fully fledged soldier, and go off at a whim on his own adventures. The harder he worked, the sooner that time would come.

So he tried to settle down; he said goodbye to his brother and he went daily to Foubert's Academy where he became the most promising pupil; and sometimes by day he would roam those colourful streets and now and then make the acquaintance of some girl.

"Don't you forget your brother's wishes," Hanson reminded him. "It's a soldier you've got to become first—and then there's Oxford and you're at a disadvantage being a foreigner."

But during those months in London Philip did not believe there were any disadvantages he could not overcome.

Hanson came into the lodging one day where Philip sat over his books and it was obvious that the man was excited.

"Such news!" he cried. "It's a blessing the Count's not here or he'd go round cutting someone's throat."

"What is it?" demanded Philip excitedly.

"Well, there is a fellow named Thomas Thynne at court. Thomas Thynne of Longleat. Tom of Ten Thousand, he's called, because he has ten thousand pounds a year and he's one of the richest men at court and one of the stupidest, they say. He's a friend of the Duke of Monmouth—the King's own son, wrong side of the blanket, but none the less proud for all that—and set to make trouble, they say."

"Well what of this man Thynne?"

"He has just married. Very quiet it was but it seems her mother arranged it. There were too many after her money so she wanted to make sure that a man with plenty of his own got her."

"It's not . . . Lady Ogle!"

"You've guessed right first time."

Philip was aghast. "But she was for my brother."

"Not now, sir. She's the wife of Tom of Ten Thousand."

"My brother will be angry. He was determined to have her."

"Then he shouldn't have gone away and left the field clear."

"Do you think he knows of this?"

" 'Tis hardly likely—he being where he is."

"Perhaps I should tell him."

"You should keep out of trouble, young sir. What's done is done and they're married now. All the dashing Counts in the world can't alter that."

Philip was thoughtful. It was the first time he had known his brother could fail. Later he heard rumours of how the young bride, who was fifteen years old, had gone to The Hague in the company of Lady Temple so that the marriage might not be consummated, the girl still being considered too young, in addition to which she protested that she hated the husband to whom they had married her. Philip guessed why she hated him; it was because she had wanted to marry his brother. What a pity Carl John had not stayed in England to abduct her and prevent this marriage.

From time to time he heard news of the marriage. Thomas Thynne was claiming his wife's property and demanding that she be returned to him.

Philip lost interest because his brother was no longer concerned; he had had a letter from Carl John to tell him that he was now staying for a while in France and might soon be with him. He devoted himself to his studies with great fervour hoping to surprise his brother by his progress on his return.

But he never had an opportunity to do so for Carl John had other matters than his brother's education on his mind. The first indication Philip had of this was when Captain Vratz, one of his brother's men, called at his lodgings.

Philip leaped at the man and cried: "My brother! Where is my brother?"

"Still in France, young sir. But I'll swear it won't be long before he is in London."

"Then I rejoice. I want to show him what advances I have made. I am going to ask him to forget all about the university and let me go straight to the army."

Captain Vratz said: "Your brother is concerned in a matter of great importance to him."

"What matter!" Philip was eager. His brother only had to hint at returning and life was exciting again.

"The Count is most disturbed as to the ill-treatment of a certain young lady now living at The Hague, and I have come over here to challenge a fellow known as Tom of Ten Thousand to a duel. Once the challenge is accepted your brother will come to England to kill the fellow."

"He has said this, Vratz?"

"It is his intention."

"Is it a secret?"

"All London will soon be talking of it."

"I wish my brother were not going to fight a duel. What if he should be killed?"

"The Count! Never. It is this Thynne man who will die. Then it will be for the Count to console the widow and she will be very ready to be consoled by such a handsome gentleman."

"Still . . . it is dangerous."

"Don't you fret, young gentleman. Your brother has come through worse danger than this, I can assure you."

Philip tried not to. But it was difficult when one was outside an adventure not to fret. If he were partaking in it he would know only the excitement; as it was he kept wondering what would happen if his brother were killed. And if he killed Thomas Thynne, would that be called murder? It seemed to him that whatever the outcome, there was cause for anxiety.

Vratz returned to his lodgings to tell him he was leaving for France. He was furious because Thynne had laughed in his face and declined the challenge; and the Captain had discovered that Thynne had sent six men to France to murder Count Königsmarck.

"Go to him quickly," cried Philip. "Warn him."

"You can trust me. It won't be the Count who's murdered I can tell you that."

A few days later, Philip was surprised and delighted by another visitor : his brother had returned to London.

"In secret," Carl John told him, his eyes gleaming with a mingling of anger, excitement and love of adventure.

"What are you going to do?" Philip begged to know.

"You'll see," his brother promised him.

He did. On the following Sunday, in the murk of a February evening Thomas Thynne's coach was stopped when he was riding in Pall Mall by Vratz, but it was one of Count Königsmarck's two servants—one Pole, one Swede—who fired the blunderbuss which killed Thomas Thynne.

The hue and cry went up through London and early next morning Philip heard the excitement in the streets, and leaned out of his window to call to a passer-by to tell him the news.

"Tom of Ten Thousand's been murdered, sir. And they say it's all along of his having married a wife."

Philip was alarmed. If Thomas Thynne had been murdered, his brother was involved. He stayed in his rooms waiting for Mr. Hanson, not daring to go out.

Where was Carl John? He had not come to his brother's lodging last night, nor had he sent any message.

Mr. Hanson at last came breathlessly running up the stairs—but not to stay.

"I thought I should warn you," he said. "Your brother's two servants, Stern and Boroski, have been arrested with Captain Vratz and they have admitted to the murder they committed on the orders of your brother."

"And my brother?"

"I heard he was on his way to the Continent. Whether he has reached there I don't know. I shan't stay. There is nothing I can do . . . and they'll be coming here to ask you questions at any minute."

Hanson left him and he was alone, bewildered and afraid. His brother's servants prisoners! His brother in flight! What was happening to Carl John and what would they do to him if they caught him? And what could his young brother do alone in a foreign country?

*　　*　　*

Those were anxious days. Carl John, attempting to leave England, had been captured at Gravesend and was now waiting to face a charge of murder. Strange men came to Philip's lodgings to question him. What did he know of this affair? Had his brother confided in him? To all these questions he gave discreet answers; and when he was in difficulties feigned an imperfect knowledge of the language. Fearful as he was for his brother's safety, he could congratulate himself that he had done nothing to endanger it. Hanson was summoned to appear at the trial; and there he spoke so cleverly in Count Königsmarck's defence that it was said he had an influence on the trial. Of the murder he knew nothing; all he knew was that Count Carl John had entrusted him with the care of his young brother's education, for he wanted him to be brought up a good Protestant and felt he could become this better in England than anywhere else; he wanted him to have the best military education and he believed that this could be acquired more thoroughly in England; he wanted his brother to be educated at that seat of learning, Oxford, which he believed to be the best in the world. Such admissions although they had little to do with the murder of Thomas Thynne showed Count Königsmarck to the English as a highly discerning man.

Philip went to the Old Bailey to hear the trial; he was even called upon to give evidence which he did in a firm voice, implying that it was quite impossible for his brother to be involved in such a case. He was aware of Carl John's approval coming across the court to him. But he was frightened by the solemnity about him, by the sight of his brother—the bold adventurer standing side by side with his servants who had betrayed him.

Going back to his lodgings through those crowded streets Philip heard the name Königsmarck on many tongues.

"Of course Königsmarck's the real villain. Those others were only his tools."

"He should hang by his neck. These foreigners . . ."

Those merry streets became very sinister for Philip during those days.

And then . . . the verdict. Vratz, Stern and Boroski guilty and condemned to be hanged in chains. Königsmarck acquitted.

There was murmuring in the streets. All the men were foreigners and therefore little concern of the English, but one of them, the leader, Königsmarck, had murdered an Englishman, and the English wanted retribution.

"Hang Königsmarck!" cried the people in the streets.

And Philip, making his way to his lodgings, trembled for his brother.

*　　*　　*

Life could not go on in the same way after such an episode. For one thing, Carl John had to leave England before outraged public opinion caused the law to take some action against him or the mob decided to take the law into its own hands. He left for Sweden, but Philip did not go with him. Carl John really had believed that his brother could acquire in England the education which would be of most use to him, so he wished his young brother to stay on under the care of Mr. Hanson.

For a few weeks Philip studied miserably in his lodgings; but he was a Königsmarck and the people of London did not like one who bore such a name. "Brother to the murderer!" they declared. "The murderer who got off scot free while his servants paid for his crimes." London was not a healthy place for a Königsmarck, and Mr. Hanson made Carl John aware of this. In a short time Philip heard that he was to travel to Sweden in the care of his tutor.

They left England on a blustery March day and after a hazard-
ous journey reached Gothenburg.

*   *   *

It was pleasant to see Carl John again but it was a very restive
and frustrated brother whom Philip found. He hated to be defeated, he admitted; and the English adventure had been a
humiliating one. For a little while Carl John looked after his
estates and taught Philip to help him; but Philip was well aware
that such a state of affairs could not last. He was right. A month
or so after Philip's return, Carl John announced his intention to
join Uncle Otho William and immediately plunged into preparations. Very soon, Philip was alone, dreaming of the time when
he would be able to join his brother.

Carl John sent word that he did not expect his brother to
remain in Sweden. Although England was barred to him, other
courts were not. The most glittering court in the world was at
Versailles; Carl John did not see why his young brother should
not visit France; there, he was convinced that he could learn
more graceful manners than he could in England.

So to Versailles went Philip, and after a pleasant stay there,
he travelled in other European countries, always awaiting that
call to join his brother.

He would never forget the day the long-awaited news of Carl
John came to him. But it was not a call to join him; and he knew
then that there would never be one. Carl John was dead—not
gloriously, as one would have expected him to die, in battle, in
the midst of some reckless adventure—but of pleurisy, brought on
through exposure during a battle.

Philip was the new Count Königsmarck.

He grieved for his brother bitterly; but eventually he began
to understand that he was rich, accomplished, handsome, and
that because of these assets he would be welcomed in almost every
court in Europe.

He travelled; he indulged in many a love affair; he had become
as romantic a figure as the brother whom he had always tried to
copy. He was the darling of his sisters; he had stepped into Carl
John's place at the head of the family. He became witty and gay
and when he arrived at Saxony, the Prince Frederick Augustus
became his friend and invited him to stay at his court as long as
he cared to, for, Frederick Augustus told him, he would always
be welcome there.

News came to Saxony of Hanover, and it was then that he
heard gossip about the lecherous Ernest Augustus, the rapacious

Clara von Platen, the boorish George Lewis and the sadly neglected but very beautiful Sophia Dorothea.

Sophia Dorothea! The dainty little girl he had known was it ten years ago? He had been enchanted with her, and she with him. And now, poor girl, it seemed she was being sadly treated by that uncouth husband of hers. No doubt she was in need of a little comfort. The Count Königsmarck was very capable of supplying comfort to ladies who did not find it in their married lives.

Sophia Dorothea, naturally, would be different from all others. He knew that before he saw her again.

And when he did he was certain. On that night when he was presented to her and she stood before him in all her dainty femininity, she was the beautiful lady in distress calling on her knight-errant to rescue her.

She could rely on him; he would not fail her.

The Temptation of Königsmarck

Sophia Dorothea had dismissed all her attendants with the exception of Eléonore von Knesebeck. The excitement of the last weeks was now tinged with apprehension and she wanted to talk about it.

Eléonore von Knesebeck was sitting on her stool, her hands clasped about her knees, staring ecstatically before her.

"He was so handsome tonight. He is surely the most handsome man in Hanover."

"And like as not he knows it," retorted Sophia Dorothea.

"He would be a fool if he did not, and would you want a fool for a lover?"

"A lover! Don't use that word." Sophia Dorothea looked over her shoulder. "How do we know who listens?"

Eléonore blew with her lips to denote contempt for the suggestion. "Everyone in Hanover is too concerned with their own affairs to bother with ours."

"I wish I could be sure of that."

"And if you were ... would you say yes to Königsmarck?"

"Yes ... to what?"

"Oh, come, Your Highness is coy. He is in love with you ... and you ..."

"You talk nonsense," said Sophia Dorothea.

"Why should it be nonsense for you to enjoy your life when others so blatantly do all about you?"

"I have taken my marriage vows to George Lewis."

"And he to you. But he does not remember them, so . . ."

"Eléonore von Knesebeck! You forget to whom you speak."

Eléonore leapt up, knelt at the feet of Sophia Dorothea, took her hand and kissed it. "Your Highness," she murmured, raising her eyes in mock supplication.

"Get up and don't be foolish," said Sophia Dorothea with a laugh. They had been children together so how could she be taken seriously if she tried to play the haughty princess now? But Knesebeck did talk too much; and she was afraid. Afraid of herself?

She sat down suddenly and said in a melancholy voice : "I have never been happy since my sixteenth birthday."

Eléonore von Knesebeck nodded.

"And now?" she asked.

"I am still married to George Lewis."

"You must enjoy life as he does. You could be happy again. Why not? Should you be expected to shut yourself away . . . to look on at him and that Schulenburg woman . . ."

"Hush."

"And why? The handsomest man in Hanover is in love with you. Why should you turn from him for the sake of that . . ."

"You will be in trouble one day, Eléonore von Knesebeck, if you do not guard your tongue. I am the Crown Princess of Hanover. I have a son and a daughter. He can have as many mistresses as he likes. They say that is unimportant. But if I took a lover, what a scandal there would be! They would suspect the paternity of a child who might be the heir of Hanover."

"You have the heir to Hanover and none can doubt his parentage."

"If I took a lover the parentage of *all* my children would be suspected. They would say, 'If she sins now why not before?' "

"They would not dare."

"Are you urging me to take a lover? You are a wicked woman, Knesebeck."

"I'm a proud one and I hate to see you treated as you have been. Do you know that since Königsmarck came to Hanover you have been different . . . younger . . . more beautiful? I wonder everyone does not notice."

"I must not see him. It is too dangerous. I must make him understand that there can be nothing but friendship between us."

"You would be denying the truth."

Sophia Dorothea gave her friend a little push. "I understand you. You want to be a go-between, to carry the notes between us, to arrange the clandestine meetings, to live in danger and fear of discovery. You would enjoy that, Knesebeck. You are bored and long for excitement. Well, you are not going to have your excitement over this."

Eléonore von Knesebeck lowered her eyes but her lips were smiling. She was not so sure.

*   *   *

In his lodgings Königsmarck was thinking of Sophia Dorothea, and he could not resist talking of her to his secretary Hildebrand.

"How strange it is that she is not appreciated here, Hildebrand. When I see the Crown Prince with that stupid looking girl I wonder whether he is in fact blind. Surely he must be."

"He has none of your finer feelings, my lord Count."

"And to think that they married *her* to him. I knew her, Hildebrand, when she was a child . . . a dainty fairy of a child. I never forgot her."

"No, my lord."

"Hildebrand, you are looking worried."

"There would be trouble, my lord. The wife of the Crown Prince . . ."

"This is different, Hildebrand. There is more to this than the act of making love."

He was silent. He wanted to rescue her from her miserable life, make her gay, glad to be alive.

But Hildebrand was right, of course. This was no ordinary love affair to be entered into with a light heart. Carl John had always said that love to be most enjoyed should be a light-hearted affair. "Never become too deeply engaged, brother. Savour the joys, not the sorrows of love."

Carl John was right. Perhaps he should go away.

*   *   *

He was there that night after supper to pay court to her in the great hall. She looked so radiant that surely everyone must notice the change in her; he had seen her before she had seen him, when he had first arrived. Beautiful, graceful but listless. Now the listlessness had disappeared and to the discerning that could be significant. He knew when she lifted her eyes to his that he excited her as she did him.

In such moments he was all for reckless action. He thought of riding away with her far from Hanover. To Saxony? To France? He would not look beyond the first exciting days. And would he have anything to fear from lethargic George Lewis? They were mad dreams. She had her children and when she had spoken of them he had sensed what they meant to her.

It was a foolish dream. Here in the great hall, he knew it. There could only be a clandestine love affair—notes smuggled to the Princess, secret meetings; continual fear of discovery.

They danced together and she had an opportunity of speaking to him.

"I love you," he told her, "and would serve you with my life."

"I think people watch us," she answered.

"What are we going to do?"

"You must leave Hanover. Quickly . . . quickly. . . ."

She caught her breath as she said that, and he knew how deeply affected she was.

"I cannot leave you . . . now."

"To stay would mean . . . disaster."

"If you returned a little of the devotion I would offer you I should care nothing for disaster."

Spoken like a reckless lover! But she smiled sadly.

"You should go away," she reiterated.

"I could never leave you," he answered firmly.

But she shook her head. Then the dance was over and he could not hope for more private conversation.

*   *   *

The feelings they aroused in each other could not be kept under control. Every time she entered the great hall, every time she walked in the gardens, she looked for him. And he was never far away . . . always seeking the opportunity to be beside her.

Eléonore von Knesebeck told herself it could not be long now. They would be lovers and it was right that Sophia Dorothea should enjoy a little happiness, that she should repay her husband in some small measure for all the pain and indignity he had heaped upon her. Königsmarck's friends warned caution, but what gallant lover was ever cautious?

To Königsmarck's friends it was as though fate had decided to step in and save him from disaster when the news of the death of his uncle, Count Otho William, occurred in Italy. The presence of the young Count of Königsmarck was needed there.

He left and tension relaxed.

Without him Sophia Dorothea was desolate yet she was more conscious than any that the danger had passed.

*   *   *

Life was a thousand times more wretched without him. True, there was no fear of what recklessness might possess them both;

but how she longed for that fear to return. Without Königsmarck life was dull, dreary and not worth living. Her only hope of happiness was in her children.

She stayed late in bed; she took rides in her carriage and often the children accompanied her. All her pleasure was in them; she read a great deal; she did fine needlework for pleasure and coarser for duty; and after supper she ignored George Lewis and his friends, Clara von Platen and hers, and was surrounded by her own little court, playing cards now and then, or dancing.

To this little court came her brothers-in-law. They had always been fond of her and as they disliked George Lewis, were jealous of him, and were in constant fear that their small inheritances would go to him when their father died, they were his natural enemies. But because he was crude and coarse, because he preferred the flaccid and plump Ermengarda von Schulenburg to the dainty and charming Sophia Dorothea, they disliked him more than ever.

Charles in particular was fond of her and showed her quite clearly that he was on her side. He was charming and gay and even the Duchess Sophia was charmed by him and secretly admitted that he was her favourite son. She was not displeased that he defended Sophia Dorothea; George Lewis was an oaf and she heartily wished that Charles had been the elder.

Charles often came to Sophia Dorothea's apartments accompanied by one of his brothers and their friends. There they would discuss the gossip of the day and provide some diversion for Sophia Dorothea.

A few months after Königsmarck's departure Charles came in full of excitement.

"Such news," he cried. "A friend of mine and yours has returned to Hanover."

"A friend?" said Sophia Dorothea slowly.

"Count Königsmarck."

Sophia Dorothea felt lightheaded; she knew there was a fixed smile on her face.

"He arrived today. His first question was about you. Were you well? he wanted to know."

"It was kind of him." Her voice sounded far off, as though it belonged to someone else.

"He has implored me to present him to you this evening. May I?"

She was silent.

"Don't say you have forgotten him?"

"No . . . no. I have not forgotten him. Yes, please bring him. I . . . I shall be pleased to see him."

Pleased! A strangely mild word to express her feelings. She already felt alive again. The hatred of Hanover; the disillusion of Celle seemed trivial now.

Here was a chance to feel alive again.

Why refuse it? Why should Sophia Dorothea not discover some joy in life?

*   *   *

On invitation from Ernest Augustus George William came to Hanover. The brothers embraced warmly; they both enjoyed their meetings. Ernest Augustus because he could congratulate himself that he, the younger, was in command; George William because he had always had a sentimental attachment to the brother who, in their youth, had adored him. They were happy together because Ernest Augustus was so deeply aware of the change in their relationship and George William either unaware or deliberately blind to it.

Ernest Augustus had arranged that they should be alone, but he thought ruefully to himself that Clara would quickly discover the reason for the encounter. She had her spies everywhere; and he himself was indiscreet where she was concerned. She had a way of worming secrets out of him when he was half asleep. Oh well, a man's mistress of long standing must necessarily be in his confidence. This happened with the Grand Monarque himself; and as every Prince in Europe modelled himself on the master of Versailles, what could be expected?

"Well, my dear brother, it does me good to see you."

"You grow more energetic with the years, Ernest Augustus."

"Oh you, my dear fellow, have found life too easy in your cosy castle. It's time I prodded you to ambition. I trust your Duchess is well?"

George William's expression was a little uneasy. "She is anxious about our daughter."

"You spoilt the child—you and your Duchess between you. A pity you only had the one. She is settling down. Soon we shall hear that there is another little one on the way, I doubt not."

"Poor child. I should not want to think that she is unhappy."

"She'll settle, never fear. I have my eye on her. I am very fond of your daughter . . . my daughter now, George William. What a good thing we made that marriage. And that brings me to the point. We have to stand by the Emperor now and if we do, he will show us proper appreciation."

George William nodded as he seated himself in the chair set for him and regarded his brother. How different now from the old days when he used to say : I am going to Italy! and Ernest Augustus used to implore to be taken with him, and listened wide-eyed to his elder brother's adventures. Now it was George William who waited on the words of Ernest Augustus.

"Louis has to be vanquished. The Emperor Leopold will never forgive him for invading the Palatinate and destroying Heidelberg and Mannheim."

"Nor should we," retorted George William. "I am sure the Duchess Sophia will never forget what they have done to her family."

Ernest Augustus hid his impatience. George William was sentimental. Had he not learned yet that wise rulers did not go to war for the sake of sentiment but for material gain, and Ernest Augustus had decided that more could be gained by supporting the Emperor Leopold than remaining outside the conflict, and it was for this reason that he had invited his brother to Hanover.

He said : "The Emperor is very eager for our help."

"We are so small, compared with himself and the French and all the allies."

"Small but strategic, my dear brother. And are we even so small? Hanover and Celle combined could give a good account of themselves."

"So we should be together."

"Certainly. We are closer than ever now since my son married your daughter. Our soldiers have distinguished themselves in battle, and Leopold wants us to set an example to the other small German states. If we come in they will follow us. If we remain aloof, so will they. My wife is determined that we shall join the allies. You know why."

"She wants to be on the side of William of Orange. We know of her fondness for the English."

"She is not blind to her advantages, either. If we support William, she will ask that he does his utmost to bring in an Act of Settlement which will exclude James's son from the throne. You know what that means."

George William nodded. "But it is hardly likely that both William and Mary *and* Anne will have no children."

"It is not a very remote possibility. Sophia finds out all she can about the health of those three and it is not good. After Anne— provided William kept his promise and brought in an act to exclude the Stuart—Sophia could be Queen of England. You know what that means, George William. Your daughter—through her marriage with George Lewis—could in time be Queen of England. A little different, eh, from the Duchess of a small German state."

George William agreed. His eyes shone with pleasure. This made everything worth while. What was a little unhappiness at the beginning when everything could turn out so gloriously. He felt more comforted than he had since that September morning.

"Not only this, but you know how I have always wanted an Electorate for Hanover. If we provide the troops for the Emperor I can see all sorts of benefits coming to us."

"In any case," said George William, "it is natural for us to be on the side of the Emperor."

Ernest Augustus smiled. George William would never really change.

"Mind you," went on Ernest Augustus, "the Electorate will not easily be come by. There are eight already in the German Empire and the Emperor would have to exert his special prerogative to create another. He will though, providing he gets a good enough price for it. I have been in communication with him and we have stated our desires quite frankly. We could not afford to have misunderstanding on such a matter."

"We could not indeed."

Good brother! It was so pleasant to hear him echoing what was expected of him.

"We have not only to support the Emperor against Louis and the Turks in Morea, but he wants money too."

"How much?"

"An annual payment of five hundred thousands thalers."

George William whistled. Then he said : "Well, we can do it . . . between us."

Between us? thought Ernest Augustus. The bulk would have to come from Celle. But why not? George William had the money and it was an investment for the future prosperity of the house of Brunswick-Lüneberg.

"He also wants a force of nine thousand men."

"And for these concessions?"

"Oh, don't worry about that. I have insisted on a definite promise. The Electorate—not immediately—but definitely, and as soon as it can be conveniently bestowed. And Orange has promised to do everything in his power to place Sophia in the succession. Now brother, is that a good bargain? And are you not delighted that you married your daughter to my son."

"I can see," replied George William, "that she has made the

best possible of all matches. And what pleases me, is that we have been brought together again."

Ernest Augustus rose and laid his arm about his brother's shoulder. George William was comforted.

*   *   *

As he had known he would, Ernest Augustus told Clara what was happening.

"An Electorate," she said. "That will delight my lord."

"I have always wanted it," admitted Ernest Augustus. "I've been working towards it for years."

"That I know well. And but for your brother you would not have been so near it. I'll warrant he is supplying most of those five hundred thousand thalers—and that a number of the soldiers will come from Celle."

"And why not?"

"I agree. Let him pay. What an excellent stroke of luck that we arranged that marriage with Celle."

"It was a stroke of genius."

"I hope you remember who did so much to promote it."

Ernest Augustus laughed. "I've never denied that the Platens played their part."

"*You* have had your reward."

"You are implying that they have not?"

"Baron!" she said. "It is not a very high sounding title."

"What about Count?"

"Charming."

"And that would make you happy?"

"Try it. I'll swear you will be pleased with your happy Countess."

*   *   *

Ernest Augustus needed brilliant commanders to lead his men and his attention was directed by his sons Charles and Maximilian to Count Königsmarck.

Ernest Augustus had already noticed the Count, who had made quite a stir in Hanover. In the first place since the death of his uncle Otho William he was reputed to be one of the richest men in Europe, and he made no secret of the fact, judging by the style in which he lived.

Apparently he intended to stay some time in Hanover for he bought himself a house not far from the Alte Palais and here he had set up an establishment of such grandeur that it was the talk of the neighbourhood. He filled it with twenty-nine indoor servants; and when he took a journey, however short, he rode in a cavalcade of fifty horses and mules. Such a large company to wait on one young man was certain to attract attention. Moreover, he was startlingly handsome and sumptuously dressed. He had brought a wardrobe with him which he had accumulated not only in Saxony but in France.

Ernest Augustus heard from his younger sons that Königsmarck was the most interesting young man at court. He therefore asked that he should be presented to him.

The young man came, resplendent; his doeskin coat embroidered with silver thread; his silk waistcoat magnificent; but even more striking than his elegance were his handsome looks. He was young, clear-eyed, clear-skinned, and, Ernest Augustus conjectured, about the same age as his own George Lewis. But what a contrast! Of course George Lewis was a good soldier, and it was soldiers who were more useful to a country than dandies; but there was in this young man's bearing something which suggested that he was no fop. His elegant good looks had been bestowed on him by nature and he would have been a fool to ignore them.

Young Charles was clearly very impressed with him.

Ernest Augustus asked a few questions about Saxony and other European courts and he was interested to find that Count Königsmarck was as widely travelled as he was himself. Königsmarck was no fool; Ernest Augustus liked him.

"What would you say, Count," he asked, "if I offered you a Colonelcy in my Guards?"

"I should express grateful thanks, Your Highness, and assure you of my desire to serve you well."

"Then it is yours. But I must tell you this : there are no great financial rewards. Here we regard such a post as an honour."

"I so regard it," replied Königsmarck. "As for money . . . I have enough for my needs and do not concern myself with what a soldier should be paid."

"Then you are the man for me."

Count Königsmarck was exultant. Now he could come and go about the palace as he pleased. No one would question a Colonel of the Duke's Hanoverian Guard. This meant that he could see Sophia Dorothea more frequently, and would not have to wait to be conducted to her apartments by one of her brothers-in-law.

He was delighted. This brought him nearer to the woman he longed to make his mistress.

*   *   *

At last Sophia Dorothea was happy. Each day she saw Königsmarck and he left her in no doubt of his feelings for her. As a Colonel in the Guards he had free access to the palace, but it was impossible for them to be alone together, although sometimes when he was on duty in the gardens she would walk there and they would have the pleasure of seeing each other.

Prince Charles knew that they were in love with each other; he admired them both, and as he detested his brother he did not see why his sister-in-law and the handsome Count might not enjoy each other's company. Whenever he called on Sophia Dorothea he asked Königsmarck to accompany him and thus there was a small intimate gathering in her apartments. Maximilian—himself a little in love with Sophia Dorothea—came also; and even the youngest of Ernest Augustus's sons, Ernest, who was about fifteen or sixteen and who had a great admiration for Königsmarck, often joined them. Eléonore von Knesebeck was delighted with the change in her mistress, and that, with the Count's arrival in Hanover, their lives had been lifted out of the drab pattern, so when Königsmarck intimated that he would like to send letters to Sophia Dorothea and receive them from her, it was Eléonore von Knesebeck who assured them that they could trust her to see that these notes were delivered into the right hands.

How pleasant, thought Sophia Dorothea, to know that she was loved—and by such a gallant gentleman as Königsmarck! She was content for a while to drift along in a dreamy romantic mood, into a world of sighs for the impossible and hopes which, deep in her heart, she believed could never be realized.

Königsmarck was ardent. He assured her that he loved her as he had never loved before; not only did he tell her this but he wrote it in the notes which the excited Knesebeck brought to her.

Life had new meaning for her—but her dreams could never come true.

Let that be as it may; she must live for a while in her world of make-believe.

*　　*　　*

George William brought his Duchess to Hanover when there were to be discussions with his brother as to how they were to meet the Emperor Leopold's demands. This gave Duchess Eléonore a chance to be with her daugher and grandchildren, and although she hated visiting Hanover where she knew the Duchess Sophia at least did not welcome her, she was happy to have an opportunity to see her daughter.

She was delighted when she noticed the change in Sophia Dorothea and her fears were set at rest. Perhaps, she told herself, she had been wrong and George William right.

Sophia Dorothea greeted her warmly; the children were enchanting; and since her daughter showed no inclination to talk about George Lewis and her marriage, Eléonore asked no questions and soothed herself with the thought that the children made up for all the happiness Sophia Dorothea missed with her husband.

There was to be a grand ball and Eléonore went to her daughter's apartments to see her women dressing her. How enchanting she looked. And how radiant. She could not look so and be really unhappy. She was to wear white satin which would so become her dark beauty.

"And flowers, *Maman*," she explained. "Real flowers in my hair and no jewels at all."

"No jewels! Then you will surely be the only lady at the ball without them."

"The Countess von Platen will wear enough to make up for my lack of them," said Sophia Dorothea with a laugh.

When her daughter entered the great hall, Duchess Eléonore felt an immense pride; she glanced at George William and saw that his eyes were a little glazed. So he, too, was moved.

There was the Countess von Platen. How vulgarly dazzling in her rich red robes and her cheeks painted as deep a colour as the scarlet folds of her skirts; her magnificent neck and shoulders bare—her bosom half exposed and, as Sophia Dorothea had predicted, ablaze with diamonds.

From the dais on which she sat with Ernest Augustus, Duchess Sophia and their honoured guests Eléonore watched the play which was given in their honour, and then after supper in the ballroom saw her daughter open the ball with her father. George William was still handsome and Sophia Dorothea was, of course, enchanting. How wise to wear the simple white, the natural flowers—she stood apart from them all in charm and beauty.

The Duchess Sophia leaned forward and tapped Eléonore's arm.

"Your daughter looks well tonight."

"Well and happy," said Eléonore.

The Duchess Sophia smiled a little superiorly. She was less displeased with the girl than she had been. She was certainly beautiful and she had dignity; she would make a good Queen of England when that glorious day came, as Duchess Sophia was certain it would. She was thinking now that the Act of

Settlement had been passed in England and this excluded any
Catholic from ascending the throne which meant that with
Anne the House of Stuart would end; providing of course neither
Anne nor Mary had children—and Duchess Sophia prayed fer-
vently each night that they would not—it would be the turn of
the Hanoverians. Sophia saw herself riding into London, the
city which she had never seen but which she thought of as
Home; Sophia Queen of England.

That dance was over; the ball was opened. Eléonore, who did
not dance, but like Ernest Augustus and the Duchess Sophia
looked on, saw her daughter dancing a minuet with a very handsome man in a suit of pink satin trimmed with cloth of silver.
He was tall, quite elegant, and he in his splendour and Sophia
Dorothea in her simple white satin and natural flowers were
the most outstanding couple in the ball-room. Clara von Platen,
for all her fine gown and scintillating jewels, could not compete
with them.

"Who dances with Sophia Dorothea?" she asked the Duchess
Sophia.

"Oh it is a young Swedish Count, recently come to court.
Ernest Augustus is pleased with him and has given him a place
in his Guards. Königsmarck. Count Königsmarck."

Many eyes were on that elegant and most charming couple.
One who could not stop looking at them was Clara von Platen.

*   *   *

Königsmarck had conducted Sophia Dorothea to the dais on
which the royal party were seated. He pressed her hand in
farewell; he wished that he could sit with her, be close to her
for the whole evening. But he was more aware than she was
that they were watched.

Sophia Dorothea took her seat beside her parents, and Königsmarck, bowing low to those assembled on the dais, turned away.
As he did so a page touched his arm.

"The Countess von Platen would have a word with you, my
Lord Count."

Königsmarck bowed his head in acknowledgment and even
as he lifted his eyes he was aware of Clara's brilliant eyes fixed
upon him; he made his way to her.

"I am honoured," he said, "that you, my dear Countess, wish
to speak with me."

Her sensuality was apparent to him, connoisseur that he was.
He knew well that she was a dangerous woman, but he understood why Ernest Augustus could not do without her. She would

be as exciting as a love potion and as difficult to throw off as a drug. As they stood there smiling, each was aware of the other's physical potentialities. In any other circumstances Clara would have immediately decided on him as a lover and he would have told himself that here was a woman he must not pass by.

"I wanted to compliment you on your dancing," said Clara. "You knew that everyone was watching you. They couldn't help it."

"If so it was because I was fortunate to be dancing with the beautiful Princess."

She leaned a little towards him and he smelt her overpowering scent as she tapped him lightly on the arm. "It was *you* I was watching."

"You are very kind, Countess."

"I am . . . to those who please me."

There was laughter in her eyes; there was invitation. What a foolish young man, she was telling him, to occupy his time with the silly little Princess when all his efforts had come to nothing—she knew this because she had spies everywhere and they would have informed her if it had—when all the time there was an experienced woman waiting with a hundred delights of which he—experienced though she knew him to be—had not yet dreamed.

"How can I thank you," he murmured.

"You may dance with me to begin with."

The music started, he took her hand, and as she came close to him in the dance he was aware of her voluptuous body, her great glittering eyes, her sensuous lips. He was even unaware of Sophia Dorothea as he passed the dais; he felt as though he were rushing downhill, and so great was the exhilaration that he would not have stopped if he could.

The dance over, he left her and as soon as she was no longer beside him he laughed at himself. She was a dangerous woman, and what a sensuous one! She had disturbed him deeply; and chiefly, he told himself, by reminding him of the Princess. He loved Sophia Dorothea; he would never love anyone as he loved her; but what was a man to do? Go on in this unfulfilled way? *He* could not live on romantic dreams, if she could. He wanted something more tangible.

He would plead with her; he would make her understand that he must be her lover in fact. Why not? All about them people were indulging with abandon. Why must they be the

only lovers at the Hanoverian court who must act with such un-
natural restraint?

He must speak to Sophia Dorothea; he turned to the dais,
but his arm was caught and turning he saw Prince Charles at
his side.

"You cannot dance with my sister-in-law again tonight, Count,"
said Charles.

"But . . ."

"My dear fellow—you in your pink and silver, she with those
flowers in her hair . . . you cut such a figure. Everyone noticed.
You cannot repeat that—or there will be talk. Once was well
enough—but the way you looked at her was a little dangerous.
No, for the sake of Sophia Dorothea's reputation don't go to the
dais again tonight."

He felt deflated. He was weary of the subterfuge. He left the
ball early and went home to his mansion which was not far from
the palace.

*　　*　　*

In his room he paced up and down thinking of the evening.
It was Clara von Platen who had started these dissatisfied
thoughts. She with her allure and her unspoken promises had
made him realize what he was missing.

"This can't go on," he said aloud; and he was at his window for a long time looking out on the dark streets.

One of his pages was at the door.

"A messenger from the palace, my lord Count."

Sophia Dorothea! he thought. A letter. She felt as he did.
She was begging him to come to her. It was time indeed.

"Bring him in," he commanded.

When the concealing cloak was cast off it proved to be a
woman.

"You come from . . ." he began.

"My mistress wishes to speak to you. Will you come with me
without delay?"

"I am ready. Your mistress . . ."

"The Countess von Platen is waiting for you."

He caught his breath. He had not expected a summons so
soon . . . not a summons at all. Perhaps it did not mean what
he feared . . . what he hoped . . . it did. And yet . . .

He hesitated, for he could not banish from his mind the
vision of Sophia Dorothea's beautiful face, her dark hair adorned
with flowers, her pure white dress so charming, so beautiful. . . .

But this was a summons from the Countess von Platen; and he could not ignore it.

*   *   *

He did not know quite what he had expected but afterwards it seemed inevitable.

She was in her apartments . . . alone; and she was wearing a scarlet robe the same colour as the dress she had worn at the ball. Her hair was loose about her shoulders, her face brilliantly painted.

"Count Königsmarck," she said. "I knew you would come."

"A summons from the Countess von Platen . . ."

"Could not be disobeyed," she added.

She held out her hands to him and as she did so the robe which had no fastenings fell apart disclosing her naked body.

She was laughing at him; he heard himself laugh too. There was no turning back now . . . even if he had wanted to.

It was early morning before Count Königsmarck left the apartments of the Countess von Platen.

*   *   *

Sophia Dorothea was constantly in the company of her parents; and Count Königsmarck in that of the Countess von Platen. The whole court was whispering together about Clara's new liaison, but if it came to Ernest Augustus's ears he said nothing. He was concerned chiefly with fulfilling the demands of Leopold and earning that Electorate.

Königsmarck suffered intermittent feelings of guilt and exhilaration; he had never had a mistress quite like Clara. His remorse when he considered what he was doing tormented him and often he would swear that he would never see Clara again; then she would come to him and taunt him; and these interviews always ended in the same way. She invited him to Monplaisir; she was enjoying life as she rarely had before. She was satisfying her immense sexual appetites and at the same time humiliating her enemy and enriching herself, for she saw that Königsmarck took his turn at her card tables and lost. Why not? He had a large fortune of which she would be happy to take a share. This she was doing, and after a successful evening there were satisfying nights.

If Clara had been romantic she would have told herself she was in love with Königsmarck. When he had left her in the early morning she would lie in bed asking herself what it was she enjoyed so much: His prowess as a lover? His handsome body? His insatiable sensuality which was a match for her own? Or the fact that Sophia Dorothea was in love with him. In any case it was a situation which appealed to her senses and her character; and what more could she ask than that?

Sometimes she had a twinge of fear that no other man would ever satisfy her after Königsmarck. That brought with it a sense of fear because she was aware every night of that remorse in him; she knew that even when he was in her bedchamber he was thinking of Sophia Dorothea and that each night there was a battle to be fought to make him forget his romantic attachment to that insipid little fool who wanted him as her lover and was afraid to accept him.

Rarely had life been so amusing, so interesting, so full of triumph for Clara. Then she began to be a little astonished at herself. It was true that no other man appealed to her, and her desire for Königsmarck was growing to an obsession. At all hours of the day he was in her thoughts; and those nights when he was not with her were unbearable. Two emotions began to dominate Clara's life : her desire for Königsmarck and her jealous hatred of Sophia Dorothea.

*   *   *

Sophia Dorothea had, of course, learned of her lover's disaffection. Rarely had she felt so desolate. She was the victim of a cruel marriage; and now the man whom she loved, the knight-errant had proved his worthlessness by becoming the lover of her greatest enemy.

Königsmarck was writing notes to her which she ignored. Did he think she was a complete fool? she demanded of Eléonore von Knesebeck. Did he think that he could openly deceive her and that she was so infatuated with him that she would accept such conduct?

"I never want to see him again!" she declared.

Fraulein von Knesebeck was like a flustered hen. It had been such fun. So exciting. So dangerous! And now it was all over. She understood. Königsmarck was a man after all, and he could not be expected to be satisfied with romantic dreaming of what might be and never was. She tried to explain this to Sophia Dorothea.

"Don't make excuses for him!" stormed Sophia Dorothea. "And of all people it had to be that woman . . . that vile, vulgar creature."

Eléonore muttered that men were men and it was no use trying to change that.

She would come sighing into her mistress's apartments. "I saw Königsmarck today. He looks so wretched."

"Doubtless jealous of his mistress. Perhaps he has discovered by now that he is not the only favoured one."

"He gave me a note for you."

"Then you were a fool to bring it and had better put it into the fire without delay."

Eléonore von Knesebeck did no such thing. She laid it on the table and retired, knowing that as soon as she had left Sophia Dorothea would seize on it.

And at last she agreed to see him. Recklessly Eléonore von Knesebeck brought him to her apartment and as she looked at him—more appealing in his humiliation and misery than he had ever been in his arrogance and faithfulness—Sophia Dorothea wanted to forgive him everything if he would but promise to give up Clara.

But she was proud and she had been deeply wounded.

"Why," she demanded, "do you wish to see me?"

"To tell you how unhappy I am."

"Why? Has your mistress been unfaithful to you?"

"It has been like an evil dream."

"Evil and irresistible!" she cried. She had to be angry or she would burst into tears; she would be telling him how glad she was to see him, that she wanted to be back on the old terms . . . that she would accept anything if they might return to those.

So she whipped up her anger. "I am quite disgusted," she said. "So you have joined the grooms and pages who supply that woman's nightly entertainment! And not only grooms and pages, of course. Noble Counts join her retinue of lovers."

"You do well to abuse me. I deserve all you say of me. But now I am with you I understand full well how much I love you. I have been unable to express my feelings. I have been frustrated . . . quite maddened by frustration that I have not known what I was doing. You must believe me, my Princess. I will never see the Countess von Platen again. I will be faithful to you and to you only as long as I live. In truth, it was because I believed I must be her friend to help you that I went to her in the first place."

"You very well showed your friendship to me!" put in Sophia Dorothea scornfully, but she was in tears.

He embraced her. "My dearest . . . my Princess. . . ."

"I believed in you," she sobbed. "I would have trusted you."

"You can trust me. Never again will I see that woman. I swear to you."

The door opened and Prince Charles came into the apartment.

"You are mad!" he said. "I could hear your voices in the next apartment. Do you realize that there will be others listening?"

He looked from one to the other. "I know your feelings for each other, but you will have to be careful."

"As careful as others are . . . as Clara von Platen for instance?" demanded Sophia Dorothea.

"She is not the mother of the heir of Hanover," replied Prince Charles. "Listen to me, you are behaving foolishly, both of you. You have my sympathy, my understanding, my friendship. That is why I bid you take care. If it came to the ears of Ernest Augustus that you were lovers, you, Königsmarck, would be banished from Hanover. As for you, Sophia Dorothea, your reputation would be smirched. There would be doubts as to whether young George Augustus was your husband's son. Don't you understand?"

"I have always understood that," declared Sophia Dorothea, "and I have never been unfaithful to my husband."

Prince Charles sighed. "Who would believe you . . . overhearing what I have just overheard! And," he continued, "how can we say who has overheard it? Clara von Platen would seize every opportunity to ruin you."

"But not the Count," said Sophia Dorothea bitterly.

"That is perhaps something for which we should be grateful. Come with me, Königsmarck. You should not be here alone with my sister-in-law."

Königsmarck looked at Sophia Dorothea, and she could no longer hide her true feelings. He took her hands and kissed them. Charles turned his back and gazed at the door.

"I am forgiven?" whispered Königsmarck. "Say that I am and we will find a way to happiness."

Sophia Dorothea nodded and they were both conscious of a bleak satisfaction as they parted.

*　　*　　*

Prince Charles said : "You are a fool, Königsmarck."

"I am in love with the Princess."

"So you go to her apartments and behave in such a manner that every little spy at every keyhole can hear what you are saying, while you conduct an affair with the most jealous and vindictive woman at court who happens to be my sister-in-law's greatest enemy."

"I agree with you. I am a fool."

"And immediate wisdom is necessary. There is only one thing you can do at the moment, Königsmarck. Leave Hanover. Come with me to Morea."

"You are going to Morea!"

"I have just received orders from my father to prepare myself. I am to lead a company against the Turks. It is part of his agreement with Emperor Leopold."

"But to Morea!"

"I am asking you to leave one dangerous spot for another. You're a soldier, Königsmarck—but I believe you are in as great danger here as you will be in Morea."

Morea! The adventure of war. It had always appealed to him. But to leave Sophia Dorothea just when he had persuaded her to forgive him!

"Well?" asked Charles; and when Königsmarck did not answer, he added : "Think about it."

*   *   *

The Duchess Sophia had sent for Königsmarck.

He thought: So we were overheard. It has come to the ears of the Duchess and I am about to be banished from Hanover. He thought of the Court of France, of that of Saxony. They were far more brilliant than Hanover but he would be far from Sophia Dorothea.

Now that he had seen her again he wondered how he could have been temporarily beguiled by Clara von Platen. She was old—all of forty; she was experienced in a manner which had fiercely attracted him; but after seeing Sophia Dorothea in her fresh youth and beauty, he knew that he loved her and he cursed himself for his lapse.

Never again would he be lured to the bedchamber of that old harridan. He was going to make Sophia Dorothea happy. He did not even despair of becoming her lover in actual fact. She wanted him even as he wanted her; he had sensed that at the last meeting; and one thing the affair with Clara had done was make her aware of that.

It was going to be embarrassing if he stayed away from her much longer. Clara was not the sort to let him go easily. He was uneasy—but the immediate problem was before him. He had to face the Duchess Sophia who would very probably give him orders to leave.

He found the Duchess subdued, which was rare with her; but her greeting was almost warm.

"My dear Count, pray be seated."

He obeyed her and she gave him a friendly smile which put him on his guard. With a woman like the Duchess Sophia one could never be absolutely sure of her intentions.

"You are a friend of my son Charles?"

He was taken by surprise and recovering himself assured her that he was.

"You are older than he is, and I believe you have a fondness for him."

"This is so," Königsmarck assured her.

"His father is sending him to Morea. I am uneasy. He is young yet, and although it is his duty to fight our battles I should like to know that he had a good friend at hand. It would give me pleasure if you would volunteer to go with him."

Königsmarck's heart had begun to beat a little faster. He raised his eyes to the Duchess's face and tried to read her mind. Everyone knew that she doted on Charles and the fact that she was not by nature a doting woman emphasized the depth of her emotion for this favourite son. Yet on the other hand what did she know of the intrigues of the court? Was she aware of his liaison with Clara and that at the same time he was involved with the Princess Sophia Dorothea? Was she warning him to get out of Hanover? Yet why should she care what trouble he involved himself in? No, it was real anxiety for her son that he saw in her face.

What could he reply to her? She was a woman who expected obedience.

He was experienced enough to know that he was going to find it very difficult to evade Clara von Platen during the next weeks. How much easier if he left Hanover for a while. When he returned, doubtless she would have found a lover to absorb her as he once had.

It would be one way of easing a delicate situation.

"Since Your Highness asks it of me, I can only have pleasure in doing as you bid me."

"Thank you, Count Königsmarck," said the Duchess Sophia.

Very shortly after that interview Prince Charles left for Morea and with him went Count Königsmarck.

The Stolen Glove

ALL through the winter, while Königsmarck was in Morea, Sophia Dorothea's spirits were kept up by the letters which he sent her. It was bitterly cold and enormous fires burned in the grates; the wind whistled about the Alte Palais and in the streets the people grumbled. Many of the men were away at the war—a war which had little meaning for them and for which they had to pay through the taxes.

Ernest Augustus anxiously awaited news from Morea and Sophia was constantly reproaching him for sending her dearest son so far from home to fight the Turk. It would have been different fighting in Flanders with George Lewis, she complained. Ernest Augustus tried to soothe her, but he too was uneasy. He was paying a big price for his Electorate.

Clara was at hand to amuse him, holding brilliant courts in the palace and at her own mansion Monplaisir. She was restless, eager for news from Morea, for, she said, she was as anxious for that Electorate as he was, knowing that he had set his heart on it. In truth she was thinking of Königsmarck and longing for his return. She did not lack lovers but they failed to satisfy her. There was, she regretfully admitted, for her only one Königsmarck.

Eléonore von Knesebeck was in her element; it was her great task to see that the letters Königsmarck sent to Sophia Dorothea reached her and that those of Sophia Dorothea reached Königs-

marck. She enjoyed threading her way through Clara's network
of spies, and she congratulated herself that the Countess had no
notion that her one-time lover was now writing the most passionate letters to her rival, assuring her that to her and her only
could he give his heart.

One day Sophia Dorothea was in the act of writing a letter to
Königsmarck when messengers arrived from Morea. A hush had
fallen on the palace; it was Eléonore von Knesebeck who came
hurrying in to tell her news.

"What is it?" cried Sophia Dorothea. "You look . . . stricken."

Eléonore could not speak for a few seconds; her teeth had
begun to chatter.

"It's . . . Charles," she said. "He's been killed in Morea."

Sophia Dorothea clasped her hands together to steady herself.
"Charles," she whispered.

"It's been a terrible disaster and . . ."

"And . . . Königsmarck?"

"I don't know. I . . ."

Sophia Dorothea had run to her and was shaking her fran-
tically. "You know . . . you know and you won't tell me."

"I don't know. I swear it. Only Charles. They found his body
on the battlefield . . . his men were with him . . . all dead!"

"Königsmarck?"

"They did not say Königsmarck."

"Then what of him . . . ?"

"I don't know. I swear I don't know."

Sophia Dorothea pushed Eléonore von Knesebeck aside and
hurried down to the great hall.

*   *   *

The court of Hanover was in mourning for Prince Charles.
Ernest Augustus shut himself into his apartments and brooded,
but the Duchess Sophia was so heartbroken that she collapsed
and had to take to her bed; the doctors were called but could
not diagnose her illness, yet because she had lost all zest for life
they feared she might die; and those about her knew how deeply
she loved this son.

From Celle came George William and Duchess Eléonore to
offer condolences. Celle was in mourning too, said George
William, for everyone had loved Prince Charles.

Gloom settled in the palace. Not only had they lost Prince
Charles but there had been utter defeat at Morea. The Duke
of Wolfenbüttel had suffered terrible losses in the contingent he

had sent; and it was agreed that it would have been better if the expedition had never been undertaken.

The Duchess Eléonore spent a great deal of time with her daughter who mourned Charles sincerely for he had always been a good friend to her; and in the days following that when the grim news had been brought to Hanover she had thought she would die of grief, for then the fate of Königsmarck had not been known. She had endured terrible anxiety each hour expecting to hear bad news.

Only to Eléonore von Knesebeck could she confide her grief.

"I never surrendered to him," she said. "I denied him myself. He wanted to be my lover more than anything on Earth, Knesebeck, and I denied him that. If only he would come back . . . I would deny him nothing, nothing . . ."

Eléonore von Knesebeck tried to comfort her. "One should not brood on the past; one must hope for the future; after all hope did remain."

Yes, hope remained.

It was a bright April day when Königsmarck came back to Hanover bringing with him a fraction of the troops he had taken with him to Morea.

*　　*　　*

Königsmarck is back! thought Clara. In fact she thought of nothing else. He was more gaunt than when he had gone away; he seemed a little older, but none the less attractive, thought Clara. There'll never be another man like him for me. How did I put up with the others? Never mind. Now he is back.

*　　*　　*

Königsmarck! thought Sophia Dorothea. He has changed. He has suffered hardship. He is more serious; and when his eyes met hers in the great hall, she knew that he was even more ardent.

He would tell her now that life was short; that was a fact which had been brought home to him in Morea. She had seen the young and handsome Charles go forth to war, but she had not seen him lying on the battlefield his body shattered by a Turkish lance. If she had she would understand that life was a precious gift which could be lost at any time. Who would have thought Charles's end would come so soon, he who had been full of health and life? They must enjoy living; there must be an end to dreams.

It was not easy to meet alone, for there was danger in secret meetings, but Eléonore von Knesebeck was at hand to scheme,

and with her help they could be together . . . alone for an hour
or so.

He came to her apartment and Eléonore was there to take him
to her, to guard them while they were together. They could trust
their confidante Knesebeck, they assured each other.

Sophia Dorothea threw herself into his arms. "I feared I should
never see you again," she cried. "I could not have gone on living
without you."

"All the time I was thinking of you. I came back for you. I
fought for my life as I never have before . . . because it was for
you."

"I am afraid . . ."

"The little Knesebeck is guarding. We can trust her."

"Oh, yes, we can trust her. And I swore that if you came back
to me . . ."

He kissed her. He understood. He had been spared for her;
now there would be no holding back.

*   *   *

Clara waited for him in her apartment. Naked beneath her
robe—scarlet because the first time it had been scarlet and that
would remind him. Her face was freshly painted and in the
candlelight she looked as radiant as a young girl. She put down
the candle, which she had held close to the mirror, and let the
robe fall open while she let her hands caress her body. It was
firm and no one would guess she had borne children; she wondered anxiously whether that last trouble had changed her.
Königsmarck, the rogue, had been responsible for that. She would
tell him so. It had made her really ill at the time and no one
believed the story she had put out as to the cause of her illness.
She would have been pleased to have had a little Königsmarck,
but the time would have been awkward. At least the others could
have been Platens by Ernest Augustus, and the truth was that
Ernest Augustus was not the man he had been; and because he
had been away from court the child could not have been assigned
to him either.

She knew that it was a little Königsmarck; and there had only
been one course open to her. Dangerous! Humiliating! She had
hated it. But as she had meant to tell him, a small price to pay for
all the fun they had together.

Her skin was as soft and white as ever; the daily milk baths
looked after that.

Oh, Königsmarck! she thought. It was worth while.

Anticipation excited her. She wrapped her robe tightly about her and trembled.

"Königsmarck! Königsmarck. Hurry, Königsmarck!"

How hard it was to wait! Up and down the room she paced; taking a candle she went to the window and idly looked out, but she saw nothing except her own face reflected in the glass. Fresh and young like the face of a young girl. So it would seem to him.

But how long he was in coming!

It was some time later when she realized that he would not come at all.

*   *   *

Clara was angry but she masked her feelings. Why did he not come? Had he not understood her invitation. Didn't he know that she was the one who decided when an affair should be terminated?

Was it possible that he had a mistress at court? She knew that he had a romantic attachment to Sophia Dorothea, but that was nothing. Just kiss my hand and dream of what can never be. Königsmarck was too much of a man to be satisfied with that. It was just an airy-fairy game he played to pass the time.

Now, he had a mistress and Clara was going to find out who; and when she did she was going to see that that little affair did not progress.

He would soon be back with her.

*   *   *

George Lewis had gone to Flanders with his men and the atmosphere of the palace was always easier for Sophia Dorothea when he was absent.

She had been living excitingly since Königsmarck's return. They wrote letters constantly to each other; there was another who was in their secret and that was Aurora Königsmarck, Königsmarck's sister, who had come to live in his mansion for a while. Aurora adored her brother, approved of his romantic adventure with the Princess, and, being ready to act with Eléonore von Knesebeck as go-between, made the affair so much easier to conduct.

"For the first time since my sixteenth birthday I am happy!" Sophia Dorothea told Eléonore von Knesebeck, whom she and her dear Philip had nicknamed affectionately the Confidante.

Eléonore was delighted; she was constantly visiting Aurora Königsmarck with whom she had appeared to strike up a friendship. Back and forth went the letters. Sophia Dorothea read them and reread and tied them up with ribbons that she might keep them constantly with her.

Occasionally there were meetings and it was the delight of Confidante Knesebeck at the palace and Aurora Königsmarck in her brother's mansion to put their heads together and arrange trysts for the lovers.

Sophia Dorothea spent her time between her children and her lover and it was true that never had she been so happy. Her beauty blossomed and Eléonore von Knesebeck declared that her very looks would betray her if she did not take care.

Life had become gay, colourful, touched with delicious intrigue.

The fact that meetings were so difficult to arange made them all the more exciting when they took place. Königsmarck congratulated himself on having a place in the Guards which meant that he was often in the gardens on duty. How simple for Sophia Dorothea out for a walk with Eléonore or with the children to pass by. Then they could feast their eyes on each other and even though she could do no more than smile and he salute her, their day was made.

The children looked for him; they would point him out to her and he made a special point of saluting them. Young George Augustus would salute in return, standing very straight like a soldier, and little Sophia Dorothea would attempt to do the same.

Sophia Dorothea was walking in the gardens one day with her little daughter, Sophia Dorothea on the alert for a glimpse of her lover and had not realized how far they had walked, when the child began to whimper that she was tired and couldn't climb all the steps to the apartment in the palace.

Sophia Dorothea laughed and caught the little girl up in her arms.

There were attendants who could have carried the child, but Sophia Dorothea did not ask them to do so; and as she was about to mount the stairs a shadow fell across the sunlight and a hand was laid on her arm.

"The child is too heavy for Your Highness."

The sound of that voice thrilled her; she turned, a radiant smile on her lips.

Their hands touched as he took the child, who gazed at him in wonder and attempted to make the salute.

Königsmarck carried the little Princess up the stairs with her mother leading the way, as though, her attendants told each other afterwards, they were an ordinary couple returning home together. It was an extraordinary way to behave and a complete flouting of etiquette; but then the Crown Princess had never had much respect for the Hanoverian customs, having been brought up in free and easy Celle.

Königsmarck was putting the child down when Clara on her way to the gardens where she knew he would be on duty came into sight.

She saw in a moment what was happening. Königsmarck carrying the child from the gardens; Sophia Dorothea flushed and excited; she heard her say : "But that was good of you, my dear Count." My dear Count! So that was it. Could it possibly be that she had dared to become his mistress !

Clara was beside them. She bowed coolly to Sophia Dorothea who, with something like insolence—thought Clara—acknowledged the greeting. Königsmarck bowed low to her and Clara passed on; under her rouge she was white with rage. So this was why he did not come to her now. It was for Sophia Dorothea that he had abandoned her.

*   *   *

Clara came into Ernest Augustus's apartment where he was resting. He was growing old, thought Clara; and although his gout was improved a little he was not the man he had been.

She was fortunate to have kept her hold on him; and this she had done partly by her forceful and magnetic personality, partly by seeing that her husband had risen in importance so that they were a team who could not easily be dismissed; she had also been wise in keeping her hold on political affairs, for instance the matter of Bernstorff who was so useful to them in Celle. Foreign envoys knew that they had to placate Clara von Platen if they wished to be well received at Hanover. Yes, she had been wise, but she must not cease to be; she knew Ernest Augustus well and that if he decided to push her aside, he would do so however important she had become.

At this moment she forgot to be cautious. Her feelings for Königsmarck made her forget everything else. She cried : "Your daughter-in-law conducts herself in a very unseemly way."

"Do you think so? I have always found her gracious. Those French manners of hers are welcome at Hanover. It does us good to remind us now and then that we are not always as courteous as we should be."

"Gracious! I wish you could have seen her romping with one of your guards."

"Romping with a guard ! Impossible."

"Not impossible . . . the guard is young and handsome enough."

"Sophia Dorothea! She's a model of virtue, though sometimes I wonder why, poor girl. That reminds me, George Lewis will soon be home from Flanders."

"And not before he was needed here. Your daughter-in-law takes advantage of his absence . . ."

"Who wouldn't? And when he comes back he'll be with Schulenburg, I'll swear. Poor Sophia Dorothea, hers is not a very happy existence."

"You are foolish about that girl."

Ernest Augustus looked at her coldly. There were times when Clara went too far. She saw it, and going to him laid a hand on his shoulder and put her face against his cheek.

"You are too kind to women," she added indulgently.

"Are you complaining?"

She laughed aloud. "When have you heard me complain?"

She was thinking quickly : "It is no use talking to him. He will do nothing. And if I protest he'll think I'm jealous, jealous on account of Königsmarck. There will have been gossip and if he were to discover, who knows . . .? Well, there have been others and he knows, but one could never be sure. People could become jealous suddenly. Königsmarck was young and handsome, every-thing a man should be. It might be that Ernest Augustus might be jealous—not of Clara—but of another man's youth and vigour.

Caution. Sophia Dorothea must be humiliated, separated from Königsmarck—but at the same time Königsmarck must not be banished.

She must take great care.

* * *

George Lewis returned from Flanders and for a while Sophia Dorothea was terrified that he might wish to resume married life with her. She need not have feared. He turned at once to Ermen-garda von Schulenburg who had been patiently waiting for him. He seemed to delight in her more than ever; she was ideally suited to him—placid, voluptuous, undemanding, adoring. With such a woman he was in no mood to make demands on Sophia Dorothea.

Clara had hoped that with his return he would put an end to the intrigue—if intrigue there was—between Königsmarck and Sophia Dorothea. She had set her agents to spy on them but they had discovered nothing, for the two watch-dogs—Eléonore von Knesebeck and Aurora Königsmarck—did their work well.

But Clara was growing more and more obsessed by Königs-

marck. The fact that he was at Hanover and she was unable to
make love with him infuriated her. She hated Sophia Dorothea;
she was not sure whether she did not hate Königsmarck. There
were times when her feelings wavered between a passionate
desire to caress him and an equally fierce one to kill him.

Every day she had to keep herself in check, while she watched
and tried to plan.

Ernest Augustus left for The Hague—and Königsmarck accompanied him—to meet William of Orange who was now King
of England and one of the leaders of the war in Europe. There
was a gathering of the allies that the policy of the war might be
discussed. George William of Celle had hoped to go with his
brother but illness prevented him, and Sophia Dorothea took an
opportunity to go to Celle with her children.

The conference was not a success in spite of all the dignitaries
assembled and the brilliant entertainment which had been devised
for them, for during it Louis took Mons, which was such a shat-
tering blow that the conference was disbanded at once. While
William of Orange returned to England, Ernest Augustus, the
Duke of Wolfenbüttel and those who had been making merry
while they made plans at The Hague returned somewhat dis-
comfited to their various estates.

Louis was quick to seize an advantage, and knowing how the
Duke of Hanover loved money sent an envoy to his court to see
if he could be bribed to abandon William and become the ally
of France. Clara was kept busy, for naturally the French ambassador had had his orders to approach Ernest Augustus through
Clara von Platen. She entertained the Frenchman at Monplaisir
and graciously agreed to accept his presents.

When the Duchess Sophia heard that the French were trying
to turn Hanover against England she was angry; she immediately
promised the English ambassador her aid and no bribes were
needed for her. She would support England no matter what happened; and she thought Ernest Augustus a fool to forget that
the English throne could easily be lost for the sake of a French
bribe.

Sophia Dorothea found herself drawn into the intrigue. She
was naturally attracted by the French at Hanover, because she
was able to talk to them in their own language and she liked
their manners. George Lewis on the other hand had a great
admiration for William of Orange.

Thus there were divided opinions at Hanover and Ernest
Augustus wavered. If the Emperor Leopold had presented him
with the promised Electorate it would have made all the dif-

ference; but it still seemed as far away as ever; this was his real grievance.

Königsmarck had not returned with Ernest Augustus and each day Sophia Dorothea looked for him. It was Eléonore von Knesebeck who learned what was happening and when she did she was so stunned that she did not know how to break the news to her mistress. But Sophia Dorothea, who knew her Confidante well, guessed that something was wrong and fearing that it concerned her lover demanded to know what she had discovered.

"He will come back," cried Knesebeck. "I know he will."

"Please tell immediately what you know."

"William of Orange took a fancy to him and has offered him a high command in his army."

"You mean . . . he is not coming back . . ." stammered Sophia Dorothea.

"The King of England is very powerful; he needs good soldiers like the Count. You must remember that he is a soldier—and what good can come of this? One day you will be discovered and then what would happen do you think? It would be terrible . . ."

"Be silent, Knesebeck!" cried Sophia Dorothea and she ran from the room to her bedchamber where she shut herself in and refused to see anyone.

*　　*　　*

There was a scratching at the door. Sophia Dorothea did not answer, so Eléonore von Knesebeck came in.

"Hurry," she cried. "How dishevelled you are! Here, let me comb your hair. There is someone to see you."

Sophia Dorothea looked at her maid's face with incredulous hope. Eléonore von Knesebeck was dimpling, her eyes shining. "Quickly! Quickly! There's no time to lose. He's outside. I see you don't believe me. He must come in quickly before he is seen. Come in, my lord Count."

Königsmarck strode into the room and Eléonore von Knesebeck stood aside smiling at the long embrace.

"They said you had gone away with the King of England," murmured Sophia Dorothea.

"Did you really think I would leave you?"

"I feared . . . oh how I feared!"

"No need to fear. I shall never leave you."

"Never . . . never . . ." sobbed Sophia Dorothea.

Eléonore von Knesebeck tiptoed out and left them together.

*　　*　　*

"Königsmarck is back!" said Ernest Augustus with a laugh. "He didn't want to leave us after all."

"The man's a fool. He'd have more opportunities with the English army." Clara's lips were tight. When she had heard he was not coming back she had been almost glad. It was one way of ridding herself of him. Now here he was, and every time she saw him he seemed more attractive, more desirable; and the desire which was torment, if unsatisfied, was stronger than ever.

"Well he toyed with the idea. He'll have his reasons for rejecting William's offers I don't doubt. And to celebrate his return he is giving a grand ball. We must attend, Clara. It is only gracious. He has chosen us in place of Orange; we should at least show our gratitude for that."

"The Crown Prince and Princess have accepted?"

"I am sure they have; if not I shall tell them that they must."

"I don't think they will need much persuasion," retorted Clara.

A ball, she was thinking; a masked ball doubtless; and there would be opportunities for a little dalliance in the gardens between the host and his principal guest—at least the principal guest in his eyes.

I'll destroy her! thought Clara. If I have to destroy them both.

*   *   *

Clara sent for her sister Marie. Plump, voluptuous Marie was content in her marriage to General Weyhe who did not make too many demands, was very rich, and delighted to be connected by marriage with the most influential woman at court. When Clara sent for Marie she knew she must not disobey.

What now? thought Marie. Surely Clara did not want her to try once more for George Lewis? That was quite impossible. Everyone knew that he was extraordinarily devoted to Ermengarda von Schulenburg. However, she was soon to find out.

"You're looking blooming," commented Clara.

Marie smiled, thinking it was more than she could say for Clara who looked raddled beneath the layers of colour on her cheeks. Clara was uneasy, and when Clara was uneasy the rest of her family should be, for their affairs were all bound up in each other.

"I am pleased," went on Clara. "You are very friendly with Prince Maximilian."

Marie laughed. "Oh, he is a very gallant young man."

"I could wish you had such success with his brother."

"George Lewis behaves like a husband to the Schulenburg. What has that woman that I haven't?"

Clara looked in exasperation at her sister. *She,* Clara, much less beautiful than Marie, had managed to keep a firm grip on Ernest Augustus all these years and she was certain that if Marie had used a little more tact, a little more care, she would have held George Lewis. How much easier it would have been to bring Sophia Dorothea to disaster if Marie could have whispered the slander in his ear!

"I have been thinking of Max," said Clara. "He is very friendly with the Crown Princess."

"He imagines himself in love with her—in a light-hearted way, of course."

Another of them! With her fairy ways and her graceful French manners she inspired these men with that sort of devotion. It was irritating; but on this occasion Max's devotion might be turned to advantage.

"He dreams of her and frolics with those who are less inaccessible—such as you, my dear sister. It is a very small thing I want to ask of you and of him. I admired very much the embroidered gloves George Lewis brought back from Flanders and want to have the embroidery copied."

"She would lend you one, I am sure."

"My dear sister, we are not great friends and I do not wish her to have the satisfaction of knowing I want to copy her gloves. No, Max must steal one of them when he is in her apartments. It won't be difficult. Then he must give it to you and you will bring it to me."

Marie smiled; she was wondering what mischief Clara was brewing. But it was not for her to question Clara's methods—only to obey.

* * *

Königsmarck's ball was brilliant and the fact that the guests were masked and in fancy dress added to the enchantment of the occasion.

Clara's spies had told her what costume Sophia Dorothea was wearing and she had one made exactly like it, and before the ball she sent a note to Königsmarck telling him that she wished to see him and she thought that the ball was an excellent opportunity for them to talk together.

When Königsmarck received her letter he was uneasy, but he realized at once that he must listen to what Clara had to say.

He was in love with Sophia Dorothea but he was not the hero she believed him to be and he was well aware of this. Often he longed to be all that she thought he was; but he knew himself to be only human. She insisted on regarding him as a god. He was afraid of Clara, afraid that when they were together she would overcome his scruples and he would fall into temptation again. Sophia Dorothea would not understand how easily this could happen, nor the overwhelming sensuality of a woman like Clara von Platen which to a man of his nature was an almost irresistible challenge. Königsmarck was like thousands of other young men—vain, a little arrogant, something of an opportunist; he had not let Sophia Dorothea know how seriously he had considered accepting the very tempting offer William of Orange had made to him. He had, it was true, returned to Hanover for the sake of Sophia Dorothea; and when he was with her, he was sure that he loved her devotedly, that his happiness depended on her. Yet, he was no fool, and often he asked himself where all this could end. What could theirs ever be but a clandestine affair; and if they were exposed, who knew what dangerous situation they might find themselves in?

He had to see Clara. He knew that she still wanted him as a lover and he could not help it if while this knowledge alarmed him yet it exhilarated him.

When he was receiving his guests he recognized her at once in spite of her mask. She looked, he noticed, not unlike Sophia Dorothea; she pressed his hand as he greeted her—a reminder that she expected him to keep their tryst.

There was the joy of dancing with Sophia Dorothea, of whispering endearments together. Could they be alone during the evening? It was dangerous for George Lewis was among the guests. He would be with Ermengarda von Schulenburg—but his wife was expected to be a model of decorum.

"If the opportunity should arise . . ." whispered Königsmarck, but he was thinking of Clara. He must see Clara. He dared not fail for he was afraid of that woman.

She was at his side, suggesting a walk in the gardens. It was summer and the moonlight was enchanting. Now, thought Clara, the stage was set. He was thinking she was going to make advances and that that was the object of this meeting. It was true that she might make advances, but the main object was not for that.

"So, my lord Count, you ignore me now."

"Madam, no one could ignore you. You are the leading light of the court of Hanover and . . ."

"Have done with that!" cried Clara hoarsely. "I have invited you to come to me in a hundred ways and each you turn aside. You are never at Monplaisir . . ."

"My duties, Countess . . ."

"Now listen to me, Count Königsmarck. Ours has been no ordinary acquaintance, has it?"

"Being your . . . friend . . . could only be a most exhilarating experience and one a man could never forget."

"I can tell you you left *me* something to remember. Do you know that I could have lost my life putting myself in order after you had gone away?"

"I regret . . ."

"So did I, Count. I regretted when I found your ardent ways had left me pregnant. And my husband away . . . and the Duke away. . . . A pleasant scandal there might have been, but I well nigh killed myself to avoid that."

"I humbly beg your pardon and I am sure that after such an experience you will never wish to see me again."

She came closer to him; he was aware of her voluptuous body, her insinuations. "About that I have not yet made up my mind," she whispered.

"I shall shortly be leaving with the army," he said. "A soldier's life . . ."

"You need not go if you do not wish."

"My duty . . ."

He was telling her he did not want her and she felt an inclination to slap his face. But that was not part of the plan. I hate him! she thought. He is refusing me for the sake of that woman, that foolish simpering Frenchwoman. Well, we shall see whether he is able to continue his secret tos and fros from her bedchamber. If he won't come to mine he shall not go to hers.

"My headdress is slipping. Let us go into this pavilion that I may adjust it."

He looked uneasily at the pavilion. It was not exactly the spot lovers would choose, being a little exposed and anyone inside it would be seen from outside.

Clara put her hands to her headdress. At any moment now Platen should be coming up the path with George Lewis—that was if Platen did his part. But she could trust him to do what he was told; the point was, had he been able to get George Lewis away from Schulenburg?

Königsmarck was relieved that there did seem to appear to be something wrong with the headdress; at first he had thought she was going to suggest an embrace in the pavilion; she was capable of such a suggestion he well knew.

"Can I help?" he asked.

"I think not. Your duties in a lady's bedchamber have not usually been concerned with fixing headdresses."

She could never resist the coarse allusion. How different from Sophia Dorothea. If only it were possible for them to go away together, to marry! He believed he would be happy to change his mode of living. He was certain he would be ready to do anything for Sophia Dorothea.

"Listen! Footsteps! Someone is coming this way. Look, we'll go out of that door and we shall not meet them."

Clara stood in the moonlight, her back to the men who were coming along the path to the pavilion. She was quick enough to see that it was her husband and George Lewis.

They would recognize Königsmarck and the figure in the dress which was exactly like that worn by Sophia Dorothea.

It is working to plan, thought Clara; and her pleasure in the success of her little plot made up for her chagrin at Königsmarck's indifference.

*   *   *

"A glove, Your Highness," said Platen, stopping and picking up the embroidered glove which Clara had dropped.

"Clearly it belongs to the woman who left in a hurry just as we came along." George Lewis looked at the glove and recognized it as one he had himself brought from Flanders. He remembered being impressed by the excellent workmanship. "That is my wife's glove," he said. "Who was the man with her?"

"It was Count Königsmarck, Your Highness."

"It was. I saw him clearly."

George Lewis continued to look at the glove.

*   *   *

The following day he made a rare call at his wife's apartments.

Sophia Dorothea was surprised and disturbed to see him; but she made a pretence of indifference.

"I come to look at the embroidered gloves I brought you from Flanders. I was talking of the fine work they do there."

"The gloves!" cried Sophia Dorothea, embarrassed. "I . . . I have lost one of them."

George Lewis regarded her sullenly. "Last night?" he asked.

"No, some days ago. I will ask Fraulein von Knesebeck."

Eléonore came running to her mistress's summons and Sophia Dorothea asked her when the glove had first been missed.

"It was several days ago," said Eléonore. "I remember remarking on it."

George Lewis regarded them sullenly and at that moment the
Count von Platen asked to be admitted. He bowed to the Princess
and offered her the embroidered glove.

"It was found, Your Highness, in the pavilion at the Count
Königsmarck's ball last night."

"But . . . I do not understand. . . ."

George Lewis took the glove from Platen and threw it on to
a table.

"That is enough," he said; and with Platen left the apartment.

Sophia Dorothea and Eléonore von Knesebeck looked at each
other in horror. What did this mean?

* * *

Each day Sophia Dorothea waited for George Lewis to act
but he said nothing; and in fact after a few weeks had passed
he appeared to have forgotten the affair of the glove. He was
deeply concerned with Ermengarda and they were seen everywhere together. She could put George Lewis into good spirits
and he seemed less uncouth consequently.

Königsmarck, who had heard of the affair of the glove from
Sophia Dorothea, knew very well what had happened, but he did
not wish to tell her that he had been in the pavilion with Clara.
He was ashamed of himself for his duplicity and as a result
became more reckless than usual, anxious to tell the world how
much he loved and respected Sophia Dorothea.

At the card table in the great hall one night, when there was a
lull in the game, when he was talking of Saxony, he mentioned
how the Elector was dominated by his mistress, how his wife was
of no account; he then went on to speak of the court of Dresden
—the magnificence of the balls and banquets. They exceeded,
he told his listeners, anything they had ever known at Hanover.

George Lewis, who was sitting at the table with Ermengarda,
glowered at him, for Königsmarck represented everything that
George Lewis disliked—elegance and eloquence, all the charac-
teristics of a legendary romantic hero.

He growled unexpectedly : "If you like Saxony so much why
did you leave it for Hanover?"

Königsmarck flashed him a look of distaste. "Because," he said,
"I did not care to see a beautiful wife distressed by the conduct
of a husband who neglected her for the sake of a mistress who
was both impudent and worthless."

There was a gasp. Ermengarda tittered nervously while George
Lewis seemed as though he were about to speak but changed his
mind.

Silence followed until the cards were dealt.

*   *   *

Clara, who heard of the incident, waited for George Lewis to act. First the glove incident and now Königsmarck's outburst! The fool, thought Clara. Doesn't he know George Lewis is the most vindictive man at Hanover? The fact that he allowed the insolence to pass does not mean he has forgotten it. It will be remembered against you, my handsome gallant, for ever and ever!

She discussed the matter with Platen who was of the opinion that George Lewis simply did not care whether or not his wife was having a love affair with Königsmarck.

But, he agreed with Clara that he would put the matter at the back of his mind, to be remembered later.

*   *   *

The lovers reassured each other that there would be no outcome of the glove incident. Meetings were arranged; they made love; they talked of their dangers and in a weak moment when he felt he wished to have no secrets from Sophia Dorothea, Königsmarck told her how Clara had insisted on walking with him in the gardens and had led him to the pavilion where the glove had been found.

This aroused Sophia Dorothea's jealousy which had to be appeased; but he knew he was right to have told her because they must both be on their guard as never before against Clara.

"She is a dangerous woman," said Königsmarck. "Never let us forget that."

They thought of the disaster she could set in motion; but the fear and uncertainty made their meetings the more precious.

Feverishly they planned to meet and meet again.

A Pinch of Snuff

WHILE Sophia Dorothea and Königsmarck were oblivious of everything else but each other, Maximilian was growing more and more restive. He missed the restraining influence of Charles; he could no longer play the gallant with Sophia Dorothea; he was constantly in the company of young men as reckless as himself; and they planned how they could force Ernest Augustus to see their point of view. To Maximilian and his friends this was an amusing game to prevent boredom; but it was dangerous; they were young and high spirited and they tried to outdo each other by their recklessness. Their enemies were Ernest Augustus and George Lewis and they talked boldly in secret.

One of the chief conspirators was Count Mölcke, Ernest Augustus's Master of the Hunt; and the young Duke of Wolfen-büttel was in communication with them.

Clara, who had been an enemy of Maximilian since the affair of the pea water, had her spies about the group, and she was always hoping to prove to Ernest Augustus that their conspiracy was not merely the mischievous but childish game he thought it. Ernest Augustus was inclined to laugh at his son's antics; he was well aware of Clara's fury over the pea water, and as for the Duchess Sophia, her one weakness was for her sons—other than George Lewis—and she too was apt to be lenient.

This was infuriating for Clara, who saw herself not only baulked of her revenge on mischievous Max, but robbed of the man whom she was now convinced was the only one to satisfy her. Above all she hated Sophia Dorothea and she determined to destroy her; and it occurred to her that if she could prove Maximilian to be plotting against his father and elder brother, she might at the same time involve Sophia Dorothea.

One evening when Ernest Augustus was playing cards, with Clara beside him, he asked for his snuff box, and as it was the duty of Count Mölcke to carry this, the young man immediately produced it. Ernest Augustus was about to take a pinch of snuff when Clara laid a hand on his arm; for a few seconds Ernest Augustus looked into her terrified eyes.

In view of her concern he could not but be warned; holding the snuff between his fingers he did not immediately put it to his nose. He said : "Mölcke, take my hand, will you."

The Count took the cards and Ernest Augustus rose and went into an ante-room, Clara following him. In the ante-room he turned to her and said : "What does it mean?"

She did not answer him but called to the spaniel who was lying there.

"Give the snuff to him and you will see," she said.

Ernest Augustus did so. "You're not suggesting . . ."

"If you won't look after yourself, I must do it for you. Let me tell you, I have friends everywhere in the place . . . *everywhere*. It helps me to uncover plots and intrigues . . . in high places . . . and low."

"Clara, this is . . ."

She pointed to the dog who had already begun to foam at the mouth. Ernest Augustus stared in horror as it fell to its side, its legs twitching.

As Ernest Augustus looked on in horror, the dog's movement ceased.

"It's dead, poor creature," said Clara. "Well, at least he has taught you to listen to me."

"But it's . . . monstrous !"

"It's black treachery," declared Clara. "Mölcke should be arrested before he escapes."

"He looked so innocent when he gave me the box !"

"What use would he be to his friends if he betrayed his black guilt? Have him arrested at once. Then you will learn that you have been too confiding."

Ernest Augustus called in the guard.

"Wait at the foot of the staircase," he said, "and when Count Mölcke appears, arrest him on a charge of treason."

Then Ernest Augustus went back to the card table. "Someone is waiting outside to see you, Count," he said.

The Count rose and walked out to the guard.

* * *

How easy it was to build up a case against a group of careless young conspirators! There were servants who had overheard their rash words. It was true enough that Maximilian was jealous of his brother; he was very friendly with his cousin the young Duke of Wolfenbüttel; and the manner in which the house of Wolfenbüttel had been treated at the time of the marriage of Sophia Dorothea and George Lewis was certain to have made bad blood. The Duchess Sophia was very anxious; she disliked her eldest son and loved the younger ones; she would have been delighted to have been able to share the inheritance instead of allowing it all to go to George Lewis.

In his heart Ernest Augustus did not believe for a moment that his son would be concerned in a plot to poison him; nor did he think the lighthearted Count Mölcke capable of such an action. But it was true that there was disaffection in the family and that was something he had tolerated long enough. Knowing Clara, an idea of how the snuff came to be poisoned entered his mind. Maximilian had insulted her and Clara was never one to forgive insults. However, he would not explore that possibility and it had to be made known that such conduct could not be tolerated.

There had to be a scapegoat and Mölcke being the obvious one, he was sentenced to death. Maximilian was banished from Hanover; and as soon as he had gone Ernest Augustus realized the folly of this action, for he immediately went to Wolfenbüttel where he was received with the utmost hospitality.

* * *

Clara was delighted with Maximilian's banishment but to punish him was not as important as to destroy Sophia Dorothea.

When Mölcke had been questioned he had been urged to implicate the Princess but this he refused to do.

It simply was not true, he said, that the Princess had been present when they had talked of the injustice to the younger sons of Hanover. He would be lying if he said she were.

Clara was not satisfied with this. She sent one of the guards to the imprisoned man to tell him that there was one way of saving his life. He only had to implicate Sophia Dorothea.

This Mölcke steadfastly refused to do; and Clara was further enraged.

*   *   *

Königsmarck visited his friend Count Mölcke in his prison.

"How could you have been so foolish as to become involved?" he asked.

"It was to amuse Maximilian. We were not serious any of us . . . at least not serious in our talk of overthrowing George Lewis. It was all so much talk. I had no idea how the poisoned snuff came to be in the box. I was as surprised as anyone."

"It was put there to incriminate you, of course."

"You will have to see that the Princess is protected."

"The Princess! What has the Princess to do with this?"

"She is innocent of any plot against the Duke . . . but I am innocent of attempting to poison him, yet here I am . . . condemned as guilty. Someone wants to ruin her. I was told that if I would swear she was guilty of treason and in the plot to murder Ernest Augustus I could save my life."

"Good God!" cried Königsmarck. "She is in danger then."

"No," said Mölcke, "I refused."

"My good friend," cried Königsmarck. "The Princess has a formidable enemy in Hanover."

*   *   *

Eléonore von Knesebeck had brought him in. He embraced Sophia Dorothea with fervour.

She was in danger, he told her. Mölcke had been offered his life to betray her.

"Betray me?" cried Sophia Dorothea. "For what?"

"My precious Princess, my darling! You are in danger. We cannot go on like this."

"I have few friends in Hanover," said Sophia Dorothea. "But I have many enemies."

They embraced. Each knew who was the vindictive enemy. Königsmarck cursed his weak folly, his infidelity, his indulgence which had led him to become, though briefly, the lover of the evil Clara. And Sophia Dorothea wept for it.

*   *   *

Sophia Dorothea went to her husband's apartments—an intrusion which was as distasteful to her as it was irritating to him.

"I must speak to you," she said.

He grunted and not rising from his chair sat back and yawned.

How she hated him. He seemed more crude than ever since she was learning to know Königsmarck so well.

"Someone is trying to implicate me in this affair of the snuff box."

He did not speak.

"Don't you see how important it is?"

He shrugged his shoulders.

"You will stand by and see your wife so treated? You know who is behind this, don't you? It is the Platen woman. She offered Mölcke his life if he would admit that I was one of the conspirators, that I helped to plan your father's death. Can't you say anything?"

"What is there to say? You have said it."

"Mölcke refused to lie. He is innocent of this charge, and he would not lie even to save his life. Well? What are you going to do?"

"What is there to do?"

"Is it nothing to you that your wife is plotted against?"

"You said he refused to implicate you."

"But someone tried to tempt him to do so."

"He didn't. And that's an end of it."

"I . . . I don't understand you."

"Why should you?"

She looked at him in exasperation. "And is it nothing to you that I have enemies who would dishonour me . . . who would plot my ruin?"

"It's no concern of mine," mumbled George Lewis.

She left him in an agony of rage; and she wept for Count Mölcke when his head was cut off in the Royal Mews.

She had lost a friend—a gallant chivalrous gentleman; she turned to Königsmarck for comfort.

Banishment from Celle

ERNEST AUGUSTUS had at last attained his heart's desire. Hanover was created an Electorate and he its Elector. All the scheming of years had borne fruit. He could not have done it, he knew, without the help of his brother George William's wealth and without the aid they had been able to give to the Emperor. But the glory was his; he was richer, more powerful than he had dared hope. And for a time he forgot his worries. He did not wonder what Maximilian was doing in Wolfenbüttel; how far his brother Christian was with him; he suppressed his disappointment in Sophia Dorothea for whom he had always had a tender spot. He gave himself up to the joy of celebrating his great achievement. Clara was only too happy to help him.

* * *

Königsmarck was uneasy. He was no coward, but the Mölcke affair had shaken him. He knew that he was living dangerously as Sophia Dorothea's lover. He continually cursed himself for having made an enemy of Clara von Platen. There were times when he was sure that he would willingly die for Sophia Dorothea and others when he was unsure. If he could have married her, willingly would he have done so, and he was sure that he could have been a faithful husband. When he was with her he was the chivalrous and single-minded lover she believed him to be. There were times when he was not with her, when he was unsure.

He was an adventurer, an opportunist; he could not change his character because he was in love. How he fluctuated! There were times when he planned to run away with her; others when he planned to run away without her.

Because she was romantic and he was calculating, because she in her simplicity loved him for that ideal manhood with which she alone had endowed him, she could not truly know him. But he knew himself; and because she meant more to him than any other living person ever had, desperately he tried to live up to her ideal.

Creeping into her apartments by night, romantically scrambling from her window in the early morning ... all this was romance. But he was always aware of the dangers he ran and wondered whether this or that night's adventure would be the last. Sometimes he told himself he was a fool.

Thus it was with Königsmarck—torn between the wisdom of flight from danger and the ecstasy of living with it.

* * *

Hildebrand, Königsmarck's secretary and confidant, was waiting for him when the Count entered the house. There was a messenger, he told his master, from Saxony.

Königsmarck said he would see the man at once and when he came to him and handed him letters he took them to his private apartments to read at once.

One of the letters was from his friend Frederick Augustus, heir to the Electorate of Saxony; but as Königsmarck read the letter he realized that his friend had come into his inheritance.

His brother George Frederick had died of smallpox and Frederick Augustus had succeeded him. He needed his friends about him and there would be a welcome for Königsmarck in Dresden.

This was unexpected. The Elector George Frederick had been in his prime—a lusty man who had at this time been ruled by his beautiful mistress the Countess von Röohlitz, an imperious young woman of twenty-one who had haughtily declared that she would not live at the same court as her lover's wife; as a result the Electress had been asked to leave. She had seemed invincible until an enemy had confronted her whom she could not vanquish. The smallpox had killed her, and in his devotion to her, for he would not leave her side, her lover had caught the disease, and died less than a fortnight after her.

"I should be with my friend Frederick Augustus at such a time," said Königsmarck.

An absence from Hanover, he believed, would give him time to decide how he should shape his life, for he could not go on for ever in this unsatisfactory state. Sophia Dorothea would be ready to elope with him, he believed, and he wanted to go away for a while to explore this exciting but highly dangerous possibility.

Within a few weeks of receiving those letters, Königsmarck was on his way to Dresden.

*　　*　　*

Sophia Dorothea missed him sadly. Life was empty without him, she told Eléonore von Knesebeck.

"Sometimes I think he will never return," she said. "He will see the wisdom of staying away now that he has put some distance between us."

"He'll come back."

"If you loved me you would pray he never would."

"When you yourself will pray that he will?"

"Have done! I want to get away from the palace. Let us go for a walk in the gardens."

It was pleasant walking in the gardens which, although not so tastefully arranged as they were at Celle, were more colourful.

People curtsied as she passed, and among them was one woman who had been in great poverty and to whom she had ordered that food and clothes should be sent. She recognized the woman, looking affluent now, and paused to express her pleasure. The woman dropped a deep curtsey and murmured that she would never forget the service done to her by the Princess. She was a midwife who had recently improved her fortunes when she delivered a very important child.

"I am pleased to hear it," said Sophia Dorothea.

"But," declared the woman, "I should never forget my true benefactress and if there was aught I could do for Your Highness I should first wish to serve you."

Eléonore von Knesebeck could not allow this enigmatic remark to pass and later went to see the woman to discover what she meant. She was told that the woman had recently delivered Fraulein von Schulenburg of a daughter whose father was George Lewis. It was kept a secret, but if it was to the good of the Princess to know it, the woman had no intention of keeping it from her.

Eléonore von Knesebeck could not keep such a piece of information to herself and went back to tell the Princess what she had discovered.

Sophia Dorothea listened with a stony expression, and when she considered how she and Königsmarck had considered it wise to part while George Lewis flaunted his mistress at court and in secret she gave birth to his child, she was suddenly very angry, and without stopping to think she went to her husband's apartments.

*   *   *

She found George Lewis alone and said impulsively, "I have just discovered that your Schulenburg friend has presented you with a daughter."

"It surprises you?" he asked.

"No, but it shocks me."

"You are a fool."

"And you are a lecher."

George Lewis did not answer. He yawned and kept his mouth open.

"You have the manners of a stable boy and the morals of a cockerel. You are crude, uncouth . . . and I cannot understand why even that foolish creature can pretend to have some affection for you. She has not, of course. She thinks it clever, I suppose, to have the whole court laughing at your antics. She likes the rewards . . . and of course if you pay highly enough . . ."

George Lewis had lumbered towards her.

"Shut your mouth."

"I will speak if I have a mind to. Someone should tell you what everyone says about you behind your back. Your place is not in a court. It's . . . Oh!" He had brought up his hand and slapped her face.

She recoiled while the red mark appeared on her cheek. Then she said : "How like you. You cannot speak reasonably. You can only brawl. You belong in a tavern . . . you and your silly Schulenburg. . . ."

George Lewis was really angry. She could defeat him in a battle of words but physically he was the master and he would show her. He caught her by the throat; she screamed as she saw what he was about to do; she was on her knees; his hands were squeezing her throat and she was gasping for breath.

He was killing her; she saw the hatred in his bulging eyes. She tried to catch at his hands but there was nothing she could do; she was fainting. This, she thought, is the end. He is murdering me.

Someone had burst in from the ante-room. There were cries of dismay. George Lewis released her; she fell fainting to the floor and lay there unconscious.

*   *   *

What a scandal! A quarrel between the Crown Prince and Princess which had almost led to his murdering her!

"She is such a violent creature!" Clara told Ernest Augustus. "It is her French blood."

"It seems that the violence came from George Lewis," Ernest Augustus pointed out.

"He happened to be the stronger, naturally. I'm afraid we brought trouble to the court when we brought that creature into it."

Although Ernest Augustus was inclined to be lenient, the Duchess Sophia blamed Sophia Dorothea. "It seems that she was making a scene because of her husband's mistress," said Sophia. "Does she not realize that this trivial matter is of no importance? She is failing in her duty as a wife when she acts so foolishly."

Sophia Dorothea herself lay listlessly in her bedchamber where George Lewis was advised by his father to visit her, and this he did. He asked her how she was, as though he were repeating an unpleasant lesson, paid scarcely any attention to the reply and then sat in silence by her bed for ten minutes—presumably the time he was told he should—after which he leaped up with obvious relief and left.

Sophia Dorothea was weeping quietly when her mother-in-law came to her bedside.

"Please, do be calm," said the Duchess Sophia. "We know where that other bout of temper led you. I have come to tell you that as soon as you are fit to travel—which the doctors tell me will be in a day or so—you are coming with me to Herrenhausen for a rest. I am sure that is what you need."

Herrenhausen! And with the Duchess Sophia!

If she were not so listless that she did not much care what became of her she would have laughed with bitterness or wept with despair.

*   *   *

Herrenhausen—that little schloss surrounded by parkland and approached by avenues of limes—was greatly loved by the Duchess Sophia, and since there had been more money to spare she had enlarged it and beautified it to some extent, although she had by no means done all she intended to. She was happier at

Herrenhausen than anywhere else; there she could lead a life which appealed to her; there she could invite men and women whom she admired for their intellectual attainments and who would have no place at Hanover where, it might be said, Clara von Platen ruled. Here she could read the literature of many countries, for she was a skilled linguist and besides German spoke Dutch, French and Italian—and of course—and best of all—English. She liked to discuss art, philosophy and literature and it was always at Herrenhausen that she had an opportunity of doing this.

To Herrenhausen she came with Sophia Dorothea. Perhaps, she thought, I could make something of the girl. She is intelligent, more so than George Lewis ever could be; and she has been brought up to have an appreciation of art. But the girl was what Sophia called hysterical, which she believed was due to her upbringing at Celle. The Duchess Eléonore of Celle might be much admired for her culture, but she had brought up her only child in a sheltered atmosphere leading her to believe that life was much simpler than it was. Sophia Dorothea was expecting every marriage to be like that of her parents. In the days when Sophia Dorothea had lived at Celle her father had doted on her mother and there was complete accord between them. It had taken years of hard work and careful planning to smash that harmony and it was being done, but Sophia Dorothea was not there to see it and she still looked for that perfection in her own marriage which she had seen in her parents'.

The Duchess Sophia did not invite guests to Herrenhausen at this time. She wanted to talk very seriously to her daughter-in-law, to imbue her with a sense of her position not only in regard to George Lewis but as the future Electress of Hanover.

They talked as they did their needlework, for the Duchess believed in sewing for the poor and that no time should be wasted.

"You have been very foolish," she told Sophia Dorothea. "George Lewis might have harmed you."

"He has already done so."

"Nonsense, you'll soon recover from a few bruises."

"The indignity . . . the humiliation!"

"Nonsense. We shall order that the incident is forgotten and so it shall be."

"His behaviour with Fraulein von Schulenburg will not be easily forgotten."

"There you are foolish. I cannot understand how wives become dissatisfied with their husbands. No amount of infidelity on the part of my husband would disturb me. It is not bad taste for a man to associate with mistresses—particularly if he be in a high position."

Sophia Dorothea stared at her mother-in-law. "I have never heard such views expressed, nor did I ever expect to."

"That is because you have not been brought up in accordance with the rank which is now yours."

"I had a very happy childhood. I love my parents dearly and they love me. What could be a better upbringing than that?"

"To be given an understanding of reality and what actually goes on in the world. Now you have been handicapped by your home life, but you have learned your lesson. I should like you to understand that I will not tolerate your quarrelling with your husband on the trifling matter of his keeping mistresses. It shows obstinacy and bad temper and is most unbecoming."

"And what of George Lewis? Was his behaviour becoming?"

"He is a man, and not to be judged by his wife. You acted foolishly and I must beg of you not to do so again."

"I want to go and see my parents. I believe I should quickly be well again if I could."

"We shall see about that. I shall ask the Duke if he will allow it."

"Let me go back to Hanover and speak to the Duke."

"There is no need for that. I will tell him of your wish and we will ask for his consent. Now I beg of you, continue with your work. These garments are taking far too long. We will beguile the time in conversation, and I will tell you what is happening in England now."

Sophia Dorothea was thinking: Yes, that is the answer. I will go home to Celle. I will take the children with me and I will tell them everything that has taken place. Then they will not let me return. Oh, yes, I shall go home to Celle.

"And is it not an extraordinary state of affairs," the Duchess was saying. "James fled . . . and William . . . the man to whom he married his daughter . . . now on the throne. Of course if Charles had had a legitimate son, this would never have happened. I knew there would be trouble when Charles died. Now, listen carefully: If William and Mary are without children and Anne is too . . . do you know what that would mean to you?"

If I told dearest Maman and Papa everything they would not refuse to let me go back, Sophia Dorothea was thinking. When they know that he came near to murdering me . . .

"Are you listening? Or is it too much for you to contemplate? I admit it could be quite bewildering when it is first presented to you. I am next in the line of succession, for James's boy doesn't count. After Anne, I should be Queen of England. I can think of no greater honour. And the point is that when I die George Lewis would be King and that would make you Queen of England."

"Queen of England," repeated Sophia Dorothea, scarcely knowing what she said. That was the answer—home to Celle and once she had reached that sanctuary never to return, to stay there forever.

*   *   *

Ernest Augustus was sorry for his daughter-in-law. He would be sorry for anyone married to George Lewis and she was such a pretty creature. If she wanted to go home and visit her family, so she should—and take the children with her.

When she heard that her daughter was coming, the Duchess of Celle made delighted preparations; but Sophia Dorothea's attitude had betrayed her real intentions and Clara's spies had kept her well informed, so she hastened to inform Bernstorff that he must prepare Duke William.

Clara and Bernstorff met between Hanover and Celle, and Clara explained that the haughty young Sophia Dorothea, after showing that she herself had no love for her husband, had made a disgraceful scene with him because he had taken a mistress. She was now coming home to tell Maman and Papa all about it.

"You owe a great deal to Hanover," Clara reminded Bernstorff, who was ready to concede that point. He was now a landowner and could, if he wished, end his career at Celle and settle in an estate of his own. Clara had however pointed out that Ernest Augustus would frown on such an action. Bernstorff had been well paid for his part in arranging the marriage and it was his duty now to remain at his post to serve his patron for the sake of honour . . . and further financial reward.

So instead of living on his estates he contented himself with adding to them and making sure that Ernest Augustus's wishes were remembered at Celle. It was Bernstorff's task constantly to make friction between the Duke and Duchess, always to be ready to point out when the Duchess appeared to assume control. He had been successful, for George William now scarcely ever discussed state business with his wife and almost childishly insisted on having his own way even to his detriment.

Eléonore was saddened by this rift between them and turned more and more to her daughter and grandchildren whom she saw as often as possible. But of course these visits were not frequent enough. The Duchess Sophia had never liked her and she consequently never felt welcome at the Alte Palais or Herren-hausen; and although Sophia Dorothea came to Celle with the children as often as she could, naturally her duties as Crown Princess of Hanover prevented those visits being very frequent.

"You must tell George William that his daughter is behaving in a recklessly foolish manner," insisted Clara. "She has alien-ated Ernest Augustus by plotting with the younger sons—even against her own husband. She shows her dislike of her husband and then becomes hysterical because he takes a mistress. It would be as well, you might tell George William, that when his daughter pays this visit he takes her to task for *her* behaviour."

Bernstorff assured Clara that she need have no fear. He would prepare George William; so they parted and Bernstorff rode back to Celle, planning the complaints he would lay before his master while Clara made her way back to Hanover.

* * *

The Duchess of Celle was delighted to have her daughter with her. She waited impatiently for the trumpeter on the tower to announce the arrival and before the party from Hanover had reached the drawbridge she was running out to embrace her daughter.

"My dearest! And how are you? You look pale! Is it just the journey?"

The Duchess knew it was not just the journey and anger momentarily choked her joy—anger against those who had dared make her darling unhappy.

"And the children!" Tears filled the Duchess's eyes. "What a little man George Augustus is! And where is my darling little Sophia Dorothea?"

She kissed the little girl. "So like you, my love, when you were a baby. No, Master George Augustus, I have not forgotten *you* !"

The children were well. She need not concern herself with them. It was her daughter who puzzled her. The nurses took the children to the apartment prepared for them and Eléonore herself led Sophia Dorothea to that suite of rooms, so familiar to her, and watching her daughter sit on the bed in the alcove and look round the room, her eyes resting on the four cupids, Eléonore knew that Sophia Dorothea was wishing that this was not merely a visit.

She sat on the bed beside her daughter. "It is wonderful to have you back, dearest."

Sophia Dorothea was crying quietly. "I was so happy here . . ." she murmured. "Never so happy . . . anywhere else."

"My darling."

"Oh, Maman, if you had not been so good to me, if you had loved me less, if I had not had the perfect mother perhaps I should be able to bear all this more easily."

"Tell me everything."

"I want to come home," sobbed Sophia Dorothea. "I want never to go away but to say with you for the rest of my life."

While Eléonore rocked her daughter to and fro as though she were a child, she was making plans for the future.

*   *   *

The three of them were together in the room which used to be the schoolroom. There at the table Sophia Dorothea and Eléonore von Knesebeck had worked at their lessons; they had sat in the window looking out over the moat, ecstatically sniffing the scent of limes in flower or watching the branches dip and sway in the winter wind. The same schoolroom, everything so familiar, thought Sophia Dorothea but she was a lifetime away from those days of peace and pleasure.

There was her mother, bewildered as though she was wondering what could have brought the change, no longer omnipotent, or omniscient, a frightened woman, ready to plead for her daughter. It was her father who had changed from the benevolent figure of her childhood. His smile was guarded; the warmth had gone from his expression. Sometimes when he spoke it was as though he were repeating a lesson.

Her mother was saying : "But surely you have no wish that our daughter should submit to these insults. . . . And more than that ! George Lewis might have killed her."

"You take these matters too seriously, my dear. Sophia Dorothea has only to behave with dignity . . . take the example of her mother-in-law."

"Clara von Platen has never taken precedence over the Duchess Sophia," put in Sophia Dorothea.

"And has this woman over you?"

"George Lewis ignores me and is constantly with her."

"You are too impulsive. Keep out of their way."

"But," said the Duchess Eléonore, "our daughter is being insulted by George Lewis and this woman."

"I tell you, you are making trouble where it does not exist. And I have not heard very good reports from Hanover of your conduct, daughter. It would appear that you have been indulging in conspiracies—dangerous conspiracies—with your brothers-in-law."

"That is lies . . . made up by my enemies."

"Still, it is unfortunate that you should have been suspected. You must have been indiscreet."

"You take their side against me!" cried Sophia Dorothea incredulously.

"My dear child, you have been behaving rather foolishly. You cannot leave your husband just because you decide you would rather live in your own home."

Sophia Dorothea saw the horror in her mother's face and she thought : I am not to stay here then. It is no longer my home.

She was frightened. She needed to be taken under their protection. She could not explain to them : I am afraid . . . afraid of the future when Königsmarck returns. I do not know what will happen then . . . but if you would let me stay here . . . protect me from my husband's insults . . . from my own folly . . . I can perhaps work out a life for myself. I need my mother as never before . . . I need you both.

"You cannot stay here," went on George William. "This must be a short visit . . . nothing more. Even a long stay would result in gossip."

Her mother had risen; there was anger in her eyes; but Sophia Dorothea caught her hand. She felt that the decision had been made. There was no going back now. Whatever was to happen in the future had been decided in this moment.

"Do not plead for me, Maman," she said. "I should not wish to stay where I am not wanted."

Eléonore cried : "George William, this is our own beloved daughter. . . ."

He did not look at them; he was afraid that if he did he would become weak, for he loved them, and like his daughter he would have been happy to go back to the old days of peace and contentment. But they had governed him then. He had been lazy, giving way to everything, a laughing-stock of his brother's court and of his own. He had to play the man, the head of the house whose word was law.

"I have told you," he said. "This is a short visit. Next week Sophia Dorothea must return to Hanover and her husband. And if he takes a mistress . . ." George William shrugged his shoulders. "It is a common habit. And she must look to her own shortcomings and not run to Celle to complain to us."

With that he left them.

They did not speak; they merely looked at each other. Then

Sophia threw herself into her mother's arms. Eléonore did her best to comfort her daughter. She suffered with her—the same torment and desolation.

*   *   *

Deserted by my own family! thought Sophia Dorothea. That was something she would never have believed possible. The familiar rooms had lost their charm. They were no longer that haven she had always believed them to be. There was a sinister atmosphere in what had once seemed so dear to her. She hated them, she told herself, even more than her apartments at Hanover. At least there she had not expected to find peace and comfort.

Her mother did her best to comfort her. She must go back to Hanover, she pointed out. She must try to be happy.

Try to be happy? How could one . . . married to George Lewis. Oh, it was not that her mother did not understand, only that she, like Sophia Dorothea, knew herself to be defeated.

She would have given her life for her daughter but what could she give but advice? She was no less hurt and bewildered by George William's conduct than her daughter was.

"We must leave here," Sophia Dorothea told Eléonore von Knesebeck, "and the sooner the better. It was a mistake to come. I have only found fresh unhappiness here."

Eléonore von Knesebeck made her preparations. Sophia Dorothea took a cool farewell of her father and a warm one of her mother and holding her head proudly high stepped into her coach with the children, Eléonore von Knesebeck and the few servants she had brought with her.

The Duchess of Celle watched the coach until she could no longer see it and then went to her apartments and remained there. In his study George William buried his face in his hands. He too was unhappy; but he was right, he insisted. The alliance with Hanover could not be broken for the whim of a spoilt child.

The distance between Hanover and Celle was not great and during it the travellers must pass Herrenhausen. As the castle came in sight the guards pulled up the carriage and told Sophia Dorothea that the Duke and Duchess were obviously in residence there and that the trumpeter was already announcing their arrival.

Sophia Dorothea lay back against the upholstered coach and closed her eyes. They would know that she had appealed to her parents to let her stay with them; and they would know that she had been refused. She pictured the sly looks of Clara von Platen, the stern ones of the Duchess Sophia, and she knew that in her present heartbroken state she could not face them.

"Drive on," she cried. "Straight on to Hanover."

The driver whipped up the horses. On they went. Sophia Dorothea closed her eyes and did not look at Herrenhausen as they passed.

*　　*　　*

"It's an insult!" cried Clara. "She is deliberately flouting you."

Ernest Augustus frowned. He had been inclined to favour the girl because she was so pretty, but his feelings had changed towards her since the Mölcke affair.

He did not in his heart believe she would be guilty of conspiracy to murder him; but she had been a friend of Mölcke and Maximilian. And now she was making trouble with George Lewis. George Lewis had all but murdered her, but she must have provoked the attack. And then she must run home to her parents and ask them to shelter her.

She was troublesome, that girl, and he did not care for trouble.

He shrugged his shoulders, but Clara, watching him closely and knowing him so well, followed his line of thought.

Rejected by her parents. Out of favour with Ernest Augustus. Disliked by her husband. Königsmarck far away. Sophia Dorothea had never been so vulnerable as she was now.

Was this the time to strike?

Given the opportunity, Clara would be ready.

Gossip in Dresden

LIFE at Hanover was intolerable with Königsmarck or without him. Sophia Dorothea came to this sudden decision. Previously she had been sustained by the thought that if her life with George Lewis became unendurable she could fly to Celle—now she knew that that escape was denied to her. Perhaps this was the greatest shock she had received so far. To be repudiated by her own father was something which would have seemed to her impossible. She knew that he had forced her to this marriage, but she had convinced herself that he had done so only because he had believed it would be good for her. But now he turned his back on her. Her mother was the only one in the world—with the exception of her lover—on whom she could rely; and her mother was in the power of her father.

Dearest Philip, she thought, you are the only person who can help me.

She would not stay here. She would leave Hanover; and if her parents would not have her there, there must be someone else.

She discussed her plight hourly with Eléonore vcn Knesebeck. She wrote passionate letters to her lover. Königsmarck replied that he understood that she could not continue in her present state. He thought that a flight to France might be possible. After all she was half French; if she became a Catholic she would be well received there; he would join her and as George Lewis would certainly divorce her, they would be married.

"There are the children!" cried Sophia Dorothea distractedly.
"I should lose them for ever."

No, she dared not cut herself off completely from the House
of Brunswick-Lüneberg; in such a way would she lose her mother
too. There must be another way. The answer was surely Wolfenbüttel. Why could she not throw herself on the mercy of her
kinsman? Maximilian was already there. She would be among
friends; she could take her children with her.

She talked constantly of this project to Eléonore von Knesebeck and letters came back and forth between herself and Königsmarck.

*   *   *

One of the most licentious men in Europe was Frederick
Augustus the new Elector of Saxony, and, delighted to find himself in power, he very quickly began to show his subjects the sort
of man he was. The court at Dresden was going to rival Versailles, not be a mere shadow of it; Dresden itself was going to
have buildings to equal in splendour those of the Roi Soleil. He
already had his seraglio but he was going to increase that; he
intended to live like a sultan of the Arabian Nights.

He welcomed his friend Königsmarck, and when he found
him melancholy, laughed at him and told him that the pleasures
of Dresden would soon disperse his sadness.

Königsmarck was a compulsive talker who could never restrain
a desire to amuse; it was for this reason that Frederick Augustus
enjoyed his company. At the extravagant banquets he would
often have him at his side and make efforts to turn him into the
gay companion he had once been.

Königsmarck's thoughts were busy. If he were going to elope
with Sophia Dorothea he needed all the money he could lay
his hands on. In the past Frederick Augustus had lost to him
heavily at cards when they had been in the army together and
these debts had never been repaid. Now if he could get the money
that was owing him he would be in a better position for a successful elopement.

This, he told himself, was the reason he stayed on at Dresden.
But it was not entirely so, and in his heart he knew it. He liked
the carefree reckless splendour of this court; now and then the
thought entered his mind that if it were not for his involvement
with Sophia Dorothea he would be enjoying life as wholeheartedly
as Frederick Augustus did. Yet he loved Sophia Dorothea. He
wanted only Sophia Dorothea. If he could have married her he
believed he would have settled down to raise a family, throw

aside his adventurous life without a regret as her father had done when he met the only woman in the world for him.

He was torn one way and another. Frederick Augustus noticed this and came to the conclusion that the best way to restore his friend to his gay old self was to separate him from the Princess of Hanover.

"I can't pay you what I owe you in cash," said Frederick Augustus. "Instead you shall have a post of major general in the Saxon army. That will bring you an income far exceeding my debt to you—and there'll be little tax on your time."

Königsmarck was nonplussed. His friend had flattered him, but he was already a Colonel in the Hanoverian army.

Frederick Augustus laughed at him.

"Give it a trial," he said.

Königsmarck thought of the money he would have; and while he was in Dresden he might as well take it.

It was as though he were marking time, waiting, wondering which way to jump. He knew very well that if he returned to Hanover he would have to take some action.

*　　*　　*

Once he had made the decision Königsmarck felt relieved; he was already slipping into his old ways; and in the company of Frederick Augustus when the drinking was heavy conversation became racy and reckless.

Frederick Augustus was very interested in the rival court of Hanover and who could better satisfy his curiosity than his friend Königsmarck who had recently lived there? The Elector would gather a few of his drinking friends together and, with a mistress on either side of him, would urge his friends to regurgitate the scraps of scandal they had gathered from all over Europe.

William of Orange and his wife Mary were freely discussed and Frederick Augustus was helpless with laughter at the thought of William's intrigue with Elizabeth Villiers. Having known William it was difficult to imagine him as the lover, and why he should indulge in such an affair gave rise to much ribald speculation, particularly as his interest in his male friends was well known. They discussed the possibility of Elizabeth Villiers being a blind for other activities.

It was very entertaining to laugh at the great soldier who, in the battlefield, had proved himself to be more skilful than they could ever be. Then the conversation turned to Hanover.

Königsmarck felt suddenly sad. He had been drinking more than was usual and felt a longing to be back in Hanover with

Sophia Dorothea. He knew in that moment that he loved her, that he wanted a chance to live in retirement with her for the rest of his life.

"My friend is becoming melancholy," murmured Frederick Augustus.

"I am thinking of Hanover," Königsmarck sighed.

"A fair lady in Hanover?"

"The fairest lady in Hanover is the Princess Sophia Dorothea," cried Königsmarck. "It is a shame and a scandal the way George Lewis treats her. I could murder him with my bare hands."

"Our friend has always been known for his chivalry towards ladies in distress," said Frederick Augustus with a smile. "Tell us more about the beautiful Princess and her ogre of a husband."

Königsmarck talked. He did not realize how freely; it was like thinking aloud. She should not be left to her misery; someone should rescue her, carry her away to where she could live happily ever after.

It was clear to the company that Königsmarck felt romantically towards the Princess of Hanover, but this maudlin sentiment was not as amusing as the more scandalous tales of George Lewis and his mistress and the Countess von Platen and her lovers.

It soothed his melancholy to be the focus of their interest. He had information which they sought; the stories he could tell could hold the company's interest and amuse; Königsmarck, a born raconteur, could not resist the temptation.

His glass was filled; his spirits rose; he heard the laughter as he gave an imitation of George Lewis's attempts at tenderness towards Fraulein von Schulenburg; but it was Clara who provided his greatest success. Were the stories that were being circulated about that woman true? Was she in fact sexually insatiable? How often did she deceive Ernest Augustus? Was it true that she took lovers indiscriminately—high born and low?

"She is an amazing woman," said Königsmarck. "I know from personal experience."

They must know all he had to tell about this remarkable woman. So Königsmarck, excited and elated by potent wine and flattering attention told the intimate details of his relationship with Clara von Platen.

*　　*　　*

News travelled back to Hanover. Clara's spies seized on it and carried it to her. She was being laughed at all over Europe. Her intimate secrets were secrets no longer. By God, she thought, I'll be revenged for this.

And the enemy was Königsmarck, the man she loved, the man she hated, the man she desired and the man she wanted to see ruined. Because her feelings were mixed, her rage was all the more intense.

Sooner or later the fact that the scandals of his court were being discussed throughout Europe would reach the ears of Ernest Augustus; and Clara wanted to be there first.

He was lying on his bed tired after the day's business when she went to him. He was often tired now; he was growing old and this meant that he was easier to manage; and the best time to get what she wanted was when he was exhausted. Then she could soothe him with her gentle attentions and couch her request so that he would grant it in order to have done with an unpleasant matter.

She soaked a handkerchief in a cooling perfume and bathed his forehead.

"That fool Königsmarck is talking too much in Dresden," she said softly.

"Everywhere people are talking too much."

"It's true. He has taken a post in the Saxon army. He seems to have forgotten you made him a Colonel of your guards."

"He's a slippery adventurer. I like the fellow, but don't forget he's a Swede, and if he likes to serve Saxony instead of Hanover he can."

"You are too lenient."

Ernest Augustus closed his eyes as though to imply he was weary of the subject.

"The fellow has uttered some insults about George Lewis," she said.

"No doubt he deserved them."

"Even so he is the Crown Prince of Hanover and to insult him is to insult Hanover."

"George Lewis will take care of it."

"He has insulted me and Fraulein von Schulenburg. George Lewis is angry about this."

Ernest Augustus shruged his shoulders.

"You like the fellow," Clara accused him.

"You like him too," retaliated Ernest Augustus and Clara was silent. "Why," he went on, "he's handsome, romantic. Of course you like him."

"So it seems does Sophia Dorothea. If he is her lover . . . if there is anything in the rumours then . . . that is dangerous."

Ernest Augustus was obviously more alert.

"I don't believe it to be so. She has too keen a sense of duty."

"But if it were so it could be disastrous. The son of the Princess —who in certain circumstances could be the heir—not begotten by the Crown Prince but by a Swedish adventurer!"

"She would never . . ."

"If she did, if it could be proved . . . then you would take action against him . . . against her."

"Action would then of course be necessary," said Ernest Augustus.

Clara sat by his bed exulting.

I'll be revenged, she promised herself. I'll be revenged on them both.

Tragedy in the Leine Schloss

Königsmarck was back in Hanover. His stay in Dresden had forced him to a decision. He was tired of the gay life; he wanted only to be with Sophia Dorothea. He was certain of it now. There was no happiness for him apart from her.

He was going to be bold and reckless and carry her right away from Hanover to where they could be happy together living the simple life.

He was not received with enthusiasm at court. The news of his gossip at Dresden was one reason; it had incensed the Crown Prince and his mistress and those who wanted to please them had to pretend to be disgusted too. He had accepted a commission in the army of Saxony when he had one in Hanover. Some explanation would eventually be expected of him.

When Clara saw him her desire for him made her forget her hatred. If he would come back to her, be her lover again, she would forgive him everything. As for Sophia Dorothea, the loss of Königsmarck would be her punishment. That was enough for any woman, Clara decided. How she would enjoy flaunting her enjoyment of the man in Sophia Dorothea's face; she would visit her and discuss his perfections with her as he had discussed her with his friends in Dresden.

She waylaid him and cornered him on the day of his return. Brilliantly painted, seductively gowned, she barred his way in one of the ante-rooms of the palace.

"So you are back." She stood close to him, her hand on his arm. "I am pleased to see you."

Königsmarck looked over her head. "I am honoured." His voice was cold.

"You should visit me at Monplaisir."

"I fear I have no time for such a visit."

Angry lights shot up in Clara's eyes.

"You will be too busily engaged elsewhere?"

"I hope to be," he answered.

"And if I were to promise you . . ."

"Nothing you could promise me would make me change my mind."

Why was she standing here accepting insults? Clara asked herself. Why did she not abuse him, call him traitor, gossip—and the worst of scandalmongers who betrays the confidences of the bedchamber?

She hated him and yet her desire for him was a raging torment. He bowed coldly and passed on.

*   *   *

This was the end of Königsmarck, Clara decided. She could no longer tolerate his presence in Hanover. He had made it clear that he would never be her lover again.

And if, said Clara to herself, he will not be my lover he shall be no one else's.

She saw herself every night thinking of him wherever he was with other women—Sophia Dorothea in all probability. How could she endure that? And to think that he should prefer Sophia Dorothea, that pretty little creature without character, without experience! It was not to be borne.

In the heat of passion she sat down and wrote a letter. She knew Sophia Dorothea's handwriting and she could easily do a draft which could be mistaken for it even by one who had received many letters from her. It was addressed to Königsmarck, telling him he must visit her that night at the Leine Schloss. It was imperative.

She then sent for one of her spies in Sophia Dorothea's household and told her that the letter must be given to Königsmarck with the information that the Princess had asked her to deliver it.

*   *   *

It was getting late. Ernest Augustus would soon be retiring for the night. Clara said : "I must see you alone."

Then she told him that she feared what could happen unless prompt action were taken.

"You are too tolerant of rogues," she told him. "Königsmarck has shown that he is no friend to Hanover in the last months. Now I have proof to offer you. He is planning to elope with Sophia Dorothea."

"Impossible."

"Is it? He is visiting her tonight. He'll spend the night with her making love and plans. They are going to leave Hanover and seek refuge in Wolfenbüttel."

Wolfenbüttel! The mention of that name was enough to arouse Ernest Augustus's anger.

"What a scandal! What do you think they will say of us at Hanover? They'll be rising against us soon. And all because you have refused to believe what is going on under your nose. I should have thought the Mölcke affair would have been a warning but you refused to believe ill of your beautiful daughter-in-law. She could do no wrong. No! Only receive her lover at night, only plot her elopement, only plot against you who have shown her nothing but kindness."

"Are you sure she is receiving Königsmarck tonight?"

"Absolutely sure. There is only one thing to do—arrest him when he is leaving her apartment. Then you will see that what I have told you is true."

"Yes, arrest him."

"Leave this to me," said Clara. "We do not want a scandal. I will instruct the guards who are to arrest him. We will do it as quietly as possible. We do not want the whole of Europe to know that the Crown Princess receives a lover in her bedchamber. There'll be doubt of the parentage of her children if it becomes common knowledge. Will you trust me with this arrest?"

Ernest Augustus nodded. "I know why you want to have charge of this, Clara. He's a very handsome man. You want him treated gently."

"I want to make sure that I do the best for you."

*   *   *

In the small room in the Leine Schloss Clara threw off her cloak and confronted the four halberdiers whom she had summoned there.

The light of candles threw their flickering glow on a flagon of wine set on the table.

Clara produced the document to which Ernest Augustus had put his signature.

"You will wait in the corridor close to the apartments of the Princess of Hanover," said Clara, "until you see a man emerge. He will have to pass along the corridor and you will wait for him. The Elector's orders are that he should be taken ... dead or alive."

"Dead or alive!" repeated the leader of the men.

"Fortify yourselves," said Clara, pointing to the flagon. "He may try to defend himself. He'll be a desperate man."

"We will carry out the Elector's orders, Countess," was the answer. "We'll get him ... dead or alive."

Clara left them and went to wait in a small room close by. Pictures came unbidden to her mind; she tried to chase them away and could not. Sophia Dorothea and Königsmarck together now. . . .

*   *   *

Disguised in an old jacket and a rough brown cloak Königsmarck made his way into the Leine Schloss. In his pocket he carried the note which he believed had come from Sophia Dorothea. Something extraordinary must have happened for her to take this risk; but he could not be concerned with that. He was going to be with her again; and now that he was here it seemed to him that nothing on earth mattered but that. He loved Sophia Dorothea. He was a different man from the careless adventurer of the past. He had been weak and foolish, even after loving her, but he was going to break away from the old meaningless life; he could not do it at one stroke. But now he knew he would in time because nothing else in the world mattered but their happiness. Tonight he would persuade her to leave everything and run away with him.

He entered the castle and made his way to the wing in which he knew the Princess had her apartments. He quickly passed through the rittersaal—the knights' hall—to a smaller hall close by; now he could see the door which led to the Princesses's apartments.

Swiftly he went to it and lightly scratched. It was opened by Eléonore von Knesebeck, who looked startled.

"My lord Count . . ."

"Take me to the Princess."

"Yes, yes. Come in quickly. . . . Oh this is dangerous . . . at such a time."

"I came in answer to her summons."

Eléonore looked even more surprised. Then she said : "Follow me."

Sophia Dorothea was in her bed and she gave a cry of joy
when she saw her lover and they were in each other's arms.

Eléonore von Knesebeck stood at the door, watching.

"Keep guard," said Sophia Dorothea.

Eléonore nodded, asking herself why she had not been told
that Königsmarck had been summoned. Usually she shared the
confidences.

Quietly she shut the dor and went to her own apartment. She
heard the key turn in the lock as she did so.

Sophia Dorothea was saying : "This is dangerous."

"You don't imagine I wouldn't come if you sent for me?"

"Sent for you! But I would not allow you to do anything so
dangerous."

He took the letter from his pocket and Sophia Dorothea
frowned over it.

"I did not write it."

"Then who . . . ?"

Danger, their minds warned them. Who had lured Königsmarck to the Leine Schloss tonight and for what purpose? But
they were together and they did not want to entertain any fears
of what this might mean. There had been long dreary months
without each other. They were both convinced that their only
chance of happiness was together.

"I am here . . . with you . . . what matters aught else?" demanded Königsmarck.

"Oh, how I have longed for you!"

They made ecstatic love; and afterwards they made plans.

Life could not go on as it had been. They were both certain.
Everything that had happened before was past and done with.
The future was theirs. It did not matter where they were as long
as they were together.

They would fly to Wolfenbüttel where they could be sure of
shelter. She would bring the children with her for she could not
bear to be parted from them. They were determined on flight.

"When?" cried Sophia Dorothea. "It cannot be too soon."

"It must be soon," said Königsmarck. "We dare not delay.
There are too many spies about. I cannot hide my love for you.
It must be tomorrow."

"But how?"

"I shall let it be known that I am returning to Dresden. My
reception here has been rather cold and it will seem natural. My
coach will be waiting outside my house and the coachmen will
be given instruction that they are to go to Dresden. You and
Knesebeck will leave the palace quietly dressed so as to attract

no attention. You will slip into the coach where I shall be waiting. When we are outside the town I will give the instructions to make for Wolfenbüttel instead of Dresden. And then . . . we shall be well on the way before it is noticed."

"And the children?"

"We must send for them later. To take them with us would certainly result in failure."

"I could not bear to lose them."

"You shall not. I promise you, you shall not. You know I could not fail you." She was sure he could not fail her. She lay shuddering in his arms and yet she was gloriously happy. To escape from the misery of Hanover. To be happy with her lover. That was what she wanted; that was what she needed if she were not to die of melancholy.

There was a gentle scratching at the door.

"I'll go and see who is there. Hide yourself."

Sophia Dorothea went to the door. It was only Eléonore von Knesebeck, alarmed by the length of the visit, for she guessed the lovers had not noticed the passing of time.

"If he remains much longer it will be dawn," she whispered.

Königsmarck came forward. "Our Confidante is right," he said. "I must leave now."

There was a last embrace.

"Tomorrow," whispered Königsmarck.

"Tomorrow," echoed Sophia Dorothea.

Then the door shut on him leaving a bewildered Eléonore von Knesebeck with an exultant Sophia Dorothea.

*   *   *

Königsmarck crossed the rittersaal, walked to the door which he had left unlocked that he might easily slip away and turned the handle. It was locked.

He was alert. Someone had locked the door. Why? Because they knew he would want to leave by it.

He turned, and at that moment he saw the gleam of halberds, while simultaneously he was seized from behind.

There were four of them—four figures, armed, determined on his destruction.

He drew his sword and struck out in the dimness; then he felt the violent blow on his head; he swayed and as he saw the cold steel at his heart he cried out: "The Princess is innocent. . . . Do not harm her!" Then bleeding profusely he fell half swooning to the floor.

"He's dead," whispered one of the halberdiers.

"Do you see who?" asked another.

"Königsmarck! Oh, my God, what have we done!"

Clara who had been waiting close by, came hurrying out. She carried a candelabra in her hand and holding it high above her head stared down at the figure on the floor.

"Oh, God!" she whispered.

Königsmarck, opening his eyes, saw her. "You! So it is you!" he murmured. "You evil woman. Murderess. Your revenge this. . . . The Princess is innocent. . . ."

That he should seek to defend her rival at such a moment maddened Clara.

She put her foot on his mouth and ground in her heel.

But even as she stared down at him, her feelings suffered a reversal. She knew that he was the only man she really wanted.

She cried out : "You clumsy fools. You've killed him. You were told to arrest him and you've killed him!"

She knelt down and put her arms about him.

"Königsmarck," she whispered, "you're not going to die."

"Evil woman . . . would to God I had never . . ."

So he was conscious still. He was cursing her. Then his face softened as he said : "Save her. . . . She . . . innocent. . . ."

His head fell backwards and his glassy stare was fixed on Clara's face.

"He's dead," she whispered. "Königsmarck is dead."

*　　*　　*

She looked down at her blood-spattered gown; then she hurried to the Elector's apartments. He started up in bed at the sight of her—dishevelled and bloody.

"They have killed Königsmarck," she said.

"Killed him! No!"

She nodded. "We must act quickly. His body is lying there near the Princess's apartment. He resisted arrest and so was killed."

Ernest Augustus looked at her intently; but he was too old and tired to attempt to probe her devious intentions.

Königsmarck murdered! This would create scandal throughout Europe and more than scandal. Königsmarck was of too important a family for his murder to be hushed up.

Clara followed his line of thought. "There is only one thing to be done," she said. "Leave this to me. His body must be buried before dawn and all signs of the murder removed."

Clara left the Elector and went back to the halberdiers, two of whom were badly wounded and in need of attention. They must invent some story of a street fight in which they had been hurt, she told them. The other two must hastily put the body into a hole in the grounds and cover it with quick lime. All the bloodstains must be washed away; while they were fresh it would be easy to do so. They would need help and they must get it, but inform all those who were called to their assistance that if they spoke a word of this night's work they would bitterly regret it.

They knew how terrible the anger of Clara von Platen could be. They had an example of it in the dead body of Königsmarck. They worked with speed; and by the morning there was no sign in the Leine Schloss of what had happened during the night.

*   *   *

With the help of Eléonore von Knesebeck Sophia Dorothea was packing her jewels.

"This time tomorrow," she said, "we shall be far away."

"Yes," agreed Eléonore, her teeth chattering.

"I could endure it no more."

"No. You have endured too much. But there will be such a scandal."

"I no longer care."

The jewels were packed into a case which Fraulein Knesebeck would carry.

"Let us lie down," said Sophia Dorothea. "I feel exhausted and yet wide awake. You lie down with me . . . and we'll talk as we used to when we were little."

They talked of the next day. They would be in readiness, waiting until the message from Königsmarck arrived; and then they would put on two of Eléonore's oldest cloaks and slip out of the palace. The coach would be waiting for them and in it Königsmarck. And as soon as they were safely inside . . . away to Wolfenbüttel.

"There are strange noises in the palace tonight," said Eléonore von Knesebeck.

"You are never awake at this hour, that's why you notice them."

"What should they be doing in corridors by night?"

"You are dreaming, Knesebeck. You're half asleep."

"Am I?"

"Yes. Go to sleep. I shan't. I shan't sleep again until I'm in Wolfenbüttel."

*   *   *

How long the morning seemed. At every sound they started up. But no messenger came, and the morning passed and they were still waiting.

It was afternoon.

"Something has gone wrong," said Sophia Dorothea. "He said he would send for us in the morning. It would have been easier to slip out then."

"He will send in the afternoon," consoled Fraulein von Knesebeck.

"The children will be here for their daily visit soon," said Sophia Dorothea.

"If the message comes while they are here we shall wait till they have left."

"I shall be tempted to take them with me."

Eléonore von Knesebeck shivered.

But the children did not come and there was no message; and by the time the afternoon was over they knew that something was wrong.

*   *   *

Where is Königsmarck? It was the question which was being asked all over Hanover. His servants had not seen him. They had not been alarmed when he had not returned home that night because he often indulged in night adventures. But now he had been missing for two nights and not one of his household knew where he was.

Hildebrand, Königsmarck's faithful secretary, was very anxious because he was aware that his master had been making plans to leave Hanover and that the Princess Sophia Dorothea was involved in them.

He would send to Dresden, he said, for it might be that some news of him could be found there. Königsmarck's sister Aurora was now beginning to be very disturbed; she herself would visit Dresden for, she said, she was determined to find her brother.

In her apartments Sophia Dorothea was both heartbroken and terrified.

"I am afraid," she said to Eléonore, "that the greatest tragedy of my life is about to happen."

Even at that moment Ernest Augustus had sent his guards to search Königsmarck's apartments in the hope, he said, that some clue might be found which would explain his disappearance.

*   *   *

Ernest Augustus was staring at the papers which lay before him on the table. Watching him intently were the Platens and the Duchess Sophia.

"So they were going to Wolfenbüttel," said the Elector. "They were going to our enemies."

"Traitors—both of them!' cried Clara.

The Duchess Sophia said nothing; she sat back in her chair, her hands folded on her lap, her lips tight. The daughter of that woman who had supplanted her all those years ago was in utter disgrace from which she could never extricate herself. Sophia at least would do nothing to help her. She would show George William what a fool he had been to refuse the daughter of Kings and take a commoner to wife. This slut, this Frenchwoman's brat, had disgraced her parents and she should never again set foot in the court of Hanover if the Duchess Sophia could help it.

Ernest Augustus was angry. To elope to Wolfenbüttel—that stronghold of traitors! It was too much. If she had merely taken a lover he would have forgiven her. God knew she had had enough provocation, and he was not the man to condemn others for weaknesses which he himself possessed. But in planning to go to Wolfenbüttel, she had forfeited all claim to his sympathy and help. And there it all was in the papers found in Königsmarck's apartments. No, he would have no mercy for Sophia Dorothea.

"Her parents should be informed of her guilt," said the Duchess Sophia.

"Without delay, I think, Your Highness," agreed Clara.

The two women nodded to each other. There was no rancour between them; they were agreed on this. They both urgently desired the ruin of Sophia Dorothea.

*   *   *

She walked about her apartments in a daze. She took no heed of time. She did not know now how many days had passed. There was only one thing she knew : her heart was broken, for some terrible tragedy had overtaken her lover; it was the only reason why he would desert her.

She had lost him; some intuition told her she would never look on his face again; and she was alone . . . staring disaster in the face.

"What shall I do? What shall I do?" she demanded of a terrified Fraulein von Knesebeck.

But the Confidante had no answer for her.

There was Celle. There was her mother.

"My mother is the only one left to me, Knesebeck. She would never desert me. She will come for me. She will take me home now."

*   *   *

The Duchess Eléonore was in tears. "She must come home. I will look after her. This is lies . . . all of it is lies. She has been indiscreet . . . but never wicked. She is incapable of wickedness."

George William looked in astonishment at his wife.

"Have you read these letters? Her guilt is plain. She has been Königsmarck's mistress. She was going to elope with him . . . to Wolfenbüttel."

"I don't believe it."

"You must believe your own eyes. Read these letters . . . in her handwriting. They will make you blush with shame. Your daughter so to conduct herself!"

"She was driven to it. Oh, God, I foresaw this. . . . On that morning . . . that birthday morning. . . . Life was so wonderful before that. And you gave her away as though she were nothing more than a piece of land. Your own daughter! *My* daughter! Now she must come back to me. I will nurse her back to health. I will make her hapy again."

"She shall not come here."

They faced each other. He had been primed by Bernstorff, for Clara and the Duchess Sophia had determined that the Princess was not going back to her mother. Oh no! She had sinned and they were going to see that she was punished. Not back to Celle to be petted and pampered by the Frenchwoman—that clot of dirt, who doubtless thought it was amusing that Princes should be deceived.

George William must be a man in his own house.

"I have made up my mind," he said.

"If you close your door to her my heart is closed to you forever," she told him.

But he would not give way. He was older now, more selfish. Her approval was not so necessary to him as that of his brother the Elector.

Her beautiful face was set in a stony expression as she said: "I no longer care for anyone but my daughter and my grandchildren. And all the years of happiness I had with you are without meaning, for I was mistaken when I gave my love to a man who could so heartlessly treat his own daughter."

She turned and left him and he almost ran to her crying out that he wanted it to be as it was in the beginning. They would have their daughter back; they would be together as they were in the days of Sophia Dorothea's childhood when the whole world meant nothing to them and their happiness was in each other.

But even as he moved he could hear the mocking laughter of Hanover—his brother's supercilious chuckle, the sneer of the

Platen woman, the scorn of the Duchess Sophia; and his pride was stronger than his love.·

Eléonore went alone to her apartments to pray for her daughter and to fight for her as well as she could . . . alone.

*   *   *

"I have no friends," said Sophia Dorothea. "There is no one to help me."

But she had a friend in her mother. Eléonore made no excuses for her father. He was against her and all who were against Sophia Dorothea were against the Duchess of Celle. "Rest assured, my darling," wrote Duchess Eléonore, "your enemies are mine and though all the world were against you I should be at your side. Do not despair. I shall find some way of bringing you comfort."

Sophia Dorothea wept when she read that letter. She believed now that her lover was dead, for only death, she was sure, would have kept him from her.

Her heart, she said, was broken; and doom was close at hand.

*   *   *

Count Platen came to her apartments.

He scarcely recognized the white-faced wild-eyed girl who received him. It was two weeks since the night of Königsmarck's murder and Sophia Dorothea had eaten scarcely anything and had slept little since.

"Your guilt is known," said Platen. "Many of your criminal letters are in the hands of the Elector and we know that Count Königsmarck was your lover and that you were planning to elope with him. It is decided that you are no longer welcome at Hanover."

"Nothing would please me more than to leave it. And how dare you keep me here a prisoner!"

"Your father agrees with all that is being done. The Elector is in constant communication with him. It has to be decided whether you are pregnant by Königsmarck which, you will admit, is a possibility."

"How dare you address me in such a coarse manner! You speak to me as though I am a woman like your wife."

"Madam, such insults will not help you. Everything is known."

"And where is Count Königsmarck?"

"He was killed resisting arrest in the early morning when he was discovered leaving your bedchamber."

She had known it; but the blatant truth was hard to accept. She put her hands to her face that he might not see her agony.

But how could she hide it? Everything was lost. She could see nothing about her but desolation and misery.

When Platen left, Eléonore von Knesebeck helped her mistress to her bed; and there she lay for several days not caring what became of her.

Shortly afterwards arrangments were made for her to leave Hanover, and she was conducted to the castle of Ahlden—a state prisoner.

Epilogue

THE people of Ahlden could scarcely remember what life had been like before the coming of their Princess. They would see her often riding out in her carriage, always surrounded by her guards, gracious, charming, beautiful, and infinitely sad. She was becoming a legend—a Princess about whom a spell had been woven. She was the Queen of Ahlden but a prisoner. There was a boundary beyond which she must not pass, she was shut away from the world that she had known. It was as though a magician had set an impenetrable forest about her domain and all that she loved best in the world was on the other side of it. The magician was George Lewis her husband.

He had divorced her and declared to the world that he no longer considered her to be his wife.

* * *

Sometimes they saw her at the window of her apartments standing looking out over the marsh lands across which the river Aller wound its way. In summer the sun touched the river to silver and the scene in golden light had a certain strange beauty; in winter when the land was flooded and winds howled across the marshes it was gloomy and full of foreboding.

But when she drove herself in her cabriolet in summer, she was a magnificent sight for she dressed as though she was attending a state occasion; with her dark hair flowing, diamonds sparkling in it, her gowns of velvet or satin cut in the French fashion

which she loved, she was a colourful figure and the people ran
out of their houses to watch her. In winter she was driven in her
closed carriage—riding like a Queen, none the less grand.

They curtsied to her; they cheered her; she had the gift of
making them love her.

Six miles from the Castle of Ahlden was the boundary beyond
which she was forbidden to go. The guards were there to prevent
her and, resigned, she would return to her prison.

In the beginning she had been listless, but after a while she
noticed the people in the cottages who came out to curtsey to
her; and now and then she would stop her cabriolet or order the
carriage to be stopped and ask them questions about their lives.
Their poverty shocked her; it was the one misery she did not have
to endure, and she found that by interesting herself in them she
forgot a little of her own wretchedness.

They must be helpd she said; not only with food, clothes and
fuel but their children should be taught. She set up a village
school and it delighted her to watch the progress of the children
and to attend the school on prize-giving day and award the prizes.

And thus two years passed and while she dreamed of escape
the people of Ahlden told each other that life had become more
pleasant when the lady of Ahlden had come among them.

*   *   *

Sometimes she paced through her apartments and thought of
those in which she had spent her childhood at Celle. These were
not dissimilar. From the two windows in her bedroom she looked
over the gardens to the village, as in Celle she had looked on the
moat; her bed was in an alcove and often during the first months,
waking in the night from a dream, for a few happy seconds she
believed herself to be a child again, that it was a birthday morning and that her parents would come through the door their
arms full of presents.

Then she would rise from her bed and try to raise her spirits
by planning a levee to which she would invite the nobility of the
neighbourhood, the governor of the castle and her own ladies and
gentlemen-in-waiting. Then it would seem to her that she had
indeed made her own little court when, magnificently gowned,
glittering with diamonds, she would receive them.

But it was a game of make-believe. No matter what she did,
she was a prisoner.

The happiest days were those when she received a letter from
her mother. The Duchess of Celle wrote frequently always assuring her that never would she relax her efforts to have her daughter

released. The letters contained news of Sophia Dorothea's children—the young George Augustus and the adorable little Sophia Dorothea.

"They visit me often," wrote the Duchess, "and they talk eagerly of you. I shall never let them forget you. I am working, my darling, to have you brought to me. Keep up your courage. One day we shall be together."

After receiving such a letter she would dress herself in her most magnificent gown; she would put the diamonds in her hair and would ride out through the village to the stone bridge which marked the boundary beyond which she could not go. And on such days she could believe that the future might bring some happiness back into her life.

*   *   *

Three years of captivity had been lived through when news came to Ahlden of the death of Ernest Augustus. George Lewis was now Elector of Hanover.

It seemed that Sophia Dorothea had little to hope for from her husband. He was content with his mistressses—Ermengarda von Schulenburg still held chief place—and made no attempt to marry again. He had his heir in George Augustus and now that his father was dead he was in complete command. He dismissed Clara to Monplaisir; his mother, too, was deprived of many privileges—a punishment for never having favoured him as she did his brothers. The Duchess Sophia spent most of her time in Herrenhausen watching events in England; Anne had a son, the Duke of Gloucester, who, if he lived, would be the King of England, for Mary was dead and William, it had been said for years, was half way to the grave; in any case he was unlikely to marry again and have heirs; only Anne then and young Gloucester, who had water on the brain, stood between Sophia and the throne of England. So in Herrenhausen she lived quietly, awaiting news from England. If I can die Queen of England, she said, I shall die happy.

Sophia Dorothea was apprehensive, for Ernest Augustus had always been lenient towards her; he had never hated her as George Lewis did, and had not felt vindictive towards her, but kept her imprisoned because it was politic to do so. George Lewis might keep her a prisoner for revenge.

Sophia Dorothea wrote to him begging to be allowed to see her children; her letters were ignored.

But the death of Ernest Augustus brought a great blessing into Sophia Dorothea's life, for the Duchess of Celle refused any longer to be kept from her daughter; and confronting her husband, she told him that with or without permission she was going to her daughter.

George William who sighed often for the old days of happiness at Celle which he knew could never come back because Eléonore had ceased to love him and could only despise him for his conduct towards their daughter, now put no obstacle in her way and great was the joy of Sophia Dorothea when her mother came to Ahlden.

*   *   *

After the first almost unbearably emotional encounter they talked together and planned for the future.

"Nothing now shall keep us apart," declared the Duchess. "I shall visit you regularly and we will find some way out of this trouble."

"Dearest Maman," replied Sophia Dorothea, "this is the happiest day of my life since . . ."

"There," said the Duchess. "No more tears. This is a happy event. I must tell you the news about Knesebeck."

"Poor Knesebeck. I heard they had arrested her too."

"Poor child, yes. She was sent to Schwarzfels and imprisoned there. But that sister of hers, Frau von Metsch, is a bold woman. As soon as she learned where her sister was she determined to bring her out of prison. Poor Knesebeck was harshly treated— ill fed, ill clothed and kept in a cold dreary cell. The poor child must have been half demented. You know what she was for excitement. The prison is half a ruin, but this turned out to be fortunate, for when the roof collapsed a tiler was sent to repair it. Frau von Metsch offered the tiler a reward if he would help and while repairing the roof he lowered a rope down to Knesebeck which she tied about her waist; he then hauled her up and lowered her down the wall to freedom."

"My dear, dear Knesebeck! Was all well with her?"

"Yes. Once free she made her way to Wolfenbüttel where they were only too glad to help her. George Lewis was horrified because at first it was believed she had been spirited away and the people were angry and said that George Lewis was being shown the error of his conduct. When he heard she was in Wolfenbüttel he was furious and doubled the guard here at Ahlen because he was afraid someone would attempt to rescue you."

"I hope she will be happy there."

"She misses you. She talks constantly of you all the time, how

ill-treated you have been; she says that she will never cease
to proclaim your innocence and call attention to the cruelty of
George Lewis."

"It is good to have friends."

"Knesebeck will always be that. She was indiscreet; she was
impulsive and I always feared she urged you to recklessness; but
she will always be loyal."

How quickly those visits passed, but there was the next to
look forward to and they became the highlights of their lives.

*   *   *

In the next few years two events occurred to cheer Sophia
Dorothea. Her son, George Augustus, coached by his grand-
mother the Duchess of Celle, became the champion of his
mother, a state of affairs which enraged George Lewis and made
him very harsh and unfriendly towards his son. Their relationship was impaired from that time and there was active dislike between them. George Augustus resembled his mother; he
was handsome and had inherited her beautiful eyes. One day
when he was out hunting he escaped from the company and
rode with all speed to Ahlden, where he demanded that the
drawbridge be lowered, and when the Governor asked who he
was he called in a loud voice : "I am the Crown Prince of Hanover come to see my mother."

The Governor refused to lower the drawbridge but the young
Prince stood his ground and Sophia Dorothea came out to a
balcony and for a long time mother and son stood gazing at
each other.

"I shall never never forget you!" called George Augustus. "I
shall always fight for your cause."

And Sophia Dorothea stood, blinded by the tears which
dimmed her vision of him.

But very soon the rest of the company came riding after him
and he was put under restraint and taken back to Hanover to
be severely punished by his father.

But it was an occasion to be remembered in a sad and lonely
life.

French and Polish troops invaded the country and came close
to Ahlden, and the Duchess of Celle declared that her daughter
was unsafe there and implored George William to write to the
Elector and tell him that his daughter was being brought to
Celle where her family would keep her in captivity.

George William hesitated, but Eléonore was firm and at last
he relented.

That was a day of mingling happiness and sorrow. To stand in the old rooms where she had known such joy—to be home . . . as she had always longed to be.

But she was still a prisoner and George William would not see her.

"Do not fret, Maman," said Sophia Dorothea. "For I feel that to see him would only bring pain to us both. I prefer to remember the good papa of my childhood whom I loved and trusted. He changed towards me on that dreadful birthday . . . and I do not want to think of him as he is now."

So they tried to make the most of this respite; and the Duchess pampered her daughter and sought in every way to make her happy.

"If I could have my children with me here at Celle, I could happily spend the rest of my days with you, Maman," she said.

But of course such happiness could not last. George Lewis did not care to have her so close. Moreover, the people at Celle knew she was there and they demonstrated their affection for her.

"Don't trust that Frenchwoman," warned the Duchess Sophia.

Sophia Dorothea must return to Ahlden, commanded George Lewis.

"She is too ill," replied the Duchess of Celle. "I must nurse her back to health."

Duchess Sophia at that time became obsessed by one idea. The little Duke of Gloucester, the son of the Princess Anne, had died; now between her and the throne of England there was only Anne, for she did not believe that the English would ever have the son of Catholic James to be their King. She referred to herself as the Heiress of England. William was a sick man; Anne had to be carried almost everywhere on account of her gout and dropsy. Neither of them could produce an heir. "I shall die happy yet," declared Sophia.

So the time passed and Sophia Dorothea spent a year in Celle, although during that time she never spoke to her father —nor did she see him. And then George Lewis would listen to no more excuses.

She must go back to Ahlden.

*   *   *

That stay in Celle had affected George William deeply. He had felt cut off from his wife and daughter and because Sophia Dorothea was in her old home, because he heard the sound of voices in her old apartments—and sometimes laughter—he brooded on the happiness of the long-ago days when there was no one in his life who mattered to him but his wife.

She was beautiful still—but how remote. He remembered how her eyes used to shine when she smiled at him. Now her gaze was cold. She had said she would never forgive him for the manner in which he had behaved towards their daughter, and she meant it. He felt lonely. Ernest Augustus, the brother for whom he had had a special affection, was dead; and as the years passed he saw how much happier he would have been if he had behaved differently. No longer did he discuss with Eléonore the affairs of Celle; she was aloof and expressed no interest in them. For days he never saw her, yet he was deeply aware of her; and some occasions when he felt particularly old and weak and the melancholy settled on him, he wished that he could go back to that birthday morning now more than twenty years ago when because of his weakness he had ruined his own happiness and that of his wife and daughter.

Bernstorff was still his chief minister yet George William had never learned that he was in the pay of Hanover; he still listened to him; he could still be persuaded. He was too old, he believed, to change his ministers now.

But he turned more to his wife; and although he would not admit his remorse he spoke of their daughter.

"Poor child," he said. "My poor little girl."

Eléonore turned to him eagerly but he knew that it was not his friendship, his companionship, his love that she wanted; it was only his help for their daughter.

He added a codicil to his will and showed it to his wife.

"When I die," he said, "our daughter will be one of the richest heiresses in the world."

"It will do her little good while she is a prisoner," was Eléonore's answer.

He grasped his wife's hand and looked at her pleadingly. "I am going to do everything I can to bring about her release."

He saw the pleasure in her face; he wanted to put his arms about her; he wanted to see her joy because everything was going to be between them as it had been when they were young.

But he knew that she was not thinking of him; this change in his attitude pleased her only because of the good it could bring to Sophia Dorothea.

*　　　*　　　*

He would visit Ahlden. He would go to his daughter; he would tell her that he had failed her as a father and that was all changed now.

Bernstorff pleaded with him. Was it wise? Should he not first consult with Hanover? Not only would George Lewis be against him but the Duchess Sophia.

George William hesitated. He was feeling ill, for he was after all an old man, being seventy years old.

"Wait at least, Your Highness, until the weather is more clement."

"I will wait a while," said George William. "But I am determined to free my daughter."

Bernstorff bowed his head. Hanover did not want interference from Celle. He reported to George Lewis. The Countess von Platen was of no importance now; she was at Monplaisir, never seen abroad, suffering it was said from a terrible illness which racked her body with pain and which had already blinded her. He had heard that she walked about her house through the rooms in which she had once entertained so lavishly, murmuring the name of Königsmarck.

George William never went to his daughter. While he was planning his visit he caught a chill; he became very ill and Eléonore nursed him.

He died begging her forgiveness for his weakness.

She kissed his cold face and thought of the handsome lover he had once been, of the long-ago happy days, and she was overcome with grief, not so much for him, she realized, but for the loss of an ideal and the knowledge that her daughter had lost all that the long-denied support of her father could have given her.

*   *   *

Shortly afterwards Clara died. For weeks before the end she lay in her bed at Monplaisir and although she was totally blind she cried out that she could see Königsmarck at the foot of her bed. His face was pale, his clothes blood-stained and he was calling her "Murderess".

She must tell everything, she cried. She must tell the story of that night for that was what the ghost of Königsmarck was urging her to do.

So she told the story—of hatred and jealousy, of cruel revenge, missing nothing; and those about her bed remembered it and some wrote it down that the mystery of what happened on the night Königsmarck disappeared might be solved.

So died Clara.

*   *   *

It is all deaths and marriages, thought Sophia Dorothea. That was because when each day was like another although the days seemed long, the years flew by. It was her mother who came to tell her that her son George Augustus had married Caroline of Ansbach and that Crown Prince Frederick of Prussia had fallen in love with little Sophia Dorothea and although his father did not approve of the marriage, Frederick was determined to have her.

"Good matches, both," said the Duchess of Celle.

*　　*　　*

Twenty years after the night of Königsmarck's murder the Duchess Sophia died, her great wish ungranted. She had said that she would be prepared to die if only it could be as Queen of England. All through the last years of her life she had studied the news of England; she had read of the illness of Queen Anne; she had sat at Herrenhausen hoping that every messenger who came to the castle brought news from England.

But death came instead; and two months later Queen Anne herself died and George Lewis of Hanover became George I of England.

*　　*　　*

Now she, Sophia Dorothea, was the Queen of England, but she remained the prisoner of Ahlden.

The last years were made a little happier by her daughter who wrote to her and would have visited her had she been allowed to.

It was comforting to know that her children remembered; and she herself was growing old now.

The greatest tragedy of those years was the death of her mother, and Sophia Dorothea herself lived only three years longer.

On a misty November day in the year 1726, she took to her bed, and in her delirium she talked of the past.

She thought she was sixteen and it was her birthday and that she was sacrificed to a monster like a child in a fairy tale.

Her hair, now streaked with white, fell about her shoulders; her eyes were wild.

"No," she cried. "Don't let me go to him. He will kill me. He will destroy me . . ."

Then she began to weep pitiably.

"George Lewis," she cried. "How dared you condemn me. You will never forget . . . though I am gone."

Those about her bed shivered. The curse of a dying woman was to be feared.

Then she rambled again, called to her mother, to the Confidante, to her dearest Philip, to her babies. . . .

The mist from the marshes crept into the palace like a grey ghost, like death.

And she lay back on her pillows in the room which had been her prison for more than thirty years; when she had come to it she had been young and now she was an old woman of sixty.

It was a wasted life, said those about her bed. Poor cruelly treated lady.

In the village of Ahlden the bells began to toll and the people went openly and told their children how she used to ride about the countryside with her black hair streaming over her shoulders and the diamonds gleaming in it and about her throat—the fairy prisoner Princess of Ahlden who was in truth not only the Duchess of Hanover but the Queen of England.

BIBLIOGRAPHY

Memoirs of Sophia Dorothea, from the secret archives of Hanover, Brunswick, Berlin and Vienna with letters and other documents. (2 volumes)

Love of an Uncrowned Queen, Sophia Dorothea; and her Correspondence with Philip Christopher, Count Königsmarck — W. H. Wilkins

The First George:
In Hanover and England
(2 Volumes) — Lewis Melville

A Constitutional King:
George the First — Sir H. M. Imbert-Terry

Notes on British History — William Edwards

The Four Georges — W. M. Thackeray

The Four Georges — Sir Charles Petrie

The House of Hanover — Alvin Redman

A History of Four Georges and William IV — Justin McCarthy

The Dictionary of National Biography — Edited by Sir Leslie Stephen and Sir Sidney Lee

British History — John Wade

The National and Domestic History of England — William Hickman Smith Aubrey

Letters of Lady Mary Wortley Montague